DIRTY DOGS

If you like this story

Go to:

DirtyDogsWrestling.com

Write A Review

Join The Team

Like And Share

or

Share A Story/Anecdote

DIRTY DOGS

DirtyDogsWrestling.com

First Edition
10 9 8 7 6 5 4 3 2 1

Printed in the United States of America

Publisher's Cataloging-in-Publication

Morgan, Boss Dirty Dogs / Boss Morgan. -- 1st ed. p. cm.

LCCN:
ISBN-13: 978-0692366592
ISBN-10: 0692366598

1. Fiction 2. Wrestling 3. Sports 4. Comedy 5. Suspense

Testimonials

Hey Greg, you bum! You just made me stay up all night with your damned book! The freaking baby is going to wake up in less than an hour, and I haven't even showered! The only bad thing about the book is that if and when it becomes a movie it'll probably get shortened.

~ George Yu, Wrestler and Attorney

John started reading your manuscript yesterday and can't put it down. He finished it early this morning. He said it was great!!

~ MaryAnn Myers, Writer (John is her editor)

The way I tell a good book is when I can't put it down. This qualifies as a very good book. And there's a character for everyone to love and to hate.

~ Fredd M., Wrestling Coach

Outrageously funny, this misadventure of a desperate coach and his band of wrestling misfits doesn't disappoint. An "E ticket" attraction for sports enthusiasts everywhere.

~ Mike O., Wrestling Coach

You hit a home run with this one. A must-read for wrestlers, sports fans, and anyone who likes a good story with unpredictable characters. If I didn't know the author, I'd still recommend it to everyone I know.

~ Bruce Trammell, All-American Wrestler, Coach and Entrepreneur

I couldn't come up with or remember anything substantive to complain about—I was too busy reading quickly to find out what happens.

~ Gary Thomas, Director of Marketing, Cleveland Indians AA Farm Team

A tribute to all the whackos in the wonderful sport of wrestling.

~ Peter Cimoroni, Entrepreneur, Wrestler and Coach

I loved the story. I loved the characters. It had a great ending. It's a fun read. I didn't want it to end. I'd enthusiastically recommend it!

~ Mary Cimaglia, Designer and Avid Reader

I thoroughly enjoyed it, and it made me laugh out loud. One of the best reads I've had in a long time.

~ Judee Nerren, Magazine Publisher and Avid Reader

Boss Morgan

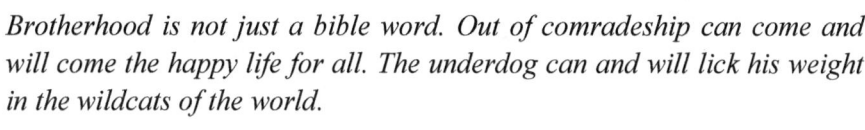

Brotherhood is not just a bible word. Out of comradeship can come and will come the happy life for all. The underdog can and will lick his weight in the wildcats of the world.

~ Heywood Brown, Novelist, Author and Journalist

BOOK 1

Preseason

○●●●●●●●●●●●●●●●●●●●●●●●●

1. ATTITUDE

GOLDEN BEAMS FROM the rising sun illuminate a flight of birds shadowing their leader. Wings harmonize, dart sideways, dive down, and swirl up. Climbing, the symphony surges faster and faster, soars higher and higher, builds to a crescendo and plunges, free-falling back to earth. Pulling out of their dive, they level off into a smooth glide, skimming the treetops lining the winding road below. A dark station wagon flickers through the alternating patches of light and shade. Tires screech around the curve, cut across the road and squeal into the next bend. Spinning rubber veers from the blacktop and sprays the roadside dirt and gravel.

Red taillights flash. The grungy, old wagon bears down on a flowered Volkswagen Beetle driven by a blonde with long flowing hair. Punching the steering wheel with the heel of his hand, the driver blasts the obstruction. He looks ahead and eyes the freeway on-ramp. *Fucking women drivers,* he thinks and stomps the gas pedal. Black smoke explodes from the tailpipe, heaving the steel wagon inches from the Bug's bumper. Plunging into the passing lane, the station wagon jets ahead. He takes a peek at the male driver decorated in beads and a headband, cuts in front of him, across his lane and makes a screaming turn onto the ramp launching the front wheel cover to the grassy shoulder. Another blast of smoke rockets the wagon up the incline, the driver mumbles, *Fucking hippies.*

At the top of the ramp, the wagon is neck and neck with a red semi, the last in a long line of identical trucks bunched like train cars. The wagon's driver glances back and forth from the savage bears painted on the side of the trailer to his vanishing lane. *Gas or brake?* He guns it. Jabbing his finger at the undersized space, he looks over his shoulder at the trucker and steers the wagon left. The truck driver brakes. Behind a smoke screen, the wagon lurches into the fast lane and begins passing the next painted semi trailer picturing growling, clawing tigers and wild lions biting into the necks of their prey. *Fucking truck drivers,* grunts the station wagon operator. He accelerates down the long caravan of trailers portraying circus acts: trained elephants and horses, playful monkeys, colorful clowns, freaks, the high-wire act, the man on the flying trapeze, and leading the motorcade, the fearless lion tamer holding an array of menacing beasts at bay with a whip and chair.

***

The wagon angles to the curb, blocking two lanes. Illegible black letters blemish the swinging door. Stepping his left foot on the doorstep, the hulk stands, poking his burr head above the car. Dan Sangha reaches to his backside, grabs a hand full of trousers and pulls them from the crack of his ass while studying the mass of people leaving the airport baggage terminal. He snatches a pad of paper from the passenger seat, and scribbles "GORNI" in letters large enough to fill the page. Ignoring the horns of the vehicles blocked by his wagon, he pushes his mangled, bottle-thick eyeglasses back into place on his crooked nose and cauliflower ears, holds the makeshift sign up with both hands and points it at the exodus.

A diminutive, wiry youth sits next to several pieces of luggage organized from largest to smallest. The dark-skinned teen sees Dan's sign and waves his hairy arms. He nimbly slips his backpack over his shoulders, hooks the straps of a bag over his head, lifts a smaller bag to his black, furry mustache and grips it with his teeth. He tucks an oversized duffle bag under each arm and lifts the final two suitcases with his hands. Dan watches the waddling pack mule bump his way through the crowd.

"Gorni?" asks Dan.

Gorni grunts and nods his flushed face. Beads of sweat roll down his forehead over his bushy unibrow and splash on the lens of his glasses. Dan half hops and half skips to the back of the wagon to open the cargo door.

He jerks on the handle. The door does not budge. Taking a step back, he delivers a front kick, and it pops open. He lopes to the driver's seat. Gorni loads his gear and shuts the door, but it swings open.

Dan watches in the rear view mirror. "Slam it." Gorni slams the door. It bounces open. Dan shouts, "Harder!"

Gorni takes the door with both hands, winds up and smashes it into the frame. It swings open. Dan bounds from his seat. He takes it in both hands, lifts and gently pushes until the latch clicks.

Orange clouds silhouette the O'Hare International Airport. The last shimmer of sunlight is laid to rest. Dan and Gorni chug through the twilight toward the twinkling Chicago skyline.

***

The vehicle works its way through a maze of dark streets, decayed buildings and leftover stench from the day's sun-baked garbage. The deeper the two occupants advance, the more eyes they attract. Black street characters yell threats. Gorni rolls up his window and pushes down his door lock. A bottle strikes the hood and explodes glass shrapnel. Dan presses the gas pedal and picks up speed. The light turns red.

A street gang clusters on the sidewalk corner, smoking, drinking malt liquor and passing around a bottle of Black Velvet and a joint. The wagon breaks to a screeching stop. Heads turn. Breaking the circle, the leader struts off. One by one, the hoodlums follow and converge on the wagon. Dan blasts his horn and floors it. Black smoke engulfs the spinning rear tires; they catch and the wagon lurches. Two thugs dive out of its path. One refuses to move. Dan swerves and knocks him aside with a glancing blow. The rest chase after and launch a barrage of bottles, cans and curses.

***

The wagon parks in the middle of the only two empty spaces in front of a run-down apartment building. Dan blasts the horn. A few onlookers stare. He opens his door and stands with his hand on the horn. He sounds it again. And again, and then shouts up at the building, "Robbins! Robbins!" He instructs his passenger, "Watch the car. I'll be right back."

Dan's body parts flail in all directions as he sprints toward the apartment complex. Several black youths move toward the station wagon.

Gorni ignores their approach and opens an Iranian magazine. A fist knocks on the windshield. Gorni lowers his magazine and peeks.

Dan hurries along the length of the shabby corridor, shouting, "ROBBINS!" and stopping to check each apartment number in the dimly-lit hall. He finds the apartment and pounds on the door with his fist. After a series of locks unlatching, the door opens. Dan struts in. A mature black man pokes his bearded face out of the apartment and checks the hall from end to end before shutting the door and locking it behind him.

Several bodies of various ages lie around the dark living room listening to a Tina Turner recording. A persistent baby's cry pierces through the music. A half-naked girl gets up from the couch and wanders down the hall. Dozens of televisions and stereos are stacked along the walls of the front room and dining area.

The bearded man shouts to the back of the hot, sticky apartment, "Adam! Dan is here!" He turns to Dan. "We really appreciate this."

"No problem," replies Dan, smelling something he cannot identify.

The bearded man opens an envelope and removes the sheet of paper inside. "We talked to the judge and everything's cool," he says, handing the letter to Dan. "He just needs to contact this person when he gets settled in down there."

Dan glances at the name and pockets the note while eyeing the food spread over the kitchen counters.

Scratching his salt and pepper beard, the man points toward the food and asks, "Something for the road?"

"No thanks, I'm fine."

Adam Robbins enters with a woman clinging to each arm. His white tank top and gold chain accent his dark-brown muscular arms. The man-child lays a prolonged tongue-laden kiss on each girl. Dan studies the way each of the men gives Adam their custom handshake and says good-bye.

"Take care yo'self, Nigger."

"Nigger, you the best of the best."

"Nigger, you's gonna makes us proud."

The bearded man takes Adam in his arms. "Life only gives so many chances. When they used up...they used up. Don't be rolling dice for what's left."

One of the men wraps his arms around the two girls who walked in with Adam and squeezes. "And don't you worry. We'll watch after everything."

Dan exits the kitchen, his cheeks bulging, a half-eaten drumstick in one hand and a few slices of white bread in the other. The gorilla-sized youth flashes a wide, pearly smile at Dan.

"You ready?" asks Dan, spraying food from his mouth.

"All set," says Adam, eyeing Dan's rumpled, untucked, and mismatched clothes. "We gonna have to do some stylin', Coach."

Dan nods and swallows. "Where's your bags?"

"This is it," answers Adam, picking up a full-length, black leather coat from a chair and draping it over his arm.

"Let's go." Dan rushes to the front door, tucks the bread under his arm and grapples in vain trying to figure out the series of locks on the door. The bearded man steps forward and aptly unlatches the locks and opens the door. Dan leads the way down the hall.

The older man yells after them, "Be smart. You take good care of my little brother."

Dan, imitating Adam's friends, raises a fist in the air and yells back, "Uh. Yep. Right. Right on, Nigger."

Emerging at ground level sucking on the chicken bone, Dan's eyes fix on the wagon's empty passenger seat. Next to the wagon, a mob is swarming. He tosses away the bone, breaks into a run and bowls into the rabble, knocking bodies out of his path. "What's going on?"

Two hefty black thugs hold Gorni on the ground. The bigger of the two has his knee digging in Gorni's chest and a vice grip on his Adam's apple. The other bully's sneaker is posted against Gorni's head as he tries to pry a wallet from Gorni's clutched hands.

"Get off him. What's going on?" asks Dan. The gang is caught off guard. They freeze. Dan struts forward. Several take a step back. Dan keeps moving. "What happened? I said get off."

One attacker lets go of the wallet and retreats. The big ruffian, with a huge afro atop the body of a sumo wrestler, keeps his grip on Gorni's throat.

"Who the fuck are you, the Lone Cracker?"

"Get off."

"Fuck you mother fu—"

5

Dan bolts forward, grabs two hands full of the afro and jerks. He twirls like a hammer thrower, extending the man's body in the air. Dan spins around and around and around. Each rotation pushes the crowd back a step. Without warning, the body is airborne. It arches across the night sky, crashes to the ground, skips, and crumbles to a halt. The bully grabs his skull and cries out in pain. Dan turns to the open mouths and extends two fists full of bloody hair above his head and bellows a deranged laugh. "Ha! Ha! Heh! Heh!"

The bully's partner lunges forward and hurls a roundhouse. Dan ducks the haymaker, comes up behind and traps the assailant in a choke hold. The victim flails his arms and kicks, trying to break Dan's grip.

Dan sinks in the choke and swings his catch around, facing the startled eyes. "Think you're tough? When I was in Mongolia during the winter, it was so cold your skin would burn and peel off just running to the next building. Each morning, the Mongolians would crawl out of their yurts, grin at us through the window, rub snow on their arms and legs, and then take off for their ten-mile run through the frozen snow—naked!"

Dan releases. The limp body flops on the ground. "Those guys were taught martial arts from the day they're born. When they turn twelve, they're sent in the wilderness to kill a bear with their bare hands, to prove their manhood."

He takes a couple of strides toward the pack. They take a couple of steps back. "One night, they were making fun of Americans, calling us wimps and pussies. I told them they were a bunch of Mongolian slant-eyed bastards, so eight of them jumped me. I got a concussion, twelve stitches," he says, pointing to a long, deep scar above his right eyebrow, "the whole side of my face was crushed. I lost half my teeth, and I was bleeding from my nose, mouth, ears, and eyes where they gouged me. I had a dislocated shoulder, a slab of broken ribs, and they shattered my left knee. And I won the fight. Ha! Ha! Heh! Heh! I put six of them in the hospital, and two got away. So how do you want it? All at once, or one at a time?"

The wide-eyed gang stands petrified. One punk has had enough talk and reaches under his shirt. An uneasy feeling interrupts his urge. He freezes, scans the crowd and finds Adam's dark, cold eyes boring through him. Adam's hand is positioned inside his coat. The unconscious body on the ground begins twitching back to life. Everyone looks at the convulsing body.

"That's called the funky chicken," says Dan. "Anyone else want to dance? My card is open." He raises his hands and sprinkles what is left of the bloody hair from his clenched fingers. "So who's first?" Dan eyes the biggest, baddest looking one, tugs his pants up, and swaggers toward him. "How about you?"

The big guy breaks too fast, loses his footing, and slips to the ground. Dan closes in. Adrenalin pumps. Moving with the speed of a trapped animal, the big guy scrambles to his feet and runs. He glances over his shoulder to see if he is being chased and keeps running. Dan moves toward another. He shies away.

Turning to Adam and Gorni, he says, "Okay, let's get out of here."

Gorni lifts his bruised body and stuffs his wallet into his back pocket. He retrieves his shattered eyeglasses from the street and fits them on his bloody nose. A drop of blood drips and splashes red on his ripped shirt. He staggers to the station wagon. Adam grabs the door handle away from Gorni and takes the front seat. Gorni retreats to the back. Adam eyes Dan as he starts the engine.

Dan looks at Gorni in the rearview mirror, held in place by a piece of coat hanger wire wrapped around the mirror and hooked to the support post. He turns and lifts the sagging upholstery, hanging from the ceiling, out of his line of sight and asks, "Gorni, you okay?" Gorni weakly nods his head yes. Dan looks in his eyes. "You sure?"

Gorni shouts back, "YEAH!"

Adam continues to stare at Dan.

"Let's get out of here before they have time to think about it," grunts Dan. He backs up, drops the gear shift into drive, and peels out. "Gorni, a wallet's not worth dying for."

"Not wallet."

"Well, the money."

"Not money."

"What else is in your wallet?" There is no answer. Dan pulls another drumstick from his pocket and holds it up. "Gorni, you hungry?" Gorni shakes his head. Dan shrugs and bites, ripping a chunk of meat from the bone, and then acknowledges Adam's gaze. "What?" he asks through a mouthful of breaded chicken.

"What the fuck's Mongolia? I mean, was that shit you said back there for real?"

"Yep," echoes Dan. "That worked pretty good. Gorni, this is Adam Robbins. Adam, this is Gorni. I'm training Gorni to be our team manager."

"No. No manager. I Gorni Balevan, I wrestle."

"Yeah, yeah, yeah," answers Dan, chomping and shredding another mouthful.

○○••••••••••••••••••••••••

2. D-Town

DAN'S BROWN CLUNKER slaloms around the other vehicles as he makes his way down Main Street. The small rural town is decorated with college students, fast-food restaurants, book stores, clothing stores, movie theaters, and bars.

"So, this is D-Town," says Adam.

Dan approaches the intersection at the end of Main Street. The light turns yellow. He accelerates. It turns red. Dan blasts his horn, speeds across the intersection and through the antiquated gateway. A sign splits the road:

Welcome to Dover University

Home of the Fighting Dogs

In the foreground, a weathered statue of a savage mongrel in an aggressive stance greets visitors. His short, tapered snout widens into a broad head. Snarled lips wrinkle the nose and bare a mouth of teeth dominated by oversized upper and lower fangs. Devil eyes glare from his growling face. Fur stretches tightly over his skull, accenting his taut, flexed muscle striations and menacing flattened ears. Hackles run down the back of his thick neck, over his broad shoulders and along the ridge of his back, which narrows to a small waist and then blows up into dense, powerful haunches and legs.

Dan delivers his customary wave to two concealed campus security officers. They casually return the gesture, ignoring his speed. Adam shields his face and marvels the man behind the wheel. Ignoring an exit-only sign, Dan jerks the wheel left and whips into a driveway, cutting off the vehicles leaving as he spurts across the parking lot toward an early century architectural relic. He parks in the spot reserved for President Hardon, tucks his folder of mish-mashed papers under his arm and dashes through the ivy-bordered entrance. Papers slip free and swirl to the ground. Gorni retrieves the papers while Adam swaggers behind Dan into the offices of the Dover Athletic Center.

Dan rushes through the dingy office complex, saying a hurried short-to-the-point "Hi" to everyone. A sign next to his office door reads "Dan Sangha Dover Wrestling Coach."

The dark office is a museum of wrestling paraphernalia. Photos, posters and awards cover every inch of wall space. Trophies, plaques, and stacks of books fill the counter space, window sills, and shelves. Dan sits at his wooden desk in the center of the square room, barely visible behind piles of magazines and papers. Two statues adorn the front corners of his desk: one, a miniature version of the same Dover Dog they passed at the entrance gate, and the other, a classic sculpture of two intertwined wrestlers. A hodgepodge of papers, cups, and plates hide the rest of the desktop, while a TV, VCR, and towers of videotapes fill the top of a small table beside Dan.

Dan searches through the mess, pushing, pulling and lifting papers until he uncovers a telephone. He wedges the earpiece between his shoulder and the side of his head, dials a number and begins opening and frisking the drawers of his desk. "Hi Cindy, I'm back. ...huh? I stopped last night and napped at a rest area. I'll be home in a couple of hours. ...uh-huh. ...I have a coaches' meeting in five minutes." Dan opens the center desk drawer and digs in, searching through the contents. "What? I'll be there. I wouldn't miss it for the world, but afterward I have to come back to the office and make calls. Okay, I promise. See you after the meeting." He hurriedly fits rings and watches on his fingers and wrists as he finds them in the open drawer. "What? Okay, put her on. Hi, birthday girl. Huh? What? Maggie? Maggie, put Mollie on. ...Happy Birthday, sweetheart. So when does the party start? Uh-huh. I'll be there. Listen, that boy from class, he bother you anymore? Good. Remember the Mongolian death grip if he tries anything. Okay. Okay. I'll see you soon. I have to go now—bye."

Dan fits the tenth and final ring on his last empty digit, turns to Adam and Gorni, and raises both hands. "See this?" Dan stands and walks around the desk. "This is what it's all about. This is why you're here." Dan shoves his hands in their faces. "These are like Super Bowl rings. We win the conference championship, and everybody on the team gets one. Everybody."

Dan checks one of his four watches, turns, takes off his jacket, hangs it on the coat rack and disappears out the door. He pops his head back in. "Wait here."

***

A grizzled pickup truck rumbles through a middle-class neighborhood plucked from the early twentieth century. A hood ornament of a cowboy riding a wild bucking bronco adorns the point of the truck. It parks in front of an old, three-story Victorian home. The driver, a middle-aged cowboy, hobbles to the rear of the pickup. A younger version slides from the passenger side.

Calloused hands grab a stuffed paper bag and a rolled-up blanket from the bed of the truck and hand it to the boy. Taking the boy in his arms, the craggy cowboy sings a series of yodels at a whisper. Then, holding the boy at arm's length, the man looks into the younger eyes and searches for the right words. "Remember, Bronk, nobody's bigger or better—they're just different." The boy nods his head. "Call coach and let him know you're here. I love you, Son." The old man lifts an almost new hat from his head, and swaps it for his son's ratty hat. "Here. I broke it in for you." He stretches the boy's old hat over his head, winks, and mounts his truck. "Now you be good to yourself. 'Cause if you ain't, nobody else will be." The man's glassy eyes stare at Bronk in the mirror. He toes the gas pedal and rolls off into the sunset.

Bronk stands alone. "You, too." His body deflates as the truck disappears around the corner. "Bye, Daddy."

He trudges up the sidewalk. Over the front porch hangs the sign "DOG POUND." Bronk reaches the steps to the front porch and spots another sign that at one time read "Freshmen Upstairs." Someone has crossed out the "n" and added an "at" to create: "Freshmeat Upstairs."

Bronk climbs the steps to the second floor and approaches a black youth pumping out pull-ups on a bar attached to the door frame of his room. He is dressed in sweats, with extra weights fitted to his wrists, waist and ankles.

"So, what's the deal? Do I just pick any room to bunk?" asks Bronk.

The youth stops pulling and hangs. "Freshmen are in the attic." He gestures with his eyes and a head nod toward a narrow set of stairs at the end of the hall.

"You bluffin' or you mean it for real?" asks Bronk.

"For real," he laughs.

Bronk climbs the stairs, opens a door marked "Puppy Pound" and enters a large single room broken up by several beds and dressers. He drops the rolled-up blanket on the bed by the window and then dumps the guts of his paper bag. A lasso, clock, two shirts and underwear, a pair of jeans, a can of dip, wrestling shoes, and a plastic bag of toiletries spill onto the bed. He sets the dip, clock, toiletries, and lasso on the dresser, throws his pants and underwear in a drawer, and hangs his shirts on the empty curtain rod.

The guy from downstairs settles in the Puppy Pound's doorway and watches. Returning to his bed, Bronk unrolls his blanket revealing a bottle of Jack Daniels and a miniature spittoon.

The black beefcake pounces across the room to the dresser. "Sure you brought enough? You're only staying nine months." He picks up the lasso. "Plan on catching your food?"

Bronk carries the whiskey and spittoon to his dresser. "Want a shot?"

"No thanks, I was just going for a run. You want to join me?"

Bronk christens his spittoon. "No, I don't go in for runnin'."

"Name's Rick Ballsinger. But everybody calls me Balls." They shake hands.

"Hi, Balls. I'm Bronk."

Balls practices his grip on the lasso as Bronk cracks open the Jack Daniels, swallows a swig of whiskey and extends the bottle. "Sure you don't want a shot for the road?"

"Don't drink." Balls twirls the rope above his head and casts the running noose across the room. It falls harmlessly on the floor next to a chair.

Bronk pulls a Marlboro pack from his shirt pocket and offers one to Balls.

"Don't smoke either." Balls retrieves the rope.

"Each to his own poison. Here, let me show you how it's done." Bronk takes the lariat into his hands. "See, you loop it like this." He demonstrates the grip and begins twirling it above his head. "You bring it around and throw your hand forward like you're crackin' a whip. See? And then when it feels right, you release." The noose casts across the room and ensnares the chair. "I need to make a call. You got a phone?"

"Sure. C'mon, I'll show you around."

***

Dan sits, resting his chin on the heels of his hands. His fingers curve along the side of his head and drum against his skull, displaying his rings and watches. It is standing room only. The athletic director presides at one end of the conference table and the football coach at the other end. Dan sits to the side in the middle of the long table. An empty plate sits in front of him. His eyes constantly shift back and forth between the coaches on either side. When the coach on his right turns his head to check the time on the wall clock, Dan snatches a grape from his plate.

The meeting is dead silent, except for the speaker, Bill Bohr. He has the stature of an old war general and the polished, manicured appearance of a small-time politician. "To sum up, I can say in my twenty years as athletic director, I've never seen anything like this. As of the end of last school year, we are broke. Our future is in the hands of the board of trustees, who are having its financial meeting as we speak. My advice to you is to anticipate the worst. Expect a severe cutback in funds." He takes a dramatic pause and looks into the eyes of each of the coaches seated around the table. "I only hope that by working together through this dire state of affairs, we can achieve a prosperous future full of blessings and good fortunes. But for now, we need all your prayers and cooperation. Any questions? Comments?" he asks, looking around the table. "Okay then, meeting is adjourned."

Dan exits the conference room. Gorni is waiting in the hall. "Telephone."

Dan quickens his gait to a gallop, bursts into his office and knocks Adam's feet from his desk. Adam jerks awake. "How was the meeting?"

"I've listened to the same speech every year for twenty years." Dan picks up the phone with one hand and turns the light switch on the desk lamp with the other. "Hello?" says Dan flicking the switch of his desk lamp on and off repeatedly without any success.

"Hello, Coach Sangha, this is Bobby Ryder."

"Who is this?" Dan reaches up, tightens the light bulb and tries the switch again.

"It's me, Bobby Ryder."

Dan settles for the dark. "Yeah, Bobby, what can I do for you?"

"I've decided I want to go to Dover and wrestle for you. I'm ready to sign anytime you want."

"Uh-huh. Okay. Okay. Bobby, I'm leaving now. Listen, I'll be there in six hours—no, no—make that five hours. I'll see you in five hours. Just hold on. Bye." The instant Dan hangs up the phone, it rings again. "Hello."

"Coach, this is Bronk. Well, I made it. I'm here in Dover. What am I supposed to do?"

"Be in my office at nine o'clock tomorrow morning. Bye."

"What about now?" asks Bronk.

Dan spells, "B...A...R...Bye."

What? Hello, Coach?"

"Yep."

"I'm over here at the Dog Pound. What am I supposed to do?"

Dan shouts the letters, "B...A...R!" and slams the receiver down.

A dashing young man strides in and bounces around Dan's office like he is looking for a place to lift his leg and mark his territory. He has everyone's attention, except Dan's. "Hey Dan, what's going down, clown?"

"That was Bronk Pokard I was just talking to. He's the guy I recruited to beat you," boasts Dan, spinning his chair around to the ranking board leaning against the TV table.

"What the hell kind of name is Bronk? Where do you find these guys?"

13

"Same place I found you," Dan says, taking Joe Kerr's name tag from the first slot and replacing it with Bronk's name tag. Then, he puts Joe's name tag at the bottom of the weight class. Dan spins back to his desk and begins shuffling through his papers.

Joe examines the ranking board. "What's this? Your new toy? Don't you think you should find something to do with your time that would work off that belly of yours?"

Adam sits up, ready for a reaction.

"Good idea. I'll wrestle you."

Unconcerned, Joe walks back around the desk and tears a piece of Scotch tape from the tape dispenser. "Quit dreaming. You're just a fat old neolith."

"A neolith? What's that?"

"A paleolith."

"A what?"

"A fossil."

"Oh. That's not so bad. Why didn't you just say that?"

"Face it—you've got a fork sticking in your rump. Lucky you got married while you had some hair left," says Joe, lifting the phone receiver. "Here—you need to call the men's hair club before it's too late." As he hangs up the receiver, he tapes down the telephone connection button.

Dan looks through his paper stacks. "I want you to take Bronk uptown tonight and show him a good time."

"I can't. I, uh—I got a bad back. Besides, I have a date tonight. I just came down to pick up my tuition check."

Dan covers Joe's check with his forearm and opens the top drawer. "Plans have changed. I had to give that money to Bronk." He slides the check in the drawer and shuts it.

"You can't do that. You promised me that money. I earned that money."

"You know the situation. I only get one scholarship. Where's your team spirit? Don't you want a better team? I'll give you free books."

"Books?"

"I'll make you a deal. You chase Bronk back home, and you can have his money next semester."

"Oh, no you don't. I get my money now, or I don't wrestle."

"You going to take him uptown tonight or not?"

Joe lifts the stapler from Dan's desk. "Don't change the subject. Anyway, I can't tonight. I told you, I have a date."

"What's the matter? You can't handle pressure?"

"I don't babysit for free." Joe strolls to the coat rack and coughs.

Adam watches Joe staple the end of Dan's jacket sleeve shut with each cough.

"How much you paying me to show this kid a good time?" asks Joe.

"What pay? I'm helping you with your education. You're in public relations. This is on-the-job training."

"Face it, Dan, you're cheap. Come on, Coach, the school gives you money for these sorts of things. Don't be avaricious." The word stumps Dan. He eyes Adam and Gorni for their reactions. Joe gets on his knees and clasps his hands. "Please. Pretty please. Pretty, pretty please, with sugar on top. Sir."

"Okay, since you put it that way. I'll give you ten dollars, but make sure you spend it on Bronk. Adam and Gorni are witnesses."

Dan takes out his wallet, opens it, and as he reaches for the money, Joe snatches the wallet and runs to the other side of the desk. Dan gives chase. They circle the desk one way, then stop, change directions and circle the other way. As they round the desk, Joe removes a wad of bills and tosses the wallet aside. Dan retrieves his empty billfold, but before he can resume the chase, Joe grabs the ranking board and lifts it above his head, as if he's going to smash it. Dan grabs a long, heavy pair of black scissors from his desk and cocks his arm, threatening to throw. Joe lowers the ranking board and uses it like a shield. Stalemate.

A blonde couple, wearing matching clothes, cuddle in the doorway. She swings from his arm, mesmerized by his leading man's looks. He smiles. Perfect white teeth accentuate his tanned face. "Hi, Coach."

Dan and Joe hold their positions. "Ben. Ben Wussle. We were just talking about you. You know Joe, and this is Gorni, and this is Adam."

"Great. And this is my girlfriend Tara." Ben shakes Gorni's hand. "Hi, Gorni."

"Adam is the guy I recruited to beat you, Ben," reveals Dan.

Ben smiles and extends his hand to Adam. "Hi, Adam. It's nice to meet you."

Adam refuses to shake Ben's hand, stands and stares him down. "It's Mister Robbins to you, boy."

"Sure. Whatever, Mister Robbins," responds Ben, rolling his eyes. Tara jerks free from Ben's arm and storms out. There is a prolonged silence. Ben shrugs. "She always does stuff like that."

"Okay, everybody get the fuck out. I have to get going," orders Dan. "Joe is taking you guys uptown, and he's paying. Now beat it."

Ben announces, "C'mon, my car's outside." Everyone heads to the door.

"Not you, Gorni. You wait in my car," directs Dan. When they exit, Dan sets the scissors down and begins putting his jacket on. Outside his office door, he hears a noise. With one arm in the jacket sleeve, Dan freezes. He listens. It is silent, then—

"Woof, woof, woof."

He focuses his eyes on the open door. Joe sticks his head in and yells, "DOGFACE!"

Dan scrambles, grabs the scissors and hurls. Joe ducks the metal projectile. It whizzes past his head and thuds into the drywall. Joe runs, barking all the way down the corridor.

Dan runs to the doorway. "Tomorrow at practice, it's me and you."

"No pay. No play. DOGFACE!"

Dan glares at Joe until he turns the corner. The phone rings as Dan slips his other arm into the stapled sleeve. His arm is stuck, and he spins in a circle trying to get his arm through. Dan answers with his free hand and looks at his blocked sleeve. "Hello? Hello?" He shouts louder. "HELLO." The phone continues to ring. "Hello? Who is this?" Dan switches his attention from the sleeve and studies the phone. He notices the tape, removes it and yells into the phone. "Who is this?—Oh, hi, Cindy. I was just going to call you." Dan stretches his leg and closes the office door with his foot. "Uh...I got some bad news." He grimaces, swallows and continues. "Listen, Cindy, I have to go to Cleveland. I know I promised. I'm sorry. I'll be back tomorrow morning, and I'll make it up to her. I promise. Tell Maggie and Mollie I—hello? Hello?" Dan slowly drops the telephone from his ear and puts it to rest on its cradle. He plops in his chair. There's a soft knock at the door. The doorknob turns. Dan grabs the stapler and prepares an ambush. The door cracks open.

Bill Bohr, the athletic director, steps in. "Dan?" Bill sees the stapler in Dan's cocked arm, raises his hands in surrender, and backs into the corner.

Dan lowers his arm. "Oh geez, Bill. I thought it was someone else. Come in. I got something for you." Dan walks around his desk and forces his fist through his stapled sleeve, ripping and shredding the material. He grabs a folder and confidently hands it to Bill. "Here's my adjusted budget."

"That's what I wanted to talk to you about."

"I cut it to the bone."

Bill listlessly pages through the folder.

"What? The airfares to nationals? I think the kids deserve to go first class."

"I don't know how to tell you."

"Everybody in the country flies, but hey, if it has to go, it has to go. We can rent a bus or even drive the school vans."

"The board of trustees dropped the wrestling program."

"Dropped? What? What does that mean?"

"They've withdrawn all financial support, effective immediately. I'm sorry, Dan. You have to return all scholarships issued. The university vehicles are off-limits, and cancel any equipment orders you've made."

"What about Duray?"

"I notified Duray so he could start looking for another assistant coach position."

"My salary?"

"There is none. I think that's everything. Oh yeah, your credit cards." Dan opens his wallet and sifts through it, slapping down a variety of credit cards. "Your program was my pride. If there's anything I can do— anything—my door is always open. I mean it. Oh, your car keys." Dan removes a set of specially tagged keys from his key chain and hands them over. "Stop in and see me tomorrow. There are some things we need to go over. I'm sorry." Bill drops his head and shuffles out.

I can't believe what I just heard. Dan grimaces. His thumb and first finger slip under his eyeglasses and massage his eyes and the sides of his nose. He drags his feet to his chair and crumples into it. His body goes limp, his head slumps and the color drains from his face.

His eyes slowly track around his office from memento to memento. *It's over. Just like that.* Each remembrance splinters his heart. *What is that?* He can't identify the strange sensation smoldering in his gut. He removes his glasses, closes his eyes, covers his face with his hands, and runs his fingers though his hair when he drops and buries his head.

He picks his head up, and peeks between his fingers at his reflection in the glass-framed picture of a much younger Dan standing on top of the victory podium. He stares into his aged, sagging reflection. Thoughts stream behind his blank face. He realizes the staggering consequences of what just happened and pounds his desktop with both fists. He rises and trudges across the room to confront his double. His stinging eyes penetrate beyond his mirror eyes. "Ahhhh!" he howls, and punches his likeness. Glass shatters, and the frame falls from its hook. Dan rages around the office, dismantling, maiming or destroying every piece of memorabilia in his path, until he finds himself back where he started. Looking at the mess, he collapses in his chair, breaking the silence with a, "Shit."

A lone stack of magazines, missed in his rampage, totters and collapses, sliding across the desk in front of his face. His eyes focus on the top magazine cover. The headline reads: "KANE'S CHICAGO TEAM FAVORED FOR AN UNPRECEDENTED TENTH STRAIGHT NATIONAL TITLE." Below the headline is a photograph of the Chicago team carrying Kane on their shoulders. He holds the national championship trophy above his head with one hand and signals number one with the other. The team stands above a large Roman numeral "X" covering the bottom half of the cover. Below, the caption reads "The Chicago Cats, coached by Dave Kane, challenge the rest of the country for a college record 10th consecutive year."

The magazine cover has a calming, sobering effect. Dan looks around the destroyed office and then back at the cover. He tears the cover from the magazine, folds it and slips it in his inside coat pocket. Opening his desk drawer, he folds Joe's check and tucks it in his shirt pocket, lifts a duplicate set of tagged keys from the drawer, picks up a folder and storms out.

○ ○ ○ ●

3. B...A...R...

A SKATEBOARDER SLICES down the road through a string of evenly spaced spotlights cast from the streetlights above. Blair "Doc" Borne frantically flaps his arms and teeters above the fluid flow of the board. He glides toward the intersection, passing a long line of stationary vehicles waiting for the signal change. Doc's baggy, worn sport jacket hangs open, whipping in the wind, revealing a T-shirt that reads "WRESTLING" over a picture of a buff wrestler with a surfboard in one arm and a bikini-clad girl wrapped in the other, above the caption: "CALIFORNIA STYLE." Earphones band across the top of his head, splitting his red mohawk into two kinky humps. His shredded jeans sag, exposing his multicolored boxer shorts.

Doc goes into a clumsy squat, makes a sharp turn toward the sidewalk, loses his balance and bounces off a car trunk. He wavers, regains control and squeezes on the bicycle horn attached to his belt. The honk signals the pedestrians crossing the sidewalk in front of the dark alleyway, and they skip out of his path. Doc's body straightens. He lifts his sunglasses and makes out a vehicle parked in the shadows just beyond the mouth of the passage. He reaches his hands skyward, elongates, sucks in his stomach and aims for the narrow gap between the car and the brick wall. His rear end bumps the fender and bounces him into the wall. He ricochets between the car and the wall and shoots out into the slanted alley toward a giant chuckhole. His body goes one way, and the headstrong board goes the other. He leans hard—harder. The wayward board's wheels cut, graze the edge of the rut and tack across the alley. His goofy body fights to regain balance, floundering as he weaves around a trash can, dodges a brick, crouches and curves around a pothole. Reflexes take charge of the disobedient skateboard and bring the high wire act under control. He straightens, accelerates by taking a couple of digs with one foot on the road surface. The clicking sound quickens as the wheels spin over the uneven bricks. He lifts a Walkman, connected to his headphones, from his coat pocket, leaps a discarded box and lands on a guardrail protecting a breaker box. He changes tapes on his Walkman as the bottom of the board slides down the length of the steel railing and takes flight. The skateboarder's legs squat and take the shock of the landing. Without slowing, his foot flips the board into the air, and he grabs it. The momentum carries him from the alley to the Main Street sidewalk, where he is swept away by a surge of bodies.

The street is alive. Everyone is juiced. An infectious energy permeates the human river. Like a vial of werewolf blood shot into the jugular on the night of the full moon, it is irresistible, heightening the senses, releasing the wildness and commencing the hunt. All succumb to the contagion of a new school year.

***

Bronk twists the top off a can of dip and stuffs a pinch of smokeless tobacco between his cheek and gum as he walks down River Drive. He slides the can back in his jeans' rear pocket where a well-worn ring marks the round can's resting place. His eyes transfix, consuming the animated images, a collage of lights, colors, fashions and ethnic groups. Frenzied lines of people file in both directions along the sidewalk. Feminine skin abounds. Cars and trucks cruise. The constant hum is accented by shouts of hellos, insults, pick up lines and an occasional horn blast. Multihued lights sparkle from every building front. Restaurants and bars dominate. Pairs of lawmen patrol. They appear sporadically and wave or nod to their brethren in uniform whenever they cross paths.

Bronk wanders down the sidewalk and stops at the main intersection. Main and River Street signs cross above his head. The potency and wonder of the scene hold his gaze as he steps off the curb. A horn blast! Bronk's head snaps toward the sound, and his eyes fill with grill and headlights. He does a belly flop back to the curb out of the path of a speeding, swerving brown station wagon driven by Dan. Bronk lies on his stomach. He adjusts his hat and is confronted by a big toe poking through a hole in a shoe resting on the back end of a skateboard.

Doc peers down. "Hey dude, what kind of drugs are you on? I want some."

Bronk looks up as he climbs back to his feet. "He sure had the spurs to that."

Doc presses down with his toe and tips the skateboard upright into his hand. The light changes yellow. He tosses the board, runs, and jumps on the rolling board. Crowds move. The "walk" sign flashes green. Bronk checks both ways and steps off the curb. Raging police sirens saturate the air. A red Harley-Davidson Super Glide darts into the intersection against the traffic signal. Brakes screech. Horns blast. Bumpers crash. Halfway through the junction, the Harley veers and angles toward Bronk. He freezes, unsure of which way to move, and begins backpedaling.

The Harley driver's nude body is capped with a kamikaze helmet and goggles over his coal black, shoulder-length hair and beard. White underwear flap from the sissy bar. The driver blasts his horn, jumps the curb and parts the human mass on the sidewalk. Bronk cannot move fast enough and extends his arms in front of his body. His hands catch the handle bar, and the force knocks him back into the wall of the building. The motorcycle turns up the sidewalk, bores its way through the crowd and turns the wrong way down a one-way alley. The wailing police car slows for the crowd to part and resumes the chase down the alleyway.

The streets are abuzz. Bronk pulls himself together and climbs to his feet. He gazes through the window and does a double take. A tall, graceful frame launches pizza dough into the air. The dough saucer twirls up, spins for an instant just below the light fixture, then falls and makes a delicate landing on the back of her long, slender fingers.

A white chef's hat corrals her strawberry blonde hair, and a white bib apron wraps around her athletic frame. Her green gaze meets Bronk's stare. She flashes a fresh smile, acknowledging his interest, and then she flips the dough again. This time, she catches it behind her back. Twirling the dough on one finger, she moves the dough like a baton from hand to hand around her head, body, and legs.

A flashing red light reflects on the window. He turns his head. Across the street, a sign with three giant red letters blinks repeatedly. Bronk reads the letters: "B…A…R… Bar." In much smaller white letters, "River" sits above the large flashing red "BAR."

A candy apple red Corvette with custom plates that read "Wuss" pulls to the curb in front of the River Bar. Behind the wheel, Joe checks himself in the mirror and runs his fingers through his hair. Scrunched in the passenger seat, Ben and Adam open the door and spill out. The River Bar doors fly open, and several students run from the bar screaming. White foam oozes out the doorway and down the sidewalk.

Joe lifts himself from the front seat and tosses the car keys across the top of the car to Ben. Joe lights a long, slender cigar, sucks like a baby on a bottle and blows a perfect smoke ring. "Ahhh—just like sucking on a wet tittie."

Ben examines the red curb. "You can't park my car here. This is a no parking zone."

"No problem," says Joe, as he points and nods to two police officers on foot patrol. "All the cops know me. It's okay." The officers wave and nod back, then pause in front of the River Bar and watch through the window.

Adam turns his face away and hikes down the street in the opposite direction.

"Adam, we're going in here," yells Ben. Adam lengthens his stride and disappears into the throng. Ben follows Joe into the River Bar.

Bronk takes a long, concentrated look at the stunning pizza thrower until she notices him. He smiles, tips his hat and canters off. He trots across the street and pulls up at the bar's front door. Across the front of the River Bar hangs a Day-Glo banner announcing, "BEER FIGHTS TONITE - Enter at own risk." Bronk holds the front door open for Billy "Pug" Pugliano. Pug is dressed in gym shorts. Each of his stubby arms drapes over the necks of two girls who support him. He carries a beer bottle in each hand. His barrel chest rests on a well-developed beer gut. Bronk trails behind Pug.

Hundreds of drenched bodies in rain suits, wet suits, parkas, umbrellas, snorkels, diver's masks and just plain T-shirts and shorts pack the large open front area next to the bar. The back half of the barroom is a step higher, and a pool table stands in the center surrounded by games, tables and televisions. Flashing lights are dimmed and the deafening music turned off. The volume level of the crowd falls as all eyes focus on Uncle Burt, the bartender, climbing on top of the bar. He is a little older than the rest. A Dover Wrestling T-shirt is stretched over his thick, slightly pudgy upper body, and a whistle hangs around his neck. He extends his arms, spreads his hands above his head and looks skyward until there is silence. "Are we having fun?"

Everyone screams.

"Brothers and sisters of Dover," he shouts, imitating a fire-and-brimstone preacher. He drops his eyes and looks over his "congregation" with a wild, crazed stare. "I come to bury last year, not praise it. We are gathered here to celebrate the new school year. If I had all the rock 'n' roll in the world, I'd throw it in the river. If I had all the booze and drugs in the world, I'd throw them in the river. If I had all the sinners in the world, I'd throw them in the river. Now, open your hymn books to page 69 and let us sing together 'Meet Me at the River.'" Cheers and laughter explode. Music blares and the lights flash.

Several big-busted, T-shirt-clad sorority girls open the front door and file in. Bronk steps aside to allow them entry and then tags behind them as they burrow through the pit of half-naked, soaked bodies. Uncle Burt, still on top of the bar, spies the new arrivals and glances to the end of the bar where Willie "Pump" Kinsman is seated. As thick as two men put together, he is a massive hairball with an XXXL-sized head. Sitting on a stool, he devours a pizza and chugs beer from a pitcher-sized mug inscribed "Pump."

Uncle Burt motions to Pump and directs his attention to the new girls. His eyes feast on their attributes, and with a confirming nod of his head, he gives the thumbs down signal. Uncle Burt lifts his whistle to his mouth and blows.

Everyone screams, "BEER FIGHT!" The air turns liquid.

The primary target is the dry newcomers. Bronk laughs at the girls in front of him getting a beer shower until he is included. Like an angry bull teased by the rodeo clown, he charges the bar, grabs the plastic cups of beer and starts hurling. He is chucking with the best of them when a bell sounds. Everyone stops, except Bronk. He is heaving with a fury. The bell sounds again. Bronk looks up at Uncle Burt, sensing something is amiss. Uncle Burt points to a sign posted behind the bar. Bronk reads.

BEER FIGHT RULES

1. GO ON WHISTLE
2. STOP ON BELL
3. BARTENDERS AND SEATING AREAS OFF LIMITS - <u>VIOLATORS WILL BE REMOVED!</u>"

Pump points his finger at the last line. He drops his slice of pizza and stands, revealing his massive size. Bronk assesses the situation, drops the cups from his hands and cracks a good ole boy smile.

"Drinks on the house." proclaims Uncle Burt.

The stampede pushes Bronk to the bar right in front of Uncle Burt, who feeds cups of beer to the ravenous horde. Joe and Ben share the stool to his right. Pug and his girls occupy the stool to the left. Pug's arms are draped across the bar, and his face rests in a beer puddle.

Uncle Burt slides a beer to Bronk. "You a new puppy?"

"Reckon so. I just got to town, if that's what you mean."

"Welcome to the River Bar. Home of the Dover Dogs Wrestling Team."

"Howdy partner, I'm Bronk."

The name 'Bronk' perks Joe's ears. Bronk reads Uncle Burt's Dover Wrestling T-shirt. "You wrassle?"

"Just the female heifers, if you catch my meaning." Uncle Burt winks.

Joe interrupts. "So what's going down, clown?"

"Huh?"

"So you're *the* Bronk Pokard?"

"Yeah."

"Dogface told me all about you."

"Dogface? Who's Dogface?" asks Bronk.

"Dan. Coach Sangha."

"You call Coach, Dogface?"

"Sure, he's one of the guys. Unc!" shouts Joe, holding his hand in the air. "A round of tequila for the team." Catching Uncle Burt's eye, he accents his order with a wink.

"I never met him, but I heard Coach was an animal."

"Sure, when he wrestled. But now, since he's coaching, he's a marshmallow. So, you never met Dogface?"

"Nope, my daddy worked everythin' out."

Uncle Burt sets three shots of tequila in front of the boys.

Ben and Joe raise their glasses and shout, "Tequila!"

Bronk raises his glass. "What does Coach think of this?"

"He loves it."

"Yeah, the crazier the better," adds Ben.

Bronk nods his approval. "Think I'm gonna like this place." He clicks the other two glasses with his. "Here's to it." The three throw down their shots like old pros.

"Unc, bring us another round and put this on my tab," says Joe.

"What's with him?" asks Bronk, staring at a snoring, slobbering Pug.

"That's Pug."

"It's a little early to be in the barn, ain't it?"

"Watch." Joe sets a beer next to Pug's head and chants, "Pug, beer." Joe repeats it slowly at first and then faster and faster. "Pug, beer. Pug, beer. Pug, beer." Pug's eyelids flutter.

The whole bar area begins chanting. "Pug, beer!" Pug blinks and slowly raises his head. Joe lifts the beer and waves it back and forth under Pug's nose. Pug sniffs. His eyes blink open. He clutches the beer, tips it up, and chugs it down in one smooth gulp.

Pug belches, "Oh, man. Gotta love it." His eyes float up into his head, and he goes limp. His face splats on the hardwood bar top.

"Ah, another satisfied customer," announces Uncle Burt.

An undulating roar turns everyone's head toward the front door. The same red Harley from the sidewalk rumbles through the doorway. The driver, Sam Kruger, is a sensual brute. His rock-hard body is now clothed with boots, skintight jeans and a form-fitting T-shirt that reads "No Jap Shit" on the front and "Harley-Davidson Forever" on the back. Kruger turns the ignition off and walks his Harley to the bar. "Barkeep, a pitcher of beer to go. And make it quick. I'm in a hurry. Woof, woof, woof." Everybody barks back in response.

Kruger admires his physique in the mirror behind the bar. Uncle Burt passes the pitcher over the bar to Kruger. Joe intercepts the pitcher and snatches it from Kruger's grasp.

"Give me the pitcher," says Kruger. Joe holds the pitcher of beer out of Kruger's reach. "C'mon, give me the pitcher," demands Kruger. Joe plays keep-away. "Joe, I'm warning you. C'mon don't fuck around. Let me have it."

Joe glances to Uncle Burt, who cannot resist and blows his whistle. Everyone screams, "BEER FIGHT!" Joe pours the pitcher over Kruger's head. Kruger, forsaking all regard for his person, uses his body to shield his Harley.

Ben sits at the bar alone. A beer splash soaks the side of his head. He sits staring at his girlfriend, who is hanging out with another guy in the dry area of the tavern. The bell sounds.

Kruger is infuriated. He quickly removes his beer-soaked shirt, revealing his hairy, chiseled chest and six-pack stomach. He wrings out his shirt and tenderly wipes his bike. "You guys got no respect," says Kruger, admiring his muscle tone in the mirror. "You got no respect for nothing."

"Uncle Burt. Uncle Burt," belts out Mini D, a short stump of muscle with an infectious smile. He wears gym shorts and a clear rain coat. An umbrella hat sits on his balding head. His tattooed arm is hooked around the neck of a taller, leaner body. They squeeze between Bronk and Pug. "Uncle Burt, this is my little brother Dickie."

"You are so dumb," replies Dickie, pulling his Stroh's beer cap down to cover his face.

"What? What did I do?"

"I told you not to call me Dickie."

"It's your name."

"Richard. Richard is my name. You are too dumb to be a Mango. It makes me wonder about Mom sometimes."

Mini D continues, "This is Uncle Burt, the living legend."

"Thank you, Mini D, thank you. Here, take this off my hands," he says, setting down a tray of drinks. "The drunks are calling."

Mini D chugs a beer and eyeballs an open purse next to him on the bar. He checks right, then left, and walks his fingers into the purse. He checks around before removing his prize and hanging his clenched hand at his side. Behind Mini D and Dickie, a cluster of girls has gathered to admire Kruger's Harley and get a closeup of his body.

Joe moves in to keep order. "Safety first, girls, safety first. Holy bakery, Kruger, you need to install a ticket machine on your bike so the girls can take a number."

"I'm not talking to you."

One of the girls notices Dickie's oversized Dover Wrestling T-shirt. "Are you a wrestler?"

"You better believe it, baby. They call me 'the man of a thousand moves.'" All the girls giggle.

Kruger peers up from his motorcycle to see who is stealing his audience. He walks straight over. "You're no wrestler," he counters, grabbing Dickie's narrow chest in a bear hug. Kruger's sculpted arms bend Dickie over backward and drop him on the beer-covered floor. Kruger flexes and poses for the girls.

"What's with you man? asks Dickie.

"C'mon you're a wrestler. Wrestle."

Dickie gathers himself, climbs to his feet, stalks in and tries to grab Kruger's leg. Kruger catches Dickie and physically manhandles the smaller, weaker foe. He slings Dickie around, slamming his body against the stools and bar and into the spectators. He flips his opponent through the air. Dickie splashes and slides across the flooded floor as Kruger raises his hands to his cheering fans. Dickie coils and launches a surprise attack from behind. Kruger turns, catching the lunging Dickie and using his momentum to toss him airborne. His body splats and slides all the way across the beer-soaked floor to the other end of the bar.

Mini D enjoys the lesson his big-mouthed brother is getting. He calmly works his way across the floor to the restrooms. He pauses, makes sure everyone is engrossed in the rasslin' match and enters the ladies' room. Inside, he opens his hand, takes the cap off the tube of lipstick lifted from the purse, and hurriedly writes on the mirror: "Mini D is the best LOVER!"

For a finale, Kruger presses Dickie above his head, spins him in a circle like the professional rasslers and throws him. Dickie's body collides with the wet slip-and-slide floor and skims across the entire length of the open bar area. Cheers prompt Kruger to follow Dickie and step on his neck. He holds Dickie's face in a beer puddle with his boot. Kruger's rigid face cracks a smile as he looks at one of the pretty spectators. "Hi, blondie. I love you, no shit. Want to buy me a drink?"

Mini D approaches. "Okay, Kruger. That's enough."

"What's it to you?"

"I don't know. Maybe because he's my brother?"

Taking his foot off Dickie's neck, Kruger exclaims, "You're Mini D's brother. Gee, you should have said something." Kruger helps Dickie to his feet. He manufactures a broad smile, clasps both hands above his head and flexes to the audience in triumph. "What can I say, Mini D? Your brother is a wimp."

"Yeah, and only faggots ride Harleys," says Dickie.

The onlookers freeze. Silence falls across the bar area. Kruger's eyes go vacant, and a creepy smile etches across his face. Uncle Burt hurdles the bar and stands in front of Kruger. "Okay, big-time wrestling is over. It's time for all good little wrestlers to call it a night." Kruger pushes

Uncle Burt aside and reaches for Dickie. Uncle Burt grabs Kruger by the back of his black mane and jerks him to an abrupt stop. "Cool it." orders Uncle Burt. Kruger's eye vessels gorge with blood as he mad-dogs Dickie.

Mini D restrains his brother and nudges him away in the opposite direction. "C'mon, forget about him."

Kruger points and makes sure his words are heard. "This ain't over."

"What a jerk. Do you believe that guy?" asks Dickie.

Mini D drags his brother to the girls' restroom. "C'mon, I'm going to teach you how to meet chicks. It's like real estate—the most important thing is location, location, location." Two cute coeds exit the girls' room. Mini D steps forward and announces, "Hi girls, I'm Mini D, and I'd like you to introduce you to my brother—"

"You're Mini D...*the* Mini D?" ask the giggling girls.

"One and only. Would you like to join us at the bar for a drink?" The girls look at each other, size up Mini D and his brother, and move to the bar.

Joe leans on the bar next to Bronk. He waves to get the bartender's attention. "Unc, another round of tequila for the team."

"This will have to be it. I got an early meetin' with the coach, uh Dogface in the mornin'."

"I thought you were a real cowboy."

Uncle Burt delivers a round of tequila shots. All the glasses are raised in unison followed by a toast. "Tequila!"

"Uncle Burt, bring another round for the team. This one's on me," orders Bronk.

Joe wraps his arm around Bronk's shoulder. "You are all right. You are a Dog." He instructs Uncle Burt, "Just keep 'em coming. Woof. Woof. Woof." Everyone barks. Joe squeezes Bronk and pulls him close. "Look, Bronk, you can take this for what it's worth, but don't let Dogface take advantage of you."

"What d'ya mean?"

"Well, Dogface has been known to do some pretty unscrupulous things."

"He's a four-flusher?"

"For example, what did Dogface give you to come to school here? Tuition?"

"No, he didn't give me nothin'."

"Nothing. You're kidding right?"

"No."

"That Dogface, he's been bragging about you up and down, telling everybody how you're going to put Dover on the map, and he got you for nothing."

Another round of drinks arrives. Everyone lifts a shot glass and shouts, "Tequila!"

Joe pats Bronk on the back. "You poor puppy."

"What?"

"Dogface is a dog ass."

"Why?"

"Dogface does that to freshmen." He gestures to the group around the bar. "We all have full scholarships." Joe points to the front window. "See the Corvette? The one they're towing?" Ben looks and takes off running. "That was Ben's bonus for signing to come here." He takes the rolled wad of bills from his pocket and slaps the money on the bar. "Dogface gave this to me earlier tonight and told me to show the guys a good time."

Uncle Burt delivers a tray of shots. Hands grab and lift a drink. Everyone shouts, "Tequila!" and drinks.

"Next round's on me," says Bronk, patting Joe on the back.

***

A herd of empty shot glasses covers the bar top surrounding Bronk and Dickie. Dickie fights to keep his eyes centered and focused. His unoccupied face is devoid of color. It's late. The crowd is beginning to thin, and Pump naps at the end of the bar.

Bronk stands on his stool and raises his shot glass high above his head. "Birds do it and fly. Dogs do it and die. And…and…uh, I can't remember, so here's to it." He downs the shot. It hits him like a bullet between the eyes, and he falls backward into the waiting arms of the Dogs. They slide him back on his stool.

Two policemen enter the River Bar. They look at the drunks at the bar. One officer waves to Uncle Burt while the other takes his two hands, covers his ears, then his eyes, and then his mouth. They resume their customary route to the back of the bar. Three preppies enter and approach the bartender.

"What brings the basketball team here?" asks Uncle Burt. "You guys slumming?"

"We want a bottle of your best champagne," says the tallest one, slapping a one-hundred-dollar bill down on the bar.

"I think I have a bottle in the back cooler. Hold on and I'll get it."

The threesome stares at Bronk. One by one, he picks up every empty shot glass on the bar and licks the last drop out of the bottom.

"He's not a real cowboy," comments the tallest preppie.

Bronk sizes the big mouth up in the mirror behind the bar and thinks, *Shit for brains, that's why they have mirrors behind bars, so no one can git the drop on you.*

The largest of the three adjusts the flipped-up collar of his shirt, leans forward, and sniffs Bronk. "He may be cow shit, but he's definitely not a cowboy." Dickie spins and uncontrollably vomits on the tailored, monogrammed shirt. "Ah." screams the basketball player as he stiff-arms Dickie and knocks him off his stool.

Bronk spins and stuffs his knuckles in the mouth of the big guy and drops him like a roped calf. A voice shouts, "Fight!" The big guy's buddies stop chuckling and attack. The crowd along the bar backs up and forms a semicircle around the foursome. Bronk's wrestling instincts take over. He ducks a punch, steps into and behind the man and locks his hands in a bear hug. He back arches and throws, launching the body over the bar, crashing into the mirror and stacked bottles of booze.

Breaking glass turns every eye in the place toward the fracas. Police charge to the rescue from the back area and begin fighting their way through the pack. The third preppie jumps on Bronk's back and applies a stranglehold. Bronk grabs the arm around his neck and uses it to throw the man to the floor, headfirst. Bronk stands over the limp body.

A policeman walks up from behind, wraps his nightstick around Bronk's throat and commands, "Everybody freeze."

Bronk grabs the stick with one hand, works his hips in close, and hip tosses the man. His backup raises his nightstick and clubs Bronk's skull. Reacting to the attack, Bronk spins and swings, decking the officer with a right hook. His eyes bulge from their sockets when he sees the man he just punched is a cop. The guy thrown into the mirror climbs on top of the bar and leaps on top of Bronk. The first policeman thrown to the floor fumbles for his whistle. Bringing it to his mouth, he blows as hard as he can for help.

Everybody screams, "BEER FIGHT!"

Beer fills the air. The brawl turns into bedlam.

○○○○●●●●●●●●●●●●●●●●●●●●

4. Eat My Dust

CLOUDS BLANKET THE night sky, screening the moon and stars. Headlight beams cast the only light. Red brake lights flash as the station wagon slides to a stop facing a mailbox. The headlights switch to high beam, and after a moment, the wagon peels out.

"It's one of these along here. You watching?" asks Dan.

"Yeah, yeah," says Gorni.

"You looking for the number?"

"I loook. I loook."

There is an awkward silence as Dan continues to slow and flash his brights at each mailbox and then speed off.

"Dis Boobbee Rydar, he goood?" asks Gorni.

"Heh, heh, does Howdy Doody have a wooden dick?"

"What is wooodeen deek? Who Howday Doooday?"

"Forget that. Bobby Ryder is the number one high school wrestler ever—anywhere, anytime. He's won it all and dominated on every level. And he's coming to Dover. Un-fucking-believable."

"HERE IS. TURN!"

Dan brakes and jerks the steering wheel. The brown bomb's tires screech as the car turns into the mouth of a driveway bordered by two overgrown evergreen trees. The wheels catch gravel, and the wagon skids toward the far tree. Dan steps on the gas and tries to accelerate out of the slide. A tree branch catches the driver's side mirror, rips it from its support and leaves it dangling by control wires extruding from the top of the car door. The spinning wheels catch and thrust the wagon forward, free of the tree, hurling down the private drive. Dan sees the rear end of a car blocking the drive and jams the brakes to the floor. They lock up. The brown battering ram skims over the gravel surface. CRASH!

The porch light switches on, and the front door opens. Bobby Ryder bounds out the front door. Moving catlike across the porch, he settles in the most advantageous spot to observe the driveway. He is followed by his parents, Mr. and Mrs. Ryder, and a fourth figure brings up the rear. Dave Kane.

Dan spots Kane. *What the fuck? What's that motormouth doing here?* He hurtles from his seat and marches up the driveway. Gorni stops to inspect the damage. The station wagon's front bumper has slid under the rear bumper of a long black limousine, smashing the wagon's front grille. A small jet of steam whistles in the night air.

Dan stops at the bottom of the porch steps and announces, "Just a scratch. Nothing to worry about."

Dave Kane leads the way inside. College wrestling's most successful coach strides to the front room. His tanned, fit physique models a tailored scarlet blazer and tie that accent his silver shirt and slacks. Last year's championship diamond ring sparkles from his right ring finger. His impeccable, professional appearance impresses and intimidates. Mr. and Mrs. Ryder, wearing a suit and dress, follow.

Dan walks in, pulling papers from his folder. "I got here as soon as I could." Everyone takes a seat around the coffee table. "Here's the Letter of Intent." Dan sets the document on the coffee table and slides it in front of Bobby.

"Would anyone care for a drink?" asks Mrs. Ryder.

"No, thank you, Mrs. Ryder," responds Dan.

Kane pushes the letter back to Dan. "What a marvelous suggestion, Debbie." He stands and walks toward the kitchen. "Do you need any help?"

"Dave, sit."

"I'll have my usual."

"I made a pitcher of martinis," says Mrs. Ryder, prancing to the kitchen.

"Vodka," announces Gorni.

Everyone pauses and stares at Gorni. The strange, hairy little man smiles. Kane returns to his seat. Dan slides the Letter of Intent back to Bobby, hands him a pen and points. "You sign here."

Mr. Ryder interjects, "Excuse me, Son. Dan, my wife and I know our son wants to attend Dover. However, Dave has been kind enough to stop, so maybe it's best we talk it over."

Mrs. Ryder returns with a tray of Martinis and extends it to Kane, who reaches for a long-stemmed glass. Dan snatches the glass from his grasp and tosses the entire contents into his mouth and swallows. Mrs. Ryder is visibly disturbed. She is ready to say something when Kane touches her lightly on the wrist.

Ignoring Dan, Kane opens his leather briefcase and begins to set up. "I've taken the liberty to put together a comparison chart, so we can see where the best opportunities are for Bobby." He assembles a high-tech portable easel and looks at Dan. "Now Dan, I want you to correct me if I'm wrong."

Dan's face is devoid of expression. Kane looks into Mrs. Ryder's eyes and then looks at Dan's empty glass. Mrs. Ryder lifts the pitcher of Martinis and refills Dan's glass. Dan robotically lifts the glass and swallows.

Kane begins. "First and foremost in Bobby's future is his education. Everyone knows Chicago's education is second to none, bar none. Twenty-one of our departments are nationally ranked and…"

Dan sits motionless and stares forward. Mrs. Ryder refills his glass again. He mechanically lifts and swallows. His body continues to function, but he is not aware of the drink, Kane, Bobby, or sitting in the Ryder's house in Cleveland's suburbia.

A man dressed in a red, hooded warm-up stands in front of a cinder block wall. Minimal light from a nearby emergency exit sign strikes the edge of the hood and casts a black shadow where a face should be. A faint, almost inaudible chant infiltrates the sanctuary. The chant builds and grows louder and louder. "Kane. Kane. KANE!" It vibrates through the arena, penetrates the dark refuge and disturbs the hooded man's meditation. He savagely lunges forward, smashing his face into the cinder block wall once, twice, a third time.

The arena is dark, except for a ring of light encircling a wrestling mat in the middle of the floor. The zealous crowd claps and stomps in rhythm to the deafening chant. "Kane. Kane. Kane!" Cheers break the crowd's cadence when a competitor sprints to the center of the mat. It is Dave Kane.

The hooded man strolls to the edge of the ring of light. The entire gym thunders and shakes. "SANGHA. SANGHA. SANGHA!" Dan Sangha strips off his red warm-up. His thick hand sweeps up, removes his glasses and drops them matside.

Dan walks to the center. Blood trickles from his forehead, forks around his eye and oozes down his nose and cheekbone, dripping simultaneously from his snout and chin. The combatants shake hands and glare into each other's soul. Raising his hand, the referee blows his whistle and swipes his arm down to signal the start. The two pit bulls ram foreheads.

"...To summarize, Chicago produces the leaders who run this country and the Olympians and professional athletes of tomorrow. The sky is the limit. Okay, Dan, it's all yours. Dan?" Dan sits in a hypnotic trance. "Dan...Dan...Dan, you ole dog, you okay?"

"Huh?"

"Dan, it's your turn."

"My turn?" Dan looks around the room. Everyone is staring at him. Kane's easel supports a board divided into two sections. The Chicago side is filled with information, and the Dover side is blank. Dan looks at the drained glass in his hand then at the empty pitcher.

Kane points at his board. "Dan, you can start where I left off—team competition. What does your team have to offer?"

Snapping out of it, Dan shouts, "We got Balls!" Mr. and Mrs. Ryder's eyes pop from their aghast faces. They stare at Dan and then at each other.

Dan realizes the impact of what he said and clarifies, "I mean Ballsinger, Rick Ballsinger and Joe Kerr. They're both returning all-Americans. 'Balls' is a nickname, heh, heh."

Dan sweats profusely as he examines Kane's comparison chart. He does a quick study and then gives a halting, unrehearsed response, addressing each issue in no particular order. He looks at Chicago's competition schedule. "We wrestle everyone Chicago does." He sees

Chicago's coaching staff of ten. "I'm the coach." Dan reads nine national championships in a row. "We finish in the top twenty every year."

"Excuse me, you didn't mention your assistant coach, Duray," says Mr. Ryder. "One of the reasons Bobby was interested in Dover was because he would have the opportunity workout with a three-time national champion."

"He may not be returning. It's up in the air," says Dan, returning his attention to the chart. He observes Chicago's first-rate facilities and academic programs. "Dover is a small school. We have our own wrestling room and a couple of nationally ranked college programs."

Beads of sweat drip from Dan's nose and chin. He notices Bobby will receive a full scholarship. "Uh, we can give Bobby tuition." Dan lifts Joe's damp tuition check from his sweat-soaked shirt pocket and slaps it on the coffee table. The room is dead. "And we can get him a job."

Mrs. Ryder breaks the stillness. "How about some wine and snacks? We have Beaujolais, White Zinfandel or Cold Duck."

Dan smiles like an accepted member of the family. "What, no Mad Dog? Heh, heh." His laughter turns hollow. "Dover Dogs, get it? Woof. Woof." An awkward silence returns. "Cold Duck would be fine."

Mrs. Ryder exits to the kitchen. Mr. Ryder turns to his son. "Well, Son, what do you think?"

"My heart is still set on Dover."

"It's your choice. Mom and I just want what is best for you."

Kane places his hand on Bobby's shoulder. "Well, stud, anywhere you go, I'll wish you the best of luck. I just want to know one thing. What can I do to change your mind? I want you to be a Chicago Cat when we set the record this year. You name it, and it's yours."

"Geez, I'm sorry, Coach, but my mind is made."

The color drains from Kane's face. Losing is not a part of his makeup. Unsure of what to do or how to behave, he does nothing. He sits back and eyeballs a sweaty, gleaming Dan.

Dan basks in victory and a beaming smile stretches across his flushed face. Mrs. Ryder returns from the kitchen with an opened bottle of Cold Duck and a tray of assorted crackers and cheeses.

"So, have you decided?" asks Mrs. Ryder.

"It's still Dover," answers Bobby.

Mrs. Ryder forces a smile and sets the tray on the coffee table.

"This calls for a celebration," says Dan, sliding the Letter of Intent to the left of Bobby, then to the right and finally in front of him. He hands Bobby a pen. Bobby takes it from his wobbly hand. Dan glances at Kane in triumph. Bobby puts the pen to paper. Dan lifts the bottle of wine. "This calls for a toast."

Mrs. Ryder fights to be gracious. "Just a moment, Bobby. Wait until I get the glasses." She returns to the kitchen, clasps her hands and looks up at the ceiling as if in prayer. She begins to shake and puts both hands on the countertop to steady her trembling body. Gathering her composure, she picks up a tray of wineglasses and starts back through the swinging door, then stops in her tracks.

Dan is already celebrating. He has the Cold Duck tilted to the ceiling and guzzles directly from the bottle. Mrs. Ryder returns to the kitchen through the swinging door unnoticed. She returns the tray of glasses to the countertop and reevaluates before marching back into the front room. Bobby sees her and picks up the pen.

"Just a moment, Bobby. Let's enjoy some cheese and crackers." She smiles and watches.

Dan stacks the cheese and crackers like a crooked heap of checkers. When he attempts to pick the miniskyscraper up, it crumbles; the pieces scatter and sprinkle from his palm onto the coffee table, chair and carpet. He opens his mouth wide and stuffs the entire contents of his hand into his face. Raising the Cold Duck in the air, he sprays cheese and crackers as he blubbers, "To Bobby's future." He snorts and laughs and then takes another swig from the wine bottle.

Mrs. Ryder cuts in. "Mr. Sangha, you must have hundreds of stories of your travels as a wrestler. Would you be a dear and share some of your memorable experiences with us? We'd love to hear them."

"Sure, be glad to," slurs Dan, spraying more crumbs from his mouth. "Once, I was the biggest guy in India. I walked down the streets of New Delhi when I was there for the World Championships. There were people all over the place. There weren't any buildings, just people all over the place. And I was the biggest one." Dan chomps on some cheese and crackers. "And they didn't have any cold Coke either, just warm Coke. And when I finished eating an apple, I threw away the core, and about a dozen people started fighting for it. Did you ever see a dead cow with a million flies on it? Heh, heh." Dan takes a gulp of wine. He offers the bottle with floating crumbs to Mrs. Ryder. She declines. "I went to the john. All there were, were holes in the floor. So, I squatted over this hole, and a woman came in, pulled up her dress and squatted at the hole next to me. I thought I was in the wrong john, so I yanked up my pants and ran out. Heh, heh, later, I found out that men and women use the same john." The memory sets off a fit of laughter.

Only Bobby and Gorni laugh in response. Dan sits up straight, begins breathing deeply and fully, and blinks his eyes repeatedly. He stands and asks, "Speaking of the john?"

Mr. Ryder points to the hallway opening. "Down the hall, second door on the left."

Dan gets his bearings. He shoves the wine bottle into Mrs. Ryder's chest. "Here." He takes a step, leans, and loses his balance, falling across the laps of Mr. and Mrs. Ryder. Kane helps Dan to his feet, and aims his shoulders in the right direction. Dan stares toward the hall, shakes his head and blinks his eyes. He staggers to the hall and then bounces from wall to wall down to the bathroom.

Dan yells, "Gorni." Then louder: "Gorni. Get in here."

Gorni looks at everyone and shrugs; he stands and walks down the hall to the bathroom.

Mr. and Mrs. Ryder look at one another, at Kane, and then down the hall.

Dan sways over the toilet, urinating and singing, "Gorni, Gorni, boroni, Gorni. Gorni, Gorni, boroni, Gorni." Gorni stands by, watching Dan's face turn pale. Dan gleams and turns to look at Gorni with bloodshot eyes. "Heh, heh. Well, Gorni, how's it going? Huh? Huh?"

"Good, but no more drink anymore."

"Yeah, I know. Now, I want you to get out there and keep your ears open. Watch Kane and don't do anything to screw this up."

Gorni returns to his seat. Everyone sits quietly and smiles politely, pretending not to hear the faint moan. A guttural bellow turns their heads. Each heave precedes a bottomless purge. This is followed by a series of hollow bull roars that soon turn into a spasm of dry heaves. Each retch gags its listeners.

Kane's confident posture is back.

***

Gorni and Kane carry a half-conscious Dan down the driveway and deposit him in the back seat of the station wagon. Dan slobbers and mumbles incoherently. Gorni walks around to the driver's seat.

"Whatever it takes," says Kane, lifting Dan's feet in the car. "You ole dog. Still a lightweight when it comes to the booze. Well, better luck next time." He wipes his hands, shuts the door and then leans into the passenger window. "Tell Dan if there's any damage to the limo, I'll send the bill to the school." Kane turns and struts back to the Ryder's house.

Dan rolls over, mumbling, "Fucking motormouth. I blew it, to a fucking chatterbox—"

"It over. Forget."

"I just needed one like Ryder…just one…just one…"

"Keys," says Gorni, reaching over the seat.

Dan stuffs his fingers into his pocket and hands Gorni a handful of cheese and crackers. He turns his back and cuddles into a ball, murmuring, "Just one…just one…"

Gorni climbs on the back of the seat far enough to reach Dan. He rummages in Dan's coat pockets and salvages the keys from a cracker and cheese mess.

***

Dan drives as Gorni takes his turn sleeping. He pulls into his driveway, and parks. Dan drags his exhausted body from the front seat, shuffles to the front door, and turns the knob. It is locked. He fumbles through his keys in the dark, picks one out, inserts it and turns. Nothing. It does not move. He studies his keys with a puzzled look and tries the same one again. It still does not work. He checks his watch and rings the doorbell. There is no response. He tries knocking. No answer. He knocks harder. Nothing.

○○○○○●●●●●●●●●●●●●●●●●●●●

5. Do the Hustle

THE RISING SUN'S rays warm Dan's sleeping face wedged between the car door and seat. His weary, unshaven face feels the radiant heat, and his closed eyes sense the light. Opening his eyes unleashes a flashback of the previous night. Reclosing his eyes, he pulls his jacket he has been using as a blanket over his head.

He sits up, slips the magazine cover from his jacket pocket, unfolds it, and looks at Kane and his Chicago team. His eyes drift away. Climbing from the makeshift sleeping berth, he stretches, takes a last look at the magazine cover and releases it. A breeze tumbles it across the lawn. He mopes to the front door, tries the doorknob, inserts his key and turns, but it does not budge. As he slips on his jacket, he checks his watch. He takes a deep breath and rings the doorbell. He tries again, waits, then knocks and listens. Nothing. He pounds on the door hard and loud. Neighbors peer out their windows. Dan backs away from the door and stares up at the master bedroom window. A hand closes the curtains. Dan's shoulders droop. He retrieves the morning paper from the driveway and retreats to the car.

Dan climbs back in the driver's seat and opens the paper. His drawn face hangs over the front page headline: "Wrestler Wrecks Bar." Under the caption, a photograph of Bronk being subdued by several policemen fills the page. Dan's dreary, deadpan eyes consume the picture from top to bottom and from side to side. His lifeless eyeballs begin to smolder as they dart around the photograph. He cannot believe what he sees. Over and over, faster and faster, his eyes retrace their path. The extinguished embers of his soul begin to glow. To confirm what he sees, he moves his finger around the page and counts to himself, *One, two, three, four*. Fresh air blows on the hot embers. *Five, six, seven...maybe eight.* The hot embers ignite and burst into flame. His eyes are aglow, and his spirit burns bright with renewed energy. A gust slaps the magazine cover to the windshield and whisks it away. Dan leaps from the front seat and chases it.

***

Dan barrels past the secretary, barges through the athletic director's office door and blurts, "I need a favor."

"Sure, Dan," says Bill, looking up from the morning newspaper. "What can I—what happened to you? You look terrible."

"Listen about them, you know, dropping the program. I was wondering if I can keep the program going."

"I'm sorry but it's out of my hands."

"I hate to let the guys on the team down." Dan leans across the desk. "This season is the last chance for a lot of them."

"Look, if it were up to me, you'd be the last to go. But this goes beyond me. This decision came from the chancellor and the board of trustees."

Dan walks around the desk. "We're right there," he says, holding his thumb and index finger a quarter inch apart in front of the AD's face. "This could be the best team in school history. This could be the year we beat Kane."

"It's a financial decision. There's just no money."

"Could I do it on my own?"

"What do you mean?"

"What if I raise the money?"

"How are you going to do that?"

"I don't know, but I'll do it."

Bill speaks slowly, "Well, I don't see why not." He thinks his way through what Dan is asking. "As long as you cover all the costs and there are no rule violations—"

"Great."

"Wait a minute, I didn't say—

"Unbelievable." Dan turns to exit. "Heh, heh, heh. Unbelievable." He stops abruptly at the door. "Oh, one more thing. Can we...you know. Is there any way we can keep this just between the two of us?"

"Besides President Hardon, the chancellor and board, I don't see why not."

Dan turns and bolts.

"Wait. I still have to get their approval." Bill scoops up the newspaper from his desk and runs after Dan shouting, "Did you see this morning's paper?"

Dan speed walks down the passageway and shouts back, "Yeah."

Bill postures outside his office, shaking the paper above his head, and yells, "What do you have to say about this?"

Hitting full stride down the corridor toward his office, Dan bellows, "Did you see how many policemen it took to arrest him? If I had nine more like him, we'd be national champs."

"It's not the type of publicity you need."

"Practice at three. Practice at three. Practice at three."

***

The noon sun's searing rays pelt the roadway. Heat waves slither above the cooking blacktop. Dan exits the Pizza Time establishment with a giant triangular slice of pizza drooping over the fingers of one hand and a manila folder in the other. The bonfire of purpose eyes his next prey. He folds the wedge of pizza in half and stuffs the entire lump into his swollen cheeks, leaps into the street, freezes, sidesteps, and then using his folder like a matador's cape, he dodges, dips, and ducks around the oncoming traffic. He leaps to the opposite sidewalk and catches his balance.

Dan charges the River Bar entry and smashes his face, stamping an imprint of his sauce-covered jowls on the locked door. He attacks the wood door with a clenched fist and then cups his hands around his eyes and looks through the window. "Uncle Burt. Uncle Burt." he hollers, knocking on the glass.

Inside, the intimidating pounding summons Uncle Burt from a deep sleep. His hand grasps air until it finds a string and pulls. The spotlight illuminates his nude body sprawled on a pool table. He rolls over onto his back, revealing an unclothed feminine shape next to him. Unable to open his eyes, Uncle Burt slides off the pool table and blindly staggers to the front door, rubbing his eyes.

"Who is it?"

"It's me. Open up," snaps Dan.

"What the hell? What time is it?"

"Let me in. I have to talk to you."

"Come back later."

"It's important."

Uncle Burt struggles with the lock and cracks the door open, shielding his slit eyes against the flood of light. "This better be good."

Dan's hand swipes the door wide open, exposing Uncle Burt's nakedness. He barges into stale beer stench and gags, "Ehhh...What's that smell?" His eyes peer crotchward. "You have an erection."

"No shit, Sherlock, I always got a hard-on in the morning 'till I take a piss."

"You shouldn't be walking around like that."

"Hey, I was asleep." Uncle Burt scratches his head. "Never mind. What do you want?"

Dan spies the unconscious, raw, curvy torso spread on the pool table. He darts to the pool table, inspects the sleeping flesh and ponders, "How can you fuck in here with that smell?"

"Please, Dan, what do you want?"

Dan gazes at the woman. "What's it like doing it on a pool table?"

"C'mon, Dan, what's so important?"

Without warning, the stark-naked woman rolls from her side to her back and spreads her legs, aiming her most private patch at Dan's face and moans, "Ohhh, go Burt go, go Burt go, ohhh, mmm..."

Uncle Burt smiles. "She must be dreaming."

"More like a nightmare." Dan's eyes are locked on her. "I wanted to talk to you alone. I didn't know there would be three of us." He peeks at Uncle Burt's erection, back at her arousing bush, and then down at his own swollen crotch. "Uh, five of us."

Uncle Burt smirks as he takes a mental picture of Dan boyishly ogling the erotic pose with a red saucy goatee and a swollen stiffy. "Enough." Uncle Burt pushes Dan back to the door and into the street. "Look, let me piss and I'll buy you breakfast. Meet me at the Dover House in twenty minutes." The door shuts, and the lock latches.

Dan turns to face the world with fresh vigor and exposes the bulge in his pants. Three young coeds point and giggle. Red-faced, Dan covers his crotch with his manila folder and schleps off.

***

The Dover House restaurant is full of suit-and-tie-clad executives doing lunch and students catching a bite between classes. Uncle Burt sits at the far end of the counter, legs crossed, sipping coffee and turning the pages of various sport sections from the nation's major newspapers. His hair is disheveled, his face unshaven. Sleep lingers in his eyes. A ratty housecoat exposes his chest and jockey shorts, and threadbare dog slippers loosely cover his feet.

Dan enters and bulls his way to the front of the waiting line. A trace of pizza sauce remains on his cheek and chin. He scours the crowd for Uncle Burt and makes his way to the counter. The only empty stool is at the opposite end. Dan approaches the man next to the vacant seat, taps him on the shoulder and asks if he would move down. One by one, Dan imposes on each diner to scoot over and works his way to the stool next to Uncle Burt. Before Dan can sit, a pretty coed slips in front of him and parks.

Uncle Burt notices Dan and points to a vacant stool hidden from view at the end of the counter. "I was saving this for you."

"I knew that was there." Dan sits. "Just the man I want to see."

Uncle Burt holds up his hand. "Just a minute." He continues reading.

"I just need to show you something."

"Give me a minute."

Dan fidgets. "I just—"

"Just a minute."

Dan squirms as the waitress delivers Uncle Burt's breakfast. He taps his fingers and toes, watching Uncle Burt devour the sports page. His breakfast goes untouched. Dan stares at the steam rising from the plate of food. His nostrils fill with the aroma of fresh cooked bacon. He reaches across Uncle Burt's paper and lifts a slice from the plate.

Uncle Burt's eyes break from the sports page and track the bacon from his plate into Dan's chomping mouth. "You want breakfast or lunch?" asks Uncle Burt.

"I don't want to eat. I want to talk."

"Can't talk on an empty stomach. How about coffee?"

"I don't drink coffee. I'll have juice." Dan helps himself to a slice of toast and another piece of bacon and makes a sandwich.

Uncle Burt puts aside the newspaper and takes the ketchup bottle in hand. "I can't eat in front of you. Remember, it's my treat." Shaking the bottle up and down, he drowns the rest of his breakfast in red sauce.

"I hate ketchup."

Uncle Burt orders across the counter at the moving waitress. "Sweetheart, another bacon and egg special." He winks at Dan. "Hold the coffee. Oh, and a large tomato juice."

Dan starts, "Okay, two things. First, how'd you like to be my assistant coach this year?"

"You already have an assistant coach—Duray."

"This is going to be the best team ever. We're going to surprise a lot of people, and it could be the year we beat Kane. We can do it together. It'll be fun."

"What are you going to do with Duray?" asks Uncle Burt.

"He's gone."

"Good, I never liked that guy."

"He was a three-time national champion and four-time all-American."

"But Duray wasn't a Dog. He was a jackass." Uncle Burt thinks for a moment. "Where did he go?"

"Don't know."

"Why do you want me?"

"You have a way with the guys. They'll listen to you."

"Thanks. I appreciate that. Why did Duray leave?"

"Budget cuts."

"Oh, I see you want an assistant for free. I'll have to think about that one."

"Hey, it could be a lot of fun. And look, I'm putting together a wrestling program, and I'm selling advertising space." Dan opens his folder and removes a sample program. "You want to run an ad for the River Bar? You'll get everyone there after a home match."

"I already get everyone there after a match." He watches Dan sweat for a moment. "Okay, let me see what you got."

Dan slides an information sheet in front of Uncle Burt and begins turning pages in the sample program. "We're selling full pages, half pages, and quarter pages."

"What's a full page going for?"

Dan bubbles over with excitement. "Five hundred for a regular, seven fifty for each of the center tucks and a grand for the back cover."

Uncle Burt thinks it over. "A thousand and seven fifty. Hmm, okay, put me down for the back cover and both center tucks."

"Whoa, that's great. That's unbelievable. The back cover is a grand, and both center tucks would be fifteen hundred. That's a total of twenty-five-hundred. Heh-heh, unbelievable."

Uncle Burt returns to his sports news. "Yeah, that ought to cover the damage your new recruit, Bronk, did to my bar. So, now we're even."

"Huh? Wait a minute."

Something catches Uncle Burt's eye. He snaps the print close to his face. "Will you look at this? Do you believe this?"

Dan tries to follow. "What? Believe what?"

Gongs from the town clock disturb the air as they do every hour. Uncle Burt changes directions. "Never mind, got to go. Nice doing business with you. Let me know when your deadline is for those ads." He shovels a final fork of eggs into his mouth, swoops up his coffee and newspapers, bolts to the door and funnels out with a dozen other students.

Dan yells after him, "Practice at three. Practice at three."

The waitress delivers the breakfast special and pulls out her check pad and pen. "Okay, let's see, that's two coffees, two specials, and a juice...comes to...plus tax...carry the one...that's $16.03." She tears off the check and hands it to Dan and smiles. "Plus a tip. Uncle Burt always leaves a nice tip."

"I don't drink coffee."

6. Got to Survive

DAN SITS AT his desk, studying a class schedule. Mini D stands behind, looking over his shoulder. Dan points. "Okay, see this class? You go to this class, but you don't have to go."

"What?"

"It's fixed with the professor. You make sure you go," says Dan, winking. "But you don't have to go. Understand?"

"Huh?"

Dan speaks with deliberate slowness. "Okay, okay. What I mean is, you tell everyone you're going to class. You go to class. You don't miss a class. But you don't worry about going. Got it?"

Mini D shakes his head and shrugs. His baffled face breaks into a smile as Balls, Gorni and Uncle Burt enter, dressed for practice.

"Look, Mini D, I'll take care of this class. You just pass crayons. Now get out of here and get ready for practice." Mini D exits, and Dan turns his attention to Balls and Uncle Burt. "Heh-heh, it's like a fucking sauna outside today. Take them to the football stadium and put them through cals until they can't do any more and then run stadium stairs until I get there. Make it tough. Remember, your job is to make them quit." *And chase away the pussies.* They nod and walk. Gorni gets up and follows.

"You stay," commands Dan.

"I practice."

"No, you stay and help me."

"I wrestle. I workout."

"No. You stay. You manager. Get the ranking board and follow me."

Gorni's rigid jaw tightens under his red flushed face as he stomps across the office. He grabs the ranking board so hard the sudden jerk unhooks and spills several of the name tags.

"C'mon, we don't have all day."

Gorni drops to his knees and struggles, retrieving the fallen name tags through his blurry eyes.

The athletic director knocks on Dan's open door and steps in. "Excuse me, Dan, may I have a word with you?"

"Sure, Bill." Dan nods his head. "Gorni, go to the wrestling room and wait for me there." Gorni trudges down the hall.

"What is it?" asks Dan, gesturing for Bill to sit.

"I ran the situation by the president, chancellor, and the board. They said you have to make a choice. They'll find you a new job with the university and keep you on the payroll, or you can keep the team, provided you are responsible for them, financially and ethically. However, they can't do both. They'll approve one. The decision is yours."

***

Bronk's bloodshot eyes squint as he steps into the blinding light. An officer carries his cowboy hat and escorts him from the police station. They stop on the front steps, and the officer extends the hat. Bronk takes it and fits it on his head. *Damn. Shit-Damn.* He removes it and feels the egg-sized lump on the back of his head.

"That nightstick of yours left its mark," he says.

The policeman cracks a smile. Bronk's forehead has a rare scrape from his right eyebrow to his hairline. A cut runs across the swollen bridge of his nose and has drained into two black-and-blue eyes. His bloodstained, buttonless shirt has several tears and hangs open. The policeman gives directions. He sends Bronk off with a pat on the back. A red bandana dangles from his rear pocket; the tip bounces with each boot step.

***

Dan saunters into the football stadium with Gorni in tow. Over a hundred drenched die-hard bodies run up and down the long rows of the stadium's wooden bleacher seating. Several fainthearted dot the sidelines with their hands on their knees, upchucking the remains of their lunch to a constant chorus of moaning, groaning, and retching. *This is good,* thinks Dan. He signals Uncle Burt to blow his whistle.

Everyone stops, and Dan announces, "Okay, one more up and down as hard as you can, and that'll be it. Line up." Everyone scrambles. "Ready." shouts Dan. He gives the signal, and Uncle Burt blows his whistle.

Those who can, attack the stairs. Blocking the pain and fatigue, they sprint as fast as they can. Each stadium step takes its toll. Those reaching the top touch the brick wall, turn and head back down past their fallen comrades. The trip down is more perilous. For those who misstep, the fall is faster and farther.

Balls leads the way to the finish. Those following him crumble to the ground as they step off the stairs.

Balls moves among the fallen, shouting encouragement. "Anything that doesn't kill you just makes you tougher. C'mon, we're the Dogs. Woof. Woof. Woof." Everyone who is capable barks in unison.

Uncle Burt blows his whistle. Everyone is quiet.

"Okay, now we're going to run the cross-country course. Balls will lead you."

Someone shouts, "But you said this was it."

"That's right. That's it for the stadium stairs. Now it's time for the cross-country course."

Another voice shouts, "How far is that?"

"Depends on the weather," says Dan, pointing to Uncle Burt to blow his whistle. "Ready?"

Someone mouths off, "I didn't come here to run cross-country. I came to wrestle."

"Oh, right. What was I thinking? How could I be so thoughtless?" responds Dan. "Forget the cross-country course. Balls, run them out to the lake and back."

Someone moans, "That has to be fifteen, sixteen miles or more."

A few dissidents throw in the towel and walk off mumbling, "Fuck this. This is bullshit. I'm out of here."

Dan retorts, "That's right. If you can't handle the pressure, and you want to pack it in, let Uncle Burt know you're checking out. We don't cut anyone here. This isn't for everyone. The rest of you, keep the man in front of you in sight so you don't get lost."

Uncle Burt blows his whistle, and they are off. Balls leads the way out of the stadium.

Dan runs after them shouting, "Run this like it's the national finals, like everything you do. Finish number one." He runs back past a crowd of quitters gathering around Uncle Burt. "C'mon, Gorni, my truck."

A long single file of runners streams down the country road. The leaders begin crossing a bridge. At the rear of the pack, Pump, Ben, and Adam jog together. Just before the bridge, Pump ducks off the road and disappears into the tall, grassy brush. Ben slows and looks back and forth between the runners and Pump. Adam pushes Ben into the bushes, and they follow Pump.

Balls turns and runs to the rear of the group and shouts, "This isn't the Dogs. Come on, let's go." He turns and races back toward the front. "The Dogs are up there. Let's go."

***

Dan's red pickup truck creeps down the road, approaching the front-runners from the opposite direction. Gorni is behind the wheel. Dan stands in the bed of the truck with his head peering above the cab and instructs Gorni, "Slower. Slower. Slower…"

Dan squats and reaches into a bushel basket of red crabapples. Armed, Dan springs up and launches his attack. He hurls the golf ball-sized fruit with uncanny accuracy. Red projectiles ricochet off the runners' heads, backs, asses and legs. They scatter, cover their heads with their arms and serpentine down the highway until they are out of range. They stop to rub the stinging red welts left by the inspirational fruit.

Dan bellows, "Hurry up. You understand about being number one."

In the distance, black storm clouds announce their approach with a thunderous overture.

***

Bronk opens the door and bounces in from the steam bath to the air-conditioned athletic center. His thirsty eyes scout the unfamiliar territory. He removes his hat and uses his red bandana to wipe the sweat from his forehead and inner rim of his hat. A row of concession machines lures him. He opts for a bottle of Coke and a bag of peanuts. He takes a swig of Coke and watches a girl lumber down the corridor carrying a couple of oversized aluminum suitcases. He runs her down and corrals her.

"You're the pizza girl."

"Gee, I never heard that one before. You some type of mystic cowboy or something?"

"You don't remember me from last night?"

She looks at his two black eyes. "Let me see. Who is that masked man?"

"You're more entertainin' than a rodeo clown."

"I'm not sure what to make of that. Is it my makeup or the way I'm dressed?"

"Shoot, you're as pretty as a red filly in a flower garden on a spring day."

Jas walks away.

Bronk pursues her. "Whoa—hold your horses. What're ya rushin' off for?"

She holds up her cases. "Got places to go, people to see."

"What's more important than someone in need?"

She stops. "Okay, what do you need?"

"Well, I'm a stranger in these parts. How do I get to your place?"

Jas walks away.

Bronk runs her down. "Boy, you're touchy."

"Not normally. But yes, considering I don't know who you are, and you look like you just had a night out with Freddy Kruger, the Evil Dead, and the Terminator all rolled into one."

"Bronk's my name and I need to find Dogface."

"Who?"

"Coach Sangha."

"Oh, so you're a wrestling cowboy."

"Among other things. What do you say I tag along?" He takes a case from her hand. "I can help you carry these cases. What's your name?"

"Jas. You can help until we get to the back door. I'm taking these across campus to the clinic in a university vehicle. No riders allowed."

"Well, Jas, what d'ya say we saddle up to a drink later?"

"Saddle up?"

"If the saddle's a problem, we can go bareback."

"Is that a ten-gallon hat you're wearing?"

"Yeah."

"I figured it would have to be that big to get your head in it."

"The hat, that's just for balance."

"Balance?"

"That's how cowboys stay on longer."

"That's not saying much, considering you only have to ride a bull eight seconds to win, and hardly anybody can do it. If you have a meeting with Coach Sangha, you better get to it. But he won't be in his office. He's at practice. Better try the wrestling room, down that corridor. Follow it to the end." Jas stops at the exit door and takes back her case.

"Okay, one last thing." Bronk bites the plastic bag and tears the top off the bag of peanuts. "Could you help me with this? It's easier with two."

"What's that?"

Handing her the peanut bag. "Just pour these in here."

Jas sets down her case, takes the bag and pours the peanuts into a funnel formed by his hands cupped around the bottle opening. The peanuts slide deep into the Coke, hiss and float back to the top. Bronk wipes his hands and licks the remaining salt from his finger tips. "Thanks."

Jas lifts her cases and opens the door with her rear. "Oh, and some friendly advice. If you're meeting with Coach, you better watch your nuts."

Bronk watches the door close and thinks, *About as warm as an icicle.* He tilts the Coke bottle, fills his mouth with crunchy Coke-soaked peanuts and strides down the hall.

***

Dickie treads alone on autopilot. He clutches his gut, slows to a stuttered step and stops, resting his hands on his knees. Collapsing to his knees, then to his hands and knees, he sprays vomit from his red-hot face.

Dan's truck stops next to Dickie. The sick dog picks his head up. The bed is full of spent bodies that could go no farther.

Dan is behind the wheel. "Dickie, what are you doing here? Do you know you're the last one, and you're about two or three miles behind the rest of the team?"

Dickie uses the side of the truck to lift himself upright. Arms reach out and pull him into the truck bed.

"You know, Gorni needs an assistant. Do you want to be his assistant?" asks Dan.

Gorni glares at Dan. A blast of wind blindsides the truck. Rain droplets dot the dusty paint and pelt the passengers. Dan makes a sharp u-turn and accelerates, then slams on the brakes, crashing everyone into the back of the cab, and then peels out, throwing everyone to the back of the truck bed. A flash of lightning. A crash of thunder. Sprinkles give way to a stinging, cold downpour.

***

A drenched female jogger plods through the cloudburst. Her voluptuous breasts bob in rhythm beneath her soaked T-shirt.

"Oh God, will you look at them bounce," says Pump, sitting with Adam and Ben under a dense, umbrella-shaped tree shielding them from the torrent of water missiles. Pump lights a joint and inhales until there is a burning tip.

"You like the ladies?" asks Adam.

"Don't let him fool you. He's married with kids," interjects Ben.

"Is that right, Pump? You got a ball and chain?"

"I got three of them and another one on the way," laughs Pump, taking another quick hit before passing the joint to Ben.

"No shit. What'd you do, get hitched in junior high?"

"We were married out of high school. I got in some trouble and had to go before a judge, and he gave me a choice: jail or the service. I spent six years in the Air Force," explains Pump.

Ben inhales, takes repeated deep breaths in and holds them as he extends his arm to Adam.

"No shit. My judge sent me straight to prison. You see any action?" inquires Adam, taking the rolled joint from Ben.

"Not the kind of action I like to talk about," says Pump.

"What's that supposed to mean?" asks Ben.

"I didn't see anything with a skirt or bullets," says Pump. "I was a supply sergeant."

Adam brings the reefer to his lips and sucks with the force of a whirlwind.

Ben raises his voice above the human vacuum and asks, "What the hell does a supply sergeant do?"

The rush of air is deafening, demanding Pump and Ben's attention. They turn their heads and watch the human Hoover. The red-hot head burns down the paper shaft of the joint. Pump lifts his eyebrows, expecting the suckage to end any moment. Ben watches Adam's black face turn red as the joint devil continues to draw in and expand his lungs. Pump and Ben look at each other, unsure of what they are witnessing. The joint burns down like a fuse. Adam's face turns purple. The roach burns down to nothing and disappears between his fingers and lips into the black hole. He begins snorting, holding the smoke in, and fighting his body's attempt to breathe. He collapses to his back, rolls on his side and goes into spasm. Ben and Pump look at each other and then at Adam shaking, jerking, and trembling.

Unsure of what to do, Ben moves closer and asks, "You okay?"

Fighting to hold his breath, Adam shakes his head and waves Ben off.

"How about you, Ben? How's your girl—what's her name? asks Pump, watching Adam.

"Tara. She's okay," says Ben, moving to get a better look at Adam's face.

"She still busting your balls?" asks Pump.

Adam snorts, coughs, and rolls over to his back. "She ain't right, mannn," he says, exhaling a smoke cloud.

"Hey, she's a hothead if that's what you mean," says Ben, returning to his seat. "She's got spirit. I like girls with spirit."

Adam shakes his head. "That's just U…G…L…Y, ugly."

"You serious? You like her like that?" asks Pump.

"Like her like what?"

"Bitchy." answers Adam.

"She good in the sack?" asks Pump.

"I'm not one of them kind of guys."

"What kind of guy?" asks Pump.

"You know, I don't talk about my girl that way."

"Why not?" asks Adam. "Everybody else does." He laughs.

Ben throws an angry stare in Adam's direction. "Shouldn't we be going?"

Pump looks down the road and sees the first runners heading to the finish. "Too early. Let's not make Dogface suspicious."

"I ain't afraid of no Dogface," injects Adam. "But I don't fuck with rats or cockroaches."

"You don't have to worry about rats or cockroaches around here," adds Pump, "just snakes."

"Snakes?" says Adam, sitting up. His eyes bubble, searching the surrounding grass.

"What's that?" asks Pump, pointing at a stick protruding from the grass.

Adam bolts to his feet and darts toward the highway

***

Gorni stands in front of the ranking board hanging on the wrestling room wall. Dan reads a name aloud from a list. Gorni finds the matching name tag, removes it and adds it to the stack in Dan's hand.

Uncle Burt enters with another list and hands it to Dan. "These are all the guys who checked out."

"Here," says Dan, as he grabs the new list and pours his name tags into Uncle Burt's cupped hands. "Give these, the quitter's accommodations."

Uncle Burt walks to the corner and deposits the name tags in the trash can.

Gorni lifts a name tag from the board and holds it up for Dan's inspection. "This one?"

"Leave it."

Gorni puts Joe Kerr's name tag back on the top rung and lifts another tag. "This one?"

"Keep it, but put it at the bottom." Gorni hangs Bronk's name tag at the bottom of the weight division.

Bronk struts in. "Where is everybody?"

Dan keeps his back turned to the young man. "Who wants to know?"

Chewing a mouth full of peanuts, "Bronk's my name and wrasslin's my game. You Dogface?"

Dan gets in his face. "You missed your meeting this morning."

"I was locked up."

"And now you've missed practice."

"I was in jail all night, and I just got out, and I don't have—"

"Excuses are like assholes—everybody's got one, and they stink."

Bronk walks toward Dan. "You must be Dogface. Look, I've scratched my head over this, and the way I figure, I'm gonna be your next champ." He points at the weight class on the ranking board. "And if you want me, you're gonna have to come up with some aid."

"We got all kinds of aid. We got Gatorade…lemonade…Band-Aids…"

"Cut the bull, Dogface, I'm talkin' cash—dinero."

Dan points at the ranking board. "See that? Where's your name?"

Bronk studies his weight class. He starts with Joe Kerr's name, at the top, and counts down to his name. "Number fifteen. Is that a lucky number?"

"Nope, only number one gets the jackpot around here. No consolation prizes. You want money? You have to chase everyone ahead of you home, and I'll give you their money."

Bronk looks the ranking board up and down and then sizes up Dan.

Dan asks, "You understand about being number one?" There is a prolonged silence. "Of course, you could wrestle me."

"What d'ya mean?"

"You score a point on me, and I'll match anyone's aid on the team."

"Now you're talkin'." Bronk takes a swig of Coke and peanuts.

Uncle Burt closes his eyes and shakes his head. Dan walks to the center of the mat. Bronk sets down his Coke and follows behind. Dan stops and turns. Bronk extends his hand for the customary handshake. Dan smacks Bronk in the head, launching his cowboy hat airborne.

They square off. Dan paws and slaps Bronk's face around like a punching bag, reopening the cut. Blood leaks from the bridge of his nose. Fingers scrape Bronk's eyes. Bronk knocks the hand away, lowers his level, and attacks. He shoots in deep on Dan's hips. Dan knocks him off with a hip shift and counter shoots. Bronk catches him with a chin and underhook, and rips a cow catcher. He cranks Dan's chin with one hand while punching the underhook arm across his back. For a moment Dan teeters, then regains his balance. He checks, controls Bronk's hands, climbs back to his feet and slips his head out of Bronk's hold. Bronk shoots. He's in deep, but Dan's hip sprawl squashes the attempt. He jerks Bronk down to the mat and applies a choke hold. Bronk gags for a few seconds and goes limp. Releasing the choke, Dan spins behind. The air revives Bronk, and he builds to his base. Dan delivers an incapacitating heel to the groin, threads his left leg around the kid's left leg and drives his hip bone into the sensitive kidney area. Bronk lets out a yelp and plants an elbow into Dan's face, which is hanging over Bronk's back. Dan punches, scraping his knuckles across Bronk's face, bloodying his nose and mouth. Seeing an opportunity to strike, Bronk bites down on Dan's forearm as it slides across his mouth. Undeterred, Dan rips his arm through the bite and screws Bronk's head around in the opposite direction of his trapped hips until his head is turned facing backward. The maneuver immobilizes Bronk. He screams. Dan strains and squeezes another piercing cry of anguish out of Bronk.

"You ready to listen?" There's no reply. Dan applies the clamps, and Bronk wails in agony. Dan asks again, "You listening?"

Blood flows from Bronk's face. His glazed eyes burn. He grunts through the choke hold, "Yeah."

"First, no more missed meetings and no more late to practice. Be punctual. Second, no more fights. And most important, don't EVER call me Dogface. Got it?"

Bronk strains and utters, "Okay."

"Now, when I let go, you're going to get up and report to the trainer for your physical, right?"

"Yeah."

Dan relaxes and untangles body parts. Bronk grimaces and grabs the back of his neck. His wrenched body crawls to his hat. He struggles to get to his feet. His left leg keeps giving out as he limps to his Coke.

"What's that?" asks Dan.

"Coke with peanuts."

Dan takes the bottle from Bronk and holds it eye level. "I thought of that when I was a kid." Dan turns the bottle on its end and drains it. "Aaahh." He drops the empty bottle in the trash bucket. Uncle Burt grabs a few paper towels and hands them to Bronk. Dan stares at Bronk. "Burrrp. Now, beat it."

Bronk hobbles out with hat and paper towels in hand, and his chin buried in his chest.

Dan feels a new sensation. He wipes his nose with his hand and notices a trace of blood. *Hmm,* he muses as he stretches his neck, *my first bloody nose.*

"That was a hell of a cow catcher for a high school kid," observes Uncle Burt.

"Heh, heh, he's strong as fuck," brags Dan. "We got one."

Dickie's head is buried in the hallway fountain between the wrestling room and the locker room. He dry heaves. A lame Bronk shuffles from the wrestling room. Babying his back, he leans against the wall and slowly slides to a sitting position. He wipes the blood from his mouth and nose as Dickie's body gags and contracts. He removes his head from the fountain and sits next to Bronk.

"Rough practice, huh?" asks Bronk, applying pressure to the bridge of his nose.

"Yeah, but this is from the tequila last night. When I got back to the house, I hugged the toilet and puked all night, then I went to bed this morning and puked in bed. When I got up, I puked in the shower, and now this. I got so wasted last night, even Pump looked cute."

Balls and Mini D enter the hallway from the locker room. They are still dressed in workout gear and carry red towels. Mini D holds his towel by each end and spins it tightly, as if he is getting ready to snap it.

Balls holds the two ends of the towel looped around his neck. "You want to go lift some weights?"

Mini D pounds his chest. "When I go on the mat, I want to feel like I'm wearing a suit of armor."

Bronk slips his hat on. "Don't believe in it."

Balls nods his understanding. "Discontent in men is the first step to progress."

Dickie jerks, scrambles to his feet and races to the fountain. He retches and chokes. "Oh God, I think I'm dying."

"Just remember, little brother, anything that doesn't kill you just makes you tougher." Mini D high-fives Balls.

"That's a good one. You have my permission to put it on my tombstone." Dickie sits next to the fountain.

Bronk watches Balls and Mini D bound off down the hall. "What the hell does that mean— 'discontent in men is the first step to progress'?"

Doc, Pug, Kruger, Adam, Ben and Pump file out of the locker room, pushing and shoving. Pump crosses the gym floor and exits. Adam and Doc swagger to the far corner of the gym toward some black dudes waiting under one of the exit signs. They talk. Doc opens his black bag, and they walk off into the shadows.

Kruger goes to the water fountain and leans over the yellow gastric juices slopped in the shallow basin. "Oh man. How am I supposed to rehydrate my parched flesh with this shit."

Pug pushes Kruger aside. "Like this." Pug turns the knob and gulps from the waterspout.

Ben turns his eyes away. "You're sick."

Kruger cast his eyes at Dickie. "Pussy."

"Faggot," mutters Dickie under his breath.

Bronk watches the upperclassmen joke and jostle each other all the way to the gym. "I don't get it. It's like they didn't have a drink last night."

"They didn't," reveals Dickie. "My brother told me. Joe had it fixed. When we drank tequila, they drank shots of water."

"WATER!"

Joe sits in the bleachers with Pug's three girls. They share a beer and wait next to a red cooler. Pug, Ben, and Kruger enter the gym. The girls crack open a fresh, cold one and hold out the dripping red can for the winner. The boys walk nonchalantly across the floor, then simultaneously make a break.

Joe plays announcer. "And the race is on. Ben takes an early lead, but Kruger cuts him off at the bleachers. From the rear, Pug bounds the steps and trips Kruger from behind. Ben recovers, grabs Pug's shirt, and pulls himself to the front. Kruger tackles Ben, crawls up his back, and reaches for the prize. Pug leaps on top of Kruger, stretches his hand, and snatches the beer from Kruger's grasp. It's Pug by a hand."

Pug grabs the prize and guzzles the contents in one continuous swallow.

Ben grabs a beer from the cooler. "Second's not bad."

"What do you mean second? You were third," says Kruger, swiping the can from Ben's hand.

"Well, third's not bad."

"There were only three of us. Third is last."

Ben grabs another beer and changes the subject. "Sure is easy this year. Dan's getting soft."

Kruger swallows his mouthful. "Yep, that's what happens when you get married. You get fat and make babies."

Pug cracks open another beer. "Yeah, no gusto." He chugs his beer, lifts his leg and rips a blustering, wet fart. "Ahhh."

"Voice has changed but breath still smells the same," says Joe, fanning the odor from his nose.

"Oh God." The girls and wrestlers alike pinch their noses and run from the inflating, dank aroma. Pug wallows in his creation, finishes his beer, picks up his cooler, and catches up to the girls. Bronk canters across the gym floor, mad-dogging Joe.

Joe feels the sting of Bronk's eyes and turns to confront him. "Well, if it isn't the Duke. How'd your meeting with Dogface go?"

Bronk stops in his path. "We came to an understandin'. I chase everyone home in my weight class, and I get their money."

"You believe that?"

Bronk bumps chests. "Your name's at the top."

Joe backs off. "Sorry, I don't talk shop outside office hours." Joe sidesteps and tries to pass. Bronk steps in front of him and blocks his way. Joe tries again. "Excuse me."

Bronk pushes his nose in Joe's face. "And when's that?"

"Each day, 3:00 – 6:00 in the wrestling room. Oh, by the way, you may as well forget about the rest of those guys. You're looking at the bank."

"That's what I figured." Bronk maintains his position.

Joe pushes Bronk away. Bronk moves back in his face. "Looks like you just opened for business." Bronk grabs two handfuls of Joe's shirt. Joe grabs back, jerks and lifts, and foot sweeps, crashing Bronk to the floor.

"Timber." Kruger laughs aloud.

Joe stands over Bronk. "You're not down on the farm rasslin' cows anymore, Duke."

Bronk sits on his bruised tailbone, stunned.

Joe stares into Bronk's challenging eyes as he climbs back to his feet. "Whoa, Duke, hold your horses. I know what you're thinking—"

Halfway up, Bronk catapults into Joe, tackling him to the floor.

Dan and Uncle Burt enter from the far end of the gym. They stroll across the floor, watching the tussle. Dan grabs Joe by the neck and jerks him off Bronk.

Dan looks down at Bronk. "Want some aid?" He clutches him by the neck and lifts him to his feet.

Dan holds the two and baits them like a couple of fighting dogs. He moves them close; they start swinging. He pulls them apart; they stare each other down. Fight. Stare. Fight. Stare. Dan's grip squeezes their necks like a choke chain. They grimace and cower.

Dan pulls Joe close. "Quit screwing around." He jerks Bronk toward him next. "I see we have to wrestle some more." Dan thrusts them apart, propelling them in opposite directions.

Bronk glares at Joe. "I'll see you tomorrow at practice."

Dan delivers a lusty smack to the back of Bronk's head. "Go get your physical."

Bronk hoofs it to the exit, staring down Joe the whole way.

Joe straightens his clothes and looks at Dan. "Okay, you got me for free."

"Okay, shows over. Everybody out." shouts Dan.

Dickie's been watching from the sidelines, staying close to the fountain. He feels another retch coming and runs.

From the far side of the gym, Kruger yells, "See you tomorrow, sickie Dickie."

With his head buried in the basin of the wall fountain, Dickie lifts his hand and holds down his middle finger. "Read between the lines, faggot."

Dan heads toward the locker room, and Uncle Burt meanders behind. "You were right. This could be fun."

"I think I'm going to let you run practice for a while. They're not ready for me," says Dan, walking past Dickie.

Uncle Burt stops. "You know, Dickie, I want to thank you and let you know that you were the inspiration for my newest event. In the spring, I'll be promoting beer slides—in your honor, of course. You were great last night, and beer slides are the stuff legends are made of. I can see it now…"

***

Bronk hobbles down the hall, favoring his left leg. He checks each door until he finds the training room. Turning the knob, he enters and looks around the complex. Walking through the deserted maze, he pokes his head in each room, looking for someone.

"Hey, what're you doin' here?"

"Trainers are usually in the training room," answers Jas.

"You're the trainer?"

"I'm one of them. What do you need?"

"Coach sent me down for my physical."

"You just missed the doctor, but I can get you started."

"So you're the trainer? Guess that means we'll be seein' a lot of each other."

"Only if you're getting the snot whipped out of you."

"Ain't likely."

"You look about the same weight as Joe Kerr."

"He couldn't throw a wet blanket."

"We'll see," Jas replies, handing Bronk a card and pen. "Fill this out." She moves to the counter and opens the upper cabinets. "Let's see, we're going to need your blood pressure, a blood sample, and a flu shot."

"No one said anythin' about any shots."

"Just standard stuff."

"How do you get the blood sample?"

Jas holds up a hypodermic needle with a syringe. "This."

Bronk swallows with a dry mouth. "Any other ways?"

"What? You already give enough blood today?"

"Just feelin' a little ragged, that's all."

"Okay, have a seat on the table and pull up your sleeve."

Bronk rolls up his shirtsleeve and begins sweating and trembling. It's suddenly difficult to get enough air, and he takes a few extra deep breaths. Jas turns with the blood pressure monitor from the countertop, and Bronk heaves a sigh of relief at the reprieve. She wraps the cuff around Bronk's upper arm, pumps the inflation bulb, and then loosens the valve on the pump. She listens through the stethoscope as the pressure cuff deflates and analyzes her readings. "Something's not right. Let's do it again." This time, Jas watches Bronk as she pumps and listens. "You okay?"

"I'm feelin' a little...lightheaded. I think it's the tequila from last night."

"These readings can't be right. I'm going to have to have the monitor checked. Okay, what do you want to saddle up to next—blood sample or flu shot?"

"Take your pick," says Bronk, breathing quickly and heavily.

Jas notices his labored breathing. "You afraid of needles?"

"Nah, let's get it over with."

Jas moves to the counter and removes the lid from the drug vial. Taking the syringe in hand, she looks back at Bronk as she removes the plastic cap covering the needle. A tingling sensation numbs his fingers and toes. She pushes the needle through the rubber top into the fluid. A sudden flush of heat fries every inch of his skin. Turning the vial upside down, she pulls back on the plunger, draws the vaccine into the syringe, and then gives a couple of gentle taps to the barrel of the syringe with her fingertip. Slowly pushing the plunger, she stops when all the air is out of the syringe and the dosage level is correct. She moistens a cotton ball with alcohol and wipes a spot on Bronk's upper arm near his shoulder. Chills numb his rigid body. Taking the needle in one hand, she pumps a squirt in the air. He sits paralyzed. Her other hand pinches up skin where she's going to give the shot. Bronk's stiff body shakes. She inserts the point. Bronk's eyes float up into his half-mast eyelids, his lower jaw drops, and his body slumps forward onto Jas. His head falls limp over her shoulder as her arms grab him and struggle to support his dead weight.

"Okay, joke's over." Jas stares at the needle sticking out of Bronk's arm. There's no sound, no movement, no change. Jas assesses her situation and takes a deep breath. She grunts and heaves, straightening Bronk and sending him falling back onto the examination table. She finishes the injection and removes the needle, hovering over the limp body. *Hmm, classic case of needle phobia.* She applies pressure and a Band-Aid. *I better get a blood sample while he's out.*

○○○○○○○●●●●●●●●●●●●●●●●●●

7. Rent

MINI D'S EYES shift back and forth over a fanned hand of playing cards. He sorts a card, then another, and then rearranges three into a new grouping and spreads his hand on the table to a bunch of hoots and hollers from the other players. Bronk, Pug, Doc, Adam and Ben sit around the kitchen table. Bronk spreads his hand for all to see. He is followed by Adam, who shows his cards, leaps to his feet and performs his end zone dance.

Bronk quick draws two imaginary six-shooters from his hip, empties them into Ben and sings, "Happy trails to you." then blows away the pretend smoke rising from the barrels. The survivors celebrate with a round of high fives.

Ben bounces across the front room. "I guess I finished sixth."

"That's great, Ben. You finished ahead of Gorni, who doesn't understand the game, and me, someone who has never played before," says Dickie.

Ben joins Balls, Dickie, and Gorni, who play another game. They take turns flipping the top card of the deck and doing the number of push-ups indicated by the number.

Ben turns the top card. It is a joker. "What do I do with that?"

"That's a bonus card. You turn another card and double it," explains Balls.

Ben slides another card from the deck. An ace. "What is that? Two push-ups?"

"The ace is fifteen. That's thirty. You're in a lucky spot. Let's trade places," orders Balls.

Bronk pulls a cigar from his shirt pocket and cuts off the tip with his pocket knife. Adam shuffles and begins dealing a new hand. Another roommate, loaded with luggage, squeezes down the stairway. He stops at the door and announces, "Well, I'm out of here."

A series of comments follows him out of the door. "Take it easy. See you at the River. Don't be a stranger." Adam uses the distraction for an opportunity to tuck a few cards under his thigh. Bronk flicks a wooden match with his fingernail, and the head bursts into flame. He holds the fire to the end of his cigar and puffs until his head is engulfed in smoke.

Mini D waves the smoke away from his face. "Put that shit out."

Dan's red pickup skids to a stop in the vacant lot next to the house. A shroud of dust erupts, camouflaging his assault on the front door.

"It's Dan!"

Everyone makes a frantic scramble except the new guys, Bronk, Dickie, and Gorni. Balls relaxes and breathes deep.

Loud stomps pound up the steps, across the front porch, and stops at the front door. The knob turns, and the door flies open. A cloak of fine sand veils the entrance. Dan steps forward and appears out of the cloud of dust. He checks left, then right, and makes a beeline for the kitchen. As he passes Bronk, he snatches the cigar, crumbles it in his hand, and tosses the shredded remains in the garbage.

"I'm here for the rent." shouts Dan.

Two oversized red refrigerators sit next to each other about a foot apart. He opens the first, ransacks it with his eyes, and then leans in and rummages for a snack.

"Where is everyone? At class?" asks Dan.

Turning away with his mitts holding their limit, he closes the door with the heel of his foot, exposing Mini D wedged between the two iceboxes. Dan walks into the front room and drops heavily onto the sofa, sending it sliding back toward the wall and squashing Ben and Adam hiding behind it. Dan freezes. "What's that?"

"What's what?" asks Dickie.

"Quiet," says Dan. "Be still."

Everyone is quiet. Crushed behind the couch, Ben and Adam grit their teeth.

Dan senses something in his body. "Feel that?"

Everyone shrugs and looks at one another, baffled. A faint pounding thuds above them. Each hit sends a pulsation rippling down the walls, across the floor and up through their bodies.

"Feel that?" asks Dan, holding still. "There it is again. Anybody know what that is?"

"Earthquake?" asks Dickie.

"We don't have earthquakes in this part of the country—Shhh." Dan listens hard. The hammering grows in volume and frequency. "What is that?"

"Termites?" asks Dickie.

"Better not be."

The thumping and vibration intensify. A sledgehammer pounds rhythmically and sends trembles through the ceiling. All eyes slowly roll up, fixed on the ceiling.

"What is that?"

"Kruger's with a girl," answers Balls.

"Balls, go get him. I'm in a hurry."

A hidden voice shouts, "It'll only take a minute."

"Who said that?" asks Dan, looking around.

Groans silence everyone. They increase in volume and harmonize in synchronicity with each thump. The repeated force of the bludgeoning shakes the ceiling. Old paint chips quiver free and snow down. Glassware clangs and cabinet doors rattle. Moans give way to screams, which build to ear-piercing cries.

"What the hell is he doing to her?" Dan can't take it any longer. He dumps his food on the coffee table and scrambles to the staircase. He climbs the stairs three at a time, yelling, "Kruger. Kruger. Kruger." Dan opens Kruger's door. It cracks open slightly but is stopped by a latch lock. He shouts, "Kruger, what are you doing in there? Open this door. It's me." Dan takes a pen from his pocket, slips it through the slender opening, lifts and undoes the latch.

The door flies open. Dan's eyes fixate on the nude coed sprawled across the bed. He's dumbfounded and tongue-tied. "Uh. Are you…uh. Are you okay?"

"I was."

He looks around the room and begins to hunt. "Where's Kruger?"

The exquisite young woman covers the fork of her long graceful legs with both hands. Her arms pinch and plump up her bosom.

Dan pushes aside the red curtains, glances out the window and then around the room again. He can't help staring at her engorged nipples. She quickly rolls over turning her bulging breasts away. He rummages the closet, then peeks. He follows the pleasing line up her well-formed legs, over the curve of her fleshy rump and down to her cleavage. Moving across to the bed, he gets on all fours, lifts the bed skirt and searches under the frame.

She looks over her shoulder. Dan is nowhere in sight. She turns back and sits up as Dan's face rises from under the bed and settles between her knees. Seized, he slowly inhales, stealing a whiff of her womanly scent. His eyes roll up to meet hers.

She screams, "Pervert. I'm calling the cops."

Dan stomps down the stairs and out the front door. "I have to go to the office and make calls. Tell everyone rent is due. Bring it to practice tomorrow."

Everyone pops from the hall closet, the bathroom, between the refrigerators and behind the sofa. Dan peels out in his truck. The rear window displays a black sign with red "For Sale" lettering.

The boys run back to the table. "New deal," declares Adam. He gathers and counts the cards. "Hey, there's only forty cards here." One by one, each of the boys pull cards from their hiding places and toss them on the table.

○○○○○○○○●●●●●●●●●●●●●●●●●

8. Roughhouse

PUG THRUSTS ONE arm deep into a sleeve, plunges his other arm into another sleeve, pulls the heavy-duty rubberized suit over his body and pops his head through the hole at the top.

Standing at the next locker, Kruger pulls his hair back and ties it in a ponytail. "So then, I hear him stomping up the stairs, shouting, 'Kruger. Kruger.' and I'm thinking, 'No, not the closet—that's the first place he'll look' and then I think, 'Not under the bed—that's the second place he'll look.' Then he's pounding on the door and jiggling the latch, so it's out the window. I'm hanging from the sill, and I know he can see my hands, so I shimmy down to the very end of the sill," says Kruger, "and I hang by the fingertips of one hand. He's banging around the room looking for me—"

"And you're hanging outside, naked as a plucked chicken," finishes Pug, slipping his legs one at a time into rubber pants.

Kruger shuts his locker and struts off. "I'll catch you in the room."

Adam opens his locker and jumps back in fright, colliding with Kruger. Kruger looks, reaches in the locker, and pulls out a black and red rubber snake, holding it up and wiggling it. Recovering from the scare, Adam jerks it out of Kruger's hand and chases a snickering Ben and Pump around the locker room, beating them with the rubber viper.

Gorni is seated on the bench, bent at the waist tying his shoes. Joe positions himself, standing with a towel wrapped around his waist. His towel slowly begins to rise from his crotch and nudges Gorni in the side of the head. Bewildered, Gorni tries his best to ignore the enlarged body organ. Kruger marches past and whips Joe's towel off, revealing a clothes hanger under the towel.

Kruger enters the wrestling room and pauses at the door to crack his knuckles. The stale dungeon is wall-to-wall brown mats with black circles and has two sets of double doors; one set leads to the inner hall and the other set to the outside. A couple dozen python-sized ropes dangle from the ceiling. The walls are decorated with wrestling posters, pictures, and motivational slogans. More than a hundred hopefuls are spread around the room talking and joking, and a few test their skills.

After his territorial gaze, Kruger spits his gum into a dented and scraped red bucket, and stalks through the room. He stops to watch Doc practice his throwing technique on a reddish cylinder-shaped dummy with "Crash" written across its forehead. Doc sports a pair of sunglasses and his Walkman. He straightens the dummy, steps, lifts, throws and slams it to the mat with a thunderous thud that echoes through the room. Kruger tracks on and then halts to watch Mini D and Dickie scrap. They butt heads and fight for a grip. Dickie pushes away and breaks his stance. He straightens and points to Mini D's shoelaces. When Mini D looks down, Dickie tackles him.

Dan enters. Uncle Burt shouts, "Okay, let's get started."

Balls runs to the front of the room and begins a series of calisthenics mixed with basic wrestling movements. Dan pulls Gorni from the ranks. He starts his stopwatch, then grabs Uncle Burt's whistle. He turns to Gorni and holds the watch in his face. "One hour," he instructs, shaking the whistle, "then blow the whistle." Dan walks to the thermostat and adjusts the temperature control switch to its highest setting. Uncle Burt points out Adam to Dan. At the far corner of the wrestling room, Adam has isolated himself and does his own routine.

Dan looks at Adam and then back to Uncle Burt. "Coaching lesson number one. Watch and learn." Dan strolls to the far end of the room, followed by Uncle Burt. He stops next to Adam, watches him do a couple of push-ups, and then gives him a tap in the ribs with his toe. Inflamed, Adam snaps his head to see who belongs to the foot. Dan smiles. "Hey nigger this is my corner. Yous gonna make us proud and bees the best over there," says Dan, pointing to the team with a hitchhiker's thumb. Uncle Burt rolls his eyes.

Adam shakes his head, climbs to his feet, and walks. "Don't be hatin'."

Dan proudly turns to Uncle Burt. "See, I know how to talk to black guys. What'd he mean— 'don't be hatin'?"

***

Dozens of glazed, sweaty backs pump up and down. One by one, they begin to crumble, unable to complete another push-up. Dan marches through the puddles of sweat and orders everyone, "Push-up position and stay up." Dan steps on a back and strides from back to back to back like crossing a creek on stones, until one collapses. Dickie. Dan gets in his face and yells, "Go stand with Gorni. That just cost everyone five more minutes." Everyone groans. "Okay, Balls, we're in overtime."

Balls increases the pace. Oxygen-deprived muscles fail, agitated emotions unleash, and iron wills crumble. Bodies and minds quit and admit defeat. Balls ups the ante again and kicks it into a higher gear. Dan stands next to Uncle Burt, watching man after man give in and give up. The pressure of Balls' tempo breaks the minds and bodies of everyone but a handful of the fittest.

Dan turns to Uncle Burt with a tear in his eye. "God, I miss this. What I wouldn't give to do it one more time."

Gorni watches the time and peeps the whistle. Dan grabs his whistle, blows an earsplitting blast and changes gears. "Okay, everybody gather 'round." Everyone mumbles and grumbles as they collect around Dan. "Shut up." He raises his right hand and points to the wall behind him. "See that? Every champion in Dover's history is listed on that wall. That's why you're here. You get your name on the wall, you become a part of history. You become immortal." Dan pauses for a moment to let it sink in. "Now, if you got the guts to stick it out and do what I say, you'll get your name up there. You're not babies anymore. Mommy's not around to wipe your ass. We don't have training rules. You're here to eat, sleep, study, and wrestle. You're not here to have fun." Dan throws his whistle. The metal missile sears the air and nails Kruger in the chest. "And you're not here for sex." Kruger grabs the burning, stinging mark, and rubs it.

Dan walks over and taps the ugly red bucket in the corner with his toe. "This is the spit bucket. Use it." Dan takes a long, penetrating look into the eyes around the room, raises his eyebrows and bellows, "ROUGHHOUSE!" and opens the door to leave.

Before Dan can step out, skirmishes break out all over the room. Kruger drops on the unsuspecting Dickie and begins twisting his arm and cranking his neck. Joe pushes a stupefied Bronk over Pug, who is on his hands and knees; the shove trips Bronk to his back. As Joe and Pug jump on top of Bronk, Doc looks for the pin. Ducking, one of the new guys avoids a miscalculated assault by Mini D. Balls stands in the middle of the fray, deflecting everyone's attempt to grab him. Using the throwing dummy as a battering ram, Pump flattens Ben to the mat, then passes the dummy to Adam. Pandemonium reigns.

As Joe and Pug hold Bronk down flat on his back, Doc smacks the mat, signaling Bronk's shame. Balls redirects two bodies and runs them into each other. Mini D dives and misses, coming up empty-handed again. Ben climbs to his feet just in time for Adam, who swings the dummy like a baseball bat and clubs him across the chest, knocking him back down to the mat. An enraged Dickie breaks free. Murder fills his eyes. With Dickie in hot pursuit, Kruger sprints across the room and latches onto one of the ropes hanging from the ceiling. He swings high into the air. At the peak, he reverses his direction, swings back and plants both his feet squarely into the sternum of an onrushing Dickie. He is laid out, clutching his chest.

**

Dan holds the door open as wrestlers file out. Uncle Burt follows the last couple of grapplers with his cupped hands full of name tags. Dan lifts the bottom of his T-shirt, and Uncle Burt dumps the name tags into the pouch.

Dan takes one last look into the room before turning the lights out. He pauses and looks at Gorni lying in the middle of the floor. He has been mummified, wrapped with athletic tape from head to toe. He wiggles and moans as Dan flips the light switch. Darkness extends over the surface of the room. A thin sliver of light from the closing door spotlights the mummy until the door shuts leaving the ball of tape squirming in darkness.

○○○○○○○○○●●●●●●●●●●●●●●●●

9. Dan Talk

BRONK AND DICKIE run shoulder to shoulder. They cruise through a red stop sign and turn from the country road onto the final stretch of highway. Dover gym is in sight. Joe and Kruger round the corner, followed by a dozen other runners jockeying for position. The two veterans gain on the freshmen.

Bronk glances over his shoulder and picks up his pace, pulling away from Dickie. Joe and Kruger pass Dickie and close their eyes and snore as they pass a struggling Bronk. Red faced, he pumps his elbows, pulls alongside the pair and matches their gait stride for stride. A paralyzing coughing attack forces Bronk to the side of the road.

Dickie passes the incapacitated Bronk, then the large group rumbles by. Out of nowhere, Balls flies to the front to take the lead and win the contest.

Inside the wrestling room, Dan scrutinizes the ranking board. There are two or three name tags in each weight division. He lifts the only name tag below Balls from its hook and passes it to Uncle Burt, who hands it to Gorni, who drops it into the spit bucket.

***

Bronk enters the locker room from the showers. One towel wraps around his waist and another drapes his head like a hood. He slouches across the deserted locker room and plops on the bench in front of his locker paralyzed in thought.

At the opposite end of the room, Gorni removes a full garbage bag from the trash container. He unrolls a new bag and snaps it in the air, opening it and giving it shape. The sound wakes Bronk out of his funk.

Bronk spins the dial on his lock, "Hold on—I got somethin' for you." He opens his locker and grabs his cigarettes from his shirt pocket. He walks to Gorni, crushes the red pack in his hand and drops it in the garbage.

***

A hand releases a wad of junk mail into the trash can. The other arm supports a beautiful, blonde three-year-old. Maggie's legs wrap around her mother's swollen, melon-shaped belly. Cindy carries Maggie across the kitchen to the stove. They have the same honey blonde hair. Swathed in her morning robe, Cindy's tousled hair covers her face, except for her large nose and a cigarette dangling from her voluminous lips. Her unpolished fingertips lift a bottle of milk from a pot of steaming water. She sprinkles a few drops of milk on her wrist and then hands the bottle to her daughter.

Dan enters the kitchen. "She's too old for warm milk."

"It's the way she likes it." Cindy lifts the coffee pot from the warmer and pours two cups of coffee. "When you going to get me a microwave?"

"They're not good for you. They destroy all the nutrients," replies Dan, sitting at the breakfast table.

Cindy sets a mug of coffee in front of Dan, removes a small bundle of mail from her housecoat pocket and drops it next to the coffee. Dan rifles through the mail. *Bill, bill, bill.* He rips the paper wrap off the latest edition of the College Wrestling News magazine and stares at it. Kane shares the front cover with his new prize recruit, Bobby Ryder, dressed in a scarlet and silver warm-up. Dan ignores the coffee, pockets the bills, and rambles down the stairs toward the door.

"Where you going?" inquires Cindy.

Dan opens the front door. "I got some things to take care of."

He makes a U-turn, runs back upstairs into the family room and picks up an old rocking chair. Mollie, an older version of Maggie, comes running from the couch in front of the TV, clutches the chair and engages in a tug of war for it.

"You promised to clean the gutters and mow the lawn today," Cindy reminds him.

"I'll do it tomorrow," he says. Mollie starts crying.

"What are you doing?"

Dan yanks the chair from her hands. "I'm getting rid of some of the junk around here." He holds the chair up and away from her outstretched hands.

"That's her favorite chair."

"Sorry, but I'm donating it to charity." Dan removes the stained seat cushion and gives it to Molly. She throws it on the floor and bawls. He carries the chair down the stairs and out the front door, shutting it behind him.

Cindy follows, opens the door and yells, "You're driving me crazy. You keep telling me you're going to do something, and you never do it."

Dan lugs the chair to his truck and wedges it in the bed of the truck with a dozen other items. "Something came up."

"How do you expect to be a great coach if you never finish anything?"

Dan adjusts the "For Sale" sign in the truck window. "Gotta go."

"You know what it is? You're like a feral animal—you just do what you want to do. Makes me feel like you don't care. Love is belief in one another. Love is commitment. You make me feel like nothing."

Dan starts his truck, and announces, "I don't drink coffee." The items piled up in the bed wobble back and forth as the truck accelerates.

Maggie clutches Cindy's neck as they climb back up the steps. She stops at the top. Her dreary eyes gaze over the kitchen and family room. Piles of dirty dishes, pots, pans, and open food containers fill the sink and cover the countertops. The floors are buried under mounds of toys, clothes, pillows, books, games and newspapers. Mollie sits on the couch, hugging her cushion and watching television.

***

Dan lifts the last item from the bed of his truck parked at the curb. He carries the television through the door under the pawn shop sign and sets the TV on the corner of the cluttered counter. He carefully slides the TV further onto the top of the display case. The pawn broker counts out a stack of bills and hands the wad of money to Dan. Dan gives the TV one more nudge to make sure it's secure and displaces an object, which sets off a chain reaction that pushes a lamp off the far end. The pawn broker helplessly watches the lamp fall and shatter. He takes back a few bills and hands the rest to Dan.

***

The athletic director, Bill Bohr, marches double-time down the shadowy corridor on a mission. He carries a folder in his hand and a stern look on his face.

Uncle Burt blows his whistle. The wrestling room silences and all heads snap to attention. Dan removes his bottle-thick glasses, held together with tape and paper clips, and places them in a well-worn spot on the ridge of the wall mats that encircle the room. The moment Dan turns his back, Uncle Burt takes Dan's glasses, puts them on and walks behind him, mimicking his every move. "Okay, I want everyone to pick a drilling partner. This is your most valuable piece of equipment, so pick a good one." A small crowd gathers around Bronk.

"C'mon you're mine," says Balls, grabbing Bronk's hand.

"No way," protests Pug, grabbing his other hand.

"I saw him first," counters Balls, as he begins dragging Bronk away.

Pug pulls the other arm. "Shit, man, I said he's mine." They start a tug of war.

"You're both wrong," says Joe. He takes Bronk's arm and pulls him from the other two.

"This hamburger is mine."

The door opens, and the athletic director steps in. He remains at the door and announces, "Excuse me, Dan—pardon the intrusion. May I speak to you for a moment? I'll wait in the hall."

Dan returns to retrieve his glasses before Uncle Burt can replace them. His hand gropes his special spot, but there are no glasses. He casually walks along the wall running his finger the length of the rim of the mat and lectures. "Now, your drilling partner is not your buddy. THERE ARE NO BUDDIES IN HERE. This is your personal dummy for beating on." Dan continues feeling along the ridge as he drives his message home by alternating between a babyish falsetto and a loud gruff voice. He whines, "Oh, don't hurt me. I'm your friend," then shouts, "THERE ARE NO FRIENDS IN HERE. YOU DON'T HAVE FRIENDS IN HERE!" Dan backtracks in his hunt for his glasses and continues his speech, warning them against bargaining with each other. He reverts to the high-pitched tone: "I won't hurt you if you don't hurt me," then immediately bellows, "THAT'S BULLSHIT! Now we're going to start drilling, and you better hurt your partner because when it's his turn…"

Dan returns to his starting point. A perplexing look besets his face when he finds his glasses in their original location. He positions his glasses on his bewildered face.

"Okay, I have to step out for a moment. Uncle Burt is going to show you a move that can fuck someone up for life. Then, I want you to practice it on each other."

The wrestlers look around at each other, dumbfounded.

"I'll be right back."

Dan steps into the hall and joins Bill Bohr. The instant the door closes behind Dan, Bill starts, "We have a problem. The president came to my office fuming over this." Bill removes a photograph from his folder. "Apparently, this fellow streaked down the middle of the playing field from goalpost to goalpost during Saturday's football contest. He's been identified as one of your wrestlers."

Dan looks at the eight-by-ten print. A nude motorcyclist sits on a red Harley with underwear waving from the sissy bar. He has jet-black hair and a beard extending straight back from his head from the force of the wind. Dan studies the man in the picture, tilts his head and rotates the picture. "Hmm, I'm not sure. It could be anyone under all that hair. Who do they think it is?"

"C'mon Dan, it's obvious."

"Let me look into this."

"Dan, the president is furious. He's going to have someone's head, either the guy's in the picture or yours."

"I just need a little time to check it out."

"You have to take action. Are you going to sacrifice the whole team for one fellow?" asks Bill. They stand, looking into each other's eyes and weighing the gravity of the question. "Oh, I almost forgot." He removes an envelope from the folder. "We received this from Chicago. It's some sort of automobile repair invoice, and they reference you. Do you know anything about this?"

Dan snatches the envelope from Bill's hand. "I'll take care of this. Thanks. I'll get back to you about the photo." He turns and enters the wrestling room.

Uncle Burt approaches. "What's up?"

Dan hands him the photograph. "Take care of this." Uncle Burt looks at the image with a warped sense of approval. Then, Dan hands him the envelope. "And file this."

Uncle Burt reads the Chicago Cats letterhead. He walks over and drops it in the spit bucket. "Filed."

Dan takes charge. "Okay, party's over. Everybody get a partner; we're going live. Gorni, you go with Dickie. Kruger, you're going with me."

***

The team files into the locker room. Their beet-red faces drip sweat pellets. They fan out to their lockers and shed their soaked, torn, and bloodied T-shirts.

Kruger brings up the rear, limping like he has been jumped by a gang in a dark alley. Bright cherry blood trickles from both nostrils, and he clutches his right shoulder with his left hand as if his arm would fall off if he let go of it.

Dan and Uncle Burt trail behind, round up the strays and make sure everyone is in the locker room.

Dan stops at the doorway. "Team meeting. Everyone listen up. The season's around the corner, and now's the time to stop screwing around and get down to business. Unfortunately, a couple of individuals have put the program in jeopardy, so I'm imposing a curfew tonight."

The wrestlers moan and grumble. "But it's Halloween."

"Tonight, there will be no drinking." Dan glares at Pug. "No fighting." He frowns at Bronk. "And no motorcycle riding." He stares angrily at Kruger. "I want everyone in bed by eleven. Any questions?"

Pug chimes in, "No problem. I was planning on being passed out by ten."

"And one more thing: Kruger, you're not captain anymore."

"I never was a captain."

"Well, I was thinking about it, so you can forget it."

"Fuck you, Dogface," mumbles Kruger.

The room is stunned. Everyone looks at Dan.

"What?" The awkward silence is broken by Dan forging into the mass of sweaty bodies toward Kruger. The wrestlers part to make a path and hold their breath. Dan stops inches from Kruger. "Did you say something?"

There's a long pause. "No."

"I didn't think so." Dan turns and walks back to his spot. "Remember, don't do anything you wouldn't want your parents or me to see on the front page of tomorrow's newspaper." He takes one more look and turns to exit. "Have a good time, and don't eat too much candy."

Dan and Uncle Burt stroll down the hall. Uncle Burt twirls his whistle around his finger.

"How's it going?" asks Dan.

"What do you mean?"

"Do you like coaching? You having a good time so far?"

"Haven't missed a day yet."

"Have any ideas on what to do with Kruger?"

"I'm working on it."

"Did you hear about Duray?"

"What?"

"Chicago picked him up as an assistant coach."

"You're kidding. What the hell does Chicago want with him?"

"Duray knows Balls better than anyone."

"They could have ten Durays; they're not going to beat Balls," says Uncle Burt, swinging the whistle up and catching it in his teeth.

"I'm just letting you know what we're up against."

"I'm more concerned about the election next week. I'm voting for the first time. Who are you voting for?" asks Uncle Burt.

"Who's running?"

"It's Reagan versus Mondale," answers Uncle Burt. "A former governor and incumbent president against a senator."

"So, we have a choice between an actor and a lawyer. You vote for the lawyer, you know you're going to get screwed. You vote for the actor, you get the performance of a lifetime."

"Maybe I'll wait until the next election."

○○○○○○○○○○●●●●●●●●●●●●●●●

10. Stray Dogs

MAIN STREET LOOKS like the back lot of a movie studio in full production. The town and campus residents have turned out in costume for the annual Halloween bash. Bronk is in his customary cowboy garb, and Dickie is dressed as a boxer. An afro wig, two extra large boxing gloves, a silk robe and shorts decorate his body and face covered in black makeup. They fidget outside the beverage store, check up and down the street and then nervously peek inside. Mini D swaggers from the carryout with a brown bag cradled in his left arm. He is dressed as Shirley Temple with a five o'clock shadow, a giant lollypop in his free hand and a foot-long cigar protruding from his mouth. Mission accomplished, they bore through the multitude on the crowded sidewalk and break from the horde down a side street.

They approach a large house with a fancy sign identifying it as "The King's Court." Several residents lounge on the front porch and keep a beer keg company, while others are scattered in small groups around the grounds of the house. Three members of Dover's basketball team drink beer and sit on a rock fence that borders the front of The King's Court and runs along the sidewalk. They push off the fence and barricade the sidewalk, blocking Mini D, Bronk and Dickie.

"Hold it. Where do you think you're going?"

"A party," answers Mini D.

"What party is that?"

"The Dog Pound," explains Mini D.

"What a bunch of losers."

"Yeah, maybe we should party here. It looks like the basketball team really has it going on," retorts Dickie.

"You are going to have to find another way."

"What d'ya mean?" asks Dickie.

One of the players points down. "This is King Carter's sidewalk. You can only use it with King Carter's permission. And if you don't have permission, you need to cross the street and use that sidewalk over there."

Several other basketball players wander down to observe the exchange. A tall drunk walks up from behind. "Will you look at these guys," he observes, goosing Mini D. "And what are you supposed to be, sweetheart?" he asks, pinching Mini D's cheek.

"A gangster disguised as Shirley Temple," answers Mini D.

"And what about you?" the drunk asks Dickie.

Dickie dances, bobs and weaves, and delivers his line: "I pity the fool who steps into the ring with me. I float like a butterfly and sting like a bee." He shakes his glove in the big drunk's face. "Now you best be chicken or you's gonna get a lickin'."

The basketball players burst out laughing and part to let the trio pass.

"That was pretty good," says Mini D.

"I practiced all day."

They walk a few steps, and Bronk stops the boys. "Hold it." Bronk returns to the pack. He walks up to the big mouth. "Hey, you forgot to ask me."

"Okay, honey, what are you supposed to be?"

"None o' your fuckin' business." Bronk scowls into his eyeballs. Mini D sets his paper bag on the curb.

The drunk grasps the intensity of Bronk's stare. "You're a little light in the ass to give me any shit. You best move along, boy."

"'Boy'? You callin' me 'boy'? Why, I've been from Maine to Spain, from Austin to Boston, I got a yard o' cock, a bushel of balls, and enough hair on my ass to weave an Indian blanket and choke two grizzly bears. And you call me 'boy'?"

"Hey, I don't want to hurt you." The teammates all laugh. "Run along."

Mini D steps in front of Bronk and forces him to make eye contact. "Hey, forget these guys." Bronk stares back at the drunk. "C'mon, we got a party to go to." Bronk continues to mad-dog. Mini D squeezes Bronk's shoulders. "Remember what Dan said." Bronk looks at Mini D, the drunk, then back at Mini D and gives in. The threesome turns and saunters down the sidewalk.

"And take your midget with you," adds the big drunk.

Mini D turns. "What'd you say?"

"Ohhh, did I hurt the little dwarf's feelings? Ahhh, how about this one—you're too little so I'm going to throw you back." All the roundballers break out in jeers.

Mini D turns and hands his cigar and lollypop to Bronk. The big mouth looks around, soaking up the approval of his teammates. He turns back to face Mini D, and his mouth is met flush with a fist. Everyone stops laughing. Mini D fakes another punch and dives in at the tall guy's ankles, tripping him to the ground. He leaps on top, straddles him and peppers his face with a series of machine-gun hits.

The rest of the squad jumps Mini D. Bronk pulls one off with his left hand and throws a right fist of knuckles, flattening him. He pulls a second from the pile with his right hand and delivers a left hook knockout blow.

Dickie stops one cold with a blindside haymaker to his right temple. A big, broad smile cracks the tall basketball player's face. He stands, towering over the miniature Ali. Dickie looks at his fists and realizes his oversized boxing gloves have no impact. The giant moves toward Dickie, who backs up, lowers his head and bull rushes, ramming his head into the guy's solar plexus.

Reinforcements stream down from the house and overrun the three wrestlers standing with their backs to each other in the middle of the free-for-all. Police sirens scream. The three manage to stay on their feet and battle back. Flashing lights turn the corner. Everyone gets their final licks in and scatters. Mini D snatches up the paper bag. The trio sprints down the road, laughing all the way. Pumped and exhilarated, they gradually slow to a walk as the sirens fade.

Bronk high-fives Mini D. "You were on him like flies on shit."

"Way to go, bro. You hit that guy so many times he thought he was surrounded."

"C'mon, let's get to the party."

They shadowbox down the street and then break out in unison, "I've been from Austin to Boston, from Maine to Spain…"

Kruger's motorcycle rumbles to a stop, halting the parade. "Mini D, hop on."

"You should've seen it, Krug, it was awesome."

"Can you tell me about it later? I need your help with something—it's important. C'mon, get on."

"Sure," says Mini D, straddling the seat.

"Hey, our bottles," reminds Dickie.

Mini D removes his bottle and hands the bag to Dickie. Kruger throttles. Mini D yells, "See you guys at the party."

***

Bronk and Dickie breeze up the steps to the Dog Pound's porch. Music blares from inside. Dressed as W. C. Fields, Pug has a jar of Vaseline in one hand and liberally applies the gelatinous contents to the inside edge of the front door frame. He works industriously with the precision and scientific aplomb of a master craftsman. He steps back and admires his creative genius.

"What's that for?" asks Dickie.

"Ah yes," says Pug, impersonating W. C. Fields, "I can see how this could be a point of confusion for the inexperienced. This assures we get the fat chickadees in."

On the wall next to the door, Doc paints bright yellow letters that read "Admission = one bottle." Underneath, he paints "Hair of the DOG" next to a yellow arrow pointing down to a huge trash can full of ice. He wears a white doctor's jacket with a stethoscope around his neck and a cockeyed reflector on his head. Groucho Marx glasses, bushy eyebrows, a mustache, and a cigar complete his costume. After a final stroke, he sets the paintbrush across the top of an open can of yellow paint on the floor.

"Just pour in your admission."

Dickie holds up a bottle of MD 20-20, twists off the cap and pours the contents over the ice.

Doc fakes a frown, "Pug, if your parents and Dogface read in the paper that you drank MD 20-20, what would they think about that?"

"They'd think I'm a sissy," answers Pug in character. Bronk opens a bottle of tequila. Pug sniffs and comments as W. C., "Ah yes, someone just uncorked dinner."

Bronk empties the contents. The smell of the tequila reaches Dickie. "How can you drink that? Just the smell of it makes me gag."

A line begins to form. Doc stoops, waves his cigar in the air and does his Groucho walk, examining the ladies. The girls giggle. "Women should be obscene and not heard." He stops and confronts one girl. "I never forget a face, but in your case, I'll make an exception." Addressing everyone in line, he quips, "A man is only as old as the women he feels." Finished with his performance, he returns to the house.

Pug breaks away from his chore at the front door and assists the female arrivals. He turns on the W.C. Fields charm. "Ah yes, welcome my little doggie-doos. Step right up. Step right up. Don't be shy. Move a little closer." Pug relieves each guest of her bottle and does the honors. "Let's see what we have here. Ah yes, the Lord's cure-all. A little wine and we're feeling fine; some whiskey and we're getting frisky; and a bottle of gin— now we're ready for sin." The last girl in line presents a bottle of water. He recoils. "Aaaah, I never touch the stuff. It rusts pipes and fish shit in it."

***

Kruger's Harley is parked roadside. He and Mini D are in the bushes a few feet away.

"I was afraid to touch him, so I just left him and got you."

Mini D leans over, turns his head, puts his ear to the small dog's mouth and listens.

"What do you think?"

"I can't tell. Shut up." Mini D listens harder. He takes the small dog's head in his hands, covers the dog's mouth and nose with his mouth and blows. He blows and listens, blows and listens, repeating the process until he pronounces, "He's breathing, I think."

"What do you mean, you think?"

He gently picks up the limp, bloodied dog and carries it under the street light. "The blood has clotted. That's good."

Kruger rambles nervously, "I didn't see him. He just came running into the street. I tried to avoid him, but before I could do anything, he was under my front tire. And you know, after what Dan said, with my luck, it's the president's dog or something."

"Let's take him back to our place."

Kruger removes his leather jacket and tenderly wraps it around the miniature dog. Mini D cradles the bundle in his arms like a baby.

Kruger straddles the Harley seat. "Why does this shit always happen to me? I didn't want to hurt the little guy. I love dogs more than people."

Mini D slides on the back half of the seat. "Hey, it's okay. Maybe this was meant to happen. Sometimes good things come from bad things. You know what I mean?" Mini D thinks he hears a sniffle from Kruger but isn't sure. "You crying?"

"No—no way. You kidding me?"

Mini D pulls a Kleenex from his fake breast and offers it to Kruger.

Kruger takes the tissue. "You say anything—to anybody—and I'll kill you." The Harley rolls out slow and smooth.

***

Dressed as Batman's arch nemesis, the Joker, Joe strides up the walk, bounds the steps in one leap and slides across the porch. Posed at the front door, he delivers his line to all the costumed revelers on the deck. "It looks like this party needs an enema. Ha, ha, ha, ha," laughs a demented Joker, reaching for the doorknob. The door flies open. A dozen hands grab and grope a gorgeous Marilyn Monroe and then push her out the door into Joe's arms. "Ha, ha. How do I get sooo lucky?"

Marilyn breaks from his grasp and smears his makeup with a slap. Tears gush down her cheeks. "Get away from me, or I'm calling the police."

Joe holds both hands in the air, still in character. "Look, no hands."

"Leave me alone," she says, sniffling.

Joe backs off and gives her space. "Hey, I just want to make sure you're okay," he says, circling to face her. "Then, you can go wherever you want."

"Don't come near me," she threatens, holding her hand out and backing away.

"If somebody in there did something to you, just point him out. I'll kick his ass."

She folds her arms across her heaving chest. "Please, leave me alone."

"I'm sorry. Won't you accept my apology?"

"Get away from me," she says, turning her back to Joe.

"C'mon, let me apologize for those guys."

"No."

"Hey, I don't want to make excuses, but they've been drinking, and this is the last chance to get crazy before the season starts. So come on, accept my apology."

"They're pigs."

"Yeah. You want to talk about that?"

"No."

"C'mon, you can tell me about it."

"I'm warning you," she says, trying to catch her breath.

"C'mon, what happened?" Joe hands her his oversized red handkerchief. "Look, being a girl, you know you take a risk anytime you come to the Dog Pound, right?"

"I guess."

"You're a lovely girl. You don't want this to ruin your Halloween, do you?"

"Nooo."

"So come on, what do you say? Accept my apology. You can put this whole incident behind you and enjoy the rest of the evening."

She looks at Joe, sizing him up. "Well..."

"Come on now, let's see that beautiful smile." Marilyn wipes the moisture from her cheeks, gives in and cracks a smile.

"Look at you. You are a hottie. You don't need to lower yourself to these guys' level."

"I know."

"So, you accept my apology?"

"Well."

"C'mon."

"Okay."

Joe puts his arm around her. "That's great. Now you're on your way to having the greatest evening of your life." He shifts to the Joker character. "Ha, ha, ha. Tonight Dover, tomorrow the world! So now that we got that out of the way, how about a blow job for the Joker?"

"But, I don't even know you."

"The night is young." Joe slides his arm around her waist and pulls her hips tight to his.

"All I did was open the fridge for a drink, and they grabbed me like a piece of meat," she says.

"Ha, ha. That's why." Joe laughs in realization. "The drinks are out here. The food is in the fridge. You never come between a wrestler and his food," he explains. "Allow me." He opens the front door.

***

Kruger and Mini D rumble into the vacant lot next to the Dog Pound and roll around behind the house to the back door.

Doc pulls Ben, dressed as the Tin Man, and Gorni, in a munchkin outfit, out of the back door onto the back stoop. Doc has one hand on Ben's shoulder and the other on Gorni's. "You are being recruited for a mission. This mission, should you decide to accept, will play a huge part in the success of our annual Halloween bash. An event that the best of the best party dogs look forward to and dream about for the entire year. An event whose reputation acts like an invisible magnetic force, enticing and alluring the most beautiful babes from the whole campus. The mission...replenish the food supply."

Kruger leads the way up the back steps and creates a path, abruptly splitting Doc and his recruits. Mini D carries his motionless bundle into the house.

"Are you with me? Can I count on you?" asks Doc.

Gorni, the munchkin, agrees. "Sure. Do Howday Doooday have wooodeen deek?"

"Huh?"

Ben, the Tin Man, asks, "What do we have to do?"

"You guys are great. How many people you think are here?"

Gorni shrugs. Ben suspiciously answers, "Maybe sixty, maybe a hundred."

"So, what do you say, a dozen of the monster pizzas?"

Ben clarifies, "Hey, I don't have any money."

Doc replies, "It's a party—my treat. I just need your help when they get here."

Ben cautiously responds, "You just need us to help with what?"

"I just need you to carry the pizzas in and distribute them."

"So we carry the pizzas in and distribute them, and that's it?"

"That's it. Now you go and have a good time, and I'll find you when it's time."

Gorni shrugs and smiles. Ben nods his acceptance. "Just carry? You got it."

Doc slings his arms around his comrades' necks and walks them back into the house. "You guys are Dogs, you know that?" They smile and everyone barks, "Woof. Woof. Woof."

As they step through the door, Kruger intercepts Doc. "Got a minute?"

"You guys go on, enjoy the party. I'll catch up with you later." Doc watches them bark their way down the hall and comments as Groucho Marx, "I wouldn't belong to any club that would have me as a member."

"I need something. I've had a rough day and I don't want to feel any pain for the rest of the night."

Doc turns and walks the opposite way down the hall to his room. He opens the door and flips on the light. He sets his black bag on the bed and opens it. Kruger steps in, looks back down the hall and shuts the door.

Ben and Gorni work their way through the kitchen and stand watching the uproar in the front room with their heads bobbing to the blaring music. Pug pushes them aside and fights through the bouncing, twitching, oscillating mob to the stereo. With a single finger, he punches the stop button, silencing the deafening music. The sudden stillness stuns the dancing crowd. A few continue dancing.

"Everybody listen up," announces Pug. "Time for the beer-shooting contest. All contestants report to the kitchen."

A few protests come from the crowd. "It's not fair. No one's got a chance against you. You drink all the time."

Pug shifts into his part as W. C. "I certainly do not drink all the time. I have to sleep, you know. Okay, let's crank this baby up." Pug pushes the play button and spins the volume dial to its limit.

Several individuals parade to the kitchen. Bronk collects Dickie. "Sounds like something I can saddle up to."

The contestants file into the kitchen past Doc talking on the phone. "Yeah, I'd like to order a dozen monster pizzas with the works. Delivered. 715 Cascade Street. How long? ...Okay, see you then."

"This is Bottom Street. Cascade is the next block over," informs Ben.

"Oh, yeah. Right. It's okay, we'll meet them outside."

"For all you beer-shooting rookies, Pug is the undefeated champ," announces Joe.

Pug struts back and forth before the contestants, holding a giant mug above his head. The silver mug has Thirsty Dog emblazoned across the front and a dozen champions' names on the back. Pug's name is listed for the last three consecutive years. "Now Pug will demonstrate how it's done. It's all yours, Pug."

Pug demonstrates as he talks. "First, you want to puncture the bottom of the can. So you start by turning it on its side so you don't spill any." Using a church key, Pug takes the pointed end and pierces the sideways can. He lowers his nose to the opening and takes a long sniff. "Ahhh, the smell of brain food," he says as W. C.

"Brain food?" a contestant asks.

"It made Bud…wiser. Now you slip your finger under the pull tab ring and cover the opening with your mouth. On the starter's signal, you tilt the can upright, pull the tab and suck beer. Like this." Pug tilts the can upright and pops the tab. Before anyone can count to two, the can hits the floor to a room full of oohhs and aahhs.

Gorni picks up the can, and a little foam oozes out. He shakes the can, which contains nothing but foam, then holds it up and peers inside.

Pug proclaims as W. C., "Ah yes, a beer a day keeps the doctor away," and then accents his comment with a loud belch.

"Just foam, baby, just foam. If any beer pours out or you upchuck, it's an automatic disqualification, " instructs Joe. "The defending champ gets a free pass to the finals, so the rest of us will have a single elimination tournament to see who challenges Pug."

Joe watches the baffled Gorni continue to inspect the can. He looks through hole in the bottom, then down the hole created by the pull tab. He sticks his finger in and feels around, then shakes the can. Joe opens the fridge, lifts out a six-pack and shakes vigorously as he walks to Gorni. "Here." Joe extends the six-pack and points to Gorni. "You," he instructs, "practice." He repeats, "You—practice," and slaps a can opener on top of the six-pack.

Joe feels Marilyn's fingertips squeeze his rear. "Okay, everyone put your name on a piece of paper and drop it in the hat," he instructs, grabbing Bronk's hat from his head. He hands the hat back to Bronk. "You take care of this. I gotta work up a thirst, if you know what I mean." He nods at Marilyn and winks. Joe's arm wraps around her waist, and he pulls her tight. As they slither off, Joe slides his hand over the cheek of her ass to its crevice and follows it down between her legs.

Bronk waves his hat in the air above his head and shouts, "Last chance. Last call to enter the shooting contest."

Jas emerges from the frenzy. "You can sign me up." She wears a long flowing white gown topped with a Greek warrior's helmet and carries a spear.

"Whoa, hold your horses. I don't know if women can enter this contest."

"How about goddesses?" she asks, poking Bronk with her spear.

"Goddesses?"

"What are you afraid of, Bronk?"

"Afraid? I ain't afraid of nothin'. It's just that shootin' beer is a guy thing."

"You afraid of losing to a girl?"

"Ha. How can you be afraid of something's that never gonna happen?"

"Then how about a side bet?"

"What?"

"I'll bet you twenty dollars that if we go against each other, my can hits the floor first."

"Nothing but foam."

"Nothing but foam."

"Make it fifty."

"You're on."

Dressed in a black-and-white nun's habit and headpiece, Pump waddles into the kitchen. He carries a notebook-sized Bible in one hand, and a large cross hangs around his neck and bounces on his pregnant looking belly. "Sorry I'm late, but my wife wouldn't let me dress until the kids were in bed. Am I in time, or do I have to beg to get in the contest?"

Gorni takes a seat on the floor next to the stereo. He removes a beer from its plastic ring, tilts the can on its side and punctures the bottom. A geyser shoots from the can, showering him. He covers the spraying hole with his mouth. Beer gushes from his nose until the jet stops, then he tilts the can, pops the top and chugs. After a couple of swallows, he chokes and spits up.

Pug approaches with his entourage of girls. "Hey, Gorni, I'd like you to meet the bitches. This is Bitch Number One, Bitch Number Two and Bitch Number Three. Ain't they great?"

Gorni nods. "I like beaches."

"And this is the one, the only Gorni." The bitches look at Gorni's wet face and the beer droplets dripping from his nose.

"Oh look, he's crying."

"I think he's cute."

"Shit, man, you want a date?" asks Pug

"What?" asks Gorni

"You…want…a…date?"

Gorni's eyes widen. "Does Howday Doooday have a wooodeen deek?"

"Go ahead, choose one."

Gorni looks over each and then points at Bitch Number One. Pug pushes Bitch Number Three forward. "Have a good time," he says dragging the other two into the dancing fray.

In the kitchen, Bronk draws two pieces of paper from his hat and announces. "Okay, the first two contestants are Mini D—"

"Here," answers Mini D.

"And," He reads the second name. "Jack Meoff." No one responds. "Jack Meoff." he shouts. Everyone giggles. There's no answer. He shouts louder, "JACK MEOFF!" The giggles turn to jeers. "JACK—" Bronk stops, realizing the joke.

"Sorry, no takers," Mini D informs him.

"Watch out for his brothers, Jerk and Whack," warns Jas.

Bronk pulls another name from his hat and reads, "And Pump." He turns to Jas. "I feel dumber than a cow pie."

"Don't feel bad. Last year they got Ben with Peter Goesinya, Goes…in…ya."

"I get it."

"And the year before that, they got Doc with Ima Diclicher."

A can splats on the floor and Pump wipes his mouth, then belches. He slaps his belly like a bongo drum.

Mini D casually continues to sip his beer. The competitors look at him with disapproval. When he feels the sting of their stares, he lowers his beer. "What? I just do this for the free beer."

"This calls for a celebration," adds Pump, opening his Bible and removing a flask from its snug bed in the cutout pages.

"Okay, next two," announces Bronk, drawing two pieces of paper from his hat, "Doc and Jas."

Jas cups both her hands and strikes Pump's belly, slapping out an improvisational rhythm and spouting, "C'mon, give me some luck. Jas needs a new beer mug."

Pump lifts his habit, exposing his beach ball belly. "Go ahead—I got plenty to spare." Jas rubs and caresses the orb, coaxing it as a witch standing over her boiling brew.

Bronk leans close to Jas and whispers, "What d'ya say after the contest, we hang out?"

"You never give up do you?"

"Ain't a horse that can't be rode."

"Or a cowboy that can't be throw'd. I have two rules. I never date anyone from the team I'm a trainer for, and I don't date guys shorter than me."

***

Several empty cans lay next to Gorni. He pierces another can and gets another beer shower. Persevering, he lifts the can to his mouth, takes several gulps and then chokes and sprays beer from his mouth and nose.

Bitch Number Three sits next to Gorni and bares her soul. "Oh, Gorni, I try and I try, but I just don't know what the Bitch Master wants. He says do this and I do this. He says do that and I do that. But I'm still number three. I'd do anything to be number one—anything. What can I do, Gorni? What can I do? You know, Gorni, you're not like the rest of the guys. You're nice. You listen."

Gorni smiles and slips the stereo headset over his nodding head. Bitch Number Three continues to pour her heart out. Gorni raises another can and chugs and chugs. His eyes widen. He tilts the can on its side and sees nothing but foam. He throws his arms in the air and hugs Bitch Number Three.

***

Two cans smack the floor, one an instant before the other. Doc celebrates, "I won. I won." Everyone stands and stares in silent disbelief. "Who are you going to believe, me or your own eyes?" asks Doc, in character.

Another silence lingers. "Okay, it was worth a try. I'm out and Jas advances," concedes Doc, pulling two names from the hat. "Next up are Joe and Ben. I'll run down Ben."

"I'll find Joe," volunteers Bronk. He walks from room to room, yelling for Joe.

Doc finds Ben on the porch. "What're you doing?"

"I was watching for Tara. She's due anytime now."

"C'mon, it's pizza time. Get Gorni and meet me back here."

Ben works his way through the crowd to the stereo. Gorni lies in a pile of empty beer cans. His eyes are closed, and his wide open mouth drools. Bitch Number Three pleads her case to the unconscious stiff. Ben nudges him with his foot. "Okay, it's time." Gorni doesn't move. Ben grabs Gorni and shakes him. "C'mon, it's pizza time." Ben rips off the headphones and shakes vigorously.

He returns to the front porch with the news. "Gorni's passed out."

"We have to recruit someone else, quick." Doc looks at his watch. "Shit, we're running out of time."

Adam sports a knit cap, and a hooded sweatshirt with the hood pulled over his head. His entire body is draped by an ankle-length trench coat. Military boots pop out from under the garment with each stride up the sidewalk toward the Dog Pound.

"Here comes Adam. He'll do it," says Ben. "Hey, Adam, what are you supposed to be?"

"You can't tell?"

"C'mon, what're you supposed to be?"

"You a fool?"

"Joe." Bronk walks out onto the porch. "Joe. Anybody seen Joe?"

"I think I saw him going upstairs," answers Ben.

Bronk makes his way to the stairs and strides to the top. Balls' door is cracked open. Bronk peeks in and does a double take. Balls sits on his bed with his legs crossed, and his eyes closed.

"C'mon in," he says without opening his eyes.

"Sorry, don't mean to disturb you. I'm lookin' for Joe."

"You're not disturbing me."

"What's that you were doin'?"

"Meditating."

"What's that? Some sort of ponderin' or chewin' over somethin'?"

"It's different for everyone. For me, it's a way to relax, empty my mind, and focus on just one thing."

"I don't see why you'd want to do that when there's a party."

"You have a point," says Balls, smiling.

"So what're ya focusin' on?"

"An alligator."

"An alligator?"

"They're survivors. Along with the shark, they may be the oldest species on earth. Their only goal is to kill so they can live. When they're hungry, they attack low, grip something with their teeth and then roll and try to rip it off whatever it's attached to. I find by meditating on the gator, I'm able to bring a lot of his fighting instincts to my wrestling."

"No shit."

"No shit. So what animal do you identify with?"

"More'n likely it'd be…a wild stallion."

"Good choice. By the way, Joe is in there," says Balls, pointing at the door across the hall.

***

Doc, Adam, and Ben stand in front of the house at 715 Cascade Street. Doc spots the red pizza delivery Volkswagen Bug at the stop sign. "There he is." The Bug peels around the corner and darts down the street. Doc grabs Ben and Adam and pushes them into the overgrown bushes next to the house. He pulls them into a huddle. "When he gets halfway up the sidewalk to the house, I'll run and hit him, and you guys grab the pizzas."

Ben stammers, "But. But I…"

"I have a better idea," says Adam.

The pizza man removes all the pizzas from his back seat and cautiously stacks the red boxes twelve high. Ben and Doc slip from the bushes to the road and stroll along the side of the road toward the delivery vehicle. The pizza man gets a good grip, lifts the pizza boxes, turns and whistles as he strides up the paved walkway. Ben and Doc turn and follow behind the delivery man.

Adam leaps from the bushes and shouts, "Hey, pizza man!"

The pizza man turns his head toward the voice. Adam slings his trench coat wide open, exposing his nakedness from the waist down. The pizza man stops in his tracks. His eyes focus on the large swinging male organ, and his jaw drops.

Ben stands motionless. "He's a flasher."

Doc is transfixed. "That' s a good costume."

"Now. Now. GO!" hollers Adam. Doc snaps out of it and elbows Ben. Ben regains his senses, sprints and snatches the chimney of pizza boxes. Doc follows with a football block to the back, knocking the delivery man to the ground. He looks up to witness the threesome running between the houses and disappearing into the shadows.

***

Bronk opens the door. "Joe, you're up." Bronk's body is silhouetted in the doorway as the light from the hall spotlights Joe and Marilyn, naked and twisting on the mattress.

Doc climbs the stairs and runs along the floor, announcing, "Pizza time. Pizza's here. It's pizza time." He glances over Bronk's shoulder, pushes him aside, lifts a disposable camera from his white jacket pocket and flashes a snapshot of the bed scene.

"Get out of here," shouts Joe. He sits up and steps over the side onto Dickie, whose head is sticking out from under the bed. Dickie screams.

"Pizza time!" scream voices from the closet. The closet door bursts open; four bodies bottleneck in the doorframe and then spill onto the floor, fighting, grabbing and pushing to be the first to their feet.

Pump rises from the top of the pile. As he ambles to the hallway, he offers his review. "I expected a lot more. I'd give it maybe three stars out of five."

"Maybe three and half," suggests Mini D as he sprints past Pump.

Kruger follows them, carrying a video camera with a little red flashing light. "I'm going to make you a star," he promises Joe.

Pug, the last in line, stops and squeezes both of Joe's nipples. "Honk, honk. This sex scene needs an enema." He runs out cackling.

Joe looks back at Marilyn covering herself with the sheets and says as the Joker, "Life as a famous criminal isn't what it's cracked up to be."

***

Hands grab slices of pizza and scatter, emptying the boxes as fast as they are opened. Joe and Marilyn sit on the couch eating. A stunning girl dressed as the Catwoman slinks through the front door and stalks toward Joe. With both hands on her hips, she demands, "Where have you been?"

"Susan, I've been looking all over for you."

"We were supposed to meet at the River Bar over an hour ago."

"I was there and didn't see you. I figured I screwed up and got down here as fast as I could. I just got here a couple of minutes ago."

Susan points a firm finger in Joe's face. "Joe."

"Honest, Susan. You can ask anybody. Honest."

Susan glares at Marilyn. "Who's she?"

"You can't tell? That's Marilyn Monroe."

***

An all-black Monte Carlo glides to a stop and double-parks on the street in front of the Dog Pound. Reflections from the street lights and homes swirl across the tinted windows as the driver's door swings open. The caped crusader and boy wonder step from their Batmobile, walk to the rear and open the trunk. Batman reaches in and lifts out a shotgun. He slings it across his chest with one hand on the stock and the other on the trigger.

"Let's get this over with," he says, with a nod toward the Dog Pound.

Robin marches up the walk, clearing a path for the black cowl. Everyone on the front porch stops and watches the pair. Batman pauses at the steps and lifts the gun above his head. He cocks the rifle by pumping the gun barrel, points it straight up and fires a round. A mad scramble clears the porch. The green, red, and yellow sidekick boots open the front door for Batman to make his entrance. He walks to the center of the front room as Robin steps over Gorni's passed-out body and turns the music off. All eyes turn in Batman's direction as he lifts the rifle above his head again and pumps. Every eye freezes on the shotgun. Robin casts a menacing stare at Bitch Number Three, who is still yapping at Gorni.

Batman raises the shotgun, braces it to his shoulder and crosses to Susan wagging her finger in Joe's face and threatening, "You're such an asshole." She stops mid-sentence when the masked man sticks the shotgun muzzle in Joe's face.

"You got the wrong man."

"Shut up!" orders Batman.

"Carter, is that you?"

Carter digs the end of the barrel into Joe's forehead and backs him across the room. "I'm only going to say this once." The wall stops Joe. Carter prods, pinning Joe's head to the flowered wallpaper. "When I take this gun from your head, you do exactly as I say, or I'm going to redecorate." Carter lowers the red bead mounted at the end of the barrel to Joe's mouth. "We on the same frequency?" Joe nods. "Open your mouth." Joe purses his lips. "You think a little red will liven up this room?" Joe opens. Carter sticks the end of the barrel past his teeth and slides it down his tongue. "Just think, if I pull the trigger, your last taste would be buckshot." Carter jabs with the gun and knocks Joe's head back into the wall. "When I take away your pacifier, you're going to do exactly as I say. Right?" Joe nods. Carter removes the barrel from his mouth and walks backward, aiming at Joe's head. He stops.

"Strip."

"What?"

"Strip—naked."

Joe removes his shoes. "Hey, you want me naked, you don't need that gun," says Joe, with a flirty wink.

"Show me some skin."

Joe pulls his shirt over his head, exposing his wiry, sinewy upper body. Carter motions with the gun to drop his trousers. Joe undoes his belt, unbuttons, unzips, and steps out of his pants. He stops and stands in his briefs.

"You know, if I take my undies off, I'm going to ruin all the women in here for the rest of you guys."

Carter lowers his aim from Joe's head down to his crotch. Joe scans the room, drops his head, takes a deep breath, and pulls his shorts down to his ankles. Carter points the shotgun at the ceiling, takes a dramatic pause and pulls the trigger. Click! Carter and Robin burst out laughing.

Pointing at Joe, Carter lets out, "I got you. Ha, ha. I got you."

"That's your idea of a joke?"

Adam shakes his head, muttering, "College kids." He strolls out to the porch, picks up a box of abandoned pizza and chomps down on a piece as he heads across the lawn. He takes a surprised second look and stops chewing. Backing up, he bends at the waist to get a good look. Smoke puffs from the tailpipe of the double-parked black Monte Carlo. Adam saunters to the idling vehicle and looks around. He opens the driver's door, takes a quick, systematic sweep of the interior, tosses the pizza box in the passenger seat and slides in. He shifts to drive, shakes his head in bemusement, *College kids,* and gives it gas.

Kruger shouts over the crowded room, "Time for some real entertainment!" He pushes the power button on the stereo and slides a cassette tape into the slot. "Wipeout" blasts from the speakers, and Kruger takes over the floor. Every part of his body jiggles, shakes, and gyrates in perfect sync to the music, and at the opportune moment, he grabs two handfuls of his T-shirt and shreds it from his torso. Screams erupt from his captivated audience.

***

Jas rubs, pats, and slaps Pump's exposed belly. "C'mon, baby, one more time. Don't fail me now." Jas abruptly breaks from her good luck charm, grabs a can of beer and takes her position next to Pug.

"C'mon, Pug, you win four in a row, you get to retire the mug—it's yours for life."

Everyone chants, "Pug. Pug. Pug. Pug."

Both contestants assume the starting position: mouth covering the hole in the can, finger under the tab. The room goes silent. The starter jabs, "Go." They jerk their heads up and back, their Adam's apples pump up and down, and then they slam their cans to the floor. All eyes make a spasmodic shift from the cans to the starter to get the decision. He takes a prolonged stare at the beer cans on the floor, lifts both to check for excess beer, looks around at everyone and points at Jas. Boos rain down on the decision. Jas jumps in celebration and retrieves her trophy mug.

Several chorus, "Cheater. Cheater. Cheater."

Others point and poke Pump. "Why d'ya help her?"

"Yeah, traitor."

"You should have come dressed as Benedict Arnold."

"Loser."

A naked Joe smacks Bronk in the back of the head. "It's your fault. You let her in the contest."

"Hey, it cost me fifty dollars."

"Speaking of my fifty dollars, when do I get paid?" butts in Jas.

"How do I get to your house?"

"Ha. Yeah, right. Just follow the yellow brick road, Shorty," says Jas. She glides into the front room and hoists her mug above her head for all to see. Three seconds later, she joins the rest of the audience mesmerized by Kruger's dance. Down to his briefs, he points his butt at the spectators, and moves to the slower sensual music. His fingers reach back and tuck the cloth in the crack of his ass to create a thong, which elicits another round of screams.

"The guy puts Chippendales to shame. I'm standing here naked as a newborn, and no one's even sneaking a peek. Who says it pays to advertise?" Joe complains to Bronk, who can't take his eyes off Jas. "You can forget about her. Guys have been trying to tap that for three years. I don't think she likes sex or guys or something."

Pug joins them. "I can't believe I lost to a girl."

"Join the club," respond Joe and Bronk in unison. Bronk's eyes follow Jas as she works her way through the crowd and slips out the front door.

Pug's thick tongue slurs, "I didn't prepare right. I underestimated her."

"No shit," says Joe.

"I'll see you guys later," says Bronk, squirming through the bodies, "I got a date."

***

Bronk watches Jas walk up the steps, cross the porch, and unlock her front door. *Now what?* One by one, the windows in each room of the house turn from black to white. Bronk snaps his fingers and takes off.

He returns to the street in front of Jas's home, carrying the bucket of yellow paint and brush from the Dog Pound porch. He starts from the yellow lines in the center of the street and extends a new set of yellow lines to the curb, over the grass, up the sidewalk and steps, and across the porch to Jas's front door. *She wants a yellow brick road. She gets a yellow brick road.*

Bronk sets the paint can and brush out of sight. Returning to the front door, he takes a deep breath and raises his fist to knock but hears loud music blaring from inside. He leans over and peeks in the window. Jas's buff body bounds by wearing just her spoils of war. The raw form flitters and whirls about the front room in a graceful, rhythmic frolic. Her firm, muscular rump and legs launch and land with a festive expression of joy. Every leap whips and swirls her strawberry hair and bounces her firm, upturned breasts. Her arms and hands improvise with her new prize.

Forgetting herself, Jas becomes the dance. Her robust sensual movements transform into an exotic, ritualistic rejoicing. She finishes, bent at the waist, bowing her head while extending the mug heavenward. Bronk is hypnotized by her sacred, private moment. Only one thought goes through his head: *Yep, she's a redhead alright.*

A loud screech of tires. Bronk turns just in time to see a red blur plowing straight at him. He backs against the front door. A car crashes into the porch. The height of the porch and its supports stop it inches from his thighs. Bronk looks into the car. Pug is passed out behind the wheel.

Two hands cover Bronk's eyes from behind. "Don't turn around," says Jas. Bronk tingles from the touch of her hands and the thought of her nude body. She continues, "Take Pug home and put him to bed. Tell everyone to say they don't know anything about Pug's car. Then, come back and you'll be my witness. We were having coffee when it happened. Hurry." The door closes behind him.

Bronk helps a mumbling Pug from the car seat. "I was making a beer run. I don't know what happened. I was following the yellow line and the next thing I know..."

11. Buck$ Fever

"AND THEN THIS fucking bear starts fucking with me. If I slow down a little, he slows down little, if I run faster, he runs faster. He stays just close enough so I feel his breath on my neck, and it smells like shit. Every few strides, he snorts this primal growl that sends a chill down my spine and raises the hair on the back of my neck, like some sort of survival instinct, and all I can think to do is run. At one point, I glance back, and I swear he's grinning. He's enjoying this. It's like he's playing cat and mouse.

"Well, we run through the forest, and I have this perfect tunnel vision, and I'm dodging every branch and jumping every fallen tree, you know, hitting every step just right, when out of nowhere, I'm overcome by this unbearable fatigue, uh…no pun intended. But I know if I stop, the game is over, and the bear would have his way with his new toy. So I push on, and in a flash, all my sweat just evaporates. My mouth goes dry. My lips crack and start bleeding. Every nerve in my body feels like it's on fire and cries out to stop. I figure this must be what it's like in hell. Anyway, all I know is I can't give in, so I try blocking it out, you know; I try to take my mind someplace else. But now I can't breathe—that's one of my hang-ups, suffocating, claustrophobia whatever—and all my body's systems just start shutting down. My head fills with this intense pounding like some sort of countdown. Now I'm begging, *Oh God, help me. Please help me.* And I go into this strange sort of autopilot. I feel nothing. I hear nothing. It's like I'm there, but I'm not in my body, and I'm still moving, but it's like I'm a part of everything, or I'm at one with everything or some shit, and I get this warm feeling all over and everything's great, and all is bliss. Total bliss.

"Now it's like everything's okay. There's no pain, and I have this perfect vision, and I'm floating and seeing everything there is to see. Up ahead about a hundred feet slightly to my left, I see this gorge, and I set a course for it, thinking it's my chance for an escape. I'm pumping away, but the closer I get, the wider the gap gets to the other side. So I'm thinking, *I need more speed, faster…faster…*but it's like I don't have a body anymore. The gorge is getting closer and closer, and the jump is getting farther and farther. So I'm thinking, *Okay, then focus; focus on your form, run perfect, be perfect.* I take my final strides to the edge and leap as hard and high as I can, and it's like a dream within a dream. I'm airborne, but now I'm above, looking down at my body in slow motion, and at the peak of the jump, my body just stops and hangs there, suspended over these raging rapids below. Water crashing over car-sized boulders. Now I'm thinking about how good that water would taste, and zap. I'm back in my body thinking, *I don't think I am going to make it,* and the next thing I know, I'm crashing into the side of the far bank face first.

"I'm stunned, and I begin to slide and then free-fall down this cliff. My hands just start grabbing for anything. I slide a good body length or two before my fingers hook a lone branch. So I'm hanging there by one hand and catching my breath, and it seems almost worth letting go just to taste the water below. My grip loosens, and I'm hanging by my fingertips when this growl focuses my eyes toward the opposite bank. The bear's going crazy pacing back and forth and staring at me, like he's trying to figure out how he's going to get to me. He never takes his eyes off me, and when he catches my gaze, he begins scratching and thrashing dirt and branches into the air and getting all riled up; then, he sprints to the edge as if he's going to leap. Just the thought of him jumping on me scares the shit out of me. And he knows it.

"So now he gloats and poses and lets out a thunderous roar. This pisses me off, so I tighten my grip and start climbing to the top of the ridge. I pull myself up on flat ground, roll over and start searching the other side for the bastard. I take my time and look all around, but no bear. So I start scanning the woods in the background, searching all over for him, but he's nowhere. Then I go to the edge, figuring maybe he tried to jump and fell in, but no bear anywhere.

"So I'm feeling pretty good now. I'm thinking I made it. I survived. And this feeling of euphoria sweeps over me, and I start radiating light from every pore. I'm glowing like a firefly. So I'm all excited, and I turn to get going and there's the bear, as big as a house, right in my face. He rears, cocks his claws and springs forward, and before I can blink, his jaws snap like a steel trap on my head and then—I wake up."

Dan and Uncle Burt trek through the predawn woods. A light snow has dusted the forest. Uncle Burt is layered and bundled for subzero weather, while Dan leads the way in a pair of camo gym shorts and a fanny pack. His entire body is painted from head to toe in camouflage. They are armed with bows, arrows, and knives.

"So, what do you think?" solicits Dan.

"It's fucking cold out here."

"Right before dawn is the coldest time, but once the sun is up, it'll warm up pretty quick. So, what do you think about the dream?" persists Dan.

"You need professional help."

"Fuck you. Asshole."

"What do you want me to tell you?"

"Forget it—just forget it," barks Dan.

"C'mon, I was just fucking with you."

Dan breaks a brief silence. "I don't know. What you do think? What would you do?"

Uncle Burt shrugs. "If it were me, I'd get the hell out of there. But if I were you, I'd kick some bear ass."

"Fight a fucking bear. That's real good advice."

"No, seriously—it sounds like you got to confront him and fight."

"You fucking idiot. I would last about ten seconds."

"Hey, it's a fucking dream. You can do anything you want in a dream."

"What do you mean?"

Uncle Burt continues, "The trick is realizing you're in a dream. When you realize you're in a dream, then you just use your imagination and anything's possible. Once I was dreaming I'm falling into this bottomless pit, and there I am falling and falling, and the farther I fall, the more afraid I'm getting about going splat at the bottom. And I start wondering if I actually hit the bottom and die, am I going to die in my sleep? Then I realize, *Hey, this is a dream*, and I stop falling right there. I think, *I got to get back to the top*, and the next thing I know, I'm flying. I practice a little and before you know it, I'm fucking Superman."

"So the next time I'm dreaming the bear is chasing me, I just fly away?"

"Hell no. You stop and wrestle his hairy ass."

"Wrestle a bear?"

"Hell yes. He may be a bear, but it's your dream."

"Okay, so how do I know when I'm in a dream?"

Uncle Burt coaches, "What I do is give myself an instruction right before I go to sleep that if I dream, I realize it's a dream."

"And that works?"

"It does for me. I look forward to sleeping just so I can fly. And then there are other possibilities if there are any girls in the dream. Maybe that bear in your dream is female, and she's horny—or better yet, maybe it's a horny gay bear. Have you thought about that?"

Dan acts oblivious. He hardly breaks his stride as he plows through the thick brush and undergrowth. His strength and power bulldoze a path, but as he pushes forward, the foliage whips back. Uncle Burt follows Dan's footsteps, but the thicket still hinders him. He trips, stumbles and fights every step forward. Dan's half-naked frame knifes through the thicket like a paddle through water. They break through to a small clearing.

"That's it. I have to stop."

Dan pushes on, "It's not much farther."

"That's what you said half an hour ago. How much farther is it?"

"About half an hour."

"I need a break. I have to catch my breath." Uncle Burt sits and leans against a tree. Sweat drips from his nose. His labored exhales create steamy vapors.

"We can't stop now. We have to get there before dawn."

"How do you do it?" asks Uncle Burt.

"What?"

"Never mind. I don't know how I ever let you talk me into this. I could be having my cock sucked right now."

Dan retorts, "Yeah, and the Pope's Jewish."

"Instead, I'm in the middle of nowhere, playing Davy Crocket."

"C'mon, we have to go now."

"What so important we have to kill ourselves just getting there?"

Dan beams. "I've been scouting this buck for two years now. He's got the biggest rack in seven states. You bag a rack like that, and it can mean a lot of money from hunting equipment sponsors. We have to be in place before dawn if we're going to have a crack at him."

"Look, why don't you just go on and pick me up on the way back?"

"Can't do that."

"Why not?"

"We've brushed against everything and contaminated this whole area. A deer won't come within a mile of here."

"Hey, right now I don't care."

"Are you sure?"

Uncle Burt confirms with a nod. Dan walks to the edge of the clearing and looks back. "Don't wander too far from here. I should be back around midmorning. You got water?" Uncle Burt nods again. Dan turns away from the clearing, then stops. "Oh, and watch out for snakes."

"What the fuck? What am I supposed to do if a snake comes?"

"They won't bother you if you don't bother them—most of the time."

"Wait a minute. What do you mean 'most of the time'?" Dan keeps walking, ignoring the question. Uncle Burt asks one last question. "What should I do if I shoot something?"

Dan glances back, and laughs uncontrollably. He turns and buries himself into the growth. Even after Dan is well out of sight, Uncle Burt can still hear his distinctive cackle.

Uncle Burt fidgets and tries a variety of positions to get comfortable. Unable to find the right spot, he unzips his coat, slides his hood off, and uses it as a cushion between his head and the tree trunk. He sits in silence, hypnotized by the full moon. The black sky sparkles. *I never knew there were so many stars.* A twinkling, dense belt quivers and channels across the night sky from horizon to horizon like a glitter rainbow. *I wonder if that's the Milky Way.* Overwhelmed by the eternal vastness of the heavens, he feels his heart flutter. He is cooling off, so he zips up his coat and refits his hood. Breathing deep and full, his senses heighten and his awareness peaks. Totally attuned to his environment, he can hear the forest come to life. *It must be close to sunrise.*

A loud crack spins his head in the sound's direction. He looks but sees nothing. Another loud snap followed by a series of quick steps spins his head in the opposite direction. *There's something out there.* He holds his breath and listens. "Anybody there?" After a brief silence, he calls out again, "Dan? Dan is that you?" The silence is deafening. "Okay, stop fucking around." Apprehension swells and fills him. "Okay, I'm warning you."

He thinks about the bow leaning on the other side of the tree. Not wanting to arouse suspicion, he stretches his hand toward it. His awkward reach and grab tangle the bow in some low-hanging branches. *Just like taking an empty hanger from the closet—it always catches another hanger. A little jerk should do it.* Uncle Burt jerks the bow, but the branch will not give. He begins to panic, and the fight is on. Playing tug of war with the tree for his bow, he thrashes about, entangling his bow. *Yeah, just like the closet. Okay, now what?* He takes a moment to look around and wonders if anyone is watching, then begins removing a branch at a time.

The process of freeing the bow prompts a reevaluation of his position. Testing several locations for a strategically better spot, he practices reaching for the bow and loading an arrow, comparing which technique is faster, quieter, and feels the best. He settles on holding the bow across his lap with one hand and holding an arrow on top of the bow with his other hand. *Okay, now I'm ready.* He begins a slow scan of the area as the first glow of daylight cracks the horizon.

***

Dan's relaxed, camouflaged torso drapes the fork of a large tree branch. Indistinguishable from the tree bark, he lounges ten feet above the ground, clearing unwanted twigs with his hunting knife. He takes a deep breath, and shifts his eyes to embrace the sliver of sun as it crests the horizon. Wetting the tip of his finger with his tongue, he holds it up to test the wind's direction and casts a glance upwind. His nostrils flare as they draw air in short inhalations. *Prime time.* No sooner has he completed the thought than he hears a familiar rustling right on cue. Ever so slowly, he turns his head toward the sound. A lone doe takes a few steps from the woods and stops to graze. Acting as if she is out for a routine morning stroll, she feeds in a clearing separating two dense thickets. Between bites, she casts cautious looks in all directions. Dan is careful not to move or make a sound. He knows the big boy is rutting and could be right behind her, looking for a chance to mate. The doe leaps as if spooked and makes a hasty exit, scampering into the opposite wood.

Dan readies his bow and loads an arrow sensing the buck is near. An occasional clacking of antlers hitting branches reaches him. A lone form begins a calculated descent through the terrain funnel. The shadowy outline advances through the thick growth of underbrush, never allowing a full view. A sense of intelligence and intuition guides his movements, stopping every few regal steps to scout. The closer he gets, the better his size can be estimated. A glimpse of his rack dilates Dan's eyes and halts his breath. *He's a monster.*

The buck breaks off the doe's trail and angles away. Dan grabs a set of antlers he has hanging in the branches and slams them together until the male deer disappears. The rattling intensifies from a grinding into the clacking that simulates a buck fight. After about thirty seconds of rattling, Dan rakes one of the horns through the tree branches and gets ready for action. He sits with bow and arrow in hand, listening and watching for any sign—nothing. The stillness continues. Dan wonders if he has let enough time go by to do the rattling scenario again. He tries a few choppy, aggressive grunts on his deer call and waits. Nothing. Dan cannot believe he has missed his chance. *What if another hunter brings down the giant buck? Shit. Maybe a doe sound.* In desperation, he tries a few estrus bleats and waits.

After moments of torturous silence, Dan grabs his set of antlers to start rattling again when he spots a shadow retracing the same tracks as the first buck. *Déjà vu all over again. He must've circled around. Pussy. He doesn't come for a fight, but he shows up to get laid.* The buck makes his way toward Dan, moving faster and more aggressively this time. He approaches the clearing where Dan first saw the doe. Dan strategizes, knowing the buck will not stop in the clearing. *He's too smart for that, but he will stop before he crosses the clearing.* The magnificent buck breaks into a run, then pulls up and stops right at the edge of his cover. *This is the best shot I'm going to get…wait…wait…when he looks away…*

An innate impulse snaps the buck's head in the air. Something is amiss. He sniffs the air; his radar ears rotate 180 degrees. He whirls with a snort, and focuses his attention in the direction of Dan's tree. The buck begins a critical search for the source of his angst. His keen eyes penetrate the surroundings below Dan, who lies motionless, not even risking a breath. Coming up empty, the buck turns and examines the scenery in the opposite direction. *Now.* Dan draws his bow. An eerie calm comes over the ancient archer. Consumed by his task, he becomes the arrow puncturing the buck's life force. The buck feels the threat. His reflexes swing his head and fix his eyes. Dan releases and the arrow takes flight. Their eyes meet. After a resounding thud, the buck darts off.

Dan waits until the buck is out of sight, then he drops from his branch and runs to examine for blood. Excitement swells as he searches the ground in anticipation. He covers the entire area and escape route but sees nothing. *I'm sure this is the spot.* He squats and begins a closer examination, going over the entire tract again. On second thought, he is not sure and looks around, trying to solve the puzzle. He replays the scene in his head and reevaluates. *Maybe he was more this way.* As he turns and rises, an arrowhead almost takes his eye out. *Unbelievable!* His arrow has split a sapling no thicker than a quarter. Half the arrow extends from each side of the baby tree. A soft, grayish-yellow substance coats the tip of the arrowhead. Dan picks the substance from the tip and fingers it. *Buckskin.*

***

The sun shines brightly on Uncle Burt's face as he purrs away in peaceful dreamland. He is curled up with both hands tucked between his legs like a little boy, and the bow lies neglected on the ground a couple of feet away. His eyeballs twitch under their lids. Loud snorts and hoofing summon him from his deep sleep. His eyes slowly crack open to see two giant bucks clashing. Their supersized racks lock in bitter combat. The uncontrolled fury escalates across the clearing toward him. The ex-wrestler's reflexes respond; he rolls and then leaps out of the way as the struggle crashes his resting spot, exploding branches and chunks of bark in all directions.

They aggressively hoof the ground, angle their heads and ready for another attack. A startled Uncle Burt labors to get his bearings. His eyes find the bow and arrows. He scrambles on his hands and knees, grabs his weapon, and quickly crawls out of harm's way. Clack! Another thunderous clack. Two massive racks entwine and seize up, forging a natural trap. The lathered bucks writhe about, unable to separate. Uncle Burt's hands shake as he loads the arrow and raises the weapon. Trembling uncontrollably, he draws, aims, and launches the lethal missile. The branched horns disengage, liberating the pair. They rabbit off, their white tails bouncing and darting to a fade.

Uncle Burt leans back against a tree. He takes several deep breaths to slow his pounding chest as his dazed mind pieces things together. An uncanny silence descends after the fracas. Collecting himself, he takes several uneasy steps forward. He feels violated. Fear fills him as he takes in the razed battle scene. Small trees have been knocked down, bushes trampled, branches ripped from trunks, and the landscape flattened to waste. He gazes around the ruined tract and replays the incident frame by frame in his head. When he gets to the part where he released his arrow, he thinks, *Here. They were here.* He studies the demolished scenery and spots something. He looks closer, slips off his glove and touches the dark spot with his bare fingertip. He brings the smear close to his face and studies it. *Blood.* He follows the escape path and searches. He finds another droplet. And then another.

***

The midmorning sun is up and the snow has melted, except in the deep pockets of shade. Dan walks at a melancholy pace, tracking something. He carries a bundle under his right arm and his bow in his left hand. He comes to an abrupt stop in the shade of a giant oak on a crest overlooking a shallow gully. His eyes pop and his jaw drops. *Un-fucking-believable!* Directly below, Uncle Burt struggles to pull a lifeless giant buck by its enormous rack through the brush and shrubs. *He got my buck. He got my fucking buck.*

Every few steps, Uncle Burt stops, gets a fresh grip and pulls. Blood covers his arms up to his elbows; his bow and blood-drenched coat lie across the buck's claret-soaked torso. Another tug and the buck slides a few feet farther. Uncle Burt stops and catches his breath. He looks around until his eyes find the original trail of blood and follow it up the embankment to the crest where Dan is standing. Uncle Burt unknowingly stares right at the camouflaged Dan and wonders how he is going to be able to pull the deer up the slope.

Dan steps forward, tossing him the bundle under his arm. "You're going to need this."

Startled, Uncle Burt jumps a foot into the air and exclaims, "What the fuck? You trying to give me a heart attack?"

"What? Did I scare the big, brave hunter?"

"You can't just go around popping out like that with no warning or nothing. What if I had my bow and shot your camouflaged ass?"

"I'll take my chances."

Uncle Burt picks up the bundle at his feet and examines it. "So, what's this?" he asks.

"It's a deer drag. You tie the deer in that end, slip on the harness, and then you can pull the deer like a dog sled."

"Geez, they think of everything, don't they?"

Dan jumps from his mound and surfs down the leaf-covered dirt ramp. "C'mon, I'll help. First, we need to field dress him."

Uncle Burt is at a loss. "Field dress him?"

"Yeah, we have to gut him," Dan explains.

He rolls the buck on his back, grabs his penis and scrotum, and with one slice of his knife, he disembodies the buck's organ and testes pouch and tosses them at a dodging Burt. Dan cuts around the deer's rectum and zip ties it shut, then punctures the lowest part of the deer's belly between his rear legs. Dan expertly inserts his left hand and holds down the deer's insides as his right hand guides the blade, slicing the buck wide open from his groin to his breastplate. He carefully removes the bladder and rectum and then turns the buck on its side. While lifting the ribcage, he severs the tissue holding the organs in place. He rolls the buck to his other side, severs the remaining tissue under the opposite ribcage, and neatly pulls out the innards, emptying the contents of the cavity. The sight of the wet, steamy pile of guts sickens Burt. Dan rescues the liver and heart from the gut pile and drops them in a plastic baggie.

Lifting the clear plastic baggie eye level, he examines them. "The liver and heart make good eating." Uncle Burt can't suppress his gag reflex any longer. As he turns away, the contents of his stomach erupt and spew forth. Dan listens to Uncle Burt's retching and gagging followed by spasmodic, noisy belching. He tucks the baggie containing the heart and liver in his fanny pack and mumbles, "Fucking virgin," then shouts, "fucking virgin!"

Dan bundles the buck in a plastic tarp. Uncle Burt joins him and helps secure the buck in the wrap.

Uncle Burt can't contain himself. "Where's your buck?" he asks.

"What do you mean?"

"I mean, we went deer hunting, and I got mine. Where's yours?"

"Let me see now. How many times have you been deer hunting?"

"Oh, you mean this is like beginner's luck."

"No. It's more like a fucking miracle."

Uncle Burt's excitement boils over. "You should've been there. I was sitting at the base of the tree where you left me and the sun's blinding me, and I notice this movement out of my peripheral vision. I turn my head real slow and out of nowhere, the buck walks into the clearing. I figure he can't see me because the sun's blinding him, too. He stops to munch down on something right in front of me. And I'm thinking, *This is the last breakfast for this bad boy.* So I raise the bow and just when I start to draw, he stops chewing and looks me dead in the eyes as if he's going to eat me for breakfast. I froze. It was terrifying—like he was possessed by the devil and his black eyes were looking right into my soul. Then I snap out of it, pull back the arrow and shoot, and I know I hit him, but he takes off running like nothing happened."

"I go after him and lose him, but there's a trail of blood, so I follow it. About half an hour later, I catch up to him hiding in a small grassy area surrounded by a thicket, and he's just standing there bleeding. So we stand there and he's giving me the ole evil eye, mano a mano, and I'm thinking about how I'm going to kill the bastard. So I charge him and start beating him in the head with my bow and he takes off running again, but he can't run so fast now, so I run him down and jump on his back. I try pulling the bow across his throat and choking him, but he just keeps running. And then I remember my knife, so I pull it out and I'm holding on with my left arm, stabbing with my right, and I keep stabbing until he stops and crumples to the ground."

"Why didn't you just shoot him with another arrow?"

"I lost the other arrows. Boy, I can't wait until I have his head mounted and hung in the bar. You know all the pussy this is going to get me."

"Pussy?"

"Girls eat this shit up. Man against beast, life and death and all that."

They tie the last knots, and Dan holds the harness for Uncle Burt. He starts to slip on the shoulder straps, then stops. "Hey, isn't this like cooking? I mean, if I cook, then aren't you supposed to clean up? Since I got the deer, shouldn't you drag it out?"

Dan shakes his head, "I already did the cleaning. This is more like taking out the garbage, and that job always goes to the lowest man on the totem pole. Besides, if I drag this buck out, I keep him."

Uncle Burt straps up and begins pulling. He follows the original blood trail up the embankment. Dan leans against a tree and rubs to and fro, and up and down scratching his back and watching Uncle Burt tackle the slope. He has a difficult time getting footing and slips and slides every step. When he can get secure footing, he uses the leverage to pull the carcass a little higher up the slope. After a drawn-out struggle, he stands at the top, pulling with all his might to lift his buck the final few feet. "I could use a little help here."

Dan replies, "We don't want to go that way. The truck is in that direction." Dan points and begins walking downhill in the opposite direction.

Uncle Burt's nonplussed. "Well fuck, you could've said something a little sooner."

"You could've asked."

They walk along side by side. The load is a lot easier to pull going downhill.

Dan changes the subject. "So how do you like that bow?"

Uncle Burt shrugs. "It's okay."

"You know, a bow adds more than a month to the hunting season. I bought that one brand new for $400. It's the best bow on the market. I could let you have it for say $300."

"What's with you lately? Every time we get together, you're hawking me something."

Dan thinks about his answer. "Money's low and with the baby coming and all, I'm just trying to get rid of some extra stuff, you know."

"Yeah, you're probably horny as hell with Cindy knocked up. How long has it been since you got laid?"

"Five months."

Uncle Burt's head is spinning in disbelief. "Five months? How long has Cindy been pregnant?"

"Five months."

"I thought you could still have sex after they're pregnant."

"You can."

"I get it. If I were her, I wouldn't want some animal like you pounding me, either. I'd be afraid the baby would come out with brain damage or his head would be all dented up."

Dan sighs, "She doesn't believe in it."

"What?"

"She believes sex is just for procreation."

"You mean you only get to have sex when she wants a baby?"

"Yep. Three times, three babies."

Uncle Burt's flabbergasted. "Wait a minute, you've only had sex three times since you've been married?"

"You got it."

Uncle Burt looks at Dan incredulously. "Holy shit. No fucking way. Oh man. I couldn't handle that. That's extreme. Don't get me wrong. I could probably go without the sex, because personally, I prefer blow jobs."

"You like blow jobs more than screwing."

"Without a doubt. As I said, I could go without sex but not blow jobs. I live for that action."

Dan's curiosity gets the best of him. "What's a blow job like?"

"No fucking way. You're not telling me what I think you're telling me, are you?"

"What? I just want to know why you like them more."

"Okay the professor's open for business. First, the name is all wrong. It should be called a suck job, not a blow job. Now, whenever I get some hottie to go down on me, and it's quite often by the way, I make it a major event. You see, I'm a visual kind of guy, so I make sure the lamps are equipped with the three-way bulbs that go up to 150 watts. You want the lamps at all angles so there's no shadows. Occasionally, I'll work a camera in if they're okay with it. Next, you want lots of mirrors strategically placed around the room so you cover all the views. Then I sit back on my bed, open a can of beer, light a cigar, and I'm ready for the preliminaries.

When the suckage starts, I slide open the top drawer of my nightstand and pull out my oversized hand mirror for the closeups. So if she's on my right side, I work the mirror with my left hand, and my right hand is alternating between the beer and cigar. Now I just take it all in; it's like watching a movie. And I do this until I sense her starting to tire, and then I have about a dozen motivational quotes I use. I start moaning and saying shit like, 'Ohhh, baby you move me.' and 'you're the best.' and 'Ohhh yeah, suck it, suck it. SUCK IT!' This helps them get their second wind, and you prolong this part as long as you can.

Now, the next part is tricky because the timing has to be just right; it's right along here that they start getting lockjaw and shit, and they start thinking about bailing. And right before they actually stop, you have to start moaning and groaning and cry out, 'I'm almost there, oh, ohhh, go, go, go—' Now you find out what they are made of. If they got heart, they bear down and hang in through all the pain and shit until you come, and if they quit, you just roll them over and fuck them."

"Sounds like it's all about you. Don't they complain? I mean, they don't get off, do they?"

"Well it is all about me. I'm not looking to get married—I just want to have some fun. You see, women break down into groups: first, you got the drivers, who want to dominate and just want you to give them head, so I don't waste my fucking time. Then, you have the women's libbers who want to negotiate equal time. Maybe someday I'll consider someone in this category if I fall in love or something, but not at this time. Next, there's the sometimers; they're the ones you just happen to hit on when something's going on in their life and the timing is just right. I'll take a sometimer anytimer. And last, there's the sex addicts, who are willing to do anything to take care of their man. This group gets pleasure from giving you pleasure. Personally, I'm partial to this group, and I invest most of my time farming this faction of women."

Dan's mind churns. "What if they've never given a blow job before? How do you teach them?"

"The easiest way is to compare it to something they already know, like sucking on a pacifier. My personal favorite is telling them it's a Popsicle on a hot day and it's melting, and they can't let any of the melting drops fall or they get spanked. And of course no matter what, you tell them they missed a few drops and you get to spank them. That one always works good."

Dan and Uncle Burt break the edge of the woods at Dan's pickup. He hurries ahead and lowers the back to the bed of the truck. Uncle Burt takes the last few strenuous steps. Near exhaustion, he collapses and exclaims, "That was a good workout."

Dan hurries. "It's getting late. Help me load this buck, and you can rest on the drive back."

"You got enough rope?"

"We don't need rope. We'll put him in the bed."

"No way. This bad boy is getting strapped to the hood, and we're driving around town."

Dan's adamant. "It's not done that way anymore."

"Well, that's the way we're doing it. I've seen a few deer, but I've never seen anything like this bad boy. We're putting him on display."

"We're hauling him in the bed."

"You know if it were your buck, you'd strap him on the hood and show the whole world."

Dan repeats, "I'm telling you it's just not done that way anymore. Besides, the troopers and police can ticket you if they think it's unsafe, and I can't afford a ticket."

"It's my buck and I say he goes on the hood."

"It's my truck and I say he goes in the bed."

"It's my buck."

"It's my truck."

"My buck."

"My truck."

"My BUCK!"

"My TRUCK!"

○○○○○○○○○○○○●●●●●●●●●●●●●●

12. Busted

UNCLE BURT TURNS and then straightens the wheel of Dan's red Ford Ranger. Cruising down Main Street, he blasts the horn and waves to get everyone's attention. Dan slides lower in his seat. The sight of the giant blood-soaked carcass dwarfing the hood, plus Uncle Burt's staging, creates a human wake in the pickup's path. People leave the sidewalk and jog alongside, touching or holding the oversized antlers. Others become engrossed onlookers, pointing and shouting at the spectacle. Business owners and workers emerge from their store fronts to see what the commotion is about. The farther they roll, the larger the crowd grows.

Uncle Burt entertains the possibilities. "Man, they'll be talking about this for weeks or months, maybe even years."

"Nice hood ornament," shouts an onlooker.

"Fuckin' A," Uncle Burt responds proudly, and then points. "Hey, look—that's what I'm talking about."

Just ahead, a half-dozen coeds stroll from storefront to storefront, window-shopping. Uncle Burt double-parks, opens his door, steps up and sticks his head above the pickup. A few dozen curious observers gather around the vehicle to get a close look and touch the prize buck.

"Hey girls," shouts Uncle Burt. "Drop by the River Bar later for the celebration. Free beer and food."

An older woman emerges from the group of young women. She complains, "I'll have you know these girls are too young to drink alcohol."

"Hey, that's cool. You can come, too." He points at Dan. "This is my dad. The two of you can chaperone. See you about seven, and bring your friends. Oh, and don't mind the TV cameras. They'll be there filming. Just make sure you tell them Uncle Burt invited you." Uncle Burt exits with a wink to the older woman. She returns a smile and then checks out Dan, who slides further down in his seat.

"Okay, party's over. Let's get down to the Dog Pound," orders Dan.

"Hey, cool your jets. Things are just getting good." Uncle Burt smiles and waves good-bye to the older woman. "Besides, I just hooked you up with your blow job right there."

"I'm married, you moron."

"Doesn't stop most of the married men I know."

A police cruiser approaches from the opposite direction. Dan sees the cop slowing to a stop. *Ha. I warned him.*

The uniformed driver activates the cruiser's flashers and commands, "You have thirty seconds to clear the street. You have thirty seconds to clear the street." Amid moans, the crowd around the pickup begins to dissipate and trickle onto the sidewalk.

Dan snickers, "Remember, you're driving."

The officer rolls down his window. "Hi, Dan. Burt. What seems to be the problemmm?" His eyes discover the buck through the thinning bodies. He opens his door and leaps from his cruiser. "Holy mother of Jesus. What a pig." The officer moves around the hood for a closer examination. "I've never seen anything like this before. Look at that rack. This has to be some sort of record. Where did you bag this monster?"

Before Dan can speak, Uncle Burt spits out, "Down off Route 15 up in the hills behind the deserted Miller place."

The traffic is blocked in both directions, and the impatient drivers remind the officer with a few horn blasts. Breaking off the conversation, the officer goes into action, directing the cars behind him to back up. He backs up his cruiser enough to make a U-turn and cuts in front of the red pickup. Another cruiser with its lights flashing joins from the rear, providing a private escort down Main Street. The Uncle Burt and buck parade is on.

"This is un-fucking-believable." says Dan in disbelief. "You lied to the officer."

"I know. I didn't want to give away your location. Besides, I saw another giant buck and thought you'd like a crack at him."

Dan's eyes light up. "Another one?"

"Yeah, you better believe it, and he's bigger than this one. I'm surprised you never saw him."

"Maybe I did and just didn't realize there were two of them. Thanks."

***

The buck express sails down a side street through a modest residential neighborhood. Uncle Burt breaks the silence. "I been thinking about your money situation, and I might be able to help if you got a couple hundred dollars you could spare."

"How's that?"

"Well, the bar just breaks even because I give away so much beer," explains Uncle Burt. "I actually make my income, my spending money, from sports wagers."

"You gamble?"

"Well, I don't just bet. It's more like a calculated investment. First, I keep up on all the teams through their local newspapers. Then I plot them and watch for trends and tendencies. I spread my bets so if I lose, I lose a minimum of money. If I win, there's the possibility of winning big."

"And you make money doing that?"

"Well, I don't get rich, but on the average week, speaking conservatively, I'll place maybe two to three thousand in a variety of bets. If I win, I make a profit of anywhere from four or five hundred to as much as a thousand or more. If I lose, the most I lose is maybe a couple hundred, so I'm always in the black in the long run."

"So what's that got to do with me?"

"Well, I've never done this for anyone before, so I don't have any sort of track record or anything, but I would be willing to manage some money for you—you know, bet it with my money and see if I can help relieve some of that financial burden."

"You mean you want to be my bookie."

"More like a financial adviser."

"And what if you lose it?"

"There are no guarantees. This has to be money that if you lost it, it wouldn't matter. You wouldn't miss it."

"I don't know. It sounds risky."

"It is risky. I can't guarantee anything, except I'll do my best. As long as I'm able to do what I've been doing for the last couple of years and not hit a losing streak, I'll get you a nice return on your money," explains Uncle Burt.

"I don't know. I'll think about it."

Uncle Burt glances at Dan. "You know, my cousin in Columbus knows a professional wrestling promoter. You want me to see how much you could make wrestling a match?"

"That fake shit? No way."

"Okay, just asking."

"That ain't wrestling, that's rasslin'."

"Okay."

"It's bullshit."

"Okay."

"It's ruined our sport."

"Okay."

There's an awkward silence. "How much do you think they pay?" asks Dan.

"I don't have a clue. But I'll find out." Uncle Burt smiles. "So, how do you think the team is looking?"

"We have too many individuals, too many alphas."

"Everybody's a chief. No Indians. That's interesting, so what do we do?"

"We have to find a way to bring them together like a wolf pack. A pack is a lot more effective at hunting than a lone wolf is."

"How do we do that?"

"Find something they all have in common, something that's—"

A caravan of police cars speeds past with lights flashing.

"Something's up," says Uncle Burt.

The caravan fans out and surrounds the Dog Pound. Uncle Burt guides Dan's truck into the empty lot next to the Dog Pound and parks between two cruisers. Immediately, the officers approach the pickup.

"Mark called us over the radio and told us about the buck. What a whopper," comments one officer.

The chief of police arrives in a cloud of dust, hurriedly opens his door, and makes a hasty stride toward the front door when he stops to admire the buck. "It looks even bigger than Mark described. You know, I was the game warden before I went into law enforcement, and I've hunted this area for almost fifty years. I've never seen anything like that. It could be a record. Maybe we should document this."

All the policemen scramble to their cruisers, retrieve supplies, and then gather around the buck with tape measures, pencils, and cameras.

"A rack has to air-dry for sixty days before you can get an official score," cautions the chief, "so this will be a green score."

They examine the rack. "Well, are we going to do a typical or non-typical score?" one of the officers asks.

"Well it only has one abnormal point, so it can be scored either way," another officer concludes.

"Hell, do both," suggests the Chief.

The officers begin measuring and figuring and proceed with the documentation process.

The police chief steps back and shakes his head in awe. "Now, that's a wall hanger."

"So what's going on inside?" asks Dan, with a nod toward the house.

"Apparently, the boys had a party here last night, and things got out of hand. President Hardon is talking to the boys now."

"What's the president doing here?"

"They're all here: the president, athletic director, campus supervisor, me, plus a lot of other folks I don't even know," explains the police chief. "I have to get inside and see what's going on."

Dan follows on his heels. Uncle Burt holds court in the background. "...he was about fifty yards away. He just got done kicking another buck's ass, and he's acting all bad boy, strutting around puffing out his chest and showing off his rack. I get him in my sights—"

"There ain't no sights on a bow," notes one of the officers.

"You know what I mean. And then he looks right at me, eyeball to eyeball, and to make things worse, it's just before dawn, so the lighting is at its worst—"

"How'd you see his eyes if the lighting was so bad?"

"He turned his head toward me. You want to hear the story, or not? Okay, I draw the bow and then the wind kicks up, so now I have to calculate the distance and the drift…"

The president greets Dan as he enters. "What are you doing here?" Everyone in the house has been roused from sleep and mustered into a lineup along one of the front room walls. The motley crew consists of the wrestling team and a few female companions. They scratch and rub their half-naked bodies. Campus security flanks them on each side. On the floor in front of the suspects lies an unconscious naked male sprawled out on his back with a red cushion over his genitals, and his head stuck in a lampshade. His chest heaves up and down with each breath.

One of the security officers vigorously pokes the body with a nightstick and reports to the police chief. "Everyone is here, but this one's out cold. The house is all clear."

"Okay, begin the search," orders the chief.

President Hardon stares at Dan. "I asked what you are doing here."

"I came to collect the rent, but you look busy. I can wait."

"I want you off these premises now."

"This is my place. I have a right to know what's going on."

President Hardon looks at the police chief. He shrugs as if to say there's nothing he can do. The president is flanked by the athletic director and chief of campus police. Behind them stand half a dozen students. As the proceedings continue, the police officers conduct their search and then one by one, they slip out to get a look at the buck. The president approaches, raises a handful of papers and shakes them in Dan's face.

"These police reports are the end of wrestling at Dover University. After today, wrestling will cease to exist on this campus." The president returns to the lineup and pages through the reports as he begins his interrogation. "Where do I begin? We have leaving the scene of an accident, discharging of firearms, car theft, assault and battery, robbery, underage drinking and the theft of the Dover Dog from the main gate. Oh well, one place is as good as another. Does anyone know anything about Carter's black Monte Carlo. His ride was stolen from right in front of this place last night?" The group fidgets. "Well?" screams the president. "We have a witness, so you better speak up." The suspects take turns looking at one another in silence. Gorni raises his hand.

"What's your name?"

"Gorni Balevan, I wrestle," proclaims Gorni with a smile that connects his ears.

"Yes, of course you do. Now what can you tell me?"

"I like Bitch Number Three. She is good ride."

"What is this? Some kind of joke?"

Balls explains, "He just moved here from Iran and is still learning the language."

The president nudges Gorni back in line. "Thank you. Quiet now. Shhhh. Carter, do you recognize anyone?"

Carter steps forward from the group of students. "Yeah, they all look familiar. They were at the party." The president glares at each wrestler. Carter returns to his place.

The president shuffles his papers. "Will a Mr. William Pugliano step forward." Pug steps out and puts on his best innocent look. "Mr. Pugliano, where were you last night?"

"Here," answers Pug.

"You were here the entire evening?"

"Yeah."

"Then how do you explain the fact that your car was reported crashed into the porch of the residence at 7275 Coss Street?"

"It was stolen?"

"Was that a question or an answer?"

"I don't know how it got there. I was here all night."

The president grits his teeth. He examines his handful of reports and yells at Pug to get back in line. Dan wanders into the kitchen and begins scavenging. He tries to open a refrigerator door, but it won't budge. He studies the door and discovers padlocks have been installed. He scrounges through the party leftovers.

The president jerks a report from the pile and resumes. "Does anyone know anything about gunshots from this residence at about midnight last night?"

A short silence is interrupted by Carter. "Excuse me, President Hardon. If you're done with me, is it okay if I go? I have to study for an exam." The president nods his consent. Everyone watches Carter exit. A police officer approaches and whispers into the chief's ear.

The president returns the focus to the issue at hand. "Well, anyone know anything? Anyone hear gunshots?" asks the president.

Gorni proudly steps forward, "I shoot beer."

"Yes, very good Gorni, now back in line. C'mon now, everyone in the neighborhood heard the gunshots. Look, if the responsible party comes forward, everyone else will be spared. Last warning," cautions the president.

One of the deputies enters. "Chief, we searched the entire premises. There were no firearms and no Dover Dog."

The boys smile, nod, and exchange high fives.

Another officer enters. "We confiscated this," he says, handing a black bag and a videotape to the chief.

"We'll have a report to you when we determine the contents of the bag and view the video," says the chief, examining the items.

The news reverses the team's mood.

The president knows he is on to something. "Thank you, Chief. Anyone want to come forward now, so that I can protect you from prosecution? Once I receive that report, it'll be too late, and the police will prosecute you to the extent of the law. The longer this goes on, the deeper the hole you dig for yourselves."

Dan settles in the doorway to the kitchen, enjoying some leftover pizza and taking in the proceedings. The president slides out another report, smiles as he reviews it. "Last night at about eleven o'clock, a dozen pizzas were stolen from the Pizza Chef delivery person. Does anyone know anything about this theft?"

Gorni declares, "Pizza, breakfast of champions."

The president sends a fake smile to Gorni, then turns his back to the boys and motions for the delivery person. He steps forward from the other witnesses and makes eye contact with Pump, who makes a throat slashing gesture with his finger. The president sees the fearful look on the delivery boy's face and spins back to the team. They look innocent. The president sends a threatening stare, hoping to spot something that will give them away.

Turning back to the delivery boy, the president demands, "What'd they do?" He asks the rest of the room, "Did anybody see anything?" After a moment, he instructs the delivery boy, "Okay, point out the ones who stole your pizzas."

The delivery boy slowly approaches and stops in front of Doc. He studies Doc for a few moments, looks him up and down, then moves to Adam and examines him in the same manner. He repeats the routine with Ben and then shaking his head, "I don't know."

"What do you mean, you don't know? You said you could pick out the thieves."

"I know. I thought I could, but now I'm not sure. It was dark, and they were wearing costumes. I just can't say for sure."

The president yells at the delivery boy, "Get out. Go on, get out, you gutless—" He turns back to the team. "If I learn that one of you got to him, it'll be your last day at Dover." He motions the final four witnesses forward. "Okay, I don't want to mess around anymore. Pick out the thugs who jumped you."

"We know two for sure," the biggest fellow says, pointing at Mini B and Dickie. "Him and him."

"You two, step forward," demands the president.

Mini B and Dickie, the two smallest wrestlers, take a step forward. They are dwarfed by their accusers.

The president looks back and forth at the noticeable size discrepancy and sighs, "According to the police report, three wrestlers jumped and assaulted several young men from The Kings Court residence. And we have documented injuries from the hospital records. What have you to say about these allegations?"

Dickie explodes in a tirade. "That report is a lie! They blocked us on the sidewalk, harassed us, and jumped us. We had to defend ourselves."

Mini D adds, "Yeah, and then the whole basketball team emptied out of the house and ganged up on us. And I want some of that big guy. He insulted me and slandered me, and I'm thinking about getting an attorney and suing him, his team, his parents, and this university."

The president is taken aback by their aggressive reaction. His eyes shift back and forth between the accusers and the much smaller victims. "We'll have an investigation and get to the bottom of this. Now, the report says there was a third party. Who would that be?" He looks to the basketball players for some assistance. They shrug. A hand behind Gorni shoves the third smallest wrestler forward. "Of course it would be you, Mr. Gorni Balevan. You can get back in line."

The president knows his case is slipping away, so he goes to his ace in the hole. He pulls an eight-by-ten photograph from the bottom of the pile of reports. He looks at it, purses his lips and nods with confidence. He studies the image and then checks the boys. He marches to the end of the lineup, holds the photograph at arm's length, and walks down the line shoving it in each face.

"The young hoodlum in this photograph has a history of breaking the law. Fortunately, this shot captured him in one of his stunts that endangered lives, disrupted an official university event, damaged university property and broke the law. This university will be better off without him."

When he reaches the end of the row, the president sticks the print in Dan's face. It is the photo of a naked, long-haired, bearded motorcyclist streaking down the field during a football game.

It's the same photo Bill showed me.

Behind President Hardon, the boys look at one another and fight back snickers.

The president glares at Dan and buries the stake. "This deviant of society has been identified as a Dover wrestler named Kruger." The president turns back to the boys and asks, "Where is Kruger?" All eyes drop to the passed-out figure on the floor. "What a coincidence. Get him to his feet. I don't care what it takes."

Two security officers each grab an arm and lift the limp figure face-to-face with the president. "Remove that shade." A hand lifts the lamp shade and reveals a clean-shaven bald guy. The president's eyes bounce back and forth from the face to the photo: the face, the photo, the face, the photo. Is it or isn't it?

Dan peeks over the president's shoulder and shares the dilemma. "That's going to be a stretch. Could I speak to you privately?"

"Just a second. Chief, any luck finding the motorcycle in this picture?"

The chief shakes his head. "Just found a bicycle chained to the back porch."

The president's mind is scrambling. He had them in a zero-and-two count, and now he's thrown six balls in a row. He was so sure.

Dan follows the president into the kitchen and out of ear range. He looks the president in the eye. "Look, Rich, why don't—"

"It's President Hardon."

"Okay, President Hard-on."

"It's Har–don."

"Okay, President Hardon."

"The sooner I can rid this campus of you —"

"Okay, then come after me, but leave the boys alone."

"They're a bunch of criminals and derelicts."

"They're kids."

"They should be in prison, not in an institution of higher learning."

"You ought to be happy I can recruit anyone to wrestle here."

"And that's about to end."

"What's with you?"

"I want you and your team off this campus."

"I don't get it. I'm not two-faced like the rest of your employees. I tell you how it is. I thought a man in your position would appreciate that."

"I don't like you, Dan. From the first time we met, I found you to be base and primitive with the manners and style of an ape. Nothing has changed."

"You're still pissed, aren't you?"

"Enough. I'm closing the Dog Pound, and you and your wrestlers are banned from this campus."

"You know you can't do that without a hearing before the review board. I listened to all your police reports, and you don't have anything."

"The basketball team is willing to press charges."

"Are you serious? If it gets out that the basketball team was beaten up by three midgets, they'll be the laughingstock of the campus. Besides, none of those boys were injured, and it sounds like Mini B and Dickie might have a pretty good case. And you don't want to draw this out in court. The publicity would be bad for the university and all those involved."

"We'll see what we have when we get back the results of the black satchel and videotape. Until then, I'll do what I can do." The president marches to the front door, turns, and takes a dramatic pause. When all eyes are on him, he speaks. "This house is under quarantine. It is off-limits to everyone except the occupants. That means all nonresidents have to leave immediately," mandates the president, looking pointedly at the police chief.

"Okay, girls, get your things. You have to leave the premises." The chief glances around the room. "Any of you boys live somewhere else?" No one answers.

The president turns his back to the Dogs. "I am putting this house on probation." Casting an eye at Dan, he continues, "If there is any inappropriate behavior—I'm talking about the slightest infraction—I'm lowering the boom on Coach Sangha and the wrestling program." He turns to the chief. "Get the names of anyone who doesn't live here and make sure they understand that if they ever return to these premises, they will be brought up for review." He takes one more smoldering look at each wrestler, then whirls his back to the boys, and comments to Dan, "They're all yours." He marches out the door.

Dan walks to the door. The athletic director, Bill Bohr, stops him. "Sorry. I tried warning you. President Hardon is on the warpath. One more incident, and even I can't save you."

With his back to the lineup, Dan proclaims, "It smells like a brewery in here." Then turning to confront them, he demands, "Rent is due." Everyone, except the freshmen and Kruger, has vanished. "Okay, the four of you get dressed. You're coming with me. Meet me outside at my pickup." Dan shouts, "For the rest of you, rent is due."

"Dan. Come out here," summons Uncle Burt.

Uncle Burt approaches. "This is Officer Mike Ross. He's interested in buying your truck."

"Yeah, I saw your 'For Sale' sign. How much are you asking?"

"Three thousand."

"Three thousand? That seems like a good price."

"It's priced to sell."

"It looks like it's in good shape. I've been looking to buy a truck as a surprise for my son's sixteenth birthday. It has to look good, you know. Any mechanical problems you know about?"

"Nope. Runs like a champ."

"Anything else I need to know about?"

"Needs new tires."

"No problem."

"Oh, and it's a deer magnet."

The office chuckles. "Yeah, I see. Okay, you deliver the truck to me in its current condition, and you got a deal," says the officer, extending his hand. They shake on it.

The boys approach and ask, "Where are we going to ride?"

"Hop in the back."

"I'm not riding back there."

"Yeah, isn't it against the law?"

"*Now* you worry about breaking the law?"

"It's okay if you don't exceed twenty-five miles per hour," says Officer Ross.

"Just get in the bed. No sitting up on the sides."

"Where are we going?"

"It's a surprise."

Everybody climbs in. Dan looks in the rearview mirror, and the boys are sitting up on the sides. "I said sit down," yells Dan, starting the engine.

They squat in the bed and then slide up and sit on the sides. Dan backs up the truck, shifts into drive, and coasts toward the driveway.

"You can drop me at the bar," says Uncle Burt.

Dan turns to Uncle Burt. "You did a good job with Kruger. Thanks. You want me to help you butcher the deer?"

"You can keep the meat. I just want the head."

"You sure?" asks Dan, looking into the rearview mirror.

"I think I should give him a name. What do you think about—look out!" screams Uncle Burt.

Another car pulls into the driveway but swings too wide. The oncoming car heads straight toward the truck. Dan jams on the brakes, propelling all the occupants in the bed airborne and slamming them into the back of the cab. Brakes lock up. The truck slides, stopping an inch before impact. Everyone lets out a sigh of relief. BAM! The police cruiser rear-ends the truck, knocking it forward into the car. The truck sits accordioned between the two vehicles.

○○○○○○○○○○○○○●●●●●●●●●●●●●

13. Wrestler's Curse

DAN'S LOADED TRUCK crawls along the highway at twenty-five miles per hour. The boys have buried themselves deep in the bed of the truck and shield their faces as vehicle after vehicle passes and drivers blast their horns, give the one-finger salute and shout insults.

"Moron."

"Asshole."

"Where did you get your license? At the Dollar Store?"

"What drugs are you on?"

"Is it recess at the old folks' home?"

Dan plods along and reflects. *This must be what's it like when you get old.* He looks left. A car carrying four senior citizens passes at a slow pace. They scowl and shake their heads in disapproval. *Fucking dumb asses.* He speeds up, catches them, rolls down his window, and hollers, "It's the law," and sticks out his tongue.

He brakes, turns, creeps to the end of a short residential street, then floors it and serpentines up the hill. He attacks the familiar winding course and takes each curve a little too fast, bouncing the boys around in the bed. Dan glides up the series of connected turns, tacking back and forth, scaling the steep mountain to its summit. An A-frame home surrounded by trees, fields and slopes, crowns the peak. As Dan turns in the steep driveway, sparks fly from the truck's weighted down rear bumper. At the top, the driveway splits; half continues straight along the side of the house, and the other fork takes a sharp right and borders the all-glass front, separating the triangular dwelling from the front yard that slopes to the road below. The yard is sprinkled with items for sale: bicycles, a lawnmower, clothes, toys, furniture, housewares, a motorcycle and a small tractor.

There are no neighbors on the sides, but several homes face the A-frame from across the street. The boys unload and follow Dan toward the house, looking around as they go.

Dickie spots the motorcycle, "Hey, Coach, how come you never ride the motorcycle?"

"That's just for fun," answers Dan.

Looking down in the valley, the boys are treated to an eagle-eye's view of the sprawling university campus and town.

"It's like bein' on top of the world," observes Bronk, mesmerized by the sight.

"You should be here when there's a thunderstorm. It rolls in from the horizon, and you can see lightning bolts strike out in all directions." Dan lifts his arm and directs their attention. "When it clears that range, the lightning strikes are followed by a long silence, a slow rumbling, and then a boom. As it approaches the thunder gets louder and louder, and the time between the lightning and thunder gets shorter and shorter. The lightning bolts are setting trees on fire, and blowing up electric poles. There's no defense. It just keeps surging forward until it surrounds you like an artillery barrage." Dan reenacts the lightning and thunder onslaught by slinging his arms up and striking down, with each arm movement he makes a guttural imitation of an explosion. "The moment there's a blinding lightning bolt, the thunder detonates in your ears, and the house shakes and rattles. Every time there's a flash and an explosion, you think you've been hit, and then just like that; it's past and moving on. It's unbelievable."

They enter through the front door. The tiled foyer is only a few feet deep from the glass front to the back wall that supports a set of stairs running up to the main floor.

Dickie notices shoes scattered on the floor at the base of the stairs. "Do we need to take off our shoes?"

"No, that's okay," says Dan, hurdling the steps.

The boys follow.

A voice shouts from above, "Where the fuck you been? You're two hours late. You can fix your own lunch."

"Cindy, I have someone with me," Dan shouts back.

Dan's wife enters with a swaying gait and steadies herself at the kitchen doorway with her hand on her protruding, pregnant belly. After a perturbed puff of her cigarette, she politely asks, "Oh, how are you? Boys, do you mind removing your shoes?"

The boys look at Dan, who refuses to budge. They shuffle to the bottom to remove their shoes and then march back up the stairs.

Cindy warns, "Don't look at the house. I worked all week. It doesn't get cleaned until tomorrow."

Dan does the introductions. "This is Dickie, Adam, and Bronk. You know Gorni. This is Cindy."

Cindy empties her wine glass with one gulp and makes the best of the intrusion. "Give me twenty minutes, and I'll whip up something to eat. You could've let me know you were bringing someone home, dear," she chides with that wonderful, wifely pissed off expression that only the husband comprehends.

"They're here to work."

"You promised to mow the lawn and start on the driveway this morning. So where were you parading around all day today?" Dan ignores her and walks in the front room. "Don't sit on the sofa with that body paint." Dan sits on the couch next to his napping daughter, Molly.

Cindy turns her attention to the boys. "He never listens to me. He's always coming home late. He never helps around here. If he's not at practice, in the office making calls, on a recruiting trip, or hunting, he's out somewhere on his motorcycle. He's never here. His kids think they don't have a father." Cindy looks at her two daughters. On the floor in front of the couch, Maggie sits in a diaper, her nose inches from the screen, watching TV and snacking on HoHos. "Aren't they lovely? They take after me, you know. The next one will probably look like Dan. Don't you think he's a bad father?"

The boys are stuck. Not sure how to respond, they stare at her and look to Dan for help. Dan taps Maggie on her shoulder, and when she looks, he snatches her last HoHo and swallows it whole. Maggie searches for her missing snack. The boys glance back and forth at each other in disbelief and then stare at Cindy to watch her reaction. Confused, Maggie begins crying and runs to her mom with outstretched arms. Cindy picks her up and hugs her lovingly. "Did that big, bad man take your last HoHo? C'mon, let's see if we can find something else." On her way into the kitchen, she remembers, "Dan, you had a couple of calls on the tractor. I wrote the numbers on a piece of paper next to the mail." Dan collects the phone numbers with the mail and returns to the couch.

The boys are drawn to a wrestling statue on the mantel of the fireplace at the other end of the room. Dickie, Bronk, and Gorni gather around the classic primitive pose of two nude wrestlers intertwined in bitter combat. Adam drifts off and cases the room. The boys are not sure what to make of the statue.

Dickie comments, "That's gay. Didn't they have uniforms in those days?"

Bronk chuckles, "Remember, those guys are Greeks, if you know what I mean."

Dan's focus on the phone numbers and bills is broken. He rises and strolls across the room. "In the original Olympics, the wrestling champion was the most revered athlete in all of Greece."

"Did they really wrestle naked?"

"It was a different world. Everybody walked around naked. They didn't have hang-ups like we do today," answers Dan. "Everyone wrestled back then, from emperors and philosophers to shopkeepers and tradesmen. You've heard of Plato?"

"The philosopher."

"His real name was Aristocles. Plato was a nickname he got because he was a champion wrestler. It means broad shoulders," says Dan, amused by their expressions. "Cool, eh?"

"I could've probably been an Olympic champion back then," proclaims Dickie.

"People forget the original Olympics lasted for over a thousand years, and the modern Olympics haven't been around for one tenth of that. We have a ways to go before we catch up to their achievements," explains Dan.

"But they probably just showed up every four years and the strongest guy won, right?" asks Dickie.

"On the contrary; in the Greek society, being an athlete was the highest honor. They had training camps and worked out from dawn to dusk every day. Anyone who broke the rules was kicked out, and getting thrown out of training camp was the biggest disgrace anyone could suffer. It was grounds for being exiled from their home city."

"You're kidding?"

"No, they trained religiously. Every four years, each city-state would send its best wrestlers to a pre-Olympic training camp a few weeks before the Olympics, and they had to qualify. Only the best were allowed in the contest."

"Geez, they really had it going on, didn't they?"

"They were treated like human gods. Each day started with an oil massage, and then they would train all day. When they returned in the evening, their bodies would be caked with dirt that stuck to the oil and sweat. Helpers would scrape the oily residue from their bodies with seashells and put it in urns, which were sold to the royalty of Greece because they were the only ones who could afford them."

"What did they want with some skanky, sweaty body oil?" asks Adam.

"It was believed to have magical healing and medicinal powers. It's no different today. Our athletes are put on a pedestal and overpaid. And people pay thousands of dollars for a used baseball or a sweaty jersey."

"What's with pro wrestling?" Dickie comments.

"It sucks," adds Bronk.

Dickie continues, "Yeah, how come there's no real pro wrestling?"

"TV." Dan smirks. "Wrestling champions have always been revered worldwide until they put it on TV and turned it into a fucking circus act. Today people want the instant gratification that the modern sports and TV provide. Wrestling is one of the few pure sports left."

Adam translates, "You mean there's no pay."

"It's an amateur sport. There's no real professional wrestling, so the highest attainable level is Olympic champion."

Dickie remains curious. "Who's the best of all time?"

"A lot of wrestlers have won multiple World and Olympic championships, but none of them have matched Milo of Croton. He never lost a match and won every Olympic championship he wrestled in. Legend has it that he was so strong that he carried a full-grown ox across the original Olympic stadium field on his shoulders."

"A full-grown ox," marvels Bronk, "holy crap. That'd be like two thousand pounds."

Gorni directs their attention to the plaque next to the statue. "What that?"

Dickie sighs in frustration. "Can't you read? That's the outstanding wrestler award from the national championships." They study the plaque and then look at Dan in amazement.

Adam reaches above his head to a small ledge created by the wood grid framework that supports all the windows. "Hey, what's this?" he asks, pulling the red ribbon dangling from the ledge. He slides a small disk about the size of the mouth of a coffee mug from its resting spot. "Hey, this is heavy." He blows a thick layer of dust masking the object as the others gather around him. The dust veil lifts, revealing a gold medal. "An Olympic gold medal. Is this solid gold? It feels like it."

Dan lifts the gold medal from Adam's hand. "I was wondering where this was. There's another one around here somewhere."

"Talk about something being worth a lot of money. I bet someone would pay buku bucks for an Olympic gold medal."

Adam's comment sinks in Dan's head. He passes the medal back to Adam and thinks of his gold medal's potential value. *Could this be the answer? Could the medal be worth that much?* The boys begin fighting over the medal.

Dickie tries another tactic. "Coach, you said there's another medal. Do you know where that one is?"

Dan forces his attention back to the boys. "Huh?"

"Do you know where your other medal is?"

Dan motions to an end table. "It's probably in that drawer."

Dickie opens the drawer, revealing a pile of gold medals. He sorts through the stack. "National champion, Pan American champion, World champion, Olympic champion..."

Bronk probes. "I thought you won the Olympics once."

Dan nods. "That's right, but I won in both styles: Greco and Freestyle."

"That's gotta be some sort of record."

"Yeah, has anyone ever done that before?" asks Dickie.

Dan scurries to the couch in excitement. "Hey, you guys want to see something?" He gets down on his hands and knees and slides a five foot long intricately designed cylinder tube out from underneath. He holds it up. "You ever see one of these before?"

Adam shrugs, "What is it?"

"Adam," says Dan, "your ancestors probably hunted with this in Africa."

"What is it?"

"A blowgun."

"How does it work?"

"See these little pointed things?"

"You mean a dart."

"Right, a dart. Well, you put a dart in here like this." Dan loads a dart in the chamber to demonstrate. "And you got three seconds. One thousand one..." The boys scatter, running for cover. "...one thousand two...one thousand three." Dan lifts the blowgun to his mouth and pans around the room.

Cindy stands in the kitchen doorway. "Food's almost ready. Dan, don't shoot that in the house. I'm warning you."

The boys cautiously peek from their hiding spots. Dan spins and shoots. The dart lands with a resounding *thunk* in the bull's-eye of a dartboard mounted on the wall between the kitchen and front room. He runs across the room to retrieve his dart.

Cindy sighs, "You can't talk to him. If he wants to be an asshole, he just acts like an asshole. He'll knock somebody's eye out someday. He'll get sued, just wait and see." She turns and takes one step back into the kitchen and *thunk*. Another dart zips through the doorway, just missing Cindy and sticking into the kitchen wall. Cindy spins around. "You shot that at me."

Dan ignores her accusation, moves to the windows and calls to the boys, "Okay, everybody over here."

"You shot that at me."

As his wrestlers gather around, Dan points outside the window. "We're going to start there and expand the driveway back to the road, like a horseshoe. We'll stake that out today." Dan moves to another window. "Then in the back, I'm going to add a deck, and in here, I'm going to update and paint everything. When the house is finished, I'm going to rent a bulldozer and put in a lake down there."

Cindy slams her fist on the dining-room table. "My kids are getting piano lessons. They are not going to be bulldozers."

Dan rubs it in. "So what do you think of the lake? Like it? Nice, huh?"

Cindy grabs the blowgun out of Dan's hand and shakes it in the boys' faces. "He's got two of them. I'm not kidding you—two blowguns. You see, every time someone gets a new toy, Dan has to have one too. When the track coach, Roy Stewart, got a blowgun, Dan went out and bought two. The neighborhood kid got a motorcycle, so the next day Dan bought one."

Dan retaliates, "Hey, it's better than —"

Cindy cuts in, "Somebody showed him a compound bow when they were four hundred dollars, so Dan bought two, and now you can get the same thing for less than a couple hundred dollars."

Dan jerks his blowgun from Cindy's grasp and shouts louder than her, "Hey. It's better than cigarettes and wine."

Cindy spins to the boys. "Be careful you don't get shot." She turns her back and marches toward the kitchen. Dan reloads the blowgun, lifts it to his lips, and takes an extra deep breath, puffing out his chest and cheeks. He gets a bead on Cindy's rear end and blows. Cindy sidesteps to the table to retrieve her empty wineglass; the dart skims by her buttocks and sails into the kitchen as Maggie runs into its path. It penetrates the thick padding of her diaper, and she screams a curdling wail and runs to her mom.

Cindy screams, "Dan!"

"I don't think we are going to be able to work today," resolves Dan. "Let's go."

***

Dan breaks and cuts the steering wheel, fishtailing the rear end of his truck and creating a dust cloud in the lot next to the Dog Pound. The boys unload from the rear of the truck. A shirtless, bald, and clean-shaven Kruger vaults out of the porch door, grabs the bicycle, and confronts Dan.

"I know it was you."

"What?"

He hands the bicycle to Dan. "I want my motorcycle back in its place by the time I wake up in the morning, or I'm calling the cops. Do you know that's grand theft? You can go to prison for that."

"You have more important things to worry about."

"Like what?"

"Like wrestling season is starting in a couple of weeks. Besides, you don't get it back until you stop mistreating women."

"What's that supposed to mean?"

"I've heard you. It sounds like you're killing them. They beg you to stop, but you have no mercy."

Kruger struggles with Dan's perception. "Okay, I see how you can say that. But you have to understand—it's like wrestling."

"How's that?"

"A wrestler has to be part sadist and part masochist. Right?"

"Okay."

"First, you have to enjoy inflicting pain."

"Yeah," responds Dan, "I know what you mean. You know how far you can twist a guy's arm, so you twist it a little farther."

"Yeah right, and then you have the flipside, the masochist. You have to enjoy it when someone's pounding on you."

"Are you saying she's enjoying that?" asks Dan.

"Of course, but they won't admit it. They start crying out, 'You gotta stop. I can't take any more.' That's my signal to shift into overdrive, and then it's 'Ahh, ahh, ahhhh' then, 'ohh, ohh, ohhh' and then, 'oh Jesus, oh Jesus,' and then it's 'oh God, oh God,' and then they scream, 'Ahhhhhh,' go silent, and get the ugly."

"The ugly?"

"Yeah, you know, the expression on their face when they completely lose it."

"Huh?" asks Dan, completely lost.

It's like going overtime in wrestling, and you have to turn it up to break someone."

"Okay. Overtime," says Dan, trying to follow.

"Yeah, you know when you get to that point in the match when you don't have anything left—you don't think you can go another second?"

"Yeah."

"But, you know the other guy's probably feeling the same way, so you kick it into overdrive, and that's when they break."

"Yeah, they crack like a corn chip."

"Well, with women, that's when they get the ugly. Their eyeballs roll up in their head and their face gets all twisted, like this." Kruger does his best imitation of the ugly.

Dan recoils in horror at the expression on Kruger's face. "They look like that?"

"Yeah."

"They look like *that*?"

Kruger nods. "Yep, that's when you know you broke them."

"So you need strong legs and hips to achieve the ugly."

"The strongest."

"Here. You need this." Dan hands the bike back to Kruger.

Kruger snatches the bike and throws it against the side of the porch. "There's laws you know. You can't go around doing whatever you want." He turns and stomps back into the house, revealing a souvenir from the night before. "Faggot" is written across his back in big, red letters.

Dan turns his attention to the boys. "See you at practice tomorrow. Remember, we have the Midwest Duals in two weeks." Dan peels out and leaves another shroud of dust. The boys turn and walk to the house.

"Do you believe he shot the dart at his wife's ass?" asks Dickie.

Adam adds his approval. "He knows how to treat his woman."

"So how'd things go with Jas last night?" Dickie asks Bronk.

"Nothin' much," says Bronk. "After the cops left, I came home and hit the bunk." Bronk continues walking, deep in thought. "I hope Cindy is wrong."

"About what?" asks Dickie.

"Their next kid looking like Dan."

"I can't imagine a girl looking like Dan," says Adam.

Dickie contorts his face in disgust. "That's sick."

"That is sick. I never even thought about it being a girl," adds Bronk.

"Well, I feel bad for Dan," adds Dickie.

"Why is that?" asks Bronk.

"All his kids are girls. It's the wrestler's curse."

14. The Jungle

COLD AND CRISP, an occasional warm ray of sun shoots down between the grayish white billows. A golf ball bounces, dribbles, and rolls to a stop in the middle of Main Street. The wrestling team's two heavyweights casually walk down the yellow lines. Pump leads. Ben tags behind, constantly adjusting the overstuffed golf bag hanging from his shoulder. Pump stops over his golf ball with his hands on his hips and analyzes his next shot.

"Well, what do you think?"

Ben breaks from directing traffic. "After that drive, no more than a five iron."

Pump motions for Ben to come closer. As Ben steps forward and leans in, Pump grabs a few hairs on his head and yanks them out. He jerks back suddenly, but smiles when he sees Pump toss the fresh-plucked hairs skyward to test the wind's direction.

Pump catches the sight of a young coed in tight jeans doing her money walk down the sidewalk. "Oh, god. Will you look at that ass? If I have a vice, that's it. I tell you, you single guys got it made."

"How come you're always saying that?"

"Because if I were single, no girl on this campus would stand a chance. Eight iron."

"Eight iron—are you sure?"

"I figure your five iron is my eight iron, Gentle Ben," explains Pump. "How's things with your girlfriend?"

Ben selects the eight iron from the golf bag and hands it to Pump. "Okay, I guess."

Pump stands behind the ball and lines up his shot. Moving into position, he stands over the ball, focuses, and takes a practice swing. He assumes his stance, fidgets with his grip, and takes a last look down the street as he sizes up his shot. He exhales, relaxes, and begins his backswing.

A shop owner swaggers into the street from his all-glass storefront. He turns and runs up the street in the direct line of fire, yelling, "What are you doing? Are you crazy? You're going to break a window. Or kill somebody. Or break a window."

Pump stops. "Don't you know you never talk when someone is in the middle of their swing? Besides, you got nothing to worry about, I never hook or slice."

The store owner turns and runs back to his shop. "I'm calling the cops."

"Looks like this might be the last hole." Pump readies himself, and just as he is about to swing, he reevaluates. "I changed my mind. I think I'll try the nine iron—oh, what the hell—give me that wedge."

"Are you sure?"

Pump hands the eight iron back to Ben, and they exchange clubs. "I know you don't like to talk about your girl. And I know you especially don't like to talk about how she is in the sack, and I'm not asking to get off or anything, but I'm just wondering what the attraction is."

Ben thinks as Pump addresses his ball.

The store owner returns to guard the front of his store with a baseball glove. He paces back and forth, trying to find the best spot to protect the glass. Pump sets, winds, and unloads a beauty that sails high and down the middle.

"See? What did I tell you? No slice, no hook."

The shop owner runs out into the street and begins circling under the high shot.

"Uh oh, maybe a little draw." The higher the ball climbs, the more it drifts left. "There must be a crosswind once you get above the buildings," hypothesizes Pump.

The projectile begins its descent, and the farther it drops, the more it sails left until...BAM! It crashes into the hood of a car parked at the curb, sets off the alarm, bounces to the sidewalk and continues to roll.

"Oh shit. I'm in the rough." The ball finally rolls to a stop in front of Champs, an upscale bar and restaurant. "No, no, I think it rolled out. Hot dog. Thank you, God."

They walk down the street, following the path of the ball. The store owner yells after them, "See? I told you. I called the cops. They'll be here any minute."

Pump tips his hat to the dumbfounded store owners and observers. "Thank you. Thank you. It's a beautiful day. Thank you."

"I guess I do," says Ben.

"What?"

"You know. You asked me about Tara. If I like the sex?"

"Yeah, and?"

"I guess I do."

"Then the big question is, is it worth putting up with her?" asks Pump.

Ben nods and gives the question some thought as they approach the ball. He slides the bag off his shoulder and begins studying the next shot. The ball lies on one side of a brick alley. On the other side, a drainpipe runs down the corner of a building and discharges toward the alley.

"Umm, it's a tough lie. After this shot, what do you say we take a break and refresh ourselves at the clubhouse?" Pump says, nodding toward the Champs establishment.

"Okay." Ben hands him the putter.

"How'd you know I was going to ask for the putter?"

"It's what I'd use."

"That's what I thought," says Pump, pointing to another club. "Hand me that driver." They study the putt. It's a good fifteen footer with a bumpy terrain and an impossible read. The old brick alley has shifted and settled every brick at a different level and pitch. The mortar binding the blocks of red clay is high, low, and in some places, nonexistent.

Ben suggests, "If you play it to the right and bounce it off the curb, you might be able to ricochet the ball in the hole, like in miniature golf."

"Watch and learn." Pump leans his driver against his belly, stretches his arms out and gives a two-finger tug on each sleeve at the elbow, pulling the long sleeves above his wrists to give his hands a little more freedom. He grips the driver, addresses the ball, takes a nice, slow, short backswing and lets it rip, blasting the miniature white cannonball. It rockets across the alley just above the brick surface and buries itself in the drain pipe. "Birdie!" shouts Pump with glee.

Ben collects the golf ball and waves to Adam strutting down the alley toward them. Pump deposits his driver in the bag, slaps his hands together and declares, "Now that's the way to work up an app—" he stops, spying a familiar group of businessmen striding down Main Street.

Ben senses a shift in Pump's demeanor. "What's up?"

Momentarily forgetting his appetite, Pump ignores Ben and focuses on the advancing suit-and-tie squadron. They catch sight of Pump standing in front of the giant red "Businessman's Luncheon Every Weekday" sign. Their jovial bonding ceases. They tighten their ranks and shift to a vigorous march.

Adam joins the two street golfers at the restaurant's entrance.

"What's up, Dog?" asks Ben.

"You calling me a dog?"

"Yeah. We're all Dogs, right?"

"You mean like the team. Yeah, right."

Pump turns and acknowledges Adam's arrival. "Good, reinforcements." He shifts his eyes back to check the executive gang's advance. He replaces the buoyant look on his face with a stern mask, wrinkles his brow, and issues a steady fixed stare as they pass. The group is a mix of yuppies, young turks, and older, established professionals. The biggest one, a head taller than his peers, leans in with his shoulder and aggressively bumps Pump knocking him back into Ben and Adam.

"Hey, what's that all about?" complains Ben.

"I don't have time to explain. Follow me, and do exactly as I say," instructs Pump. He puts on his game face and marches in the bar behind the well-dressed bunch. Inside, the professionals join a larger group in suits and power ties already assembled in the heart of the large dining room. The two groups merge, exchange handshakes and pats on the back, and as cordials spread through the executive collection, competitive eyes cast glances at the out-of-place boys dressed in Dover Wrestling T-shirts and jeans.

"Good. We're just in time. Huddle up," commands Pump. Ben drops off the golf bag in the coat check and joins the other two. The college students lean their heads together, drape their hands on each others' shoulders, and listen to instructions. Pump takes an occasional peek at the kitchen doors. "Here they come. Break."

Two waitresses enter from the kitchen carrying a giant round tray the size of a hula hoop. As they approach the tightly packed gathering, they extend their arms and raise the trays high above their heads to give themselves room to squeeze through. They warn, "Coming through. Heads up. Coming through." The administrative types split just enough to allow the girls with the trays to slither through to a table in the dimly lit room.

"Now!" shouts Pump.

The command sets the boys in action. Pump charges the distinguished-looking convention and lets out his best mad dog growl. "Grrrrrr." His partners run behind with their hands pushing on his back as hard as they can. The bold tactic surprises the throng of businessmen. Pump's surge pushes the front line of bodies away from the buffet table just as the waitresses set down their trays of cold cuts, cheeses, and bread. The items have been neatly arranged and layered on the trays like a fanned deck of playing cards. Catching their balance, the businessmen dig in and fight back, stopping Pump's bulldozer strategy. Working as a unit, they dam up.

Pump orders, "Break off. Break off."

Ben and Adam retreat to the trays of food. They slip their fingers under the bottom slices, and with a few swipes, they scoop up all the meats and cheeses, shouting, "Go. Go. Go."

Pump turns his back to the swarm of professionals, and their force presses forward, driving him toward the table. His massive body acts as a natural barrier as he collects the bread and politely exits. "Excuse me, excuse me, thank you, thank you, excuse me." As he works his way through the crowd, they begin fighting for the leftover scraps and crumbs.

The attack leaves the executives thunderstruck. They glare at the triumphant wrestlers, throw their empty paper plates in disgust, and take turns bitching. "This is bullshit. The sign says 'businessmen.' Yeah, they don't even belong here."

Pump comments, "God, it's a jungle," and leads the way to a table in the corner away from the grumblings. They stand with their hands full and look at each other, unable to pull the chairs out. "Okay, who forgot the plates?" asks Pump. They look at the enemy in the war zone surrounding the buffet table and then look back at each other, realizing the solution sits right on the table. "Napkins."

The threesome sits at the table diligently creating giant skyscraper sandwiches. Ben returns to the subject of his relationship. "I've been thinking about what you said, and yes, it is worth putting up with Tara to be with her."

"Then you're hooked?" asks Pump.

"I guess."

"Well, that may be even better. All you have to do is make her fall in love with you."

Adam barely looks up from his sandwich. "You still talking about your bitch?"

"Don't call her that." Ben turns to Pump. "Why should I make her fall in love with me? She's already in love with me."

"She may love you, but that doesn't mean she's *in* love with you. If she was in love, she wouldn't treat you like that."

"Like what?" asks Ben.

Pump avoids getting into the details. "*You* know. Look, would you leave her?" Ben shakes his head. Pump continues, "Would she leave you?"

"The other morning while I was sleeping, she kicked me right in the middle of my back and knocked me out of bed onto the floor."

"That ain't right. I'd slap that ho upside the head," interjects Adam.

"You're kidding. What'd you do?" asks Pump.

"I asked her why she did it, and she told me, 'If you don't like it, leave.'"

"I grew up with whores like that my whole life, and that's what they do. They pick fights, so they can walk out and feel justified doing whatever they feel like doing," offers Adam.

They look at Adam as if he's from another planet. Pump turns his attention back to Ben. "See, you can't leave her, so you have to make her fall in love with you, or she's going to keep treating you like shit or leave you. Either way, you'll be the one suffering all the pain."

"How do I make her fall in love with me?"

Adam jumps in, "You treat her like she treats you. You pick a fight and walk out on her. Leave her thinking while you're out partying. If that don't work, you get her hooked on crack or heroin, and then she'll do whatever you want, even sell herself if you need money. Then you duplicate your efforts like a cookie cutter and start franchising. Pretty soon you got an operation on every corner like Mickey D's, and the cash flows, baby."

Pump and Ben stare at Adam in silence, then Pump continues, "Ben. Ben. Gentle Ben. Don't you know what that girl needs?"

"No. What?"

The waitress approaches. "Okay, boys, what'll you have?"

"If you would be so kind, we could use some lettuce, tomato, condiments, and paper plates," responds Pump.

"What'll you have to drink?"

Pump gently takes her elbow in his hand and pulls her close. "You going to give me a hard time?"

"Just want to take your order."

Pump releases her elbow, smiles, and asks, "What's your cheapest beer?"

"A glass of draft is two bucks."

Pump complains, "I can get a draft for a buck at the River Bar."

"This isn't 'Let's Make A Deal.' You know the rule. The free lunch is only free to paying customers."

"And how can you tell a paying customer?"

A wicked smile creeps across the waitress' face. "I can always tell a paying customer by the size of his tip."

Pump winks and begins digging in his pocket. He recovers a crisp twenty-dollar bill. He rolls the new bill into a slender green tube and offers it up like a flower. The inducement produces a state of mental conflict. Tempted, she stares at the offering and then looks around for her boss. Pump extends the twenty closer and waves it seductively in front of her face. Hypnotized, she snatches at the bill, and grasps air. She tries repeatedly as Pump outmaneuvers her and slaps it on the table. "It's yours when we're done. So, bring us some goodies for our sandwiches and a round of water." The server eyes the Jackson under his thick fingers. "It's not going anywhere. It'll be here waiting for you." She takes one more look at Pump and the boys, then exits. He watches her plump rear end as she returns to the bar. "Oh, lord, she's sitting on a gold mine. Don't get me wrong. I love my wife. She's great—the best, but it's the marriage part that kills me."

Ben asks anxiously, "Okay, how do I make her fall in love with me?"

"Come on," coaxes Pump, "you know what she needs?"

"Well, I guess she needs someone to put her in her place."

"See how simple it is? She just wants what every woman wants. A man she can look up to. There's nothing sexier to a woman than male authority," explains Pump.

"Male authority?"

"It's like baseball, Ben. All baseball fields have boundary lines. Inside the lines, you have the field of play, and outside the lines is foul territory. All you have to do is draw the boundary lines, so she knows when she's out of bounds. It's like any game. You have to know the rules and where the playing field is."

The waitress brings a tray with plates, condiments, and three large glasses of water. Pump winks. "Thank you, queenie." He watches with yearning as she bounces away. "Why, God? Why?"

"Yeah, I see what you mean. It's simple," figures Ben.

Adam remarks, "Yeah, well it's the same thing I said, except in my game, I get to be the umpire and make up all the rules." Turning to Pump, he asks, "You been here for a while. How do you work Dan?"

"You don't work Dan. You tolerate him. He's a whole different animal. When I got here, we knocked heads all the time."

"About what?"

"My attitude. I hated to work. I'd skip practice. I wouldn't listen. My grades sucked. I screwed up about every way you could. He took me into the corner and talked to me more than anyone."

"What happened?"

"One day he got tired of talking and said, 'let's roll around.' When he got me on the mat, he beat the living shit out of me. He gave me an attitude adjustment."

Ben continues to contemplate his relationship. "Yeah, attitude's important in everything."

"And you took his shit?" asks Adam.

"What choice did I have? After that beating, I started listening and re-thought a lot of things. He was the only one to stay in touch after I went into the service. He was the only one who never gave up on me. He was giving me money, and I had to take care of my family."

"How much money does he give you?"

"He promised me money this year, but he said something came up, and I was on my own."

"That's bullshit. Why you wrestling then?" asks Adam.

"It's my last year, and I love wrestling. I just don't like the work. Plus, the doctor at the hospital where my wife works made me a deal. He promised to pay for the delivery of our baby if I make All-American. So I'm depending on you guys to be there for me and push me as hard as you can," explains Pump as he puts his arm around Ben's neck. "And I can't afford a girl fucking with my partner's head because then she's hurting my family, and my family is the most important thing in the world to me. So take care of her. You guys about done?" Pump stands, slides the twenty back in his pocket and makes for the door.

Ben looking for the server. "What about the waitress?"

"Oh, that was just an illusion you saw," says Pump, putting his arm around Ben's neck, "Supporting a family is a whole different ballgame. I don't mind the responsibility. It's just that my wife was my first and only.

142

In fact, it was the first time for both of us, and she got pregnant. Let's light up that joint."

Ben collects the golf bag, and they exit Champs. A blustery, cold wind raises goosebumps on his arms. Gray, overcast clouds block the sun. Up the street, a police car sits at the curb, emitting intermittent flashes. On the sidewalk, an officer is surrounded by a crowd of witnesses telling their stories. The boys make a U-turn, round the corner, and are almost run over by Kruger on his bicycle.

"Watch where you're going," shouts Kruger.

"Hey Kruger, you should've been with us today."

"I'm late. Can't talk," says Kruger, pedaling off, his legs pumping like pistons.

Ben lights the joint and hands it to Pump.

He puffs, exhales, and takes in a long, deep breath through his nose. "Smell."

They inhale through their nostrils and fill their lungs. "Smell that?" asks Pump.

"Smell what?"

"It's here."

"What's here?"

"It's wrestling season. You can always smell it in the air. These are the last days of golf for a while. I should have been a golfer. I love it, and it's not work." Pump passes the joint, and Adam grabs it.

"Oh, no you don't," argues Ben, trying to take the joint from Adam. Adam pushes Ben away into the red brick wall. Ben bounces back, pushes Adam into the opposite wall, snatches the joint and takes off running. Adam chases after Ben down the alley.

BOOK 2

The Season

○○○○○○○○○○○○○○○●●●●●●●●●●●●

15. Cheap is Cheap

RISING SUN RAYS streak across the black asphalt and spotlight the back of the athletic center. Parking spots nearest the rear entrance are marked for handicapped, reserved, and loading and unloading only zones. A brown university station wagon and a new customized van are backed cockeyed in the handicapped spots, ready for a quick getaway.

Wrestlers congregate around the back door, listening to music, napping, and casually conversing. A beverage truck backs into the delivery space. Sliding down from his elevated seat, the driver walks to the back of his truck and opens the cargo area. He pulls out a dolly and stacks cases of soda pop as high as he can reach.

Ignoring the delivery, the wrestlers linger about, waiting for departure. The truck driver pulls the cargo door closed and wheels the overloaded dolly. A polite hand opens the back door. Nodding appreciation, he spins the dolly and backs through the doorway. Forming a line, the boys begin passing the red cases of soda pop from the beverage truck to their vehicles.

Inside, Dan exits the locker room, cleaning his ear with a six-inch medical Q-tip. His hair and clothes are wet. He slings a black field bag over his shoulder and double-times down the corridor past Uncle Burt and Gorni.

"Everybody ready?" asks Dan.

"Balls went for a run. He's in the shower."

They fall in behind Dan, who hastens for the exit. Bill Bohr pokes his head into the passageway as Dan slams into the emergency bar and opens the door.

Bill's shout, "Dan, wait up!" stops Dan before he becomes a witness to his team's soda pop theft. Not anticipating the sudden stop, Uncle Burt and Gorni crash into Dan. Bill catches up and explains, "I have a few items to go over with you before your departure."

"Can't this wait?" asks Dan with the Q-tip hanging from his ear.

"This is good news. I think. First, as of yet, the police have not been able to identify the contents of the black bag seized at the Dog Pound. And the videotape has disappeared from the police evidence room."

Dan smiles.

"I thought you'd like that. Second, I received complaints that apparently a couple of students wearing Dover wrestling T-shirts were playing golf through the municipal cemetery and down Main Street and then created a disturbance at the Champs Bar and Grille."

"Do they know if they were wrestlers?"

Bill pulls Dan aside and whispers, "Look, I'll do my best to see that these reports go no further than me, but you have to collar the boys and get them under control. Okay? What are you driving?"

"My truck."

Bill looks at Dan in shock. "Your truck?"

"And Uncle Burt is driving his van."

"Oh, okay. Good. Why do you have to drive halfway across the country?"

"It's where the competition is."

"You could find something local for a fraction of the cost."

"Yeah, I know."

"Okay. Well, good luck." Bill shakes Dan's hand and abandons a small roll of cash in his palm. "Kick some ass this week."

Dan nods, deposits the green wad in his pocket and heads out the exit. Uncle Burt holds the door open for the beverage truck driver carting the empties back to his truck.

Dan and his entourage join everyone waiting outside. All eyes are on Dan. *Which car is he driving?* Dan walks to the station wagon. The squad breaks. Dan opens his car door. Everyone else fights to get a spot in the van. Dan watches the fracas as he starts his car. The fight for the final seats escalates from pulling, twisting, and gouging, to wicked flying fists, elbows and kicks.

Dan stands and asks over the roof of his station wagon, "Who's going with me?" Everyone stops. No response. "Mini D, Dickie, Gorni, you're in the van over here with me."

Everyone looks around and wonders if anyone else just heard that. The grumbling threesome are banished with a sequence of slaps, kicks, and pushes. Balls and Bronk exit the athletic center with Jas.

"Bronk and Balls, you're in my car. Trainer, you're in the van." Feeling triumphant, Dan slides into his car seat and slams the door, jamming the Q-tip deep into his head contorting his face in pain.

In Uncle Burt's van, Kruger sleeps atop the gear bags piled behind the back seat. His irreverent snores assault the rear seat occupants, where Joe is crushed between the two heavyweights, Pump and Ben. Joe fights for space, pressing his elbows out against each wide body with all his strength, but the moment he relaxes, he is engulfed by the hulks.

The only space left for Jas is on the floor between the two captain chairs occupied by Adam and Doc. Everyone snickers as she crawls into the spot on the floor. Jas evaluates, removes a pillow from her bag and props it on the center console between Uncle Burt driving and Pug riding shotgun. She leans her back on the pillow and stretches her long legs between the second row seats toward the back of the van. She opens a book and begins to read. All eyes collect on her. *What a great spot. Wish I thought of that.*

Joe snorts, "Dan's a fox. We have a twenty-hour ride, and he's got all the small guys in his car. Hey, Trainer, trade places with me."

Dan peels out. Uncle Burt follows.

The truck driver completes his soda pop inventory count and compares his count to his clip board. He shakes his head and starts his count again.

***

The brown smoke bomb streaks down the interstate followed by Uncle Burt, who keeps the van just out of range of the grayish-black cloud spewing from the wagon's tailpipe.

Dan gives assignments. "Okay, Gorni, since you're riding shotgun, you get to be my eyes. Here." Dan opens the little black bag, hands Gorni a giant set of binoculars, and instructs, "You watch ahead; check both directions of traffic and along the sides of the highway for police cars. And every once in a while, you check the sky above the road for helicopters." He passes back another giant set of binoculars. "Here—give these to Dickie." Sitting with Mini D in the middle seat, Balls passes the binoculars back to Dickie, who occupies the rear seat with Bronk.

Dickie asks, "What am I supposed to do with these?"

"You're watching for cops coming from the rear. If we get a ticket, you're paying."

Dickie looks out the rear window and snaps back, "How's anyone going to see us through the smoke screen you're laying down?"

"You're paying," warns Dan. He stomps the gas pedal.

***

In Uncle Burt's van, Joe and Jas have traded places, and Adam and Doc have swung their captain chairs around to form a circle. They play cards, smoke cigars, and drink soda pop.

Jas lies across the heavyweights' laps, studying her cards. She chews her gum with an open mouth, distracting her opponents with the annoying smacking sound. She studies her cards and looks at Joe, the only one who has not folded. She takes a swig of pop and chews some more. Pinching the gum with her fingertips, she stretches the gum an arm's length above her mouth and wiggles it back down onto her tongue. Another look at her cards, a long drag on her cigar, and then she expels the smoke in a series of smoke rings, each one more perfect than its predecessor. This routine is followed by more chewing and an incessant sharp cracking as she pops the gum by sucking it in. Pug passes around a small flask, and everyone takes turns energizing their drinks. Ben peeks over Jas's shoulder to get a look at her cards.

Jas senses Ben's gaze. She holds her cards to her chest and pushes his face away. "No cheating."

She looks at her cards, examines Joe, and then begins blowing a bubble. It slowly grows and grows, bigger and bigger, and when it's about the size of her head, it pops and sags across her face.

Joe shouts, "C'mon. Quit playing with yourself and play cards."

Jas peels the limp, sticky gum from her nose and cheek and steers it back into her mouth. "Okay, I call."

Joe confidently lays down his full house, jacks over nines, and announces, "Read 'em and strip."

Jas follows with her full house of kings over threes. "One item of clothing, please."

Joe jerks off his designer shirt and violently throws it in Jas's face. "This is bullshit. Are we going to have to put up with all your crap every hand?"

***

Total silence fills Dan's vehicle. The mood is bleak. He thinks he hears a siren, but he is not sure. His eyes check his side mirror, but no vehicles trail behind the van. The siren sound grows louder, and he slows the wagon. *It is definitely a siren.* He checks his side mirror again. Nothing.

A disguised voice cuts in, breaking off the siren. "Okay, Dogface, pull over. Your driving days are done."

He checks his rearview mirror, sees Dickie and Bronk in the back giggling, and then notices everyone laughing. Without acknowledging the prank, he accelerates and watches the highway ahead. He decides to entertain with one of his favorites. "Did I ever tell you about the time I was in India for the world championships?"

He feels something tap him on the back of the head and reaches back to brush his hand through his hair. He captures an insect-like object and brings it to his face to examine it. He looks at the small wad of wet paper in his palm. *It's a spitball.* Just as he identifies it, another one smacks him in the back of the head.

Dan yells, "Okay, knock it off," and glares in the rearview mirror. The moment his eyes leave the mirror, another projectile hits its target. "I'm warning you," he screams. Another spitball misses its mark and splats on the windshield.

***

All the guys sit in their underwear. Jas sits on a pile of about a month's worth of laundry. Joe is down to his briefs. Beads of sweat break out and swell on his forehead. A drop rolls down between his brows, along the ridge of his nose, and drips from the end.

Jas asks, "Is there anymore pop? Hey, you guys know why it takes a million male sperm to fertilize one female egg?" She waits a moment, then delivers the punch line. "Nobody will ask for directions."

Joe takes one more long, hard look at her.

"So, what's it going to be, Clotheless Joe?" she asks.

Everyone chimes in.

"Go for it."

"She's bluffing."

"You got her this time."

"She can't win 'em all."

Joe lays down his cards. "I call. Two pair—aces and eights."

"Oh geez, I only have this." She lays down a pair of jacks.

Everyone cheers, shouts, slaps high fives and celebrates the first victory over the girl. Joe bounces to his feet and begins his victory dance.

"Oh, while you're up, you can hand over those shorts." Jas puts a third jack on top of the other two. A stunned silence sweeps through the van. The boys sit and stare at Jas's hand.

Joe exclaims, "Whose idea was this game?"

"Yours!" Everyone answers in unison.

Jas starts clapping and humming a strip tune and shouts, "C'mon, baby, let's see it. Take it off."

Everyone joins in, shouting, whistling, and clapping in rhythm.

Joe rolls his eyes, shakes his head in disbelief and executes some half-ass dance moves. Then, imitating a Hawaiian dancer, he begins performing intricate gyrations with his hips and hands. He freezes, signals two thumbs-up, and resumes dancing as his thumbs travel a hypnotic path from his face to his groin. Each thumb hooks on the sides of his red underwear and begins slowly inching his briefs down until his pubic hair is visible. He removes his thumbs, resumes the sensual dance with his shorts at half-mast, and shakes the sexy crack of his ass in every face. As a final tease, he repeatedly slides his underwear up and down before the grand finale. The van brakes, and everyone lurches forward into a human heap.

"Okay, everybody get dressed," orders Uncle Burt. A dozen hands grab for their clothes.

"What's going on?" asks Jas.

"I'm not sure. Dan just all of a sudden pulled to the shoulder. Maybe, car trouble."

Dan climbs from the driver's seat, walks around the station wagon, opens the passenger doors and commands everyone to get out. As they spill out, Dan pushes them up against the side of the vehicle and instructs them to place their hands on top of the car and spread their feet. Once everyone has assumed the position, Dan pats them down.

A highway patrolman pulls to the shoulder and parks behind Uncle Burt's van. He flips a switch that produces an instantaneous brilliant burst of blinking lights. He finishes his conversation on his radio, opens his door, stands, and fits a flying saucer-shaped hat on top of his head. He marches with a military stride toward Dan and the boys, glancing in the van on his way. The erect patrolman is an imposing figure; he stands a head taller than everyone. "Car problem?"

"No," responds Dan.

"Taking a rest stop?"

"No."

"Can I see your driver's license and registration?" Dan hands his wallet to the officer. "Please remove it from the wallet." Dan takes it out and hands it to him. Examining the license, he begins his inquiry. "You're a little ways from home, aren't you?"

"We're the Dover wrestling team. We're on our way to the Midwest Duals."

"So why are you stopped on the highway?" asks the patrolman as he eyeballs the interior of the station wagon.

"The boys were getting a little carried away, and I thought it was getting unsafe to drive."

"Most accidents on the interstate are related to vehicles pulling to and from the shoulder. Turning his attention from the wagon, he picks a paper wad from Dan's hair. "Pulling over is a lot more dangerous than spitballs. What are the binoculars for?"

Gorni volunteers, "I watch for cops."

"I see," says the officer. He pulls out a pad and begins writing as he continues talking to Dan. "You have two passengers in the van without seat belts; you need to move them to your station wagon. The shoulders are for emergencies only. Please use the rest areas for all other stops. This state has an emissions law. You need to check the smoke coming from your vehicle. It's excessive."

"It just started smoking like that."

"Uh-huh. I'm writing you a warning. You have three days to get it fixed. After that, don't drive this vehicle in this condition in my state," he says, handing Dan the warning with his license and registration. "And go the speed limit. Have a nice day."

***

An occasional security light throws down its spotlight in the pitch black surrounding the giant space-age arena. Uncle Burt follows Dan into the vacant parking lot. Dan punches it and speeds around the back to the pass gate. He parks, lifts himself from his seat, and runs to the door. The entire back of his head and shoulders are covered with spitballs. The windshield in front of the steering wheel has a perfect spitball outline of Dan's head and shoulders. He yanks at the door, but it won't budge. He hammers on the door with his fist until he hears a voice. "We're closed. You have to come back tomorrow."

"It's the Dover wrestling team. We're wrestling here tomorrow."

The door cracks open, revealing an older maintenance man in uniform. "Sorry, but workout times ended hours ago."

"We don't want to work out. We were hoping you would let us sleep on the mats." Dan looks at the old-timer. He thinks it over. "Please. We won't bother anything."

"Sorry. Something like that has to be approved beforehand."

"We drove more than twelve hundred miles. There was an accident, and we were stuck in traffic for hours. We missed our hotel reservations."

"Sorry. I got orders I have to follow." He closes the door in Dan's face.

***

A miniature clock chirps a feminine "Beep-beep, beep-beep, beep—" Jas's hand silences the alarm. She begins removing the limbs draped across her body that don't belong to her. She lifts Joe's hand resting on her breast and tosses it into his sleeping, smiling face, causing him to readjust and roll over. Once her restraints have been transferred back to their rightful owners, she sits up and stretches. Her eyes examine the contents sprawled over every available inch of the vehicle. The early dawn light exposes the litter of puppies, their body parts entangled in a random assortment of indecent places and positions. She reaches over the front seat and nudges Dan. He checks the time on his watch and shouts, "Okay, everybody up. Everybody inside and check your weight. Weigh-ins start in an hour."

***

Uncle Burt and Dan stand next to each other and watch the upper weights jogging in a circle around the perimeter of the wrestling room. Each wrestler is layered in hooded sweats, gloves, and knit caps.

Dan comments, "I don't get it. Everyone in your vehicle is over weight."

Uncle Burt shrugs and responds, "No problem. The run will put them on weight, and besides, it's a great warm-up. It'll get the engine going so they'll be ready for the first match."

"As soon as we're done, load Gorni up with all the dirty gear and send him to the laundromat. There's one about a mile down the road."

"Does he know how to drive American?"

"He can walk." Dan watches intently as the heavyweights plod around the room. He glances at the clock and then back at the wrestlers. "This isn't going to cut it." He yells to the runners, "Okay, everybody over here for sprints."

***

The arena is packed to the nosebleed sections for the finals. Ben is in a scramble with his opponent. The referee indicates two points when Ben finishes on top and takes the lead with thirty seconds left. Out of nowhere, Ben is flopped to his side and can't recover. He fights back, but his opponent traps him and slowly works him to his back. The final seconds tick down with Ben unable to get off his back. The official slaps the mat, signaling a fall with two seconds left and setting off pandemonium. The gladiators shake hands, and the official raises the victor's hand. Ben walks off the mat hanging his head. Pump sprints to the center of the mat, jumps in the air, executes a forward roll and springs to his feet. This brings the roaring crowd to its feet for the final match. He faces off with his foe, and they shake hands.

Ben finds an empty seat away from his teammates and sits. Dejected, he wipes his sweaty face with a towel.

The whistle blows, and the crowd screams as the heavyweights clash. Dan's eyes focus on Pump's match as he approaches Ben and sits.

Without looking at Ben, Dan begins, "You know you got pinned with two seconds left."

"I'm wrestling up a weight. The guy was too big."

"That's not an excuse. Now Pump has to pin for us to win. After you took the lead, you just hung on. You have to be aggressive. When are you going to learn you have to hurt people?"

The action in Pump's match heats up.

Dan leaps from his chair and yells at Pump, "Score. Drive. Drive. Drive!"

Pump's legs churn, driving his opponent off his feet and straight to his back.

***

The Dogs spill into the locker room, flooding it with the spirit of victory.

Dan yells over the celebrating, "Everyone here?"

Kruger enters dressed in street clothes with his arm in a sling followed by Pump, the last one through the door. The sweat ball carries his warm-up in hand. His entrance provokes a "Woof" cheer from his teammates. His dripping face cracks into a smile.

Dan continues, "Shut that door. Quiet. I said QUIET!" The room comes to order, and the boys cast their eyes toward the coach. "Okay, we got lucky at this tournament. We caught these teams out of shape, and they had some starters out of their lineups."

Bronk pipes in, "But Coach, we lost Kruger, and we still beat two ranked teams.

Ben adds, "And we drove twenty hours, slept in the car, and I wrestled up a weight class."

Dan glares at Ben. "What are you doing in here? You don't get pinned with two seconds left if you are in shape. Go run. I don't want to see you until you've been sweating for an hour."

"But—"

"Go. Now!" Ben exits. "Bronk, you can join him." Dan stares at Bronk until he gets up and leaves. Dan turns his attention back to the team. "Now, we really have to start working hard. Next time around, these guys are going to be gunning for us. So, I'm canceling Christmas break. Everybody will stay at Dover and work out. Hey, the season is a long-ass haul. Nobody can afford to be sick, so take care of yourselves. And no sex during the season. I don't want any of that shit." Dan looks to Uncle Burt. "You have anything to say?"

Uncle Burt turns to the group and lectures in his best rendition of Dan, "You know how you guys get sick? Kissing. Do you know how many red blood cells it takes to produce sperm? Millions. Hundreds of millions. So, no sex." The guys snicker at Uncle Burt's impersonation. Dickie raises his hand.

Dan acknowledges him. "Yeah."

Dickie asks in all seriousness, "Coach, can we jack off?" Everyone hoots and hollers. During the commotion, Joe sneaks behind Dan and empties a juice bottle down the back of his pants. Dan spins and swings. Joe instinctively ducks, and Dan's hand smacks Adam up the side of the head.

Dan spins back, faces the team, and barks, "Quit screwing around." All eyes stare at the fork of Dan's legs. His slacks are soaked from his crotch to his knees. "Okay, hit the showers and let's get out of here," orders Dan, pulling the wet, sticky material from his thighs and crotch.

***

Ben and Bronk are in their sweats, running laps around the outside of the arena. Ben complains, "This is bullshit."

Bronk responds, "It's bullshit gettin' pinned in two matches you was winnin'."

"At least I'm wrestling. You sat the bench the whole weekend."

"I got to wrestle one match."

"Only because Kruger got hurt, and Dogface bumped everybody up and put you in. At least, you got to wrestle somebody your size."

Simultaneously, the two runners see Dan and the rest of the team exit from the back pass gate and break off their run. They sprint across the parking lot and intercept them at the vehicles. Dan asks, "What are you doing?"

"Running."

"Running? You should have been taking showers. You can dress in the van."

Everyone loads up, and the van follows the station wagon out of the parking lot. As they turn onto the main highway, a window opens and someone throws some clothes and a cowboy hat from the van.

Uncle Burt follows Dan down the highway to the food district. A string of restaurants from fast food to elegant dining decorate both sides of the road. Flashing signs and thoughts of unlimited food and drinks for the first time in days get everyone in a feeding frenzy. Dan pulls into McDonald's, and everyone begins unloading.

Ben is the first to complain. "McDonald's!"

Joe whines, "Come on, Coach, let's eat someplace nice. I just beat two All-Americans."

Adam adds, "Fool, Mickey D's the best."

Dan explains, "I got it straight from Kane. This where Chicago eats all their training meals."

Joe gets to the point. "Face it, Dan, you're cheap."

Dan responds, "It's called a B…U…D…G…E…T, get it?"

Doc adds his two cents. "It's cool. We know you need it."

"Yeah, cheap is cheap," adds Joe.

Ben teases, "Yeah, toys for Dog Breath and Dog Butt."

Not sure what he means, Dan attacks back. "Ben, what kind of lights are they using at the arena? Sylvania or GE?"

"What's that supposed to mean?"

"You spent so much time on your back looking up at the lights that I thought you'd be able to tell us."

The team senses Dan's vulnerability and begins chanting, "Dog Breath and Dog Butt, Dog Breath and Dog Butt…"

Pug grabs Pump and pulls him aside for a private conference.

Dan yells, "Okay, knock it off. SHUT UP! I want everyone on their best behavior when we go in here. Remember, you represent the university. We're a team. We stick together. You don't do things by yourself. I don't want to see guys doing their own thing. There is no 'I' in team. There are no individuals. There are no prima donnas. There is no preferential treatment. No one is special, there is no favoritism. Everyone is treated the same. We do everything as a team, everyone together." Dan bullies his way to the front of the line.

Pug and Pump slip around the van and walk toward the highway.

Dan leads the team through the door and hurries to the counter. He orders, "Okay, Adam, Joe, and Balls, you won all your matches, so you can order whatever you want. The rest of you get a Value Meal, except Ben and Dickie. Ben, you get a fish sandwich, and Dickie, you get the Happy Meal."

Ben complains, "You just said everyone's the same. I hate fish."

"You looked like one tonight, flopping around on your back." A spit ball smacks Dan in his cheek. He scans the room for Bronk and notices he's standing naked with a towel wrapped around him. "Where's your clothes?"

"Someone threw my clothes out of the van. We gotta go back and get my Daddy's hat and belt buckle. And I won all my matches."

"You only had one match."

"I won it."

"Okay, you get one thing extra like a fry or a dessert or something."

Dickie pipes in, "What's with the Happy Meal?"

"How many matches did you win?"

"None."

"Besides, you get a toy, it'll give you something to do on the drive home." Another spit ball splatters on Dan's neck. His eyes slowly shift back and forth, looking for the culprit.

***

Dan has a Big Mac and fries in his left hand and a milkshake tucked under his left arm. He roams from table to table grazing, helping himself to everyone else's fries with his free hand. Another gooey spitball lands and clings to Dan's ear lobe. He snaps his head in the direction it came from. Joe and Adam are the only ones seated in his range of vision. Dan stuffs his mouth with a handful of fries and grabs his strawberry shake from under his arm as he walks toward the seated boys for a showdown.

Joe holds up both of his empty hands and implores, "Check the angle, Dan."

In a slow, deliberate move, Dan lifts the strawberry shake above Joe's head and begins to spill it. Joe sits up, tilts his head back, and looks directly into the mouth of the cup. The milkshake cup is upside down above Joe's face. The thick shake clings to the cup and doesn't budge.

After a moment, Joe pronounces, "Innocent. Innocent. Now, how about Adam?" Joe grabs the shake from Dan's hand and tilts the cup over Adam's head. "Come on, Adam, your turn."

Adam looks up, and the cup's entire contents slide out and turn his face a creamy pink. He explodes and leaps after Joe. As Dan steps between them, the rest of the wrestlers pop to their feet.

"Out of my way," demands Adam.

Dan stands his ground. "You look good in pink."

Joe breaks into a stupid white boy dance. "I may be a hunky, but I know what's funky." When all eyes are on him, he grabs Bronk's towel and tosses it to Adam. "Here you go. You can clean up with this."

Bronk goes after his towel, and everyone joins in a game of keep-away.

Outside, Pug and Pump, dodge traffic as they run back across the highway, carring a case of Coors. They open the back of the van and begin shifting the baggage.

Pump runs back across the street. Pug hustles in the restaurant. Inside the door, he stops to lift his leg and fart. "Ahhh." He approaches Dan at Joe and Adam's table. "Coach, Pump's not feeling well. He wants me to get something for him."

"Everybody gets a Value Meal." Turning to the rest of the Dogs, he announces, "Okay, picnic's over. Let's get out of here."

Mini D leads the exodus. At the door, he yells, "Last ones out ride with Dan." The Dogs logjam at the door, pawing and scrapping to ride in the van.

Pug approaches the counter. As he thinks over his order, the aroma of his gas bomb permeates the restaurant. One by one, the customers' faces wrench and their bodies cringe as they run for the exits. The entire place is empty, except for Pug, the staff, and a feeble old man. Desperate to escape the unbearable stench, the senior struggles to climb from his seat to his walker. Just as he pulls himself upright, he is overcome. He falls back into the seat and begins twitching.

The cashier leans over the counter toward Pug. "See the old man? I think he shit in his pants."

***

Swarms of snowflakes pelt down from the black sky. Each butterfly-sized flake performs its signature death dance to a final crash landing. A steady dose of snow missiles pelts the vehicles as they pull onto the highway.

Uncle Burt marvels, "Jesus, I've never seen snowflakes like this before. They're gi-normous."

Joe asks, "Trainer, you going to say anything if we get goofy?"

Jas reaches into her backpack and whips out a baggie of grass. "Here—you can start with mine." The boys start passing around the beer, and Joe fires up a joint.

There's a loud rattling in the rear of the van. Uncle Burt flips on the dome light. "What's that rattling?"

Pump wrestles with a gumball machine filled with peanuts. After a loud crack, the glass bowl pops off the top of its stand. Pump turns the bowl upright and passes it around, claiming, "You can't have beer without peanuts." He opens the window next to him and tosses out the steel stand. It hits the road with an explosion of sparks. Fireworks follow the bouncing stand to the guardrail.

***

"I lived on a dollar a day. When I was in Europe for the world championships, I toured Europe after the tournament. A loaf of bread, a bottle of wine and a woman, all on a dollar a day. I slept on the beach. It was great. Anybody else got a good story?" asks Dan. The dead silence lingers as everyone's long faces and sleepy eyes reflect exhaustion.

Riding shotgun, Gorni stares through the front windshield with eyes as big as golf balls. Terror is etched on his face. He glances at the speedometer, which reads ninety, and then immediately returns his focus forward. He raises his right hand, points ahead and states, "Can't see."

Dan explains, "It's called a whiteout, but don't worry. When it gets really bad, I know what to do."

Gorni looks out his side window. The shoulder of the road is lined with parked cars and trucks waiting out the storm. Gorni points and demands, "Look!"

Dan acknowledges, "Exactly. With everybody else off the road, we can make good time. I'm going to signal the van up." He flashes his headlights on and off. The van moves to the lane next to Dan's wagon and creeps up alongside.

Inside the van, Uncle Burt flashes his dome light on and off repeatedly, creating a strobe light effect as Mini D performs a lewd dance in the isle. Midnight lunacy on New Year's Eve fills the van. Dan rolls his window down and sticks his head and arm out as Uncle Burt pulls even and rolls down his window.

Dan frantically waves his arm and yells, "Gas! We need gas." Dan pops his head back in and announces, "Did you see those guys in the van? Now, they're mentally tough. They're winners. These road trips don't have to be so bad."

The vehicles proceed up the exit ramp and pull to the pumps at the nearest gas station. Vehicles waiting out the storm fill every parking space. Before Uncle Burt can come to a stop, the Dogs slide the side door open and make a frantic dash for the bathroom. Uncle Burt yells, "Alright, you guys stay away from Dan."

Dan bears down on Uncle Burt. "What the hell did you hit on the highway?" Uncle Burt shrugs him off. Dan continues, "You should have seen it. There were sparks everywhere. Whatever it was, it flew up and hit the guardrail."

Uncle Burt shakes his head, feigns innocence and opens the gas station door. Everyone is mobbed around the vending machines. The wrestlers vie for space, laughing, yelling, and fighting for the next turn.

The freshmen and Balls surround a grinning Dan. "Heh, heh, heh. See, those guys are mentally tough. They're having a good time."

Balls takes a banana from his bag and begins peeling it.

Dickie asks, "Dan, you want something from the candy machine?"

"Ooookay."

"What do you want?"

"Surprise me."

Dickie walks up to the candy machine and waits behind the last wrestler grabbing his treat. He inserts his money and reaches to pull the knob for a Butterfinger. A hand comes out of nowhere and pulls another knob. Dickie looks up: it's Kruger. "What'd you do that for?"

"I don't like that kind," answers Kruger, as he leans in to take the Doritos. Dickie crashes into Kruger's bad arm hanging in the sling. He clutches his shoulder in agonizing pain. "What'd you do that for?"

"I don't like that kind," says Dickie, snatching the Doritos back. Kruger is about to retaliate when Dickie makes a fist and threatens to punch his injured limb. Kruger retreats, and Dickie inserts more change.

Dan observes the team, and scrapes wax from his ears with his car keys as he shakes his head defiantly at Bronk. Dressed in his cowboy garb and hat, Bronk pleads, "Come on, Coach, just some change." Dan continues to shake his head. "Come on, when we went back for my clothes all my money was gone."

Dan examines the tip of the car key. "Everyone else managed."

"They're spending their own money. They just don't want to ask you."

"Nope."

Balls opens his bag and offers Bronk a piece of fruit. Bronk stomps off. "Toys for Dog Butt and Dog Breath."

Dickie returns and extends the Doritos bag. Dan reaches and snatches the Butterfinger.

"Hey, that's mine."

Dan asks, "Who's Dog Butt and Dog Breath?" as he holds the candy bar above Dickie's head.

Dickie reaches for the candy. "Give it to me."

"Who's Dog Butt and Dog Breath?" asks Dan, switching the candy back and forth from one hand to the other to thwart Dickie's attempts to retrieve it. Dickie stops battling and gazes at the Butterfinger.

Dan waves the chocolate bar. "Who's Dog Butt and Dog Breath?"

"They're nicknames."

Dan offers the candy bar and asks, "And?" Dickie reaches for the candy, and Dan snatches it away. "And?" The silence prompts Dan to tear open the wrapping and peel it down the side of the Butterfinger. Sticking the end of the chocolate bar into his wide open mouth. "And?"

"They're nicknames—for your daughters?"

Dan laughs, "Heh, heh, heh, Dog Butt and Dog Breath. That's pretty funny. Dog Butt and Dog Breath. Who thought that up?"

Dickie laughs along, caught up in the moment. "Bronk thought it up."

Dan chomps down on the Butterfinger and then stuffs the entire bar in his mouth.

Dickie complains, "Hey."

"I'll kick his ass Monday at practice." Dan sprays Butterfinger from his mouth and announces, "Okay, it's time to hit the road."

Dickie takes his stand. "That was my Butterfinger. I got the Doritos for you."

Dan grabs the bag of Doritos. "Thanks." He scrambles outside and yells, "Uncle Burt. Uncle Burt." He runs up to Uncle Burt. "It's getting pretty bad. When we get back on the highway, put your parking lights on and follow my taillights."

Dan's wagon turns out of the station onto the snow-covered road. Its rear end swings from side to side. He fishtails all the way down the entrance ramp onto the highway. He turns off his headlights and accelerates. Instantly, their surroundings transform from a whiteout to a visible black, snowy wonderland. The wagon plows a path for the van and streaks past all the vehicles pulled to the side of the road.

Dan follows a very long gradual curve. Up ahead the expressway narrows and enters a tunnel. Dan turns the steering wheel slightly. The vehicle doesn't respond and begins sliding toward the center guardrail. A sharp turn of the wheel swerves the rear end. Another sharp turn of the steering wheel to compensate has no impact. The rear end of the wagon spins out of control and takes on a life of its own. Dan spins the steering wheel to the right and then back to the left. No effect. He releases the wheel and lets it spin wildly. The wagon twirls like a baton down the icy highway. Dan watches, times, grabs the spinning steering wheel and punches the gas. The wagon straightens and shoots into the tunnel.

Dan shouts with glee, "Heh. A lesser driver wouldn't have made that."

***

Everyone sleeps except Dickie, who now occupies the front passenger seat. He constantly glances back and forth between the road and Dan. Dan's head nods and then jerks back upright. He blinks his eyes and shakes his head. After a spin of the radio dial, the volume blares, and Dan sings along. After a couple of minutes, the singing turns into incomprehensible mumblings, and his eyes and head sag. A head jerk, some deep breaths, and an adjusted posture wake him again. The battle lines are drawn: the sandman versus Dan. He rolls up his sleeve and rests his forearm against the freezing window. The burning feeling on his arm startles Dan awake. *It's like putting your foot in a bucket of ice water.* Soon the numbness wears off, and the battle resumes.

He leans his head toward the icy door window and presses the side of his face against the ice-cold, frost-covered glass, jolting his eyes wide open. Again, he feels his heavy lids sagging and props them open with his thumb and index finger. When this fails, he rolls down the window, letting the freezing air in. He leans his head out the window. Snowflakes pelt his face until he can't take the frigid air any longer. He pulls his head in, takes a deep breath, sits upright, and starts tapping the steering wheel like a set of drums. His eyes close and his head bends forward.

Dickie watches intently as Dan's head nods off. "Coach. Coach, you okay?"

Dan snaps awake and threatens, "Dickie, you wake me up one more time—no, I think I've had it. I need to let someone else drive."

"I'll drive."

"How long you had your license?"

"A few months."

"And you have the balls to get behind the wheel while I'm in the car?"

"Yeah. Why not?"

The black night is filled with red flashing lights. A highway patrolman pulls alongside Dan and motions for him to pull over. Dan reduces his speed, angles to the shoulder, and slows to a stop. The patrolman opens his car door and stands. He uses one gloved hand to hold the disk of his hat as he leans into the wind against the onslaught of snow and battles his way to the station wagon. Dan rolls down his window and looks into the face of the same patrolman who stopped him a couple of days earlier.

"It's the storm of the century, and you're speeding with your lights turned off."

Dan explains, "I figured it's better to get home before it really gets bad."

"Really gets bad?" asks the patrolman in disbelief.

"Oh yeah, this is nothing compared to the storm when I was in Mongolia for the world championships. And then there was the time I was hunting in the Rockies, and we had to dig out from twenty feet of snow."

"And your speed?"

"I'm afraid if I slow down, I might get stuck."

"And I'm sure you can explain driving without your lights."

"I can see better with the lights off. Really. The snow reflects the light, so with the lights off, you can actually see."

The patrolman pauses, slides up his coat and shirtsleeve, and uncovers his watch. "You have one hour to get this piece of junk out of my state. Now, get moving. Oh, and by the way, congrats on winning the Midwest Duals."

○○○○○○○○○○○○○○○○○●●●●●●●●●●

16. NO xMAS

THE WEIGHT OF Dan's bulky chest and belly pressures down on the back of one of his wrestlers. His legs wrap around the lower back, and his heels dig deep in the groin. He curls his right arm high in the air and delivers an exaggerated forearm smash to the side of Bronk's head and then scrapes his knuckles across Bronk's eyes, nose, and mouth. In concert with the crossface, he raises his left arm above his head and unloads a rabbit punch with his bony elbow into the back of Bronk's head and neck.

That's for Dog Breath, rationalizes Dan.

Dan stretches the head and upper body in one direction while rotating the hips the opposite way. The excruciating technique twists the body as far as it will go without breaking. Dan strains with all his might, squeezes a series of pops and cracks from the hapless torso and then releases. He immediately follows up with another punishing crossface.

And that's for Dog Butt, justifies Dan.

The rest of the wrestlers fake their drills and watch. *Even for Dan, this is extreme.* Dan is not wrestling. He is torturing to the brink of injury.

Bronk's rich red blood splats on the mat. Dan halts his assault and takes a deep lungful of air. Bronk has endured the beating without a peep. When he feels Dan easing up, he requests, "Hey, Dan, how 'bout lettin' me go on top for a while?"

Dan thinks it over for a moment, rolls off Bronk and positions himself on his hands and knees. He drops his chin into his hands and rests on his elbows with an insulted expression, as if anyone could entertain the absurd idea that they could hold him down.

Bronk slowly stands, bounces on his feet, and shakes his limp arms and hands as wrestlers do on breaks to free any tension. He calmly approaches Dan, who looks up at him with a shit-eating grin on his face. Bronk looks at the other wrestlers around the room and then circles, positioning himself between Dan and the door.

"Okay, you ready?" asks Bronk.

Dan frees one of his hands from under his chin and waves for Bronk to bring it on. Bronk stands and stares at Dan, gauging his attack. He aims, winds up, and buries a fist flush in the side of Dan's face as hard as he can, then turns and walks out of the room. All activity halts as all eyes look to Dan.

Dan squints and grimaces as he runs his tongue around his mouth and delivers a blood-soaked tooth to his waiting hand. "Good. Now we're getting somewhere. I think he's going to make it."

Dressed in workout gear and his arm in a sling, Kruger struts to Dickie. "Hi, Dickie," he says, removing his arm from the sling. Dickie cocks his fist and acts as if he's going to punch the injured arm. Kruger smiles and swings his arm around in circles to loosen it up. He grabs Dickie, throws him down, jumps on him, and twists his arm.

Dickie complains, "What's your problem?"

"Nothing. I just got motivated."

Dickie loses his temper. "Hey. What's with you, man?"

"I just haven't decided if I want you on the team."

"Well, no faggot is going to chase me away."

"Oops, you've gone too far. Now I have to hurt you." Kruger, forces Dickie's arm beyond its range.

Dickie screams and then grunts through his clenched teeth, "You faggot. What do you call that, wrestling or making love?"

Kruger likes this game. "Oh, so you want me to hurt you. Now I'm going to really hurt you."

"Give it your best shot, fudge packer."

"Okay, break it up," orders Dan. "Dickie, come with me. Gorni. Kruger needs a partner." Gorni jogs over. Kruger grabs him and begins beating on the smaller wrestler while Dan pulls Dickie by his T-shirt to the other end of the room and tells him, "You're down."

Dickie drops down on his hands and knees and asks, "Okay, now what?"

"Do you want to bleed?" asks Dan.

"No."

"Do you want to make other people bleed?"

Dickie looks toward Kruger and answers, "Yeah."

"Good. I'll teach you the legs. There is only one rule. Legs are for pinning, and to pin people, you have to hurt them. You do legs right, and you make people scream. You never just hang on and ride with the legs. You do that, and you get in trouble. The only rule is if you don't make them scream, then I get to make you bleed. Got it?" Dickie nods. "Okay, let's get started." Dan drops on top of Dickie.

Kruger launches the much smaller Gorni airborne and crash-lands him on the mat near Dan. "Gorni, you wrestle like a practice dummy. When we're done, I want you to mop the mats and clean the locker room."

***

Ring...Ring...Ring...Kruger fumbles for the phone, holds it to his face and answers, "What?"

"Woof, woof, woof—"

"Who is this?" asks Kruger, barely awake.

"Woof, woof, woof—"

Focusing his eyes on his bedside clock, Kruger demands, "It's fucking four o'clock in the fucking morning. Who the fuck is this?"

"Woof, woof, woof—"

"Okay, jerk-off, I'm warning you."

"It's me."

"Mini D?"

"Yeah, I got two babes. Get your ass out of bed and get over to eighteen Moss Street."

"It's fucking four in the morning."

"You want me to call someone else?"

Kruger gathers his senses. "What are they like?"

"When did you get particular?"

"Are they fat?"

"They're great."

"Are they ugly?"

"Beauty is in the eye of the beholder."

"Are they black?"

"What's with all the questions?"

"I just want to know what I'm getting myself into."

"You're getting into some pussy. See you in five, brother."

***

Mini D opens his door; tiptoes across the hall to the opposite door and stands naked in the hall, listening. He can hear Kruger's powerful thrusts pounding one after another. Mini D quietly turns the doorknob, slowly cracks an opening, and peeks in. "Ooooh, go...go. Go Kruger. Go Kruger. Go-ooooh." Kruger intensifies his efforts. The entire second floor begins vibrating and shaking. Fixtures rattle, pictures hanging in the hall vibrate, and unsecured knickknacks tumble and fall. Mini D's eyes shift back and forth. *Maybe I should stand under a doorway.* The pounding and screaming marry to a crescendo, then divorce and go silent. Mini D smiles, nods his approval and ambles down the hall to the bathroom.

He lifts the toilet seat, begins to urinate and looks at himself in the mirror mounted on the wall above the toilet. He smiles and pops out his partial with his tongue, then smiles again with several missing teeth. He leans in and examines his receding hairline. He's brushing his thinning hair around with his fingers when Kruger steps in. He's sweaty and naked, and breathing heavy. The two stand side by side, shoulder to shoulder as they share the toilet and listen to the soothing, peaceful sound of the human water fountain. They look into each other's face in the mirror and announce in unison, "I have to tell you something."

They turn their heads from the mirror and look each other in the eye.

"You first," says Kruger.

"My girl told me to warn you that your girl has crabs."

Kruger shoots back, "My girl told me to warn you that your girl has crabs."

They stare at each other and then burst out laughing at the girls' joke. The uncontrollable laughter slowly dies. They finish urinating, pause, look in the mirror at each other and exclaim in all seriousness, "We better wash. Just in case."

***

Peddling his bicycle, Kruger cuts the frigid air of daybreak with Mini D, who sits on the handlebars with his legs straddling the front tire. As Kruger stands and pumps, the bike picks up speed and hops the curb, putting them on a collision course with the Dog Pound's front porch. Just before impact, Kruger slams on the brakes. As Mini D pushes off and jumps clear, Kruger lays down the bike and simultaneously slides it under the porch while leaping onto the porch in one unbroken motion.

"C'mon, I want to show you something."

He flips on the light as they enter his room.

"What?"

"I want to show you Tarzan," confides Mini D as he opens the closet door. Out bounces a feisty Chihuahua. "What do you think?"

"Wow. That's the same little mutt? I don't believe it."

"Hey, watch it. He's not a mutt. He's a full-blooded Mexican."

Kruger pets Tarzan's head and asks, "How'd you do it? I thought for sure he was, you know, a goner."

"Yeah, I did too." Mini D holds up an eyedropper. "I squirted water and food down his throat every couple of hours until he could eat and drink on his own. And I taped his leg, like a cast, until he could walk on it."

Kruger grabs a sock lying on the floor, slaps Tarzan across the face with it, and a game of tug of war is on. Mini D picks up a large bucket-sized container and wanders around the room from plant to plant, watering.

"So did you have a good time?" asks Mini D.

"You believe this? Just when I get going good, she says, 'Slow down, take it easy. I like it slow and easy.'"

"Communication. That's good."

"Yeah, well, I don't even know her, you know. I had her head against the wall, and I'm thinking, 'I'm going to put her head through the wall.' So I go animal on her. Bam, bam, bam," Kruger repeatedly pounds his fist into his hand, "and her head's putting dents in the drywall."

"Different strokes for different folks."

Kruger continues, "She loved it. I figure most girls don't know what they want, so I just do what I want. They started all this women's lib bullshit, and now they got half the guys scared to death. That's why there's so many faggots nowadays. They're all afraid, wondering if the broad came or not. I say who cares?"

Mini D sets the water can down and picks up a pair of scissors to manicure a plant. "Yeah, well the way I figure it, I better get all I can now. In a couple of years, I'm not going to have any hair left, and then it's all over for me."

Kruger adds, "Well, I don't have time for them—none of them."

"What do you call tonight?"

"That was for my ego. It needs it now and then. But I need all my concentration for wrestling, and girls can mess that up if you let them."

"It's going to be a good year—I can feel it. I had a great dream last night. I was playing baseball, and this guy hits a fly ball over my head, and I turn and start running it down. But this ball is way over my head, and I think the only way I'm going to catch it is if I'm as tall as a building. And the moment I think that, I start stretching like a rubber band, like I was elastic or something. My legs, body, and arms stretch through the air and catch the ball. And then this giant face appears in the sky next to me and says, 'We've been waiting,' as if I could've done it all along. And then everyone I was playing with came up to me, giggling. It was like I could be as tall as I wanted just by thinking it. I could reach the moon if I wanted. It was amazing. I tingled and felt warm all over. It was even better than the high I get when I wrestle."

"Whoa, that's how I feel when I'm riding my Harley," shares Kruger. "All my senses are activated. I tingle and get warm all over, and I actually get high. I get higher from that than anything." Kruger's unconscious hand slides into his pants and scratches his pubic hair.

"Hey, maybe we should wash again," says Mini D, scratching his crotch. "You know, just in case."

***

Christmas lights decorate the snow-covered homes and yards, outlining the Dogs as they run in a single-file line through the residential streets of Dover. Every home has a celebration underway: family dinner, exchange of presents, a party. Bundled in layers of sweats, the team plods by a group of overzealous of carolers who persuade the occupants of one home to open the front door and share a moment of oneness.

Balls yells, "Indian run!"

"Oh, fuck." mumbles Pump at the end of the line. The command prompts him to break out and sprint past everyone to the front of the line. Once he secures the front spot, Ben, the next man at the end of the line, sprints his way to the leader position. Each man makes the sprint to the front when it's his turn.

Darkened, cold dormitories replace the warm, glowing homes. Silence allows the runners to hear the rhythm of their steps and breathing, and question what the hell they are doing in Dover on Christmas Eve.

The Indian run follows the road through the deserted dorms and then climbs a long, steep hill. Halfway up the incline, Pump drops out of line and rests his hands on his knees. The rest of the team labors to the top of the hill, where the road levels out for a quarter of a mile and dead-ends into downtown. They sprint the straightaway, make the turn left and sprint down Main Street. Decorations illuminate every light post and storefront with the spirit of the season. Uninhabited streets echo with the sounds of the Dogs sprinting through the abandoned city. The run ends just short of the River Bar. Catching their breath, the wrestlers walk around with their hands on their hips or their fingers interlocked behind their heads.

Dickie paces in a wide circle. "Boy, this is eerie."

"Yeah, it's the most beautiful I've ever seen Dover, and no one is here to see it," Mini D observes.

"Except us." Pug ties his shoe, stands, and stares down the street.

Balls yells, "Okay, everybody follow me," and leads the team down the street.

Now what? they wonder.

Jas, dressed as an elf, opens the front door just as they arrive in front of the River Bar. She greets each guy with a hug and a "Merry Christmas" as they enter. The bar has been transformed. Christmas decorations, lights, and a giant Christmas tree welcome the sweaty Dogs.

Uncle Burt wears an oversized red Santa hat and stands at the top of a stepladder, face-to-face with his trophy deer head mount. After a final decoration adjustment, he lightly flicks the antlers, head and shoulder fur with a feather duster. He straightens the oversized necklace and squares the attached nameplate that reads "Bad Boy," then dusts it off. Pulling a hairbrush from his back pocket, he grooms the hair of the mount, and then plugs a cord into the socket. Christmas lights sparkle from Bad Boy's antlers, and a red flashing light accents the nose.

Uncle Burt greets each of his working Dogs with a handshake and a pat on the back, leaps onto the bar, looks at his watch and announces, "Thirty-six minutes exactly. Perfect, Balls. The run you just completed allows each guy six beers and no more. Keep your sweats on and your sweat going. Dan will be checking your weight in the morning. There's a present for each of you under the tree. Oh, and Merry Christmas, Dogs. Woof. Woof. Woof." Everyone barks back.

Jas mans the bar. She trims the bar with a line of cold beer bottles adorned with black and brown bows and ribbons. Balls takes a seat at the bar. "Can I have a glass with ice?"

Jas fills a glass with ice and slides it in front of Balls. "How about a drink to celebrate Christmas? Whatever you want. It's on me."

"Thanks, but no thanks," answers Balls, reaching into his backpack. "I have my own." He pulls out a bottle, shakes it vigorously and then pours a protein milk shake mixture over the ice.

The front door opens; everyone looks and shouts, "Gorni!"

Jas glances around the bar. "Where's Pump?"

***

Pump's chest heaves. He hangs his head and walks alone with his gloved hands on his hips. A drop of sweat clings to the end of his nose and steam billows from his mouth. He stops at Main Street and looks both ways. *Nothing.* It dawns on him to check for footprints in the snow. He turns left and walks in their tracks. An eerie sensation fills him as he leisurely meanders down the multicolored lit tunnel. *There's something really familiar about this.* Trying to understand his recognition, he feels the presence of something behind him. He doesn't look and begins to jog. The crunching of the snow grows louder as something closes in from behind. Pump breaks into a run. A vehicle pulls alongside. Pump grins and breaks into a full sprint.

"Need a ride?"

Pump pulls up, looks over his shoulder and examines the van full of coeds as it slows to a stop next to him. "I don't need a ride, but I sure would like one." The girls adjust their seating as Pump walks around to the passenger side and climbs in.

"Where to?"

"Nowhere in particular. Let's just drive. Now, what the hell is the country's best-looking women's basketball team doing driving down Main Street in Dover on Christmas Eve?"

"I don't know. We got bored and decided to go for a ride and check out the lights. What the hell are you doing jogging down Main Street on Christmas Eve?"

"Dan made us stay and work out over the holidays."

"Yeah, our coach made us stay and work out because we haven't won a game yet and conference games start next week. What about you?"

"We haven't lost a match yet. Dan's just being Dan. Mmm, you guys haven't won a game yet, huh?

"Yeah, we're 0-8, but we're not that bad. I guess you could call it a slump."

"Sounds like you guys need a slump buster?"

"Yeah, right. Where do we get one of those?"

Pump smiles as if he just drew into a royal flush. "Look, I'm going to share something with you, but you have to promise you won't tell anyone. Okay?"

All the girls look around at each other and nod in agreement. Pump pulls his sweatshirt up to expose his bare belly and plays it with his hands like a tom-tom.

***

A dozen semiconscious bodies lie around the wrestling room. Uncle Burt breaks the silence. "Okay, everybody up and running." Everyone is still dressed in the same sweats they wore at the Christmas party. One by one, they climb to their feet and shuffle around the long, rectangular room.

The Dogs jog in circles around Uncle Burt, who lies on his side in the middle of the wrestling room with his head propped on his bent arm.

"Where's the lead dog?" grumbles one of the wrestlers.

"He's running late," responds Uncle Burt.

Kruger's anger flares. "This is bullshit. Why do we have to be here at six thirty on Christmas morning?"

"Yeah, while Dan's sleeping." Joe slows to a trot.

"He'll be here."

"Toys for Dog Breath and Dog Butt," Pump mutters.

"Where were you last night?" asks Ben.

Jogging between Ben and Adam, Pump asks, "You guys believe in déjà vu?"

"Days of what?" asks Adam.

"Déjà vu," explains Ben, "you know, when something happens in your life, and you can swear you've already lived it or dreamed it before."

"Yeah, I get that every time I get my hand raised after a match. So?" retorts Adam.

Pump continues, "Well, it happened to me last night. I have this dream, like a sexual fantasy, where I'm jogging down the road, and I get picked up by a van full of women. Last night, I was jogging and got picked up by a van full of the girls' basketball team."

"What are they doing here?" asks Ben.

"They haven't won a game yet, so their coach made them stay over Christmas and work out. I convinced them I could end their slump if they all slap my belly at the same time. So they take me back to their place, and I tell them the only catch is everyone has to be naked, or it won't work."

Ben shakes his head in disbelief. "No way. They fell for that?"

"It's amazing what people believe when they want something bad enough. Anyway, it all played out like my dream. We got naked, and they surrounded me and started belly slapping me. And just like in my dream, one thing leads to another, and before you know it, it's an orgy. I'd still be there if we didn't have practice."

"What about your wife?" asks Ben.

"She's visiting her parents with the kids."

"I didn't think you screwed around on your wife."

"I don't. But this was weird. I had this dream so many times it didn't seem real. It just had an energy all its own. I couldn't stop it. I couldn't believe it was happening."

"What are you going to tell your wife?"

"Nothing."

"That's right, nothing. You never say nothing," adds Adam.

"As far as I'm concerned, I just dreamed it again. It didn't really happen. And as far as you guys are concerned, nothing happened."

"I'll never be able to look at the girls' basketball team the same again." Ben slows, deep in thought.

"But this has me thinking. I have a plethora of fantasies, and they always start with me jogging. I got one where I get gang raped by a girls' motorcycle gang. In another one, I come across a women's prison bus with a flat tire. And there's the one where I get picked up by a group of strippers on their way to the national stripping contest. My favorite is the touring Vegas dancers."

Ben jumps in. "Next time you go running, let me know."

Adam makes his request. "Next time you have an orgy, let me know."

The door opens, and Dan struts in. He walks to the center and lies down next to Uncle Burt.

"I had to watch the girls open a present."

"No problem."

Dan watches the lethargic effort from the Dogs. "C'mon, let's pick it up. Let's go!"

"Dan, it's Christmas. Give them a break."

Dan whispers to Uncle Burt, "Someone in here smells like a brewery. Can you tell who it is?"

"Probably me. I tied one on last night."

Dan blows his whistle and yells, "Okay, everybody over here."

"What are you doing? Let them work their way into it. They'll be fine. Give them some time."

Dan glares at Uncle Burt as the team settles around him. He looks from face to face, examining eyes. Looking at Bronk, he orders, "Come here. Today we're working on the front headlock." Dan puts Bronk on his hands and knees in front of him and wraps his arms around Bronk's head and arm and locks hands. "I call this move the 'the equalizer.' Your object here is to pop his head like a pimple." Dan grips and compresses, and after a few seconds, Bronk begins gagging and making gurgling sounds. Dan squeezes harder. "This is what is known as legal pain." Bronk frantically taps Dan's back. Dan flexes again, releases, and stares at Bronk's beet-red face gasping for air. Bronk clutches his throat and Dan says to the team, "That's how you know if you did it right; your opponent grabs his throat when you let go." He turns back to Bronk and smacks him in the back of the head. "Don't show emotion. Okay, get your partners and drill it."

Dan watches the boys mill around and take their time. They drag to their spots and lollygag. Dan explodes, "You go out and party and come in here and drag your ass. THAT'S BULLSHIT! Okay, we're going shark bait. Get to your stations. I want one man in the middle, and he stays in the middle. Every time I blow the whistle, I want a fresh man on him. And you better go after him, or we're going to be here all day."

***

The door blows open, slams against the wall with a force that makes it rattle. Bronk stomps out of the wrestling room.

Dan follows, yelling, "I didn't blow the whistle. Get back in here and keep wrestling."

Uncle Burt tags along, a step behind Dan.

"Fuck you, Dogface." Bronk rips off his head gear and slings it against the wall. "Fuck this sport."

"You can't walk off the mat in the middle of a match. They'll penalize the team."

"Fuck the team."

"You're going to miss our annual basketball game."

Bronk storms into the locker room and slams the door behind him.

"You broke him," observes Uncle Burt.

"He snapped like a dry twig."

"I'm going to slip out the back and try to catch him when he's cooled off."

Bronk stampedes across the locker room casting aside anything in his path. His fingers coil into a fist and lash out, denting the wire front of the locker. He grabs his lock and spins the dial. Bright red blood drips from his knuckles. He removes the lock and chucks it across the room at the Dover Dog painted on the wall. He empties his locker on the floor, scoops the contents up in his arms, and storms out.

***

The team stands in the middle of the basketball court surrounding Dan, who holds a ball under his arm. "Okay, since Bronk left, I'll take his place. There's twelve of us, so there'll be six on a team. Me and Pump will pick teams. I'll go first."

"Why do you get to pick first?" asks Pump.

"I'm the coach."

"So? Why don't we shoot baskets or something to see who picks first?"

"Good idea. We'll wrestle. First to score gets first pick."

"That's not fair. If you get first pick, then I get the next two picks."

Dan thinks for a moment. "Okay, if I get the two picks after that."

"Okay, you're on. Your pick."

"Adam."

"Ben and Balls."

"Kruger and Joe."

"Pug and Doc."

"Mini D and Dickie."

"Okay, Gorni, you're on my team." Pump takes the basketball from Dan and holds it up in Gorni's face. "You know how to play basketball?" Gorni shrugs and mugs as Adam makes eye contact with Dan and nods toward their basket. Dan snatches the ball from Pump, and Adam fast-breaks toward the basket. Dan leads him with a pass. Adam dribbles, leaps, and dunks.

Dan shouts, "Two nothing. First one to eleven wins."

Ben complains, "We didn't even start yet."

Adam fires a laser pass and bounces the basketball off Gorni's chest, recovers it, dribbles and dunks.

"Four nothing."

Doc grabs the ball and passes to Pump, who passes to Ben. He dribbles down the court around Dickie, past Mini D and drives on Joe. He gets the angle on Joe, but Kruger fills in and blocks his path. Ben pulls up and swishes a twenty-foot fallaway jump shot.

"That doesn't count. He was traveling," hollers Dan.

"Bullshit. That's two to four. Your ball." Pump bounces the ball toward Dan.

Dan passes to Mini D and orders, "Get the ball to Adam."

Mini D spots Adam being double-teamed at the other end of the court. He passes to Dickie. Balls appears out of nowhere, intercepts the pass, and drives down the court to the basket. Dan sets to defend. Balls fakes Dan and dribbles in for an easy lay-up.

Dan pleads, "Foul. He fouled Dickie when he intercepted the pass."

"That's four-four."

Dan snaps at Mini D, "I told you to get the ball to Adam."

"He was covered."

"And Dickie wasn't."

"Not when I passed."

"You want to win? Do what I say. Now, get the ball to Adam."

Dan passes in to Joe, who brings the ball down the court. Ben and Pump double-team Adam. Balls moves out to cover Joe. Joe sends a look to Mini D and whips a pass to him. He looks to Kruger, who is covered by Pug and Doc, fakes to Adam, and passes to Dan standing alone under the basket. Untouched, Dan takes the pass and puts the ball up; it bounces off the backboard, hits the rim, and bounds out. Pump's wide body clears the space under the basket and grabs the rebound. He passes the length of the court to Ben in full stride. As Dickie blocks his path, he fires a no-look, behind-the-back pass to Balls, who angles down the other side of the court to the basket for an easy lay-up.

"Six-four."

Dan screams at Mini D, "I told you to get the ball to Adam."

"You were wide open."

"I suck. Just do what I say."

Dan passes to Joe, and they work it down the floor. This time, Joe passes to Dickie. Dickie looks at Dan wide open under the basket, at Adam covered by Ben and Pump, and at Kruger covered by Pug and Doc. He shakes his head and passes in Adam's direction. As he releases the ball,

Dan charges across the paint and takes out Ben and Pump with a vicious body block, freeing Adam for an easy dunk.

Ben lies on the floor screaming, "Foul. That was a foul."

"Six-six," answers Dan.

"What about the foul?"

"You didn't call the foul before when I called for a foul. Six-six."

Angered, Ben yells to Pump for the ball. Pump passes to Ben. He dribbles down the length of the court, weaving around Dan and his entire team. He pulls up and swishes a ten-footer.

"Eight-six."

"We have to take away his outside shot," yells Dan.

Ben runs back to the other end of the court and high-fives his teammates.

"I'll take care of him," says Adam.

"Now, let's work it down and get it to Adam," Dan instructs.

Kruger brings the ball down. He passes to Joe, who passes to Dan, who sets a screen and hands off to Adam. Ben slides by the screen, and Dan runs to the basket, knocking Ben down and pushing any interference out of the way. Adam follows Dan and buries another dunk.

"Eight-eight."

"We playing basketball or football?" complains Ben from the floor.

Ben yells for the ball again. Mini D deflects the inbound pass. The ball rolls above the foul line, and Dickie picks it up.

Everyone from Pump's team screams, "Shoot!"

Dickie instinctively arches the ball skyward. The ball hits the back of the rim and rockets out into Dan's hands. He tosses it to Adam and yells, "Follow me." as he lowers his shoulder and bulldozes his way to the basket. Pump and Ben take on Dan as the rest of the team grabs at Adam, trying to bring him down. A hand shreds Adam's T-shirt from his body. Arms wrap around his legs, waist, and head. Just before he is forced to the floor, he releases the ball; it sails up, catches the rim, does a three-sixty and falls through.

Dan's team scrambles back to their feet and runs to the other end to protect their basket. Dan shouts, "Ten-eight. Ten-eight."

Pump looks at his team. "Okay, let's jam it down their throats." He underhands the ball to Ben, and his team forms a flying wedge with Pump at the point, Pug and Balls to his right, and Doc and Gorni to his left. They run the length of the floor like a football play, and Ben carries the ball like the fullback to the opposite foul line. Dan's players throw their bodies into Ben's protection. Collisions stall the wedge and stop Ben's advance. He sets to shoot.

Dan yells, "The game is on the line, Ben. Don't miss this one."

Ben resets, does a double take on the basket, and shoots. Just as the ball leaves his hand, Adam comes in over the top of his downed blockers and clotheslines Ben's head, knocking him to the floor. The ball sails up, hits the back of the rim, and rebounds out past the skirmish. It falls harmlessly and baby dribbles across the floor into Gorni's hands.

"Kill the man with the ball." Dan's team converges on Gorni. He closes his eyes and throws the ball in the air. It arcs over the onrush, comes down, hits the rim, bounces above the backboard, and then falls through the hoop.

"Yeah. Oh yeah." screams Pump's team. "Ten-ten. Next basket wins."

"Okay, you see what it's going to take to win," says Dan, forming his wedge.

He hooks arms with Joe and Kruger, and they hook arms with Dickie and Mini D. They march forward to the center of the court. Dan yells, and they rush down the floor. Pump's team doesn't wait. They attack and collide with Dan's wedge halfway between the midcourt line and the free throw line. The savage onslaught breaks Dan's wedge. Balls blitzes in and slaps the ball out of Adam's hands and runs across the floor chasing it. Ben, following Balls, tackles Adam to the floor. The boys fight one-on-one to take each other out of play. Dan breaks free and sprints. Balls catches up to the rolling ball, picks it up, and sprints for the winning basket. Dan is hot on Balls' heels as he dribbles past the free throw line and launches his body. He stretches toward the basket with the ball, and at his most vulnerable point of flight, Dan sweeps at Balls' legs. He releases just as Dan sweeps his feet from under him and spins him in midair like a pinwheel. Balls loses control and crash-lands on the wood floor. He grabs his knee and screams.

***

The ceiling fixture spotlights Bronk sitting at the kitchen table. A half-empty bottle of Jack Daniels sits in front of him. A red ember burns in the shadow beneath the brim of his hat. He takes deep, repeated hits on the cigarette stub, burns it to his fingertips, tosses the butt on the floor and rubs it out with the toe of his boot. Swiping the bottle from the table, he leans his head back and exhales a thick fog that engulfs the light above the table. Tilting the bottle to his lips, he gulps the tea-colored whiskey.

The team bursts through the front door and files into the smoky room. Behind the group, a human ball of mesh gear bags packs through the kitchen and heads straight into the laundry room.

Mini D waves his hand back and forth, fanning at the haze in front of his face. "What the hell? I have to breathe this air, too."

"Hobble your lip," says Bronk, "there's no smoke down where you breathe, fuckin' midget."

Everyone stops. They stand and look at Bronk like viewing a caged animal at the zoo.

"What? What the hell you all gapin' at? I'll take all you on."

Pug circles around behind Bronk and nods for everyone to leave. As they disperse, Pug asks, "You sharing or you drinking alone?"

"Pull up a stool. Mi whiskey su whiskey."

"You got any more smokes?"

Bronk retrieves his cigarette pack from the table, digs his finger in the tiny hole, rips off the shiny top, turns it upside down and shakes. A few bits of tobacco sprinkle the tabletop.

"Shit, no."

"Just as well," says Pug, nabbing a beer from the refrigerator. "Would you like a cold one to wash the Jack?"

"No." Bronk opens the conversation.   "Assholes. What's their problem?"

"You just freaked everybody out. You were AWOL all day, missed this evening's practice, and we haven't seen you drink or smoke for a while."

"Get used to it."

"So where you been all day?"

"Out to pasture. Did you see the way they looked at me? Hell, you're drunk all the time, and they never give you any shit."

"That's true, but when I drink, I drink to forget and have a good time. When you drink, you get angry and look for a fight."

"Fuck you." Bronk jumps to his feet, kicks his chair across the room, and looks into Pug's startled face. "Ha-ha. Got you." Bronk laughs and sits in another chair. "So what have you got to forget?"

"Coming to Dover, for one."

"Hell yeah. Fuck Dover, fuck wrasslin', and fuck Dan, fuckin' asshole."

"Join the club."

Bronk lifts the bottle of Jack in the air. "To the Dan Haters Club." He takes a healthy swig and wipes his mouth with his shirtsleeve. "He works us too hard."

"Harder than anybody in the country."

"And he pushes us too far."

"Further than any of us could ever dream of pushing ourselves."

"And I'm tired of Joe's bullshit," adds Bronk.

"Go down a weight."

"I don't cut weight. Besides, I wouldn't have a chance against Balls." Bronk looks at Pug. "Maybe I'll go up a weight and challenge you."

Pug bursts out laughing. His all-out contagious guffaw infects Bronk. Feeding on each other, they hoot and holler until tears flow down their red flushed cheeks and their bodies twitch and convulse for oxygen. Every time they almost stop, they look at each other and crack up again.

"But we're all here because of Dan," screams Pug.

"He tricked me into comin' here," snorts Bronk.

"Tricked you?"

"Yeah, he signed me early. And then after I won freestyle nationals, everybody wanted me, but it was too late. Ha. Ha-ha," cackles Bronk uncontrollably.

Pug breaks up again. "He was the only college coach who stayed in touch with me after my accident."

Bronk continues laughing, forgetting what started the outburst in the first place. "What kinda accident?"

"When I was a junior in high school, I got in a motorcycle accident and broke my back in three places." One look at Bronk and he starts chuckling again.

"No shit?"

"The doctor said I'd never walk again, but my senior year, I was all-state in football and wrestling."

"Cowboy up," shouts Bronk. They jump to their feet, crash chests and bounce back into their chairs. They look at each other and break out in an overwhelming burst of laughter that shakes their bodies to the core.

"Not only did I break my back, but all my organs got pulverized," roars Pug. "When I piss, it doesn't squirt—it just drips out like a leaky faucet. Ha, ha. Ha, ha. It takes forever to just take a leak."

"Yeah, I was told if I gotta go, better not get in line behind Pug." Tears flow down their faces.

"And ever since the accident, I got gas all the time and my farts are rank," crows Pug.

"Worse than an outhouse," hollers Bronk.

Pug can't keep a straight face, even as the topic takes a more serious turn. "And then there's the constant, unbearable pain. Ha, ha, ha. The doctors tried every drug and treatment known to man to subdue it, but the only relief I get is from alcohol—and when I drink, it makes my gas worse. Ahhh."

"Shit, you're fucked up." Their bodies and tears are drained. They gasp for air, and then a renewed outbreak of helpless laughter infects them. They laugh to exhaustion and their stomach muscles hurt.

"The only time I don't drink is for practice and matches." They sit and breathe.

Doc bounces in. "Hey, Cowboy, I was invited to a Christmas party and dinner. You want to join me?"

Bronk sits still and stares at Pug. "You want to come?"

Doc breaks in, "C'mon, it'll be good for you to get out of here, get around some normal people, and laugh a little." He picks up the empty bottle of Jack from the table and drops it in the garbage. "It looks like a little food would do you good."

***

Doc and Bronk walk down a deserted, festively lit street. A lone pedestrian out for a late-night walk approaches from the opposite direction. Doc blocks the stranger's path and goes ballistic on him, shouting a tirade of vehement, hostile threats and profanity. The stranger darts into the street, runs to the other side of the road, slows to a fast walk and keeps glancing back at Doc to see if he is following.

"What's that all about?" asks Bronk.

"My life was in constant turmoil until I devised the stranger theory."

"And what's that?"

Doc explains, "The way I look at it is there's two types of people in the world: those you know and strangers."

"I'm itchin' to hear this."

"Whenever the world has you down or is screwing you over, you don't want to take it out on your family or a friend, so you pick on some stranger and lash out at them. You yell and scream at them and then just walk away."

"What does that do?"

"It's an emotional download—a dump, so to speak, and by doing it to someone you don't know, you don't risk a relationship and have to go through the awkward process of cooling down, explaining things, talking it out, and making up."

"Never looked at it that way."

"And it has lots of other benefits, too. Say you have some sort of dilemma. You meet a stranger, explain the issue, and get feedback. Usually, it's more honest and better advice because the person's not prejudiced by a relationship with you. Your friends are always going to be on your side and not want to say anything to hurt your feelings. Plus, there may be certain things you don't want your friends to know about, so you tell a stranger."

"Some things I wouldn't tell anyone," confesses Bronk.

"That's what's neat about a stranger. You'll probably never see them again." They walk in silence. "So how'd you end up at Dover?" asks Doc.

"My high school coach kicked me off the team my senior year."

"What'd you get kicked off for?"

"I wouldn't wrestle the weight he wanted me to."

"What about wrestle-offs?"

"That's how I figured it. Why should I cut weight if I can beat everybody at the weight I'm at? But he wanted to work one of his favorites into the lineup and wanted me to cut down to a lower weight, but I don't cut weight. And I couldn't go up. His son was there."

"What happened?"

"He got in my face and went on about how I was lettin' down the team, started pushin' me around, and came at me, so I laid him out."

"You punched your high school coach?"

"And his son. He attacked me after I knocked his old man down, and I put him down, too."

"So how'd you end up here?"

"Dan was the only one who called. And after he signed me, I went to freestyle nationals and beat three state champs. Every coach in the country wanted me then, but it was too late."

Doc stops. "Here we are." They stand on the sidewalk looking at the only darkened house on the street.

"I thought you said there was a party."

"There was. It must be over." Doc starts up the walk toward the house. "C'mon."

"Where you going?"

"Hey, they had a party and dinner. There must be some food left over. Let's go check it out."

"We can't just walk in someone's house."

"This is Betty's place. She's like my sister. I crash here all the time. It's okay—c'mon."

Doc stops at the front door, taps lightly on the window pane, cups his hands around his eyes and looks into the house. "No one seems to be around." Doc tries the doorknob. It turns, and the door opens. "Betty always leaves it unlocked for me." They tiptoe in and stop in the foyer. Doc looks into the front room to his left, down the hall ahead and into the dining room to his right. His head stops and freezes. "Did you hear anything?"

"No," answers Bronk in his regular voice.

"Shhh," cautions Doc, and then whispers, "they may be sleeping, so let's keep it quiet. C'mon." He leads the way down the hall to the first doorway on the right and walks into the kitchen. "Have a seat." He looks in the refrigerator. "So what do you feel like? You want some leftover turkey and fixings, or do you want me to cook up something? I make a mean omelet."

"Whatever you feel up to. They got anything to drink?"

"Here." Doc hands Bronk a cold beer. He removes several plates of leftovers, an egg carton, a package of cheese, and a container of milk. Spreading them on the countertop, he looks for the cooking utensils. "How does a Christmas omelet sound?"

***

The boys sit in front of two empty plates and a half-dozen drained beer bottles. Remains of the leftovers, an empty egg carton and plastic wrappers litter the countertop. Used skillets and mixing bowls cover the stovetop. Bronk guzzles the last of his beer and belches.

"My compliments to the chef. How'd ya learn to cook like that?"

"Over the summers, I bused at a restaurant and worked my way up to a cook."

"Well, that hit the spot."

"So what the hell happened at practice this morning?" asks Doc.

"When we went shark bait, fuckin' Dan put me in a group with Balls, Joe and Kruger, and they pounded on me. When I got tired, he kept blowin' the whistle, and before I could even get back to my feet, the next guy was tacklin' me from behind and shit. And I got so tired I couldn't even get back to my feet, and Dan got in my face and was screamin' at me and callin' me names. I blew up. That's not wrasslin'.'"

"Coach isn't here to be your friend."

"I don't care if he's my friend, but I still want him to treat me like a man."

"He does whatever it takes to get you ready. He pushes every button and attacks every weakness. Besides that, he'll always be there for you."

"Yeah, right."

"You ask any guy on the team. Dan's been there for them when no one else was. My old man's a super straight, uptight asshole. I turned eighteen before my senior year, and he didn't like my lifestyle, so he kicked me out of his house. Dan let me stay in his basement and finish high school. That's why I came to college here."

"What's your old man do?"

"He's a chemical engineer and works for the university. He's loaded; he's got patents up the wazoo."

"Patents for what?"

"Wonder drugs, experimental drugs, and shit like that." Doc looks up at the clock on the wall. "So I guess Pug told you about Balls?"

"No—what?"

"This morning at our basketball game, he blew out his knee and had to be taken to the clinic."

"No way. Is he goin' to be okay?"

"They won't know until they take x-rays and shit."

"That ain't right. Anybody but Balls."

"Yeah, it was his year. Weird how things work."

A little old lady in curlers, an ankle-length gown and slippers shuffles into the kitchen. A startled, terrified look overwhelms her wrinkled face. "Who are you? What do you want? Oh Lordy, what have you done to my kitchen?"

"It's okay. Betty said I could stop by."

"Who's Betty?"

"Isn't this Betty's house?"

"There's no Betty here. Just me and my husband."

Doc stands. "Oh, geez. I'm sorry." He motions for Bronk to stand. "We must be in the wrong house. You know, in the dark all the houses on this street look alike."

"Who's Betty?" asks the old lady. "There's no Betty on this street."

Doc pushes Bronk out of the kitchen and toward the front door. "We're sorry, ma'am—it was all a mistake. We'll get out of your hair," says Doc, scurrying out with Bronk in tow. "Delicious turkey—and by the way, your dressing was out of sight."

"It's a family recipe passed down to me from my mother," says the old lady, holding the door open. "Who's Betty?"

***

Uncle Burt swallows and sets his empty beer bottle on the bar. He asks, "What were you thinking?" Signaling the barkeep for another, he offers, "You want a beer?"

"I don't drink beer," says Dan. "I'll have juice."

"I don't believe it," says Uncle Burt, holding up his index finger, "I leave one practice early, and you put our best wrestler, our team leader, and our spiritual guide out for the season."

"We don't know if he's out for the season."

"Wrestling is Balls' life. What the hell was so important that you would risk the possibility of ending his season?"

"I was stopping him from making a basket."

"Did he make it?"

"Yeah, but he was fouled, so it doesn't count."

"I think in basketball if you make a basket while you're getting fouled, the basket counts."

"He has to shoot a free throw."

"A free throw?"

"Yeah. If he makes it, they win, and if he misses it, it's our ball."

"You're fucking crazy. You're still trying to win the basketball game?"

A cold, sweaty bottle of beer is planted in front of Uncle Burt.

"And bring a moo juice for my buddy here."

The bartender glances at Dan, snickers, and walks to the other end of the bar.

"I don't care for milk. It upsets my stomach."

"Watch the bartender and tell me what he's doing."

"He's pouring the milk. Now he's holding it up in front of everyone and saying something. They're all looking at me and laughing."

"Exactly. Pretty soon, we'll have every dollar in this place in the pot. See the tall guy at the pool table with the long hair?"

Dan does a slow three-sixty of the country bar and looks at the fellow without looking at him. "Yeah."

"How long? A minute? Two minutes?"

Dan shrugs.

"He looks like a hippie, for Christ's sake."

"Make it a minute," says Dan, chugging the glass of milk. "You know, you were right."

"About what?"

"About wrestling the bear when I dream."

"Yeah, how's that going?"

"Well, every night I do better. He still kicks my ass, but I'm starting to figure him out. I should be able to score on him soon."

"How's the house coming along?"

"Good. I got the driveway dug out, started the deck, bought new cabinets, and prepped for the paint. Oh, and I priced the bulldozer, and I'm thinking about turning the loft into a bedroom."

The barman touches Uncle Burt's forearm and nods toward the pool table. When Uncle Burt looks, the men around the table toss their cue sticks on the green felt top, pick up their coats, and stroll out the back door.

"Okay, it's time," says Uncle Burt, sliding off his stool.

Everyone in the bar dashes to the back door, herds behind Uncle Burt and Dan, funnels through the exit and stampedes into the rear parking lot. The frenzied rush is halted by a black and grey cat-sized rat strolling from the garbage dumpster. The oversized, long-tailed rodent stops under the security spotlight mounted above the back door, raises the corner of his lip and sneers. The crowd takes a rapid second look. A chill shoots up their spines. After establishing his territory, the gnawing animal ambles across the parking lot and vanishes under a parked truck. A couple of dozen witnesses position themselves around the edge of the ring of light, circling Dan and the tall, long-haired man from the pool table.

"What are the rules?" asks one of the men from the pool table.

"You pick the rules. We pick the odds," answers Uncle Burt.

"Anything goes. They fight till there's a knockout or tapout."

"I have two bets," says Uncle Burt, waving a handful of cash in the air above his head. "Even money on the winner and two-to-one odds my man can win in under a minute."

The bystanders swarm around Uncle Burt, fighting to get a bet down before he runs out of cash. Dan slouches with his hands in his pockets and smiles at the excitement. His foe's sinister, dark eyes stare down a good six inches into Dan's. The taller man bends at the waist, leaning his broad shoulders and wiry frame forward, and then he jerks his head up and tosses his hair back, revealing a face landscaped with scars. Massive, lumpy hands pull his shoulder-length hair together and tie the dirty blond strands in a knot.

Dan watches the man's exaggerated preparations. *He is a hippie.*

The tall man cracks his knuckles and stretches his fingers, then winks, blows a kiss and smiles at Dan.

He's a gay hippie.

"Bets are down," says Uncle Burt, clutching two fists of cash. "Who holds the money?"

"I'll hold the money." The crowd parts to let the source of the voice step forward. Uncle Burt holds the money out. Into the light steps the local deputy. His Elvis sideburns clash with his holster and authoritative demeanor. Uncle Burt pulls the money back.

"You got any objections?" asks the deputy.

Uncle Burt sizes up the deputy and the onlookers, wondering if it is a setup. He looks to Dan, who removes his glasses.

"We run a fair fight here, and I'm here to guarantee that."

After a brief lull, Uncle Burt hands over a handful of money. "Okay, this is the to-win money." Surrendering the second bundle, "And this is the to-win-under-a-minute money."

The deputy stuffs a wad in each of his front pockets and turns to the fighters. "When I step in and yell 'break,' it's over. Everything stops. Understood?" Both nod at the officer. He steps in the middle of the circle of light, looks at each man, and asks, "Ready?" They nod. He says, "Bring it on," steps back and adds, "start the time."

The rabble screams, "C'mon, Mac. Let's git this guy, Mac." Mac's buddies from the pool table start chanting, "Mac attack. Mac attack. Mac attack!" and all the locals join in.

The tall guy leaps forward and swings a wild roundhouse punch. Dan ducks. The fist and arm slice the air above his head and then whips back with an elbow to Dan's temple, stunning him. Before he can react, two bulky hands palm his head and position it for a knee smash to the face. The mob's collective oohs and aahs serenade Dan as he falls to his back. Going with the force of the hit, he tucks, does a backward roll across the brick alley and pops up to his feet, shutting up the hometown fans.

His adversary stares in disbelief for a moment, then charges again. Dan lowers his level, steps in on the charging Bull Moose and locks his arms around his rib cage, squeezes, and lifts him off his feet. Cries from Mac's supporters scream for him to break the hold. He pounds away at Dan's tucked head. Dan's eyes catch the deputy stepping back and blending with the crowd. His grip tightens, compressing Mac's bony barrel chest. Pain and then panic etch across the man's face when he realizes he can't breathe. Mac jams his hands into Dan's head and pries it away from his body, then drives the heels of his hands under Dan's chin and pushes his head up and away. Once he's created a gap, he delivers a short, powerful elbow shot to the side of Dan's face and breaks the bear hug. The tall guy's followers cheer him on as he circles for a moment to catch his breath.

Dan notices the deputy drifting to the back of the hooting human circle. He looks at Uncle Burt and nods toward the deputy, but Uncle Burt shoots a cautionary look back at Dan and points at his watch. Dan points to the crowd. "The dep —"

Mac interrupts Dan's warning with his chiseled fist. He follows up his punch with another assault and lunges forward.

Dan dodges him and takes off running. The rooting bodies split, revealing the deputy with his back turned as he walks toward the parking lot. Dan runs up to the deputy from behind. Before he has a chance to react, Dan grabs him around the ribcage, slips his arms under each arm and locks his hands behind the deputy's neck in a full nelson. Dan spins and catches the force of Mac's charging shoulder with the deputy's torso. Air rushes from his deflating lungs. The deputy wheezes for oxygen, makes a breathless utter, and gasps again.

Dan peeks over the deputy's shoulder, sticks his tongue out, and gives Mac the raspberries, spraying his face with saliva. Mac coils a fist, winds up and swings with all his might at Dan's head. Dan swings the deputy around and blocks the fist with the deputy's face. He spins the deputy again and smacks the tall guy in his angry face with the deputy's extended open hand. Mac unloads another haymaker, and Dan blocks it once more with the deputy's face. Repeating his maneuver, Dan spins the deputy in the other direction and smacks the tall guy's face with the deputy's other hand. With fire in his eyes, Mac grabs the deputy by the throat with one hand and hammers home the knockout punch with his bony knuckles. When Dan feels the deputy go limp, he tosses the body at Mac, who instinctively catches it. Before he can finish thinking he's left himself unprotected, Dan's fist cracks him between the eyes.

A momentary hush is broken by Uncle Burt looking at the timer's watch. "Fifty-eight, fifty-nine and sixty." All eyes focus on the two bodies lying on the ground. Everyone looks for any movement, any sign of life. "Okay, that's it," announces Uncle Burt.

The locals study the bodies. "Looks like the deputy is giving Mac head."

"Yep, looks like he sucked the damn life right out of him."

"Anybody got a camera?"

***

Uncle Burt steers the car and counts money at the same time. "Minus my cut for putting up the money, you pulled in a little over a grand tonight. Not bad for less than a minute of work. So far, that totals more than four thousand."

"I like it when you fix me up with wrestling matches. Somebody could get hurt in this fighting stuff." Dan rolls an icy cold red and brown beer bottle across his eye and cheek.

"It's all I could get. Too bad you don't want to do the pro wrestling gig."

"You ever find out how much it pays?"

"As a matter of fact, I did. You can make anywhere from a few thousand up to as much as ten grand for a main event, but there's no way you'd get a main event. You got no experience how to fake wrestling and make losing look good."

"Ten grand to fake wrestle and lose. What's wrong with the world?"

"Police chief stopped by the bar."

"You didn't say anything about this, did you?"

"No."

"You can't say anything to anybody. Nobody can know what we're doing. Nobody."

"I know. I know."

"What'd he want?"

"He said Doc's bag is full of drugs of some sort, but they can't find anything illegal. And the videotape is of Kruger banging some girl."

"What's he telling all this to you for?"

"He can't stand President Hardon and wants to work out a deal with us."

"Okay, take care of it."

"You done with that beer? I'm thirsty."

"I need it for my eye."

"Who are you kidding? You got a head like a rhino."

***

Bronk and Doc walk down the paved path running parallel to the road. An unfamiliar car cuts them off on the sidewalk as it pulls into the vacant lot and parks next to the Dog Pound. Adam gets out, opens the back door, and lifts a stereo from the back seat.

"Make yo'self useful," commands Adam.

Bronk and Doc peek into the car. The front and back seats are packed to the ceiling with dozens of stereos, electronic devices, and hundreds of cassette tapes.

"Where'd you git all this?" asks Bronk, filling his hands.

"The dormitories," answers Adam, leading the way to the house. "With everyone gone for the holidays, it's like a shopping mall. Only free."

"Nice car," says Doc, grabbing a load.

"I borrowed it for a while."

They open the front door to Gorni screaming, "Give back," and desperately running from guy to guy as they toss his wallet in a game of keep-away. Gorni lets out a piercing cry as he jumps on Ben, who barely gets off a last-second throw to Kruger. Gorni growls as he runs across the room and attacks Kruger, who hurls the wallet toward Dickie. Adam's hand releases the stereo and snatches the wallet from midair.

Adam looks at Kruger. "Why you always picking on the little guys?" He hands the wallet back to Gorni who clutches it.

"Why you always stealing?" retorts Kruger.

"Bully."

"Thief."

Adam sets down the stereo and walks toward Kruger. "What I do is none of your business."

Kruger meets him halfway, standing nose to nose. "What you got there?"

"I got everybody their own sound system. Merry Christmas."

"You bringing that stuff in the house is my business. It's all our business. We get busted with any of that shit in the house, and our season is over."

"I didn't see you thinking about any of us when you were riding your Harley," Adam snaps back.

Everyone's attention turns to Gorni. He sits staring at his open billfold, uttering inarticulate sounds with tears rolling down his cheeks.

"What's with him?"

Adam remembers the thugs attacking Gorni outside his apartment building. "There's something precious to him in that wallet."

"Yeah, like what?" asks Kruger, snatching the wallet.

Gorni screams, "My family."

Kruger looks at a picture of Gorni with his mother, father, brothers and sisters. Gorni grabs back his keepsake and holds it with a tight grip.

"Geez, what's the big deal?" asks Kruger as Gorni begins bawling.

Adam steps in and shouts in Kruger's face. An argument erupts. Everyone pushes each other and takes sides as the whole team becomes embroiled in a quarrel. Ben backs away from the dispute, climbs the stairs to his room and shuts his door. Angry shouts penetrate his sanctum. He slips on headphones and turns the volume up on his cassette player. Looking at the picture of Tara on the nightstand next to his bed, he floats away in a daydream.

○○○○○○○○○○○○○○○○○○●●●●●●●●●●

17. Come Together

BRONK LIES IN bed, staring at the ceiling with his head propped up on his interlocked fingers. His eyes discover a cartoonish face in the bumps and ridges of the textured ceiling. *Like cloud watching.* A smoking cigarette dangles from his lips. He looks at the clock. *5:01. Practice in an hour. Maybe I can catch her before she leaves.* He takes a last exaggerated puff followed by a long exhale. He crafts a point on the red-hot cigarette tip by spinning it on the bottom of the ashtray, then smashes it out. He pulls on his shirt and jeans.

Bronk's breath billows in the frigid air. He walks down the dark, deserted street and rounds the corner to Jas's house. Her front door opens. *Just in time.* Jas and Joe step out. Bronk pulls up. His hunched shoulders drop as he doesn't feel the cold anymore watching them get in Joe's car.

***

Bronk stuffs the last piece of clothing in the paper bag. He haphazardly tosses his toiletries and miniature spittoon on his blanket, folds in each side, and rolls it up. Tucking the roll under his arm, he grabs the bag in one hand, rope in the other and takes one last look around. Someone knocks at the Puppy Pound's door.

"Door's open." Bronk turns with his belongings.

Jas pokes her head in. "There you are."

"Yep, here I am."

"I was worried about you. I hadn't seen you at practice for a couple of days and thought maybe you were sick or something."

"Nope." Bronk walks past her to the stairs.

Jas notices his bag and roll. "You going somewhere?"

"Yep."

Jas follows Bronk to Balls' room. Bronk opens the door and lays his lasso on Balls' bed.

"Where are you going?"

"Home," says Bronk, descending the next set of steps.

"Home?"

"Yep."

"So you're just leaving? Not going to say good-bye to anybody or anything? Just disappear?"

"Nothing to say."

"I thought—" Jas watches Bronk walk down the front porch steps and turn up the sidewalk without a word or a look back.

***

Bronk walks backward down the side of the highway hitchhiking. Several vehicles speed past, blasting Bronk with icy air. Finally, a car brakes, pulls to the edge of the road, and stops a couple hundred feet away. Three college-age fellows look back and watch Bronk run to them. When he gets to the locked car door, the occupants smile, wave, and speed off. Bronk watches until they disappear, branding their laughing faces in his memory.

After an hour of backward walking and holding his thumb out, a red Porsche driven by a platinum blonde pulls to the shoulder and stops. As Bronk walks to the small two-seater, another vehicle pulls up and beeps. Bronk looks. It is Dan in his pickup. Bronk looks at the blonde as she turns her head, throwing her shoulder-length hair back and revealing her movie-star looks. Bronk casts his eyes to Dan, smiles, and jogs to the Porsche. Dan blasts his horn.

"Looks like I'm stuck in the gate." Bronk tosses his roll and bag in the front seat. "Could ya hold on a sec?" He runs back to the truck and opens the passenger door.

"Where you headed?" asks Dan.

"Home."

"Checking out?"

"I guess. What'd ya want?"

"Just came from the hospital. Balls asked to see you."

"Me?"

The blonde blasts her horn. Bronk takes a deep breath.

"You can go with her, or if you want to see Balls, I'll drive you home."

"You'd do that?"

"It's up to you."

***

Kruger and Mini D are bundled in layers of sweats, running down a deserted street.

Snowflakes melt on Mini D's hot face. "This is the first Christmas I've been away from my family."

"At least you got your brother here."

"Yeah, but in a way, you and me, we're like family—well, everybody. It's like a wrestling family."

"Come to think of it, that's why I hate them so much; they remind me of my family."

"Man, I still can't get used to Dover like this."

"It's like a ghost town," adds Kruger.

"A deserted ghost town."

"That's what a ghost town is. Deserted. You have to change your name to Mini B."

"What's the B stand for?"

"Brain." Kruger continues, "What a Christmas vacation. All we do is eat, sleep, shit, run, and wrestle."

"I like training like this and not having to worry about school," says Mini D, "I love it."

"What's there to love about it?"

"I just love wrestling. It teaches you about life. It's just you and one other person when you walk out on the mat, and he can make you scream or cry or anything. But there he is and there's no way you can avoid him. If you lose or get beat up, you got no one to blame but yourself. It's tough. And I figure when I get out of college, that's the way life is going to be. Every day is there; you can't avoid it. It beats you, or you beat it. Besides, what else is a guy my size going to do?"

"You could be a jockey."

"Geez, I never thought of that."

"The only thing I hate about wrestling—besides Dan—is the one day the worst guy in the room gets a move on you. He knows it's the only chance he's going to get all year, so he really makes you pay."

"I don't mind that so much. I hate the waiting. You have to wait to work out, wait to weigh in, wait to eat, wait to wrestle. It's always hurry and wait for something."

"Sometimes it scares me."

"What?"

Kruger confesses, "I get crazy thoughts, and I'm afraid I'll lose control, you know?"

"Like what?"

"I've never told anyone this, but when I have a guy's leg or arm, I look at it and think, I'm going to break this fucker off. I'm not going to act like it, I'm just going to fucking do it, you know?"

"Yeah, I get like that when I get mad. One day in practice, Dan got to me, and I lost it. I head-butted the guy I was wrestling right in the face, and his nose fell over on his cheek. Before I could blink, blood gushed from his nose like a water spigot turned on high. I felt horrible, but everybody in the room cracked up laughing."

Kruger chuckles. "Yeah, I remember that. That was cool. Well, I don't have to get mad, and I don't feel bad. I have to hurt people, or I get hypertension. It's like a release. I go to practice and say, 'Hi Dickie,' and start twisting his arm. I used to go up to freshmen and tell them, 'You don't want to wrestle me. I'll break your fucking neck.' You should've seen the look on their faces." He snickers.

Kruger tucks his red, bare hands in his pockets to warm them. He feels a slip of paper and pulls it out. He unfolds it.

"What's that?" asks Mini D.

"Girls are always giving me their numbers. I just don't have time." He crumples the piece of paper and tosses it away.

"My hair is falling out in clumps, and you don't have time. Just wait till you start going bald, you son of a bitch."

A loud screech of tires followed by a thud disturbs the stillness of the deserted town. They look down the side street. Brake lights flash, and a sedan turns the corner and speeds off. Kruger and Mini D turn and run down the tire tracks left in the new-fallen snow. A white lump lies in the middle of the highway. From a distance, it looks like a discarded pillow or quilt. It's not until they are on top of it that they discover it's a white German shepherd. The snow around the dog turns red.

"Wow," exclaims Mini D.

"Jesus, he's hurt bad."

"C'mon, quick. Help me."

"Okay, brother, but this one is mine."

***

Dan sits in his snow-covered truck with the engine running. The front door to the clinic opens. Bronk clomps through the fresh, unblemished snow cover and gets in the truck. The cab is silent. Dan turns on the wipers, and they swipe the cover of white from his windshield.

"So, what's happening?" asks Dan.

"Balls said the doc told him he was done for the season. He has to wear a cast for the next couple of months."

"Anything else?"

"He said that God threw him a curve ball."

"He said that?"

"And that adversity weakens the weak and strengthens the strong, and he was goin' to come back stronger than ever from this."

"Balls is a man," says Dan.

"He makes me feel like a pussy."

"He's set a whole new standard."

"We both know it wasn't God that put him out for the season."

They sit. Thinking.

"Anything else?" asks Dan.

"He told me a story about lions. Did you know when a lion gets too old to hunt, the pride leaves him and circles to the other side of the herd they are huntin'. And when the pride gets in place, the old lion jumps from the grass and roars. The herd reacts instinctually and runs away from the roar, right into the rest of the pride. He said it's like life. If you want to survive and live a life worth livin', you have to run to the roar."

They sit in silence.

"Anything else?" asks Dan.

"With him out, there goes our season."

"It's not over 'til it's over."

They mourn.

Dan breaks the silence. "Anything else?"

"He says the two of you chewed it over and settled on me bein' the new captain."

"You think of anybody better?"

"Joe."

"Everything's a joke to him. It's a philosophy that works for him, but he'd turn the team into a circus. Not everyone would get it the way he does, and they'd fail."

"Why me?"

"Potential. You got all the ingredients to be a good captain. You have to grow into it."

"I can't be a Balls."

"Nobody can. You have to be Bronk."

"How can I captain if I'm not a starter?"

"You got a bigger problem than that. With Balls out, we don't have anyone to fill his spot."

"You can bump Gorni up."

"Or…"

"I could go down."

"That would solve both problems."

"I don't have the best training habits. And why would they listen to me?"

"The choice is yours: I can either drive you home, or you can stay and captain this team. What are you thinking?"

"Timin' has a lot to do with the outcome of a rain dance."

"What the hell does that mean?"

"Nothin'."

"Have you talked to your dad about quitting?"

"Yep."

"What'd he say?"

"You can't tell how good a man or a watermelon is 'til they get thumped."

***

A shaft of light about the size of a roll of quarters shines through a hole onto a captivated eyeball. A knock at the door is ignored. Another knock and then a louder one interrupt the fantasy. The observer fits a form-fitting plug into the hole.

"What do you want?" asks Joe as he opens the door.

"Need to talk," Bronk replies.

"I'm busy."

"Don't look busy."

"Can't we do this some other time?"

"It's about Balls."

Joe nods for Bronk to enter. "Do they know anything yet?" He pulls a chair from the kitchen table.

Bronk sits. "He's done for the season."

"What a waste."

"Yep, sometimes you get, and sometimes you get got."

"Fucking Dan, that asshole."

"Nice place," says Bronk, looking around.

"Thanks. Is that it?"

"Nope."

"Well…"

"Dan and Balls want me to be the captain."

"No way."

"I told 'em it should be you, but they already had me hogtied and branded. So I figure the only way it's gonna work is if we work it out first. So I'm here to bury the hatchet."

"I'm listening."

"It don't take no genius to spot a horse in a pack of dogs. I don't fit, and I need your help with the guys. I was hopin' we could partner up."

"You don't want to be my friend," warns Joe.

"I don't see any other way."

"Why do you think I'm alone all the time?"

"Figured that's the way you like it."

"Friends are for fucking over," explains Joe. "Someone who doesn't know you or someone who's your enemy isn't going to let their guard down, but your friends, well, they do, and that makes them easy prey."

"I'm a big boy."

"When I was a freshman, I took a class that was way over my head. So, I made friends with the prof. I had heard he was into distance running. So I got up early one morning and 'accidentally' ran into him, and we became running partners. Every morning at six for almost five months, we'd run six to ten miles before class, and once a week, we'd go for a twenty-mile run. We became friends. I got to know his family, dated his daughter, went to his home for the holidays, all that shit—and he flunked me."

"Yeah, but you were just doin' it for the grade."

"But I never saw it coming. It was beautiful. I had no clue. Flunking his class made me ineligible. I missed wrestling that semester, but I was in the best shape of my life."

"Wouldn't it have been easier to just study?"

"Did they say why they didn't want me as captain?"

"They're afraid some of the guys wouldn't git your take on things, and you'd lose 'em."

"I may come off like a goofball, but nobody is more serious about winning than me."

"I know that."

"I'm just different. Balls thinks wrestling builds character. I think wrestling weeds out the pussies. It's survival of the fittest. The strongest survive, and nobody is stronger than me up here," says Joe, pointing his index finger to his temple. "This is where it counts."

"I figure the two of us workin' together could git it done. What d'ya say?"

"I'm listening."

"I need to get somethin' out in the open."

"Shoot."

"What's going on between you and Jas?"

"Nothing."

"I saw you coming out of her place the other morning."

"I was trying to get laid. It's been deserted around here for the last month, if you haven't noticed. I went over for a friendly visit, pretended I was too drunk to drive, and did the old pass out routine. And then you know, they go to bed and you try to sneak into bed with them. But she was on to me and had her door locked. I spent the night on the couch."

"But you got a girlfriend."

"And after that night, I called her, and she came back early. C'mon, I want to show you something." Joe leads the way into the next room. "I got a girlfriend because she's the best looking girl on campus. Nothing is better than going out with her on my arm and watching all the saps drooling."

"So she's more ornamental than useful."

"Oh, she's useful," Joe enters the bedroom and walks to the closet. "Besides the sex, cooking and cleaning, I haven't had to write a paper since I've been dating her. For me, it's the conquest. Nothing gives me more confidence than walking around town and knowing I've done half the girls on campus. I look around and think, 'I did her, I did her, I did her.' You know what I mean? I want you to check this out." Joe puts his finger to his lips and removes the plug. A small shaft of light casts into the dark closet like a spotlight.

Bronk peeks through the hole. Susan sits naked on a stool in the middle of the steamy bathroom facing the peephole with her legs spread.

She examines her genitalia in a mirror propped on a stool in front of her. Her hand guides a razor to put the final touches on a small black, heart-shaped hair patch just above her vagina. She pulls back wet strands of black hair that keep falling off her tan shoulders. Her facial features induce a hypnotic trance. Lean muscles and paper-thin skin define each proportioned body part. Joe plugs the hole and walks back to the kitchen.

"After my old man met Susan, he brought me a gross of rubbers the next time he came to visit. She's beautiful, sexy, smart, witty, funny. She's perfect, except for one thing: she loves a schmuck. Me. She'll do anything for me. She screwed one of my profs so I would pass his class."

"Doesn't anybody on this team have a normal relationship?"

"What's that got to do with what I'm talking about?"

"Nothin'."

"The point is, I should care, but I don't."

"Like I said, I'm a big boy. I can watch out for myself. Next, I'm droppin' to take Balls' place in the lineup, so we won't be knockin' heads. I figure we can train together." Bronk takes a seat at the kitchen table.

"I don't know about that—that's why I live alone. I don't want anyone to know what I'm up to. It adds to the mystique. You hungry? You want a sandwich or something?"

"Sure."

Joe opens the fridge and tosses a loaf of white bread on the countertop. He sniffs an opened package of meat and tosses it in the garbage. "So you're going thirty-four. You'll do good there. Everybody's running from Balls, so it's wide open."

" 'Cept for Bobby Ryder. He's beat everybody 'cept Balls."

Joe gathers all the sandwich fixings, spreads them on the kitchen table in front of the cowboy, and sits.

Bronk examines the dried, wrinkled lunch meat and the moldy cheese and bread and reasons, *Okay, this must be some kinda test.* "You got a knife?"

Joe stands, walks to the stove, picks up an encrusted knife and cuts a mouthful of meat from the raw steak in the skillet on the stove. He stabs the bloody morsel with the point of the blade and pitches it in his mouth.

"What's that?" asks Bronk.

Joe chews. "Steak. That's all I eat during the season." He hands the knife to Bronk and sits. "I just warm it up a little and eat it as raw as I can."

Bronk holds the knife and stares at Joe. Joe stares back. Bronk examines the ingredients and begins making his sandwich. "So, how'd you end up comin' to Dover?"

"I was being recruited by all the major programs in the country. Everywhere I went, they wined me and dined me—the best hotels, restaurants, and parties." While Joe talks, he looks at Bronk's sandwich, takes a paper napkin, and begins tearing small pieces off. "When I came here I drove down on a Friday, about dinner time. I'm beat from the drive and starving. Dan drives me to the middle of town, drops me off, says 'I'll see you on Sunday,' and drives off." Joe sizes up Bronk's sandwich and tears the napkin to the same size as the bread. "At first, I was pissed and started walking to my car to go home, but I got sidetracked by a couple of coeds and ended up having the weekend of my life. Hell, I was two days late getting home. After that weekend, I would've come to Dover for nothing—hell, I did come for nothing. The point is, this is a great place, and I would have come despite Dan."

Bronk smashes the top slice of bread down on his sandwich. Susan slinks in from the bedroom.

"Whoa, hold your horses," says Joe, nodding toward Susan, "get a load of that." *Just the distraction I needed,* thinks Joe. Bronk's eyes hang on her every move. Susan glides across the front room in see-through lingerie with no underwear. Joe lifts the top slice of bread on Bronk's sandwich, fits his perfectly sized, custom-made piece of paper and covers it with the slice of bread.

"Susan, you remember Bronk?"

"He's the guy you come home from practice bitching about every day."

"That's a little too much information."

"He says you have the best cow catcher in the country. I heard your story. Why don't you tell him the real reason you came to Dover?" She looks at Joe, waiting for him to say something. When he doesn't, she explains, "He got kicked out of school for a prank and missed the state tournament. All the 'major programs' lost interest."

Joe explains, "I got a picture of one nude guy porking another in the ass, and I replaced their faces with the principal's and superintendent's faces. Then, I snuck into school at night, made a few hundred copies, and plastered them all over the school."

"You two know each other from high school?" asks Bronk.

"Yes. You don't think any girl here would have him, do you?"

Bronk can't take his eyes off Susan. Unconsciously, he lifts his sandwich and opens his mouth to bite.

Susan cruises by, grabs it from his hands, and chucks it in the garbage. "I can't believe you would feed him that. That stuff has been in the fridge since before Christmas break. Bronk, would you like to join us for dinner? Joe was about to cook us a steak. There's enough for three."

"Bronk just came from the hospital. Dan blew out Balls' knee. He's done."

Susan is crushed. "Oh no, not Balls."

"Dan said he's gonna petition the NCAA and see if he can get Balls another season," adds Bronk.

Tears trickle down Susan's cheeks. An awkward moment follows. Everyone struggles for the right words to say.

"Fucking Dan," blurts Joe. "It's just a game to him. He just wants to break guys like he did to you in practice the other day. He cracked you like a walnut. Snapped you like a Ritz cracker. Broke you like an old nag—"

"Okay, okay, we get your point," interrupts Bronk.

Joe continues, "He thinks his job is to make you quit. If he can make you quit, you weren't meant for it, and if you survive, you're ready. Just once I'd like to get him, you know, fuck him up really bad."

"Yep, get in line," says Bronk.

"Okay, let's make a vow right now." Joe holds out his hand.

Bronk grabs it, seizing the opportunity to bond with Joe.

Joe looks Bronk dead in the eyes. "We're not going to let Dan break us. Come on, say it."

"We're not gonna let Dan break us."

Joe squeezes Bronk's hand as tight and hard as he can and jerks him close. "We're going to turn this on Dan and get him. It's payback time."

Bronk grips Joe's hand with all his might and jerks back. "The 'Get Dan' plan."

Joe nods in agreement, and with wide-eyed enthusiasm, they chant, "Get Dan, get Dan, get Dan…" until it dies its own death.

"Speaking of Dan, I got it on good authority he's performing in a pro wrestling match in Columbus, Ohio," says Joe.

"No shit."

"Do you believe that? Apparently, one of the main acts got injured."

"Let's get the team together and pay him a visit," suggests Bronk.

"That'd be a good team activity. A road trip," summarizes Joe.

"You staying for dinner?" asks Susan.

"Naw, as much as I'd like to, I got some things I gotta do, and besides, I gotta start watchin' my weight. But thanks," says Bronk, nodding to Susan and walking to the door. "See ya at practice tomorrow."

"Be there or be square."

Bronk shuts the door behind him. Susan turns to Joe. "So, now you have someone to do your dirty work."

"Like taking candy from a baby."

"So do you want dinner?" asks Susan, lifting her lingerie and exposing her manicured heart, "or do you want dessert?"

18. Rasslin

THE DOGS CROWD around the ticket booth.

Joe requests, "We'd like to get some tickets down as close to the stage as possible."

"All seats are general admission. Seating is on a first come basis," says the ticket lady.

"Okay, we'll take eleven tickets," replies Joe, sliding the money under the window bars.

The ticket lady counts the money, passes eleven tickets back and says, "Good luck." She hangs a 'sold out' sign on her window and closes the station.

***

Boos hail down on the Commie Bastard, who enters from a side stage pulling a rope draped over his shoulder. The red spotlight reflects like a beacon off his sweaty, bald head. At center stage, he drops the rope, turns his back to the audience, and lifts the corners of his scarlet cape, displaying the USSR flag embroidered with a yellow sickle and hammer. He turns and shouts from beneath his oversized mustache, "I will bury America," and then pointing to the crowd, he yells, "I will bury YOU!" Boos drown the Russian anthem playing over the speakers.

The Dogs enter through one of the ramps on the upper level. They look around at the stuffed arena.

"Okay, where do you want to sit?" asks Pug.

"Let's get as close as possible," answers Joe. They eye the standing-only section on the floor surrounding the square ring.

"Let's go," says Pug, leading the way.

The Commie Bastard removes a hammer and sickle from his belt, shakes them in the air, and laughs at the multitude of jeering faces. Hecklers shout obscene names and hiss. Others wave anti-Commie Bastard signs: "America Rules, Bolsheviks Drool," "RED is DEAD," "Pinkos are Gay." He tucks his hammer and sickle in his belt, lifts the rope over his shoulder, and marches down the ramp into the arena. At the end of the rope, a dummy of Uncle Sam is dragged by the neck through the side stage curtain and down the sloped runway.

The sight works the spectators into a frenzy. They bombard the Commie Bastard with lewd, filthy gestures. As he climbs into the ring, droves of miniature red, white, and blue Styrofoam A-bombs rain on him. He stands in the center of a mound of miniature bombs, pulling the rope handful by handful to drag Uncle Sam up the side, under the ropes, and onto the platform.

Ringside fanatics press forward, swaying the crowd control barriers to their limits. Dozens of security personnel sprint out and form a protective circle around the elevated stage. The Commie Bastard ties Uncle Sam to the corner post and bludgeons his head repeatedly with his hammer, then slashes Uncle Sam time after time with his sickle. Hysteria ravages the audience. Women faint. Children cry. Hands clasp in prayer. Fans fight to break through the security blockade.

Out of nowhere, Sergeant America, dressed in red, white, and blue camouflage, leaps into the ring and sneaks up behind the bald slasher. A thunderous cheer rises from the horde as he grabs the cape and yanks the Commie Bastard off Uncle Sam. The force of the jerk hurls the body across the ring and leaves the sickle buried in the dummy's head. The cape rips free, sending the enemy's body flying through the ropes and onto the floor. The arena vibrates with cheers. Sergeant America dives from the ring onto the Commie Bastard's back, wraps the Russian flag cape around his neck, and chokes him.

Rhythmic stomping and clapping accompany the chant, "U...S...A! ...U...S...A! ...U...S...A!" The red-faced Commie Bastard gags and fights for air. In a final act of desperation, he waves his hands and begs for mercy. Sergeant America hesitates. The Red cheat pulls his hammer from his belt and takes a vicious swing. The crowd gasps. Sergeant America falls to the floor, clutching his head. Everyone holds their breath. The Commie Bastard takes the flag from his neck, winds it around his attacker's neck, and strangles him. Sergeant America kicks and pulls at the flag until his oxygen-deprived body goes limp. The Bolshevik raises the Russian flag above his head and struts around the outside of the ring.

An overzealous woman breaks through security, rushes the dirty Red, and takes a swipe at his head. He drops his flag, grabs her like a barbell, and presses her above his head. Holding the kicking, swinging, and screaming woman above his head, he marches around, inciting the crowd to a fury. When he gets to the most riotous section, he throws the woman, flattening a bunch of the loud mouths to the floor.

The disturbance creates a gap in the security fortress. A small boy, dressed like a miniature Sergeant America, slips between two protective legs and attacks the giant Commie with tiny, clenched fists. The Commie Bastard palms the little boy's head and holds him at bay as he swings wildly in the air. The giant laughs at the pint-sized warrior, then pushes the pip-squeak to the ground and rubs his face into the floor until he gives up and breaks down crying. Rage spurs the throng to hurl food and drinks at the parading Russky. He retrieves his flag, steps on the chest of the unconscious Sergeant America, and climbs back into the ring. He waves his flag and prances around, taunting the angry mob.

The Dogs squeeze through the shoulder-to-shoulder cluster onto the main floor. Everyone bitches and complains as the boys wedge their way forward toward the stage. When the bodies get too thick to move any further, Pug goes into action. He looks at his teammates. They hold their noses, and he lets it rip. As the odor permeates the air around Pug, everyone fights to move away from the smell. The team works its way forward, fills the deserted space, and inches closer to the roped ring. When they reach the next roadblock, Pug breaks off another stink buffet and repeats the process, creating an unobstructed path.

The houselights dim, and a single light beam shines on the stage at the top of the ramp. The next challenger is shoved out into the spotlight, struggling to straighten his crooked mask. The cockeyed face protector is the kind used in amateur wrestling. It covers the face from the chin to the hairline with three large holes for the eyes and mouth. "D O G F A C E " is printed across the forehead of the brown mask in staggered black letters. A leash dangles from the collar buckled around the rassler's neck. The arena goes silent. Everyone stares and tries to figure out the oddity.

Dressed in a black suit, sunglasses, and a Fedora hat, Uncle Burt runs onstage. He swings a bone the size of a baseball bat. He does an impromptu dance, grabs the end of the leash and tugs, pulling the masked man down the ramp. The only shaft of light focuses on Uncle Burt. He waves the giant bone at the capacity crowd and then shakes it in a threatening manner at the enemy in the ring. It's a new hope. Every shake of the bone spawns a louder cheer.

Every few steps, the masked man stops, like a dog out for a walk; a yank on the leash jerks him forward. They approach the elevated ring. Uncle Burt nudges and pokes the bone into the masked man's body and face, prompting him to snatch the bone and break it over his knee. A wild cheer explodes. He flings the two jagged pieces into the surrounding darkness, rips the collar from his neck, and trudges toward the roped pit. The full house begins stomping and clapping.

"I don't know how I let you talk me into this. Let's get this bullshit over with," mumbles the masked man. He climbs the stairs, ducks under the rope, and steps into the ring.

A surprise forearm smash to the protective face cover knocks the veiled rassler reeling into the corner turnbuckle. The hated Red grabs the mask and twists it sideways with a powerful wrench to force the mask to the side of his opponent's head. He laughs as the man struggles to right his mask.

Uncle Burt steps into the ring to assist. The giant Russian grabs Uncle Burt's jacket lapels and jerks them over his shoulders to his elbows, trapping both of his arms. He spins Uncle Burt in circles, reaches deep into the back of his pants, and yanks his white jockey shorts up and out of his pants. Holding Uncle Burt up on his tiptoes by his underwear, the bald bully prances him around the ring, working the audience. When the wedgie effect peaks, he tosses his prop through the ropes. As Uncle Burt crashes to the floor, he turns his attention to the masked man.

Just as the rubberized mask is set straight, the Commie Bastard delivers a swift kick to the groin. When the masked man clutches his crotch, the dirty pinko pokes his fingers through the eyeholes. The masked man clasps his hands over the eyeholes as the referee steps in to stop the lunatic's illegal tactics. With one swipe, the Russian backhands the referee; his body goes limp, and he falls unconscious to the canvas. Turning back to the man in disguise, he moves in for the slaughter. Uncle Burt reaches in with his hand and catches the Russian's foot, tripping him to the canvas. He hurtles back to his feet, grabs the incapacitated shrouded man, and crucifies him to the ring by twisting the ropes around each arm.

The enemy's eyes find Uncle Burt at ground level. Uncle Burt realizes he's the next serving on the plate and makes a break for the ramp. The mad Red sprints across the ring and dives over the ropes. He somersaults through the air and lands with a belly splat on Uncle Burt's back. Uncle Burt lies motionless. With one jerk, the acrobat rips the underwear from Uncle Burt's still body.

A few rows of fans separate the boys from the front row. Pug detonates another gas blast, and the bodies part like it's the Running of the Bulls. The dirty pinko climbs the corner post and stands high on the ropes, waving the stained briefs above his head. As he bounds down from his pedestal, Pug's last gas bomb spreads, saturating the ring and the Commie Bastard's nostrils. He jerks his head away from the dirty drawers, pinches his nose, and holds the shorts out at arm's length as he marches across the ring toward his captive. Stopping in front of his trapped adversary, he rotates to each section of the coliseum, holding his nose and waving the underwear. When he completes the circle, he ties the underwear around his victim's head with the brown streak running down the middle of the mask.

The bald terrorist unties one arm and then the other from the ring's ropes. Grabbing a wrist with both hands, he whips the masquerader across the ring into the far side ropes. The ropes recoil the body back toward the center of the ring, where the Russian's extended arm is waiting. He clotheslines the masked man across the throat, clobbering the body to the ground with a vibrating thud. He grabs the limp stiff by the mask and arm, pulls him back to his feet, and flings him back into the ropes. This time, he dips and catches the rebounding frame with his lowered shoulder and launches his opponent skyward. Dogface's body does a complete flip; he lands flat on his back with a thunderous slam. The Russian dives on his adversary and covers his body. He looks at the unconscious referee and begins his own count.

"Dogface! Dogface! Dogface!"

The masked man pulls the underwear away from his eyes, so he can see where the chant is coming from. The Dover Dogs are ringside, shouting the nickname. Before Commie Bastard's hand can hit the mat for the final count, the bottom man flips the Russian off to the screams of the throng.

Others join in the "Dogface" chant.

Dogface stands, rips the underwear from his head, removes the cumbersome mask and tosses it aside. Dan stares at the boys. Fans make a mad scramble and fight for the discarded mask and underwear.

The Russian attacks and tries to spear Dan with a football tackle. Dan catches the blitzing linebacker with his arms, sits on his rump and kicks, catapulting the Sputnik across the ring to a crash landing.

More join in the "Dogface" chant.

The two combatants stare at each other. They walk and meet in the center of the ring. With confirming eyes, they clasp hands in a test of strength. Commie Bastard strikes first. His all-out assault bends Dan's hands back. Commie Bastard towers over the arched body, bowing it backward to its limit. He glares down into Dan's eyes and laughs when he feels Dan's bones compress. Their clinched hands begin vibrating. Dan collapses to a knee. Their arms shake uncontrollably. Dan drops on both knees. He holds. He has endured the jolt of the Russian's power surge. He straightens and strains one foot up and then the other. On his feet, he slowly bends the bald man's hands backward.

The "Dogface" chant pulsates.

The Commie Bastard's wrists are wrenched back beyond their limit, forcing him to his knees. He shakes his head in agony. The fans chant and stomp. Dan looks into the tortured face of the Russian, around the arena at the thousands of faces screaming for blood, and back at his defeated foe begging for mercy. Thinking he has won he releases the hands, and walks to his corner.

Commie Bastard waits for Dan to turn his back and walk a few steps before he grips his hammer and launches a sneak attack from the rear. The crowd roars. Dan waves to them in victory. From his corner, Uncle Burt screams and points. Dan instinctively spins and lowers his level, just in time to feel the breeze from the swinging hammer and catch the charging Bolshevik on his shoulder. He drives into the Commie Bastard and lifts him airborne. He twirls his feet toward the ceiling and pile drives the Russian, spiking his head into the canvas. Commie Bastard falls onto his back and writhes in pain, holding his head and neck with both hands and stomping the floor of the ring with both feet.

The bloodthirsty mob growls for more.

Commie Bastard rolls to his stomach and crawls. He grabs the lowest rope, pulls his body toward the perimeter, and straddles his leg over the edge. Just as the back foot is about to slide under the rope, Dan catches it and tugs. A hard yank suspends the Russian's body in the air as he clenches the bottom rope with both hands.

The "Dogface" chant echoes from the rafters.

Dan snatches the other foot and jerks until the hands release their grip. The Russian claws at the canvas as he's dragged center stage to the screams of the rabble. Dan lets go of the feet, jumps on the Commie Bastard, and wraps around him like a starving boa constrictor.

The crowd cheers at every stretch and twist Dan applies. He captures an arm and bends it across the Commie's back. Muscle striations tear down the shoulder. As far away as the upper cheap seats, oohs and aahs replace the cheers. The Russian cries out. The sinew holding his shoulder joint together crackles and pops as a chicken leg being ripped from its carcass. The sickened onlookers share gasps of shock. Dan drops the limp, lifeless arm and goes to work on the opposite upper limb. Parents cover their children's eyes. Adults turn their heads from the horror. Those who continue to watch are repulsed. Some vomit.

***

Police spearhead the entourage forging a path through the curious bystanders. Commie Bastard is wheeled out on a stretcher. His neck and head have been immobilized, and air casts enclose both arms. Two attendants push and steer while a third cares for the fallen bad guy.

A middle-aged man strides next to the rolling transport. His neat crew cut tops off his tanned, round face. A tailored designer suit fits his thick torso. His silk shirt hangs open to his navel, and a gold chain with an Italian horn bounces off his shaved chest. He gives a consoling pat with his right hand, jiggling the gold watch that dangles from his wrist. A ring with a twinkling diamond the size of a gumball encircles his pinkie. He breaks off and glides into the locker room.

"Great match," says Sid, the promoter, approaching Dan and Uncle Burt. "You were great, fabulous—the fan favorite. Your own cheering section and the 'Dogface' chant. Heeey, first-rate. And then you overcome almost impossible odds to win the bout. I couldn't have scripted it better. Not only did you win, but you sent my star, my main attraction, to the hospital."

"Do we still get paid?" asks Uncle Burt.

"Burt, that's your name, right?" Uncle Burt nods as Sid takes a check from his inside jacket pocket and holds it up with the thumb and index finger of each hand. "I did this as a favor for your cousin, and this is the thanks I get." The promoter shifts his eyes to Dan. "You were supposed to lose." Sid slowly tears the check down the middle and hands the two pieces to Uncle Burt. "Here's your check." He turns to leave, stops at the door, and walks back to Dan. "Oh, and this is for you," he says, removing a folded piece of paper from his coat pocket and handing it to Dan. "If you have any questions about this, read your contract. But you were great. If you ever want to consider a career change, I'll make you a star." Sid turns and slides out.

"What's that?" asks Uncle Burt.

Dan unfolds the piece of paper. "It's the ambulance bill," says Dan, lying down and covering his chest with his hand.

"What's the matter?"

"I feel funny. Something's not right."

"Should I get the doc?"

"What the fuck was the team doing here? I told you not to say anything to anybody."

"I didn't. Honest."

○○○○○○○○○○○○○○○○○○○○●●●●●●●●

19. Close to You

"QUIET. WE CALLED everybody to practice early to make a couple of announcements. It's all yours," says Joe, nodding to Bronk.

Bronk steps forward. "I ain't much for words, so here goes." He looks into the faces gathered around him. "First, I want to apologize for actin' like an ass and let you know it ain't gonna happen no more. Next, I went to visit Balls in the hospital and he and Dan bushwhacked me and made me the new captain."

Mini D asks above a collective grumbling, "Why you?"

"I don't rightly know. But I'm goin' down to fill Balls' spot in the lineup. I know me bein' captain ain't gonna sit so well with some of you, and I know I ain't gonna be able to be the captain Balls was. So, I asked Joe to partner up with me and maybe together we can ramrod this team. But the only thing we could agree on is we're sick and tired of Dan. The way we figure it is, we've had it with him, and now it's —"

"Payback time," interjects Joe.

"That's right. So we put together the —"

"Get Dan Plan," announces Joe.

"Right. We know none of us has a baby's chance of ridin' a bull if we try takin' Dan on one on one."

"So we team up. Us against him," says Joe.

"What d'yall say?" asks Bronk.

The room is silent.

"Well, you with us or not?" pressures Joe.

No one speaks.

"You gonna sit around gettin' saddle sores while he puts someone else in the hospital?" asks Bronk.

"Or out for the season? The next one could be you." Joe points at Mini D and then jabs his finger at the rest of the guys in the room. "Or you, or you, or you."

"So we team up. What's that going to do?" asks Kruger.

"That's the beauty of it." Joe steps to the front. "We pick our moments and act collectively and then Dan can't retaliate against any of us or single anyone out. Like at the wrestling match the other night—we acted together."

The boys consider the idea, discussing it among themselves.

Bronk seizes the moment, walks to the center of the group, extends his hand. "Together."

Joe follows, lays his hand on Bronk's and chants, "Get Dan. Get Dan. Get Dan…"

One by one, each team member joins the huddle, adds his hand to the stack, and joins in the chant. "Get Dan. Get DAN. GET DAN!"

***

Joe has the wrestling room door barely cracked open and peeks out. "Here he comes. Lights out and quiet." He shuts the door ever so gently. The lights go out, and a hush falls over the room. Everyone hears footsteps grow louder and louder as Dan nears the doorway. The doorknob turns and the door opens. Before he reaches the light switch, the door closes behind him and casts the room into darkness.

In unison, the team shouts, "Rough House!" and jumps Dan.

***

The training room is strewn with bodies. Blood drips from noses and mouths. Every wrestler sports an ice bag somewhere on his bruised body. Some have two ice bags. The entire team is spread around the training room, on the floor, on every training table and in the hot tub.

Carter enters, drawing a couple of other basketball players behind him. He dances to Joe, who is stretched out on an examination table next to the ultrasound and electrical stimulation devices.

"Give it up," orders Carter.

Joe exaggerates a look over his left shoulder, his right shoulder and then back at Carter. "You talking to me?"

"You're in my spot."

"I don't recall seeing your name."

"Tell him, Jas."

"Sorry, the head trainer says basketball players get treated first, and the doctor says Carter gets this treatment every day before practice."

Joe sneers at Carter as he slides off the table.

"Sorry. You can have it back when he's done," says Jas.

"You don't have to apologize to him." Carter pulls off his shirt, lowers his shorts slightly and lies on his stomach.

Jas squirts a white lotion on her hand and warms it by briskly rubbing her hands together. After spreading it over Carter's lower back and upper rump, she wipes the excess lotion from her fingers, picks up the ultrasonic massager, and rotates the head of the massager in tiny circles, repeatedly kneading the area covered with white cream.

"Tell me when," she instructs Carter as she adjusts the intensity level with her other hand.

"Right there," replies Carter with an eye to Joe. "Oh baby, now that's what I'm talking about."

Dan bounces in laughing. "You guys, that was great. I haven't had so much fun in years. Heh—heh, unbelievable." He examines the ice bags and chuckles. "They didn't have ice in my day—just tape." Dan runs down the doctor. "Hey Doc, you got a minute? I need to talk to you."

"Sure, Dan, have a seat in my office, and I'll be in when I finish up." Dan strolls past the team, down the corridor, and into the doctor's office.

Everyone's eyes focus on Joe and Bronk.

"Great idea you guys came up with," complains Dickie, lifting the ice bag from his swollen, closed eye.

"Yeah, if we team up, he can't get all of us," mumbles Kruger, wiggling his loose tooth.

"Hey, we got our shots in," barks Bronk, bleeding from both nostrils.

"Yeah, you really smashed his knuckles with your nose. He'll probably never play the piano again," quips Dickie.

"This is only the first round," adds Joe, "we just have to get smarter next time."

Carter chimes in, "Seems funny that the guy doing all the talking about getting Dan is the only one without a mark or an ice bag."

Everyone examines Joe and thinks, *He's right.*

A beeper goes off. "Your ten minutes are up," says Jas, wiping the head of the massager clean with a towel.

"You sure? That didn't seem like ten minutes."

"I set the timer," shrugs Jas, winking at Joe.

"Jas, you give good sound, baby," compliments Carter, "but we're going to have to invest in a new timer." Jas removes the excess cream from his back with a towel.

"Ten minutes? Carter only lasted ten minutes?" giggles Dickie.

"Basketball players are creampuffs," digs Kruger.

Joe approaches Carter. "Creampuff—that's a good name for you. It fits. Now, let a man show you how it's done."

"You wrestlers probably wouldn't know what to do with a woman. You're into grabbing and sweating on each other," says Carter.

Kruger drops his ice bag on the floor, pushes off his table, and barges across the room. "All you ballers do is play with balls—big, sweaty balls."

Carter's basketball buddies cock their bodies, ready to jump in. Jas puts her hands together in prayer and wedges herself between the boys.

Joe stabs his hand in Kruger's chest, and he drops anchor. "Hey Carter, what's this called?" Carter looks over his shoulder. Joe nudges Kruger's shoulder.

"I don't know. What's that called?" asks Carter.

"A technical foul." All the wrestlers laugh.

"Creampuff," scoffs Kruger.

Carter jumps from the table and spins Joe around. "Okay, all you wrestlers." From behind he hooks his right arm under Joe's right arm and cups his hand on the back of Joe's neck. "What's this called?"

"Half nelson."

Using his left arm, Carter scoops Joe's other arm and interlocks the fingers of both hands behind his neck. "And what's this called?"

"Full nelson."

With both of Joe's arms restrained, Carter asks, "And what's this called?" and starts hip thrusting Joe's rear end. Joe goes crazy and rips free. The wrestlers and the basketball players stand toe to toe.

"I don't know. What's that called?"

"A Dover wrestler," says Carter, diving back on the table as he snickers. The round ballers break out laughing.

"C'mon, off the bench. It's my turn," Joe shoves Carter's shoulder.

"Uh-uh. Now I get my electrical stimulation."

"He's right," says Jas, moving as fast as she can. She peels and sticks a series of electrodes at strategic spots around Carter's lower back.

"Jas, could you come in here a minute?" yells the Doctor from his office.

Jas yells back, "I'm coming."

"You're not even breathing hard, baby," teases Carter.

Jas connects a wire from the electrotherapy stimulator to each electrode, sets the pulse rate and timer, pushes the start button, and prances off.

Carter looks back at Joe. "What're you staring at?" He points at himself. "You want some more of this? You can wait in line with the rest of your homos." Carter puts his head down as if he's taking a nap.

Everyone looks at Joe glaring at the back of Carter's head. Joe rolls his eyes and winks at the wrestlers, and nods toward the basketball players. He returns to Carter with a boyish smile. Reaching down to the stimulator, he spins the dial to high voltage. The juiced pulse jolts Carter into the air. He screams and reaches, trying to pull the electrodes from his fried skin. Before he can get to the patches, the next pulse bounces him off the training table and onto the floor. The wrestlers surround him, forming a barricade between him and his teammates.

Joe stands over Carter convulsing on the floor. "He looks about done. Who's next?"

***

Kruger stands shirtless over the counter, slicing and dicing with the speed and skill of a sushi master. He uses a giant knife to scrape chunks of mushrooms over the edge of the counter and into a bowl. Oil pops and sizzles as he dumps the contents of the bowl into one of four skillets cooking on the stove. He lowers the heat a smidge, sprinkles an herb over the mushrooms, and adds a dash of seasoning. He leans over the skillet, smells his concoction, and adds a pinch of one last ingredient before returning to the prepping station and working on the next item.

He is in constant, effortless motion, at one with the cooking process as he checks, smells, tastes, adjusts, cleans, and cuts. The ballet halts when the front door opens. A magnificent white German shepherd scrambles from his resting place; his paws slip, slide, and scrape as he tries to get a grip on the slick wood floor. Barking up a storm, the white blitzkrieg descends on the opening door.

"It's okay, Kaiser," shouts Kruger, "it's just Mini D."

"Oh man, it smells great," says Mini D, petting Kaiser and cradling a bottle of wine in his other arm like a football. "Wow, your girlfriend's got a nice place."

"She's not my girlfriend. You're just in time," says Kruger, handing over a wine bottle opener. "Here—open that. The girls ran up to the store. They'll be back any minute."

Mini D works on opening the wine but watches the white shepherd. "Kaiser looks great, but Tarzan would chop him up."

"Between a German and a midget Mexican, my money is on the German."

"Hey, it isn't the size of the dog in the fight; it's the size of the fight in the dog."

"Yeah, well the only way Tarzan would chop up Kaiser is if Tarzan is packing a machete and a machine gun."

"So, what do you think of Dan making Bronk captain?"

"I stopped trying to figure Dogface out a long time ago."

"I wish I could've been captain. That would've topped off college for me. After this, I just become another little person."

"You know, when I get out of college, I want to have the big-gest, bad-dest, and best-test Harley-Davidson shop in this part of the country."

"I'll probably end up working with my dad in landscaping," says Mini D, popping the cork from the bottle, "but I'd like to coach."

"You'd be a good coach. I wish I could've had a coach like you in high school."

"My high school coach flunked me in gym class and made me ineligible my senior year. The year before, I beat the guy who won state, and he got a full ride to Oklahoma."

"What a prick," says Kruger, adjusting the flame level. "But hey, if he didn't do that, we might not be teammates now."

"Yeah, I'd probably be at another school. I got to hand it to Dan; he got me in JC and called me all the time. He coached me on how to study and made sure I was doing what I needed to be doing. He got me to believe in myself."

"I'll give that to him. My senior year I got accused of rape, but it was consensual. The school kicked me off the team. After I missed the state tournament, the girl dropped the charges. All the colleges lost interest but Dan. But he's still an asshole."

"He made me tough."

"My old man made me tough," says Kruger, checking the time, "but he's still an asshole. He always told me, 'If you're going to be a tough guy, one day you're going to run into somebody a little tougher around the next corner.' That's the way I look at it—you have to be ready."

"You're right. My high school coach was a prick."

"So's my old man. He was always getting drunk and coming after me or my mom. One day, I'll never forget was my fifteenth birthday. My mom and I had cake, and she got me a Harley-Davidson Super Glide model. I spent the whole day putting it together and painting it. A few hours later, dad comes home crocked, pulls me out of bed and lays into me, throws the rest of my cake against the wall, smashes my model, then goes after my mom. He's dragging her around the house by her hair, and I decided that was enough. I beat the crap out of him and called the police."

"What'd they do?"

"They put him in jail for the night. But here's the weird part. I had to go to court and testify against my dad. And after that, everything changed. Things were okay with him; we tolerated each other. But it was never the same with Mom. She stopped talking to me. Even today when I go visit, she just sits there and won't say a word." Kruger pauses and checks the time again. "If the girls aren't here in five minutes, we're eating without them."

***

During dinner, only the sounds of Kruger, Mini D, and their dates feasting can be heard. Several empty wine bottles are scattered around the white table cloth, mingled with the fine china, gourmet food, and candles. Only one piece of meat remains on the plate in the center of the table. Mini D and Kruger stab it simultaneously with their forks. They glare at each other; neither one is willing to give in. They begin a tug of war. As the meat slides from one side of the plate to the other, the field of battle escalates.

The girls stand and back up to the wall. With one hand free, the boys grab anything within reach and begin an all-out assault, pummeling each other with food, napkins, silverware, and dishes. Kruger runs out of things to grab, and when he ducks a candleholder, Mini D gets an advantage on the meaty prize. Rather than concede defeat, Kruger grabs under the edge of the table and charges, pushing Mini D back and pinning him against the wall. As Kruger lifts and throws, Mini D loses his footing and falls. He ends up sprawled out on the floor under the overturned table. His bellowing laughter breaks the stunned silence. Kruger tosses the table aside and helps his buddy to his feet. Mini D rips the steak and hands half to Kruger as they walk to the front porch and let the girls clean up.

"To hell with that motorcycle shop—you should open a restaurant."

Kruger puts his arm around Mini D's neck. "I can talk to you. I've learned a lot from you, and I want to give you something."

"You don't have to give me anything. I got you as a buddy, and you make me laugh. That's enough."

"No, I want to."

"You did."

"No, seriously, there has to be something I can give you. What do you want? I mean what is it that makes your heart soar and turns you on?"

Mini D thinks and states, "I want to be captain."

"I want you to know I'm your buddy—and when I say I'm your buddy, I am your buddy anytime, anywhere, no matter what."

A scared look comes over Kruger's face. He jumps to his feet, jerks his pants down to his knees and begins checking his crotch. He frantically runs his fingers through his pubic hair while his eyes wildly search.

"What is it?" asks Mini D.

"Every time I get an itch, I think of those two girls."

"What, you think you got crabs?"

"Maybe. It drives me fucking nuts."

"I heard you can use Raid."

"Raid? And it gets rid of crabs?"

"Yeah, this guy told me it worked on crabs."

"Bullshit."

"He said he used it and got rid of them."

"I'm not spraying Raid on my cock."

***

Dressed in sweatshirts, shorts and running shoes, Joe and Bronk walk shoulder to shoulder with matching strides.

"This is the best conditioning run you can do," says Joe.

"I thought you were gonna show me how to start cuttin' weight?"

"Don't worry about that. I'll show you how to sweat it off tomorrow."

"Why we walkin'?"

"We have to get to the starting point," responds Joe, looking over his shoulder.

"Where's that?"

"Just up ahead."

They walk. Joe's eyes constantly check around in all directions.

Bronk wonders, "So when you're ready to wrassle somebody, what d'ya think about?"

"I like to screw with a guy's head. He expects me to shoot, I slap him up the side of his head. When he expects me to bang his head, then I shoot. What about you?"

"I just look a guy over and ask myself, 'Can I kick his ass in a fight?' And if he looks like a wuss, no way I'm gonna lose to him."

"Okay, we're getting close. You have to be careful. If they get tipped off we're coming, they'll try some sort of ambush," warns Joe, scanning to his left and right.

"What? Who?" asks Bronk.

"We're getting near the basketball house."

"So."

"You know, Carter," says Joe, walking into the street. "C'mon, let's put some distance between us and these houses."

Bronk follows Joe to the center of the street. "What's with you and Carter?"

"We were freshmen together. The school made a big hoopla over him. He was a high school all-American in football, basketball and track. He was going to single-handedly save Dover sports. He immediately became the big jock on campus. They called him King Carter."

"Yeah, so?"

"We were in a class together. He missed a couple of classes and asked if he could borrow my notes to catch up. I said sure and loaned him my notes. And he wouldn't give them back. He stole them. He screwed me over, so I screwed his girlfriend, and it's been on between us ever since." Joe comes to an abrupt halt and stops Bronk with his arm. He cautiously examines would-be hiding places, then proceeds. "The best part is I became a college all-American before he did. Okay, we're here. Be ready."

Joe posts his hands on the rock fence surrounding The King's Court and vaults over. Bronk tags along. Joe takes precise steps, counts, and stops at a measured spot from the fence. He yells up at the second-floor window, "Hey Carter, why aren't you at the bar-b-cue?" He whispers to Bronk, "Be ready."

"Ready for what?"

Carter appears at the window, opens it, and sticks his head out. "Well if it isn't the best of the Village People. What are you yapping about?"

"I said, why aren't you at the bar-b-cue?"

"Barbecue?"

"They can't start until the rump roast is there."

"Now I know he's the cowboy, but which one are you?"

"Me? I thought you knew. I'm the all-American."

"You may act like an all-American and talk like an all-American, but that doesn't fool anyone, 'cause you really are a homo."

"Thought the high-and-mighty king would like to see if he can catch a lowly all-American."

"I already had my workout today."

"Geez, must be tough. What'd you do? Bounce that big, heavy basketball a hundred, maybe two hundred times?"

"I'd run you into the ground, gay boy."

"Wanna bet?"

"Bet what?"

"You catch us, either one of us, and the wrestling team has to show up at the basketball game dressed any way you say. And if we outrun you, the basketball team has to show up at the wrestling match dressed any way we say."

"I'll be right down."

"Okay, they're going to come at us from all directions."

"What?" asks Bronk.

The front door flies open and three bodies bolt out. Three other basketballers dash around from one end of the house, and four more race around from the other end.

Joe shouts, "Run!" He springs into a sprint, and without breaking stride, he hurdles the fence, soars through the air, and hits the ground running full speed. Bronk has to slow and makes an awkward leap, falling a few steps behind. Joe looks back; all ten round-ballers jump a section of the fence, converging on Bronk. "RUN!" screams Joe.

Bronk puts the spurs to it and gallops up next to Joe. "What are we running for?

"Running is where they're best; you got to sprint as hard as you can for the first half-mile or so."

"Why don't we just stop and kick their butts?"

"They think they're better runners than us because they run up and down a basketball court. We beat them at their game, and they're our bitches."

"I'd still rather stop and kick their butts."

"They're going to start taking turns trying to run us down. Whenever one breaks out, we have to sprint hard."

**

Uncle Burt drags a local out of his place by the arm and onto the sidewalk in front of the River Bar. Pointing at a sign hanging in his window, he commands, "Read it." The townie studies the sign. "Out loud," orders Uncle Burt, pointing at the sign. "What does it say?"

"Free beer tomorrow," reads the townie.

"That's right. Free beer TOMORROW."

"But that's what it said yesterday," complains the townie.

Uncle Burt shakes his head in disbelief. "And that's what it's going to say tomorrow."

A police cruiser slows, pulls to the curb, and parks in front of the River Bar. The officer driving stays put as the back door swings open and the police chief steps from the rear seat with Doc's black satchel.

Joe flies around the corner, screaming over his shoulder, "Faster. Another one's breaking."

Everyone backs up, clearing a path for Joe. Bronk follows, and a step behind him charges a taller, wiry guy who reaches out and hooks his fingers in the neck of Bronk's sweatshirt. Bronk feels his hand.

Joe shouts, "You going to let a wuss catch you?"

Bronk grits his teeth and does his bull charge, ripping the sweatshirt from his body. The rest of the basketball team rounds the corner and gives chase. Another one breaks from the pack and sprints forward as they pass the threesome.

The police chief strolls to Uncle Burt. "What the hell's that all about?"

"Beats me."

Everyone watches the racers' heels and elbows pumping as they sprint down the sidewalk, then turn and disappear around the corner.

Uncle Burt pats the townie on the back and tells him, "Come back tomorrow, and we'll talk about it." The townie wanders down the walk, shaking his head and grumbling to himself.

Uncle Burt looks at the police chief and motions to the sign in the window. "He doesn't get the joke." The chief reads the sign and cracks a smile. Lifting the satchel to eye level, he signals his reason for the visit. He enters and sits at the empty bar. Uncle Burt follows. A few students play pool in the back.

"What can I get you, Chief?" asks Uncle Burt, manning the bar.

The chief sets the bag on the bar. "Depends on how bad you want the contents of this."

"This the stuff?" Uncle Burt opens the bag and looks in at the confiscated videotape and Doc's drug stash. "I heard the video was missing."

"It was. From the evidence room."

"What can I get you to drink?"

"I'll have a draft and a shot of your good stuff."

"Have you watched it?" asks the chief as Uncle Burt pours the draft.

"Watched what?"

"The video."

"No." Uncle Burt slides the glass of beer on the bar.

"It was missing because the boys in the station were passing it around," says the chief, lifting the glass of beer and swigging half of it in one gulp.

"You mean they were watching it?" Uncle Burt takes a bottle from a cabinet under the bar and pours two shots.

"Are you sure you haven't seen it?" pries the police chief.

Uncle Burt shakes his head. "Never knew about it until you impounded it."

"Boys said it was the best porno they've ever seen. Said they'd watch it with their girlfriends and wives. Every one of them got horny and had to have it and couldn't get enough."

"No shit," says Uncle Burt, holding the videocassette at eye level and staring in deep thought.

"That boy's got a talent. I had a hell of a time getting it back. Now, there's nothing illegal about that, unless he doesn't have the girl's permission, or she's not of age."

"I wouldn't know about any of that." Uncle Burt and the chief click glasses and down their shots. Uncle Burt pours two more. A pregnant silence rests between the two men.

"What about the black bag?" asks Uncle Burt.

"Sent it to the lab and had it analyzed, but they couldn't really find anything that's technically illegal. But we know who his father is, and more than likely, it's something you need a prescription for."

"I've been giving this some thought."

"So have I."

"You know the arrangement I have with your men."

"They've done very well with the sports wager tips you've given them."

"Good. I think I can do the same for you. What I suggest is you hang on to this stuff until you parlay my information to a certain amount and then you hand over the bag and tape to me."

"That won't be necessary. You can have Doc's bag and the tape today. You can do whatever you want with that bag, but you hang on to that tape, and after those kids graduate, I get the tape back."

"That's it? And we're off the hook?"

"There is one more thing…"

***

"We need a moist washcloth, the larger the better," Jas explains. "You have to wring it out so it's damp but not wet."

She sits on Bronk's bed. He comes out shaking a damp washcloth back to its square form. "I don't get what this has to do with anythin'."

Jas takes the damp cloth, drapes it over the back of both her hands, and tosses it. "This simulates pizza dough." The whirling cloth spins up and hovers like a flying saucer before dropping and landing back on its launching pad. She repeats the demonstration. As she gets her feel, each toss is better than the one before.

"This will give you a sense for tossing and catching real dough. It's easier just to do it than explain it. Here you go," she says, spinning the washrag through the air to Bronk.

He makes an awkward catch and repositions the damp fabric on the back of his hands.

"Go on," encourages Jas, "you can't make a mistake."

Bronk launches his first effort. It flies off his hands across the room. "Thought you couldn't make a mistake."

"I guess I forgot who was tossing it."

Bronk retrieves the cloth and readies another try.

"Try using both hands equally," instructs Jas. This time the cloth barely leaves his hands and falls back lopsided.

"Okay, put a little more spin on it and toss it higher."

Bronk repositions it on the back of his hands and tosses. It spins up and to the right, coming down a couple of feet away. He lunges and snatches the errant facecloth midair. It's not as simple as Jas makes it look.

"You have the idea. Now practice." Jas watches. "So when are you going to start cutting weight?"

"Already started."

"How much have you lost?"

"Nothing."

"You got four days to make weight. What's your plan?"

"Joe said not to worry 'bout it, that he'd show me how to sweat it off."

"So, you hear about Dan?"

"No. What?" He tries tossing the cloth again.

"Remember when he had the doctor check him?"

"Yep."

"They're sending him to the Cleveland Clinic to see a heart specialist."

"His ticker 'bout to peter out?"

"Something's going on." She watches a twirling washcloth liftoff and return. "I think you got the idea. Now it's my turn." She stands and walks to the window.

"What's your hurry?"

"It's almost dark," says Jas, climbing out the window. "We're going to run out of light."

Jas and Bronk sit near the top of the roof outside his bedroom window. Two rectangular cinder blocks positioned side by side form four hollow squares below and to the right, just above the gutter. The security light on the side of the house provides enough brightness. Above, the stars sparkle. Jas tries to unloop the rope from the cinder blocks with a wiggle on her end of the rope. After a few failed attempts, Bronk covers her hand with his and firmly wraps his fingers around hers. With a flick of his wrist, the rope flips free of the blocks.

"This here angle mirrors ropin' a calf from a horse," says Bronk, his breath billowing in the cold night air. "Course, we're not movin'."

"You got a horse?" asks Jas, pulling in and retrieving the rope.

"A herd of 'em."

"No way."

"Yeah, on my daddy's ranch."

"You live on a ranch?" asks Jas, twirling the lariat above her head.

"More'n three thousand acres," says Bronk, watching the lasso loop drop and encircle the concrete blocks. "Geez, you're a natural."

"Growing up with seven older brothers. Sometimes I think I'm a guy in a girl's body."

"Most guys can't do it their first try, let alone six times in a row. Now all you gotta learn is two wraps and a hooey."

"Two wraps and a hooey?"

"Two wraps and a hooey," explains Bronk, "is how you tie the calf's three legs together." He enacts the maneuver with his hands. "Two wraps and a hooey."

"So, you got a girlfriend?"

"Yeah."

"You never said anything about a girlfriend."

"No one ever asked."

"What's her name?"

"Shoe."

"Shoe? Yeah, right. What kind of name is Shoe?"

"Kind that's fittin'. You want to hear our story?"

"I'm all ears."

"There's two parts: how we met and how we started hangin' out."

"How'd you meet?"

"Like most things that come along in life, it was unexpected. Like findin' a flower growin' in a field of weeds. She was a real hard case, an abused horse that—"

"A horse?" asks Jas with a sharp elbow nudge to Bronk's ribs.

"My sweetheart," says Bronk with a smile. "She had a reputation of being a herd bully, so none of the local boarding stables would take her. My daddy agreed to put her up until they could find her a home. She looked like crow bait, and she'd just as soon as bite ya as look at ya. Anytime anybody'd come too close, she'd turn around and threaten to kick, and if she couldn't turn, she'd pin her ears back flat to her head and start strikin' and bitin'. The guys all called her psycho bitch. Daddy's the only one who could go near her. He'd feed her and ride her. She'd be penned up in the horse hoosegow if it weren't for him. He's got a way with horses. Granny says ever since he was a runt, he's had a gift of understandin' horses. Communicates with 'em just by the way he moves and looks."

"A horse whisperer."

"Yeah, right," says Bronk, a little surprised and impressed she knew the term. "Daddy taught me how to handle a horse as good as anybody, 'cept for him, of course."

"My uncle has a knack with dogs. People are always coming to him with problem pets."

"Horses are wise in their own way, but they're not pets like dogs or cats. The nature of the horse is to be a part of the herd and to seek a bond. They're a lot like people in that way. When they feel safe and secure, they let you in. And when they do, you should be kind and gentle, and patient. Some are understanding and sensitive like women and some are mean and aggressive like men, but they're all innocent like children. Daddy used to have me sit and watch the herd for hours. You watch a herd real careful and you see how they interact. There's a pecking order, you know. Get to know who the bullies are, who's submissive, and who the true leader is. They're always the most balanced, the smartest, and for the most part, the calmest, but also the fiercest when they need to be."

"Okay, let's hear part two. How did she become your girlfriend?"

Bronk smiles, remembering. "We were out roundin' up cattle, bringin' 'em down from the summer pastures when she threw a horseshoe. She had tender hooves and came up lame. Daddy handed me the reins and had me walk her back while he took my horse, and him and the boys continued the roundup. So I start headin' her back to the barn, expectin' the first chance she gets, she's gonna take a mouthful, but for some reason she let me walk next to her.

"An hour or so down the trail, we began losing light, and a frigid wind kicked up and blew in a storm. The temperatures plunged. I wasn't dressed for it, and the cold penetrated my face and hands. It wasn't too long before they started stingin' and burnin'. It got to the point where I couldn't take it anymore. I was walkin' into the wind with my head down and tuggin'. My hands were frozen to the reins, and I was wonderin' if I was ever goin' to make it back to the house when 'bout that time she came up next to me. Expectin' to git bit, kicked or somethin', I turned and looked up at her, and she lowered her head and blew her breath in my face. To this day, I can still feel her warm, sweet smellin' breath. Her muzzle barely touched my skin. I cupped my hands around my face, and she kept takin' deep breaths and lettin' out the warmth. After a few minutes, the feelin' returned to my face and hands. And when we started movin' again, she took the lead, shieldin' me from the wind.

"I got a deep, clear insight that night. I don't know how she knew to do what she did, but Daddy always said if you open your heart, you can see deep into a horse's soul. Well, that night that horse opened her heart and saw deep into my soul. By the time we got back to the house, I felt so much for that mare that I decided to buy her. I didn't have the money, so I had to make weekly payments.

"I groomed her twice, sometimes three times a day, bought her some alfalfa hay and fattened her up a little, and she turned out beautiful. She got to likin' bein' groomed and got used to me bein' around, but she was still a little standoffish. One day, we was just hangin' out; I was hand grazin' her on a long line in some clover, and she walked to me and lowered her head to right about my chest level." Bronk places his hand over his heart. "And just like that," he says with a snap of his fingers, "we belonged to each other."

"Now, mind you, when I bought her, I didn't know her name, so I called her Shoe. 'Cause she threw her horseshoe. Funny thing," says Bronk with tiny smile lines accenting his blue eyes, "when I finally got her papers—it took almost a year—I looked at her name, and it was 'New Pair of Shoes.'"

"You're kidding," says Jas, hanging on his every word. She looks at him, wanting the feelings of the moment to last.

"I was mighty proud of that," says Bronk, looking at Jas with a twinkle in his eye. "You know, like it was meant to be."

Jas can't take her eyes from his. "What's she look like?"

"A big sorrel mare. Well, big for a quarter horse. She stands close to sixteen hands. Broad muscular chest and hindquarters, extremely quick and agile with a really long flaxen mane and tail. I like her mane flowin' so I don't roach it."

"Could you say that again in English?"

"Okay," laughs Bronk, "I'll interpret. She's a light reddish color with a pale yellow mane and tail that turns even lighter durin' the sunny summer days. Roachin' is when you buzz their mane. Saves groomin' it. But I don't mind brushing it."

"How much is a hand?"

"'Bout four inches."

"That's just five feet."

"It's five feet to her withers."

"Here we go again."

"That's the top of her shoulder."

"So it doesn't include her neck and head?"

"That's right."

"Is she pretty?"

"Oh yeah, she's pleasin' to the eye, like you."

Jas turns away, almost blushing.

"She's got four white socks, a short, elegant head with perfect facial markin's. A white diamond that's not too big or too small right between the most expressive eyes you ever seen. And on her muzzle, there's a snip in the shape of a heart."

"A snip?"

"A white mark between the nostrils, like that freckle," says Bronk, touching the tip of her nose. Their eyes catch and hold fast. Ever so slowly, his fingertip traces around the edge of her fleshy lips without touching. She can feel the energy. He traces her eyes with his. "Boy, I thought Shoe had expressive eyes." Caught in her trance, his hands stroke her hair and cradle her head. His lips are drawn to hers. Slowly, his half-opened lips tenderly touch hers; he closes his lips, then gradually opens them again and moves away. Before she has a chance to look, Bronk moves forward again and gives her a real kiss. When he feels her return it, he moves away, looks into her eyes and then softly, gently kisses her again.

Jas breaks and turns away, touching her mouth. "Wow," she sighs, "will you look at that moon."

Unable to sever the connection, Bronk studies her, wondering what she's thinking. Overwhelmed by a strange and surprising feeling, he ponders, *I wonder if she's feelin' the same.* He forces himself to pull his eyes away from her face. They sit unaffected by the cold night air.

"You can almost see the man in the moon's profile," observes Jas.

"Uh-huh."

"I don't believe in accidents. You ever think about why Shoe came into your life?"

"Honesty. She taught me honesty. You can't lie to a horse," replies Bronk, running his eyes down her profile. "And you gotta let 'em be who they are. They have to know they can trust you. They have to know they can trust you, no matter what."

Jas stares up at the silvery sliver of the new moon, breathes deeply and begins trembling.

Bronk puts his arm around her shoulder and squeezes her close. Gazing up at the slender crescent moon, he continues, "The night before I left for school I decided to go for a final ride, you know, like a good-bye. I rode her bareback, as I didn't want anything to come between us. We rode for a while, and I was thinkin' 'bout how tough it's goin' to be sayin' good-bye, when suddenly she reared and threw me. I landed hard on my back, and it knocked the wind out of me. Instead of runnin' off, she walked over, licked my face, and then just looked at me. It was as if she was sayin', 'I can't believe you're leavin' me.' And she stayed right there with her head by mine 'til I could get up."

Jas smiles, tilts her head, and rests it on Bronk's shoulder. He smiles at her, brushes the hair from her face, and they share the intoxicating night sky.

Bronk points and his finger traces the length of the shining sliver. "The moon was just like that, that last night." He cracks a smile. "Shoe's probably lookin' at this moon as we speak. Shoe, I hope you're happy. Been thinkin' 'bout you. I miss you."

A light burst ignites over the crescent moon, and a shooting star streaks a fiery tail across the night sky and extinguishes.

"Oh my God, make a wish," implores Jas. "You have to make a wish."

Bronk smiles, "I got everything I want."

"Go on."

Bronk hugs Jas and wishes, *I hope this lasts.*

○○○○○○○○○○○○○○○○○○○○●●●●●●●

20. Misery

"NOW THE PLAN is you do three workouts a day," explains Joe, tossing a gear bag on the bench next to Bronk. "You track how much weight you lose in a workout so you know how much you can eat and drink. But, you're only allowed to eat and drink what you lose in your workout and no more. Let's say you lose five pounds. That means you can eat and drink five pounds of stuff. You do that after each workout, and you'll drift two to three pounds a day."

Bronk strips to his underwear as he listens.

"The key," instructs Joe, "is not to starve yourself. You need to eat and drink so you have the energy to work out. You do this every day this week, and after your last workout on Thursday, you should be on weight."

"But how am I gonna feel?" asks Bronk, unlocking his locker.

"Like shit. But once you get your weight down, you keep it down. You have to work out before you can eat and drink. That's the secret. Once you're down, you stay a workout or two within weight the rest of the season until your body adjusts to its new weight and your strength and stamina return."

"You sure I can do this?"

"I know you can," says Joe, unzipping the bag. "How you dress allows you to drop the most weight in the shortest time and expend the least energy doing it." He pulls a set of long thermal underwear out of his gear bag and hands it to Bronk. "First, you need a form-fitting undergarment that covers your whole body. The first layer is very important."

Bronk slips into the long sleeve shirt, tucks it into his ankle-length bottoms, and pulls a set of thermal socks over his calves. Only his face and hands are exposed.

"Next come the plastics." Joe hands over a rubber suit.

Bronk slides into a heavy-duty two-piece rubberized plastic suit that covers the thermals.

"Now, it's important to prevent air from getting under the plastics, so you tape the ends." Joe wraps athletic tape around Bronk's wrists and ankles, sealing the plastics. "Next, you want to press the plastic tight to the body, so you put on another form-fitting sweat suit. This is where it's nice to have a turtleneck. And then you cover that with a heavy-duty set of sweats with a hooded top you can tie. The last layer consists of your running shoes, gloves, a knit cap and a down jacket. Now, you are a human furnace, and you will never forget this experience for the rest of your life."

Joe pulls Bronk's hood over his knit cap, pulls the string tight, and ties it. "You're all set."

Bronk looks as if he's about to go for a space walk. Joe advises, "The trick is to break a sweat and then keep it going and stay in the suit for as long as you can. With the workout I'm going to show you, you can drop five or six pounds—sometimes more—in less than an hour."

Bronk runs in oblong circles around the wrestling room. Joe shouts, "You have to run for twenty minutes straight. This is like throwing wood on the fire. You break a sweat and turn the kindling into a big, hot bonfire." Joe adjusts the thermostat to its highest setting and then places a cup of ice on top of it.

***

Joe jogs next to Bronk. "Okay, twenty minutes are up. You can walk." Bronk nods his wet, beet-red face and slows to a walk. "Now, you walk for thirty seconds, and then you do sprawls for thirty seconds."

Joe watches the time and yells, "Sprawls." Bronk sprawls until Joe yells, "Walk."

They repeat the sequence until Bronk's body begins to break down from the heat, and he cannot complete the sprawls. Joe instructs him to replace the sprawls with running in place. They do that until Bronk can't do anymore.

"C'mon, push," commands Joe.

"I can't. It's too hot."

"Focus on the exercise."

"I gotta take some of this stuff off."

Joe points to the wrestling mat. "Get down."

Bronk gets down on his hands and knees. Joe drops on top of him and grabs hold. "Okay, try to get away."

Bronk moves around for a few minutes until he collapses. "I'm done."

Joe works him over. "C'mon, keep moving."

Bronk lays there like a lump. "I gotta git out of this." He begins peeling off his gloves.

Joe points to a spot with urgency. "Quick, lay down right here."

Bronk lies down and removes his hood and knit cap. Joe lifts the edge of the wrestling mat, rolls Bronk up like a burrito inside a foam tortilla, and sits on him. "Now the boiler. When you feel your sweat stopping, do some isometrics. That'll keep it going. And when you can't take it anymore, holler and I'll take you out."

"I can't take any more."

"Relax and breathe," coaches Joe. "Relax and breathe."

"I want out now."

"First time is always the hardest. It gets easier."

* * *

Pump, Ben, and Adam jog past the college golf course and across the athletic fields to a cluster of dormitories. A couple of coeds exit a side door. Pump leaps a set of steps and catches the door. They bound up the stairs to the top floor and run down the hall.

One girl screams, "Man on the floor!"

Girls in bathrobes, towels, and bras and panties scurry about. Pump and the boys stop in front of an open door and run in place as they peer in. They nod their approval to the girls in their undies, dash down the hall, and take a detour through the girls' showers to a serenade of screams. They run back out, dart to the end of the hall, and rush down the stairwell, bolting for the 'emergency only' exit door.

"Hey, this is for emergencies," exclaims Ben.

Pump answers, "This is an—"

A hail of brushes, shoes, and books rain down on them. They sprint out the door, down the street, and around the corner. After about a block, they slow their sprint to a jog. A shapely figure bikes past the threesome, standing and pumping to increase her speed. When her speed is up, she stops pedaling and sits.

"Oh, what I wouldn't give to be that bicycle seat," observes Pump.

"Is that all you think about?" asks Ben.

Pump takes off sprinting. He looks back. "I think I'm beating the two of you."

Ben and Adam take off. The race is on. Behind them, a squad of campus police cars swarm the dormitory.

***

Sweat droplets rain from Bronk's brow, nose, and chin, forming a puddle on the mat under his face. He remains rolled in the mat as Joe sits on top. Bronk yells, "Let me out."

Joe unrolls Bronk. "You know, people pay hundreds of dollars for this at a spa. They call it a heat wrap."

Bronk's freed arms claw at his drenched, dripping clothing. He tears his garments away from his body like a man on fire. He can't get the tape around his wrists to cooperate and starts biting and ripping at the tape with his teeth.

"I have all the showers turned on hot. Let's go in there and undress. It'll be like a relaxing steam shower."

***

"Gorni. Gorni," shouts Dan.

"He's already going with someone," says Uncle Burt.

Dan does a critical search around the wrestling room. "Dickie, get on Kruger."

"He's too big."

"Practice your legs."

"Third period," shouts Uncle Burt. "Three minutes left. Bottom man set..." All the bottom wrestlers move to a set position on their hands and knees. "Top man cover..." The top wrestlers wrap an arm around the down man's waist and place their other hand on the near side elbow. When everyone is set, Uncle Burt blasts his whistle.

Kruger does a power stand up and springs to his feet. Dickie clings on monkey style and wraps a leg around Kruger's near leg and grabs his far arm. Kruger drives his hip into the mat before Dickie can lock his position and smashes him into the mat under the weight of both their bodies. He hangs on and rolls through, coming out on top of Kruger.

236

Dan strolls to the far end of the room, hollering his sermon. "You have to beat people up. You have to hurt people. You never let up. Be an ax and chop until they drop. Be a hammer and pound until they hit the ground. You go out every period, every minute, every second and score as many points as you can and then stick them. Then, you can stop." Dan turns, and meanders back in the opposite direction.

Kruger rebuilds his base and pops up in a tripod on both hands and both feet. As Dickie adjusts to the new position, Kruger does a forward roll, trying to peel him from his back and face-plants him into the mat. Dazed, he clings to the tumbling body and hangs on for the ride. After the roll, Dickie wraps his body across Kruger's back and tightens his grip.

Dan continues his preaching at a full yell. "You're going to have to wrestle the same guy five, six, sometimes ten or more times in your career. You have to establish dominance. Leave no doubt in their minds." Dan pauses and watches Dickie.

Kruger launches another stand up with extreme back pressure. Dickie goes with the force and pulls Kruger back on top of him into a crab ride with one arm wrapped around the waist, the other arm hooked in a half nelson, and toes hooked under each of Kruger's knees. Dickie elevates a knee with his foot and buries the half, trying to trap Kruger on his back, but with his size advantage, he just rolls back to his hands and knees.

Dan barks, "You don't give anybody a break. NO BREAKS!" He studies Dickie's technique. His volume lessens. "You kick their butts so bad they forget about you and think about the guys they can beat." The change in intensity and volume turns all heads toward Dan as everyone wonders what's up. Dan examines and analyzes Dickie's leg ride. Everyone follows his gaze.

This time, before Kruger can mount a move, Dickie buries a leg, applies pressure, and jerks out the far arm. Kruger is stuck; he can't move until he reestablishes his base. It's a stalemate. Dickie releases the arm with one hand, reaches down, and grabs the far ankle; he lifts and drives, flattening Kruger to his stomach.

"One minute," shouts Uncle Burt, watching in amazement. Everyone not wrestling focuses on the Kruger–Dickie match.

Kruger builds to his hands and knees. Dickie buries his other leg in the groin, pops his hips, and knocks out Kruger's arms, breaking him back down to his stomach. Kruger's eyes bulge in surprise and disbelief. He does an angry push-up to get back to his base; Dickie locks his hands around the far arm, buries his elbow into the back of the neck, and applies a power half. Kruger is stuck and fights to force his arm down and head up to break the top man's grip. The tussle teeters back and forth until Dickie's hands break, and Kruger regains his base.

Dan continues his coaching instruction while staring at Dickie. "You have to do it in the room. You do it in the room, you know you can do it in a match. You have to come in here every day and dominate people so severely it's not even funny. You have to make your man succumb. I repeat, make your man succumb." Everyone in the room has stopped wrestling and watches Dickie and Kruger.

"30 seconds," screams Uncle Burt, his eyes fixed on the twosome.

Kruger goes ballistic at the thought of being ridden by a freshman, Dickie no less. Dickie feels his teammate's body rising and goes back to a leg ride and cross face, releasing the pressure on the far leg. Kruger steps up with the far leg; Dickie locks his hands around it and Kruger's head, applying a cradle and bringing Kruger back to his knees. Kruger tries lifting his head and straightening his leg to break the locked hands but Dickie holds and drives forward, breaking down the near leg and driving Kruger to his side. Dickie jerks his locked hands into his chest, turning Kruger toward his back when the whistle sounds.

"Time!" shrieks Uncle Burt with a radiant grin.

Dickie releases his grip. Kruger delivers a stinging elbow to Dickie's solar plexus and springs to his feet. He stomps around the mat, rips the headgear from his head, and slams it into the wall. Dickie remains on the mat, recovering from the elbow shot. Kruger turns, pounds across the mat, and hovers above him. He extends his hand and pulls Dickie to his feet. "Welcome to the team. You're a Dog."

Dan approaches Dickie. "You hung on too much. More pressure next time." And then to the team. "Okay, that's it for today."

Kruger lumbers out ahead of everyone. Dickie tries to act like nothing happened, but he is beaming. He can't contain himself. "Did you guys see that?"

Joe acts oblivious. "See what?"

"Me wrestling Kruger."

Mini D feigns aloofness. "I didn't see it." He turns to Bronk. "Did you see it?"

Bronk shrugs. "I didn't see nothin'."

"What about it?" Joe asks.

"I rode him out." answers Dickie.

"Yeah, right," laughs Joe, "in your dreams."

"And almost turned him."

Joe shakes his head. "Do you believe this guy?"

"I did. You can ask Kruger."

"Assuming you did, you sure you want us reminding Kruger and telling him you're bragging about it?"

"I'm not bragging."

"Well, it's either bragging or dreaming. Hold up." Joe stops everyone. "Did anyone see Dickie wrestling Kruger?"

Shaking their heads, they answer, "Dreaming."

***

Dan schleps to a stool and sits. He crouches and buries his face in his hands.

"What's up?" asks Uncle Burt.

"I'll have a drink."

"Orange juice, tomato juice or Coke?"

"No juice." Dan's face emerges. "A drink."

"Okay. With orange juice, you can do a screwdriver, tomato juice, a Bloody Mary, and with Coke, you can add rum."

"Okay."

"Which one you want?"

"All of them."

"All of them?"

"Are you fucking deaf?"

"Okay, cool your jets." Uncle Burt scrambles and lines up three tall glasses in the staging area. He fills them with ice and pours Coke into the first, orange juice into the second, and tomato juice into the third.

"Can you still bet money for me?"

"How much you got?" Uncle Burt fills a shot glass with rum, then tips it and spills the contents into the glass of Coke.

"How long would it take to turn one hundred into six thousand?"

"Maybe a year." He looks at Dan, discards the shot glass and tops off the drink straight from the rum bottle.

"What can you do in a month?"

"Double it."

"That's not good enough."

"What's up?"

Dan looks around to see if anyone is in hearing distance. "This goes no further than us." Uncle Burt nods his head, and Dan continues, "The school's not paying our way to nationals."

"When did you learn about this?"

"I've known for a while, but I had a plan. I sold the truck and used that money to update and make improvements on the house. I dug out the new driveway section, and the lumber side forms are staked in place; I'm just waiting to pour the concrete. In the back, the deck footings have been poured, the posts set, the beams and ledger secured, and the joists attached. All that's left is the flooring, railing, and stairway. I laid the kitchen and bathroom bare, removed all the old cabinets, and the new cabinets are ready to be installed. When I finish the front room, the whole interior will have new paint. I'm doing all new light fixtures and outlets and light switch plates. Plus, I added a wall in front of the loft and created another bedroom. I just have to paint it, and it's done. And in the spring, I'm doing new landscaping and a fresh stain on the outside."

"What's that got to do with nationals?"

"I was going to refinance the house and raise the money that way."

"That's good."

"I had the loan guy come and take a look. According to him, interest rates have skyrocketed and property values have dropped. Even with the improvements, my house is worth less than what I owe on it."

"That's bad."

Dan reaches into his coat pocket. "What do you think you can get for these?" He sets his Olympic gold medals on the bar.

"Put those back in your pocket."

"You got any better ideas?"

"You've been the coach here for years. Let's do an alumni event, and you can hit them up for a donation."

"You can do that?"

"Sure, everybody does. I got it—we'll plan an alumni night at our last home meet. After the match, we'll put out a spread and get a few drinks in them. They'll be seeing all their old teammates and feeling giddy. And then you beg for money for the cause."

"You think that would work?"

"Hell yes. They're all out in the world working. You could probably get a few hundred from each one." Without thinking, he declares, "I'd bet Bad Boy on it."

Dan turns his head and looks up. Only Bad Boy's necklace hangs in the space the trophy mount occupied. "Where's Bad Boy?"

"Okay, I'll take care of the plans. You work on your speech."

"What happened to Bad Boy?"

"The police chief got his record wall hanger."

Both sit and stare at the empty wall.

Dan breaks their silence. "That putting a crimp in your sex life?"

"Actually, it's helped it. I'm telling everybody it was stolen, so I'm getting a lot of sympathy sex."

***

Balls steps, shifts his crutches, and swings his way down the dark hall. He stops at the boiler room door and reaches for the door knob. It opens, dodging his grasp. Out step Kruger and Dickie. Their T-shirts, shorts and red headbands are soaked through, and their face, arms and legs glisten with sweat.

"How's he doing?" asks Balls backing up to a chair.

"He's getting low on liquids, so he's burning bad before he breaks a sweat," answers Kruger.

Balls puts both crutches in one hand, lifts his injured leg and eases himself to a smooth butt landing. "You think he's going to make weight?"

"He should be pretty close after this workout," answers Kruger.

"Yeah, it's hotter in there than a sauna and steam room put together," adds Dickie.

"We drive all day tomorrow, but he'll have one more workout tomorrow night when we get there, so he should be okay.

"How's he handling it mentally?" asks Balls.

"It's his first time cutting weight, so we took that out of the equation."

"Yeah," volunteers Dickie, "when we first took him in the boiler room, he went crazy from the heat. So Kruger had me throw in my legs and hold him down to stop him from running out. When Ben and Pug got here, we held him on the stationary bike and taped his hands and feet to it. They're working him now."

"Here's a new one for the books," adds Kruger. "Tell him what you told me."

"Earlier, he said he had to go to the bathroom, so I escorted him and caught him trying to take a drink from the toilet."

"You're kidding," marvels Balls. "Maybe I should talk to him."

"I don't think his mind is very receptive at the moment. Just being here is enough."

"Yeah, he'll never forget the feeling, knowing you were here for him."

○○○○○○○○○○○○○○○○○○○○○○○○●●●●●●

21. Dog Cheap

JOE PEEKS OVER his shoulder at Uncle Burt behind the steering wheel and then returns to his huddle with Kruger and Doc in the back seat of the van. They break and casually check the rearview mirror. Uncle Burt is focused on the highway ahead. Joe eyes Kruger, then Doc. In one smooth, quick motion, he leans forward and slides a jockstrap over Uncle Burt's head.

"You want to play games? We'll play games." muffles Uncle Burt into the elastic sack.

The athletic supporter hangs upside down on his face; two straps split at the bridge of his nose, across each eye and travel around his head above his ears. He floors the gas pedal and whips the van onto the shoulder. Speeding parallel to the guard rail, the speedometer reads ninety miles an hour and climbs. Inching closer and closer, the guardrail posts blur together. The speedometer needle passes one hundred. He edges closer.

Occupants on the guardrail side of the van can't see any space, just the hazy outline of the barrier. They cover their eyes, throw themselves back into their seats, and scream in protest.

"Come on, man."

"Quit screwing around."

"Slow down, clown."

"You're going to kill us."

Uncle Burt slams on the brakes and locks them up, engulfing the van in a cloud of grayish-black smoke.

***

"When I was in Europe for the European Championships, I lived on a dollar a day, a loaf of bread, a bottle of wine, and a woman. Heh, heh, all on a dollar a day. I slept on the beach—" Dan looks in the rearview mirror. "Where's the van?" He brakes hard, jerking everyone from a nap and shouts, "Anyone seen the van?"

He finds the next turnaround and makes a U-turn. He peels through a muddy path ignoring the "No turns" sign and accelerates, backtracking down the highway.

Approaching the van from the opposite direction, he spots Gorni pumping the jack handle to lower the van while attempting to ward off Joe, who slips the jockstrap over his head. The van rests on the ground. Gorni tosses the jockstrap aside. Several of the wrestlers examine Gorni's work and simultaneously yell conflicting verbal instructions. The rest run around the van and climb on it like Monkey Island.

Dan pulls off the highway into the grassy median. Rolling down his window, he yells, "Everything okay?"

"We'll be back on the road in a minute," responds Uncle Burt.

Dan spots Doc lying on his back in the middle of the freeway. "Doc. Get in the van."

"Just trying to stop some help for Gorni." Doc climbs to his feet.

Dan spots Balls. "Balls. What are you doing here? Get out of here. You hear me?"

Everyone ignores Dan's tirade.

"You're not supposed to be here. You're not on the list. If the school finds out, they can bust me."

Gorni tightens the last nut.

"I don't have money for you. If we get in an accident, you're on your own."

Gorni tosses the jack and flat tire into the back of the van.

"Balls, you pack rat. You stay here. You can hitchhike."

Balls joins the migration back into the van. Everyone finds a seat, smiles out the windows at Dan, and waves.

Dan yells after them, "You guys didn't see a thing. Balls isn't with us. He isn't here. Understand?"

Uncle Burt accelerates down the shoulder and merges back onto the road.

Dan guns it, and the spinning tires sink up to the hubcaps. He takes his foot off the accelerator. When the wagon rolls back, he floors it again and repeats the process, creating a rocking motion that goes nowhere. Opening his door, he leans out and looks. The rear tires are buried up to the frame.

"Okay, everybody out. You have to push."

Everyone unpacks and trudges through the muck to the back of the wagon. The group lines up across the back and gets into position to push, some with their hands and some with their backs.

"Okay, on three," instructs Dan. "All together now. One...two...three."

Dan floors it. Everyone pushes. The wheels catch, and the wagon surges forward. The twirling tires splatter everyone with chunks of wet, sticky-soft mud mixed with grass.

***

Dan turns into a driveway followed by the van. The station wagon bounces and bottoms out in a giant chuckhole at the mouth of the entrance. The gravel parking lot is freckled with deep holes and ruts under a fresh layer of wet snow. A couple of broken down jalopies are parked in the back corner of the vacant lot. Dan angle parks across two parking spots next to the main office. He hurdles from the station wagon as the van parks next to him. Leaving the wagon door hanging open, he runs toward the office entrance, shouting back at the van and wagon, "Wait here."

He scurries to the front desk, looks around, and taps the ringer on the counter. A fat, unshaven guy walks out from the back room, rubbing his eyes.

"What can I do ya fer?"

"I'd like four rooms with two double beds in each room."

The guy thinks for a moment, slides his hand under his soiled fatso T-shirt, and scratches his pregnant-looking belly. "Well, let me see," he says, checking his register. "Four rooms, you say." He turns the page and lifts a half-smoked cigar from the counter ashtray to his lips. "You have reservations?"

Dan shakes his head.

"You may have lucked out." The old ashes dislodge from the end of the cigar and explode on his watermelon belly, leaving a grey blotch. He studies the register and lights a match, lifts it to the end of the cigar, and puffs aggressively. After a deep inhale, he removes the cigar from his lips and blows the match out, filling the air with smoke. "How long you want 'em fer?" he asks, reaching under the counter. He lifts a brown paper bag to his face and takes a healthy swig from the bottle wrapped inside.

**

Several hands drop a dollar bill into a knit cap. "Head shot wins."

Dan exits the office, walks to his car, and reaches for the door handle.

A lone voice shouts, "Hey, Dan."

Dan turns toward the voice coming from the outdoor balcony spanning the length of the second-floor units. A dozen snowballs pelt him. He wipes the snow from his face and looks for the culprits. The Dogs scatter.

Dan yells, "Only head shots count. Headshots are the only thing that count." He scoops the slushy snow from the car roof with his bare hands and molds it. He spins and rifles the snowball. Joe and Bronk fight for the stocking cap overflowing with dollar bills. The baseball-sized ice bomb whacks Bronk in the back of the head, knocks off his cowboy hat, and drops him to his knees.

Joe clutches the money bag and sprints down the balcony toward the cover of the corner of the building. Dan shapes another missile. Joe smiles at the thought of turning the corner and being out of range. A grenade-sized projectile explodes on the side of his face one stride from safety. He lifts his wet, red, swollen face and rallies his teammates hiding in the stairwell. "Well, what are you waiting for?"

The wrestlers come out of hiding and attack en masse. Dan slides down behind the wagon and expertly molds his artillery. He pops up, throws, and then ducks behind the wagon. As the team surrounds the wagon, Dan springs up from a different spot each time, keeping the wrestlers at bay. His arm is a bazooka against peashooters. One by one, he picks them off. A blast to the head leaves each wrestler nursing a red, puffy face, a bloody mouth, a bloody nose, or all three. The contest turns into a massacre.

His body spotted with snowball imprints, Dan turns to Uncle Burt and Jas sitting in the van. "Lock your van and come with me." He runs around his wagon, gets in, and locks all the doors except the passenger door. Uncle Burt and Jas slide in the front seat. Small chunks of melting snow drip from Dan's red, swollen face. His glasses have been knocked askew and pieces of snow glitter in his hair. "Lock the door." The Dogs converge on the wagon. Dan holds up the room keys and dangles them as he puts the wagon in reverse and backs out. "Let's see how tough they are now. It's below zero with the wind chill." Dan chuckles and waves to the guys and pulls onto the highway. "Let's go get something to eat. Those guys can freeze their asses off for the next hour."

"Okay," adds Balls from the back of the wagon.

"What are you doing in here?"

"I kind of had a feeling it was going to work out something like this."

"You're on your own. I don't know you're here. I haven't seen you. I haven't talked to you. Uncle Burt and Jas are witnesses."

They cruise a few miles down the highway and are beckoned by a family-style restaurant advertising home cooking with a flashing red neon sign. "How does this look?" asks Dan.

"Great," responds everyone in unison.

Dan pulls in and parks. He opens his door and steps out as the others climb from the vehicle and shut their doors. Dan lunges back in the car, stretches across the front seat, and locks both passenger doors. He starts the wagon and pulls out. He cracks his window. "Have a nice walk back to the hotel. That's for not warning me." And peels out.

***

The van and station wagon pull into the parking lot of the Chicago Athletic Facility, a futuristic dome structure. They park near the auxiliary entrance, and the wrestlers sling their bags over their shoulders and hike toward the door. At the entrance, a guard greets them and directs them to another entrance. They file around the building to an all-glass section and open the glass doors.

A huge sign spans the oversized scarlet and silver corridor.

Chicago Cats Wrestling Hall of Fame

Don't Just Make the Team, Be a National Champion

The passageway is a shrine to all the great wrestlers in Chicago history. Dozens of photographs of past team and individual champions plaster the walls.

"Psych 101, this is just Psych 101," says Dan, rushing through the glorified lobby.

"Hey, Joe, check this out," says Ben.

The Dogs gather around a window-sized framed image of one of Chicago's champions.

"Isn't that the guy who beat you in the national finals last year?" asks Ben.

"He didn't beat me. I blew it," replies Joe.

"Well if you had won, his picture wouldn't be up there."

Dickie studies the picture. "He looks like a dork. I can't believe you let a dork beat you."

"He didn't beat me, I—"

"Hurry up and get dressed," interrupts Dan, poking his head in from the hallway. "We only got two hours, and then they're kicking us out."

The team files out. Joe stands looking at the man who won his title.

"What're you thinking?" asks Uncle Burt, picking up a Chicago brochure.

"That'll never happen again."

"What's that?" asks Uncle Burt, studying the picture of Coach Kane on the cover of the Chicago brochure.

"I've never told this to anyone. I was winning with twenty seconds left, and I thought, I'm going to be the national champion. In that instant, he shot and scored the winning takedown. I'll never stop wrestling when I have a lead. I'll never beat myself again. And I'll never let a dork beat me again."

"C'mon, let's catch up with the team."

Uncle Burt hands the brochure to Joe. He glances at the cover and returns it to the rack.

***

Multilayered sweats make Bronk look like a brown Pillsbury doughboy. He screams, "I can't go anymore," rips free from Ben and Dickie, who run on each side holding an arm, and makes a break for the door guarded by Dan and Uncle Burt. They don't budge. They grab the ball of sweats and restrain him.

Bronk pleads, "You gotta let me out. I can't do it anymore."

Dan and Uncle Burt look into his drained face framed by the sweat-soaked cord of his hooded sweatshirt pulled tight and tied under his chin. His facial skin sags around the dark rings under his eyes and his swollen, white, cracked, bleeding lips.

Dan looks into Bronk's tortured face, turns to Uncle Burt and tells him, "I've seen worse."

"You got ten more minutes," says Uncle Burt.

"I can't, I can't." Bronk goes limp and crumples into a lump at their feet, sobbing, "I can't, I can't."

Uncle Burt nods to Ben and Dickie. They each take an arm, lift Bronk back to his feet and wrap his arms around their necks. They resume jogging, dragging Bronk's flaccid body around the room.

Balls opens the door to the torture chamber. "They said we got to be out in ten minutes."

"I'm going to check on the rest of the team," says Dan, dashing out.

He hurries down a hall in the labyrinth buried deep in the arena. Jas sits in a chair reading a book as he blasts past her and into the locker room. "Okay, we got five minutes to clear out." Dan sees Gorni. Tape has been wrapped around his body like a cocoon, from his ankles up to and covering his mouth. His head has been shaved in a mohawk. Everyone wears Chicago T-shirts, sweats, and jackets.

Adam cuts through one last lock and slips his bolt cutters into his oversized gear bag. He removes the lock from the locker, grabs all the

Chicago gear, and stuffs it into his bag, covering the bolt cutters. Mini D and Kruger write "Woof, Woof, Woof," in permanent marker on the bulletin board. Joe chases Pump around the locker room, spraying him with a fire extinguisher. Pug and Doc fight over a Chicago letterman's jacket.

"Stop it. Knock it off. Quit screwing around."

The door opens. Everyone freezes at the sight of Bronk's limp body dangling between Dickie and Ben. Uncle Burt and Balls follow behind the threesome. "They kicked us out of the wrestling room," Uncle Burt explains.

"You three hit the showers," says Dan. "Turn every shower on hot and make a steam room. Uncle Burt and Balls, make sure Bronk doesn't drink any water."

Every eye follows the droopy Bronk to the showers.

Dan paces back and forth. "Take off those T-shirts. I don't want to see anything to do with Chicago on anyone."

They shed the gear amid mumbles and grumbles. Kruger slips his Dover letterman's jacket on, completely covering the Chicago jacket underneath.

Dan poses with his hands on his hips. "You guys think you're tough? You're not in college. You're at Dover. It's a fucking Disneyland. Chicago invented wrestling. They've won almost half of the national titles and the last nine in a row, and you guys think you're going to come in here and change fifty, sixty years of tradition. You bubbleheads think that?" Dan takes a dramatic pause and looks into each set of eyes. Kruger is sweating marbles under the jacket layers. "You guys aren't a wrestling team. You're a drinking team with a wrestling problem. You're nothing. You hear? You're nothing. Every day you wrestle, you're getting worse and you're wrestling like it's next year. You suck! We got two days of wrestling ahead of us, and if we're lucky and make the finals, Chicago is going to rip you from one end of the mat to the other—"

Ben barrels into the locker room pushing a laundry cart over flowing with Chicago gear. Dickie pops from under the heap and announces, "Hey, they don't have locks on the lockers in the team room."

***

The phone rings repeatedly, waking Dan from his sleep. "Yep, what is it? ...Good, we'll see you when you get here ...Huh? Walk. We'll see you when you get here." Dan hangs up.

"Who was that?" asks Uncle Burt.

"Gorni."

"What did he want?"

"A ride."

A glow crests from the horizon just before sunrise. Uncle Burt's van pulls out of the hotel parking lot onto the highway. He drives a couple of miles and spots Gorni trudging down the side of the road. He's carrying a dozen mesh laundry bags strapped around his neck, over his shoulders, under his arms, and gripped in his fists and teeth. Uncle Burt pulls over and helps him load the gear into the van.

Gorni climbs into the passenger seat. "Thanks."

"You been up all night?"

Gorni nods.

"You're amazing, Gorni."

Gorni beams.

"How come you never challenge Dickie for a spot on the team?"

"Coach Dan say I manager."

"We'll have to see what we can do about that."

***

Everyone gathers around the toilet stall, hooting, hollering, pointing and high-fiving.

"Okay, we got a new leader," announces Joe.

Kruger clasps both his hands and acknowledges his triumph by shaking his tightly gripped hands from one side of his head to the other and back again.

"Who's next?"

Pump lumbers in from the locker room slapping his belly. "You guys come unarmed for this contest," he says as he waddles toward the commode. Everyone scatters as the wide body makes his approach and lands. He sits on his miniature throne and positions himself for an all-out effort. Hands massage his belly and his legs adjust to maximize his push power. Taking a couple of deep breaths relaxes his body. A grunt awakens it from the meditation. His body strains, shakes, turns red, and lets out a full-bodied "Arrr!" The exertion taxes his body to its limits. Veins pop from his neck. Pain etches deep crevices across his red face.

Doc coaches, "Breathe. You have to breathe."

Pump does a peppered Lamaze breath, followed by a violent outburst of unrelenting strain accompanied by a succession of grunts, whimpers, and whines. Laboring to the utmost, his face wrenches and twists. After a prolonged release, he utters a satisfied sigh and a long "Ahhh." Calm returns and a confident smile emblazons his relaxed face. Pump stands, examines his deposit, and exits. "I believe we have a new leader."

A clamor ensues. Judges rush to the bowl to make it official.

"Jesus, look at that."

"Unreal."

"It's a trophy."

Kruger steps up and starts pushing and pulling his way into the stall. "Let me see." Standing over the white fixture, he comments, "It looks like a fucking Pringle chip container. Hey Pump, you're supposed to chew before you swallow."

Joe scans the room. "What about you, Adam? You want a shot at this?"

"I don't want nobody looking at my shit."

"Okay, then it's official. Pump is King Turd for the third year in a row," proclaims Joe.

"What about me?" asks Dickie.

"You have to be kidding. That turd probably weighs more than you do."

Everyone laughs and pokes fun as Dickie approaches the bowl, sheds his shorts, and squats. He sits for a couple of seconds, stands, pulls up his shorts and exits the stall.

One of the judges strolls over and examines the results. "Oh my God." Another ruckus erupts as everyone inspects the piece of excrement.

"Will you look at that?"

"Enormous."

"What?" Pump pulls bodies from the cubicle and fights for a look. "Holy shit. The perfect turd."

Those leaving the round vessel shake their heads and spread their hands as if they are telling a fish story. All eyes look at Dickie, dart up and down his frame, and then back at his deposit in the bowl. They shake their heads. Dickie shrugs.

Pump marches across the room. "This kid's got a gift."

"I get it from my mom's side of the family," replies Dickie.

Pump takes Dickie's hand and raises it in the air. "You're looking at the new King Turd."

Dickie stares at the bowl. "Should we flush?"

Pump shakes his head. "Last time we flushed after a contest, it ran over and flooded the whole locker room."

"Flush when we leave," Joe instructs.

Balls interrupts the discussion. "Time to suit up. Warm-up for the finals starts in fifteen minutes."

"Time to kick some Chicago ass." Joe turns toward the lockers.

The mood in the locker room shifts as the team responds with gusto. "Woof. Woof. Woof."

***

Mini D storms into the locker room and kicks the trash can across the room. Dickie knocks him out of the way and grabs the nearest chair; he swings, slamming it into the lockers, and then beats it on the bench until the chair breaks into pieces. Bronk grips the bulletin board, the first thing he sees. He rips it from the wall, cracks it in half over his knee, and shatters it as he slams it against the corner of a row of lockers. Mini D jumps up and down on the trash container, flattening it. Uncle Burt frantically looks for something to demolish. Nothing to the right, nothing to the left, nothing on the walls. He grabs a four-by-six-inch sheet of paper from the floor and savagely tears, shredding it into a hundred bits. The rest of the Dogs parade in and become an audience witnessing the demolition derby.

Dan bulls in, pushing everyone out of his path as he bellows, "You drive halfway across the country and let Chicago kick your ass. That's BULLSHIT! That's not what we work and train for. That's not who we are. And now they'll be twice as tough at nationals."

"But we froze half to death waiting for you at the hotel," says Ben.

"That's not good enough. You were winning tonight and got pinned in the last thirty seconds."

Ben throws up his hands. "Who could sleep last night with all the screams and gunshots and sirens all night?"

"All you had to do was fight off your back, and we would've had a shot. But you couldn't fight for thirty seconds."

"This is bullshit, the way you treat us and then expect our best." Ben sags onto the bench.

"Ben, in there," orders Dan, pointing to the doorway that leads to the toilets and showers. Ben gets up and slugs into the next room. Dan follows.

"You know why no colleges came calling after your senior year, why no one wanted you? You wrestle with one hand around your throat."

"Uh?"

"You're a choker. A pussy." Dan points to the toilet stall and nudges Ben in the back with a stiff arm toward the can. "Over there."

Ben doesn't move fast enough for Dan, so he grabs him by the back of the neck and under the armpit, lifting and pushing Ben across the tile floor.

Curiosity gets the best of the team, and one by one they wander into the next room to watch. Dan releases Ben's armpit with his left hand, slings open the door to the toilet stall, and forces Ben's head down toward the bowl overflowing with defecation, vomit, piss and stained tissue paper. Dan lifts the hinged seat with the toe of his shoe.

"See that?"

Ben looks and can't help but think, *It's like a Porta-Potty filled to the rim.*

"I'm going to put your head in it." Dan pushes down harder.

"C'mon, Coach, quit messing around," says Ben, bracing his hands and feet. "Joke's over. C'mon, stop it," pleads Ben, his head inches from the crapper. "I'm warning you."

"I'll stop when your face is covered with shit." Dan jams Ben's head into the punch bowl of excrement.

Ben's hands grab the top of the toilet bowl, stopping his face an inch from the stinky smudge. The foul fumes singe his face. A killer look comes into Dan's eyes. He intensifies his effort and pushes harder.

"Stop," says Ben, shaking and trembling from the strain. "I'm going to get mad."

He pushes hard against the bowl and battles against Dan's hold. His head slowly rises. Dan adjusts his grip and slides his arms around Ben's neck, squeezes a headlock, and drives his head back toward the bowl. Ben catches himself, braces one foot on the back wall and thrusts, propelling them out of the stall and into the cinder block wall. Dan regrips and methodically drags Ben inch by inch across the floor. Unable to grab anything to stop his slide, he delivers an elbow to Dan's groin and wraps both arms around one of Dan's legs. Dan drives him closer. Ben braces his foot against the bowl. It dislodges the toilet and unleashes a flood of water. He jerks Dan's leg up and drives back, crashing into the stall wall, and collapsing it.

The two behemoths roll around on the wet floor, fighting for position. Dan builds to his feet first, drops his chest onto Ben's back, locks his arms around Ben's waist, and lifts him upside down off the ground. Ben's feet flail in the air above Dan's head. Dan walks him back to the bowl and lifts him as if to use his head like a toilet plunger. Ben jams his head into Dan's groin, drops his feet against the wall and pushes off, thrusting them across the room to the floor. Dan loses his grip and Ben comes up swinging, landing a fist flush on Dan's mouth and nose. Dan grabs Ben in a bear hug. He struggles free and swings wildly. Dan dodges and ducks the wild thrusts and times another step in to a bear hug, trapping one arm. Ben uses his free hand to deliver punches to the back of Dan's head.

"It's over," says Dan.

Ben continues to fight back. Dan holds tight.

"It's okay, Ben. It's over. It's okay."

Ben's arms relax.

Dan relaxes his grip. "It's okay…it's okay."

Ben breaks down crying. Dan releases. Ben sits on the floor and covers his face.

The team stands wide-eyed.

Dan turns to the team. "I hate losing to Chicago." Bright red blood sprays from his mouth. "When we meet them at nationals, they're going to pay. Somehow, someway, they're going to pay and that's it. We're not going to wrestle them, we're going to beat the shit out of them. Remember, when the tough get going…uh, the tough get going."

Everyone is numb. Dan stands and helps Ben to his feet. "Remember, Ben, the next time someone puts you on your back, they're putting your head in the toilet."

***

Two maintenance men stride side by side. Each pushes a mop handle and rolls a bucket-on-wheels down the hallway and through the doorway. In a synchronized routine, they lift their mop handles up and down, plunging the mops in and out of a cleaning solution, and then lift the wet mops and stuff them in the wringer. They push down their handles, drain the excess, slop the mop heads on the floor, and swish them back and forth.

Looking up from the floor, one of the men observes, "Will you look at that?"

In wonderment, they march stride for stride and look side to side. Every hanging picture and plaque has been tilted askew. Every standing trophy and award has been laid on its side. The entire Chicago Cats Wrestling Hall of Fame has been vandalized without destroying a thing.

"I wonder what that's about?" asks one of the men, pointing at a picture with a towel draped over it. They remove the towel and stare.

"Maybe we should leave the towel on it."

"Yeah, he looks like a dork."

"Think we should notify Coach Kane?" asks one of the men, looking around. "Hold on, the brochures are gone from the rack."

The other fellow looks around the room. "All the brochures are gone from all the racks."

They open the door to the storage room. "And all the brochures are gone, the whole inventory."

"What the hell is somebody going to do with thousands of brochures?"

"Now we got to tell Coach."

***

Curled in a ball, Dan purrs in the back of the wagon. The team surrounds the parked vehicle. Everyone gets a grip, and on Joe's signal, they violently rock and bounce the frame while screaming. Dan leaps from his deep sleep and smashes his head on the ceiling.

Gathering his senses, he asks, "Where are we?"

"We had to stop for gas."

An old-timer tops off the van and limps to the wagon, gripping the sole hose to his one pump. "What 'bout this 'un?"

"Fill it up," says Uncle Burt.

Dan holds up his hand. "No, wait. I recognize this place. We're only a few miles from Dover.

"How much do we need to get to Dover?"

"Dover ya say. Let me see. You got a good ways, figure three quarters of a tank."

"Are you sure?" asks Dan. "Seems like we're a lot closer than that."

"You want to get there or not?" The old codger removes the cap and begins pumping.

"Twelve gallons, but no more," orders Dan.

Ben climbs back in behind the wheel. Dan studies him. "How you doing, Ben? You need a break?

"I'll drive," says Dickie.

Dan ponders the proposal. "I'm going to give you a shot."

Ben fidgets about the steering column and controls, removes the keys, and steps out of the wagon. He extends his arm. Dickie puts his hand out, and Ben drops the keys in the open palm. "Dickie's been up all night navigating," he warns.

"It's okay. He can do it," says Dan. With a pat on the back, he tells Dickie, "I'm going to run in and pay the bill. Be ready to leave when I get back."

Dickie slides in behind the wheel, adjusts the seat and mirrors, and inserts the key.

Dan runs up to the wagon, whips the door open, and jumps in. "All right, take us out of here. Quick. Let's go."

When he turns the key, everything goes on full tilt. The radio blares, wipers whip back and forth, heater fans blast and hazard lights flash. Dickie looks around the dash. One by one, he turns each instrument off or down and gives a laughing Ben the evil eye in the rearview mirror.

"Paybacks are hell," warns Dickie.

He puts the car in gear and accelerates too fast; the wagon lurches forward. He slams on the brakes, pitching his passengers into the seat or dash in front of them.

"I'm not used to power brakes."

"How long have you had your license?"

"The same since the last time you asked."

Dickie pulls out. Everyone screams as he drives over the curb.

"Dickie, you okay?" asks Dan.

"Yeah, yeah, I'm okay. I thought that was the driveway. Don't worry about it."

Everyone yells instructions simultaneously. "Faster! Slower! Turn right! Turn left! Stop! Go! The other way!"

Dickie hollers back, "Shut up. I know what I'm doing." He approaches the freeway, slows, turns right and accelerates up the exit ramp. Everyone screams.

Dan stares straight ahead. "You're doing fine, Dickie."

Uncle Burt's van sits in the street and waits for Dickie to back off the exit ramp. The van follows Dickie under the overpass, up the entrance ramp, and onto the freeway. They merge onto the highway and pass a sign that reads "Dover 45 Miles."

"Shit," exclaims Dan, thinking a couple of gallons of gas would have done it.

The van pulls alongside the wagon. Mini D dances the jerk under the flashing dome light. Kruger is behind the wheel. He takes his hand from the dome light switch, smiles at Dickie, and bending just his fingers, waves and floors it.

"You going to let him beat you?" asks Dan.

Dickie punches the gas. The two streak down the deserted highway, through the early morning mist. They trade the lead back and forth all the way to the Dover exit. Kruger accelerates down the ramp. At the bottom, he slows just enough to make the turn, blows through the stop sign, and pounds the pedal.

"He's making his move," says Dan.

Dickie follows Kruger through the stop sign onto the four lane road, flexes his leg, and puts the gas pedal to the floor. The wagon kicks into passing gear. He catches Kruger, who blocks every attempt to pass by pulling in front of the wagon and denying the lane. Dickie fakes one way, guns it, and jerks back to the open lane and slips up next to Kruger. They barrel down the pavement. Ahead, the road narrows from two lanes to one.

Dickie's passengers urge him on. "You can do it. You got him. Go, Dickie."

As the rolling masses of steel race to get in front, their front bumpers take turns in the lead. Running out of road, the race becomes a game of chicken. Cries and shouts cheer Dickie on. Perspiration glitters on his face, and his white hands grip the steering wheel with all his might. In the last stretch, the passengers grimace, shut their eyes, and brace for impact. Kruger brakes and Dickie surges in front, unleashing an uproar.

"All right. You're the man. You're a Dog. The Top Dog. Woof. Woof. Woof."

"Good move. Now you got him. Just don't let him pass you," instructs Dan.

They streak down the dark, deserted road through the residential neighborhood and into town. At the far end of town, the athletic center is in sight. Kruger jockeys to the left, then the right, looking for an opportunity to pass. Dickie drives down the center of the two lanes to prevent Kruger from passing on either side. As they approach the main gate entrance, the green light turns amber, then red. Dickie brakes. Kruger jerks the van around the wagon, bowls through the red light and entrance gates, and coasts onto campus. Dickie sits at the red light without a soul around.

"You blew it. You had him. Pussy. Loser."

The station wagon pulls up to the parked van. Everyone is strewn about as if they have been waiting for hours. Kruger and Joe lean against the van with their hands behind their backs. Dan gets out of the wagon, and casts a bruising look at Dickie. Joe plants a snowball behind Dan's ear. He jerks his head and glances in the direction of the attack. Kruger and Joe are in the same position, leaning against the van with their hands behind their backs.

"Check the angle," says Joe.

Dan looks at Kruger, shouts, "Kruger," and takes off running toward him. At the last second, when he gets within range, he goes after Joe. His face gleams as he reaches to grab Joe. Pulling a hidden snowball from behind his back, Joe fills Dan's face with it and takes off running.

"Outfox the fox," crows Joe.

○○○○○○○○○○○○○○○○○○○○○○○○●●●●●

22. Pressurized

DRESSED IN BLACK with hoods and ski masks, three dark figures carrying boxes move in the shadows, darting from bush to bush to avoid the nighttime security lights. They slither in a snakelike pattern through the maze of hedges toward the back door of the Dover Athletic Center.

"Down, down, down," orders the leader as he dives behind a leafless bush.

The other two take cover just as a university security vehicle pulls into the parking lot and cruises down the side of the building with its spotlight, scanning the shrubbery. It breaks to a stop at the back door with its searchlight beam frozen on a short, woody plant with a sunburst array of stems that conceals the leader. The cruiser door opens. A black shoe steps out onto the pavement, and the security officer slides from his seat. He scans the length of the facility, breaks into a fast walk and then a jog. The hiding bodies cock their muscles, ready to bolt. Running up to the back door, the patrolman wiggles and pulls on the handle of the locked door and then returns to his vehicle. He is about to sit. A noise catches his attention. He stops and stands erect as he scans the area and listens. *There it is again*. His eyes focus on the lit bushes. Another muffled sound drifts from the shrubbery. Unsure of its exact location, he walks closer. Approaching the bushes, he leans his head and upper body from side to side to get a better view and bends forward at the waist—

His car radio blasts, "All mobile units. All mobile units, we have a 10-10 in progress at Guthrie Residence Hall, please respond. Repeat, a 10-10 in progress at Guthrie Residence Hall, please respond."

The guard sprints to his car. Jumping in behind the wheel, he glances at the bush and peels out. "Mobile unit three responding."

When the patrol car turns the corner, the three rush to the back door.

The leader demands, "What's with the sneezing?"

"I don't know," he says, trying one key in the lock. "I couldn't help it." He tries key after key from a large ring of keys. "I must be allergic to that plant or something."

"It's the middle of winter."

The third member huddles at the door. "C'mon, what's taking so long?"

"I don't know which key it is."

"Are you sure there's a key that will open the door?" The leader glances over his shoulder.

Shoving in the next key, he insists, "There has to be one." It turns.

Once inside, they shut the door, arm themselves with flashlights, and work their way down the hall to the next locked door leading to the athletic offices.

"Try the same one. Maybe it's a master."

"I don't know which one it was." He starts over, trying one at a time.

"You're not very good at this, are you?"

"Here—you do it," he says, surrendering the ring of keys.

After several tries, they conquer the lock and enter the dark offices. They make their way through the complex to an office door and open it with one try.

"See. It is a master. All you need is this one key."

They set the boxes down and pull the chairs aside so there's room for the three of them on the floor. As they remove their masks, Joe rips a box open.

"Pug, you cut, Kruger, you tape, and I'll stick," says Joe, dumping a box of Chicago brochures on the floor. Pug grabs the scissors. Kruger finds the tape, and Joe dumps the contents of another box of brochures on the carpet. They form an assembly line across the floor. Pug opens one of the hundreds of brochures piled next to him and cuts Kane's face from the front cover. Kruger has a rolled piece of tape waiting and sticks it to the back of Kane's face and hands it to Joe.

***

Bronk sprawls across his bed as if he were on the receiving end of a knockout punch. He inhales with a series of loud, harsh intermittent gulps and snores. His naked body is buried under empty ice cream Drumstick boxes and Drumstick paper wrappers. Chunks of waffle cone, chocolate, and nuts sprinkle his face, chest, and the bed. Dry vanilla ice cream cakes his lips, cheeks, nose, and chin. On the floor around the bed, piles of shredded, discarded wrappers bury a half-dozen empty boxes.

***

Bronk enters the athletic office complex, pounds down the hall to Dan's office, knocks, and turns the doorknob. It's locked. He looks around and turns to leave when Dan arrives.

"Coach, can we have a powwow?"

"Ooookay," says Dan, unlocking his office door.

"Well, I did it your way," says Bronk, sitting. "I ran. I lifted. I followed the rules. I did it in the wrestling room, and I still got my ass kicked."

"You're not supposed to like losing."

"It's worse'n gettin' thrown comin' out of the gate."

"It's okay to lose as long as you don't lose the lesson."

"Bullshit," shoots back Bronk, "how the hell would you know? You never lost."

"Good. Take the way you're feeling, bottle it up, and use it next time."

"Next time? Ryder threw me around like a baby calf."

"You have to take it to the next level. The harder you work, the harder it is to let somebody do that to you," says Dan.

"You're not listenin'. I did everything you said, and I got my ass kicked."

Dan stares at Bronk. Bronk stares back. Dan breaks the impasse. "You don't set your standards by the guys in the room. You have to work harder than anybody in the country. In the world. This isn't about winning and losing. It's about competing. You have to be the ultimate competitor. You have to train so hard that no one—I mean no one—can hang with you," says Dan, turning the switch to his lamp that doesn't light. He sits and stares at a little face next to the light switch. He studies the picture of Kane. *What the hell is that?*

"I just can't figure it. I don't know what's the matter. I never got beat so bad in my life. Not even by Balls."

Dan detects another Kane face on the lamp shade, on the empty Coke can, on his coffee mug, on the stapler, the scissors, and the phone. The Kane image even covers faces on the magazines.

"You said if I did what you said, I'd be ready for the match. I did everything you said. I lost weight. I went down. And you saw what happened."

Dan peels the Kane face off a piece of leftover donut and shoves the morsel in his mouth as his eyes scan. Hundreds—thousands—of Kane faces surround him. Kane faces in front of him. Kane faces to the left. Kane faces to the right, faces behind him, faces above him, and faces below him. Pictures of Kane's face are stuck all over the room: on every trophy head, over every face in every photograph, on posters, the light fixture, the ceiling, the walls, the floor, the door, the windows.

"Bobby Ryder threw me around like a new born. I couldn't even throw him with my cow catcher. It was like steer wrestlin' a bull. I don't think goin' down was good. I told you I was a forty-two pounder. What d'ya think?"

The Kane faces begin to swirl and spin. Dan stands and scans the room. Totally absorbed, he begins peeling faces.

"So, what d'ya think?" asks Bronk.

"You never quit. You can take a breath, but you never, ever quit."

"I'm talkin' 'bout cuttin' weight."

"You haven't done anything stupid, have you?

"What? What do you mean?"

"You didn't gain all that weight back, did you?"

"Uh…I had an ice cream."

"Your weight is okay then?"

"It should be."

"You're not going to give up and quit, are you?"

"I ain't throwin' in the sponge."

"Right now, you're swimming against the current, but when you get your weight under control and find your style, it'll be different."

"I want to go back up. What d'ya say?"

"It's human nature to look for the easy way out. Next time, this is what you're going to have to do to beat him—"

"Beat him?"

"The next time you wrestle him, you're not going to think about winning—you're not going to think about wrestling. You're going to do what you do best. You're going to get into a fight and turn it into a brawl. Think you can do that?"

"I reckon."

262

"The only way you beat kids from Chicago is to get physical," says Dan, jerking Bronk from his chair, shoving him against the wall, and getting in his face. "You get in their face and pressure them and beat the shit out of them. You don't let up for a second. You beat on them for the whole match."

"But coach, he majored me."

Dan takes Bronk by the collar, smacks him in the head, and thrusts him into the hall. Following him, he shoves him into the wall and lands an open hand smack to his temple. "So, the next time you wrestle him, you going to let him push you around and bitch slap you?" asks Dan, knocking Bronk around.

Bronk's chest puffs and his eyes blaze.

"That's it. That's it right there," says Dan, pointing his finger at Bronk's face. "You fixed your face. That's what I want to see the next time you wrestle Ryder. Now beat it. I'll see you at practice."

"But—"

"You got to eat it, drink it, breathe it, walk it and talk it as if it's a done deal."

"But—"

Dan spits out his words. "Every day, each of us has a fight going on inside between a starving chicken and a starving eagle. The chicken's a coward and lives a life full of worry, doubt, and fear. The eagle is brave and believes in himself and lives life with confidence and daring. Do you know which one is going to win?"

"Which one?"

Dan pokes Bronk in the chest. "The one you feed." He walks back in his office and closes the door, then reopens it, "Remember, pick a fight—"

A stunned Kruger stands in the door opening.

"What do you want?" asks Dan.

Kruger gathers himself. "I have to talk to you."

"Not now."

Kruger forces himself into the office. "It's about Mini D."

***

President Hardon stalks down the corridor toward the wrestling room with the athletic director in tow. "This is it," says the president, patting his brown leather satchel. "I've got him this time. He's on the scaffold, standing on a chair with a noose around his neck, and all I have to do is kick the chair out."

The president reaches for the door handle. The door flies open, forcing the president and athletic director up against the wall.

Two trainers hustle out the door, carrying a screaming wrestler. "Hurry. Faster. Faster. We have to call the clinic and get him over there as fast as we can," orders one trainer as they break into a run and disappear down the hall.

The president adjusts his tie and turns his attention back to the issue at hand. He grabs the doorknob, opens the door, and barges in. The heat and smell are unbearable. The room is wall-to-wall bodies wrestling. Hardon snaps his handkerchief from his jacket pocket and covers his nose. He walks into the center of the mat nearest the door and shouts, "Sangha, Dan Sangha."

The athletic director slides in and leans against the wall next to the entry. Uncle Burt sits against the wall on the other side of the double doors. He looks at the intruder's street shoes, checks his stopwatch, and stands. Twirling his whistle around his finger, he approaches the president. "Excuse me, you better get against the wall for your safety."

"I want to speak to Dan. I'm afraid I have some bad news."

"I'll get him, but you have to move off to the side." Casting his eyes down, Uncle Burt adds, "No street shoes on the mat."

The president gives Uncle Burt an indignant look, turns his head back to the room and shouts, "Dan Sangha."

Uncle Burt shrugs. "Okay, you were warned. I'll get Dan."

The president removes his coat without moving from the center of the mat as Uncle Burt strolls to the far end of the room and hunts for Dan. Along the way, he picks up Dan's glasses from their favorite resting spot, puts them on and approaches two intertwined wrestlers. "Hey Dan, there's someone here to see you."

Dan pops his head up, "I'll see them after practice," and then resumes grappling.

"It's the president and AD. Seems important."

Dan continues wrestling and doesn't respond.

"He's wearing street shoes on the mats."

Dan's head jerks up. He squints at the man in street clothes at the other end of the room. He takes a deep breath. The president stands in the middle of the mat with his arms crossed over his jacket and satchel, staring in Dan's direction. A blur streaks across the mat. Pump runs through Ben with a blast double leg tackle, and the two wide bodies blindside the president. The five-hundred-pound clip takes out the president's legs and knocks him to the mat into a sweat puddle. Pump keeps driving, and they fall on top of the president and smash him into the mat. The president yelps, balls up, and covers his head with both arms to protect himself from the wrestlers.

Dan stands with Uncle Burt and squints at the scene across the room. "Did you tell him to stand against the wall?"

"Yep."

"Get my glasses." He stands and walks. Uncle Burt follows.

When the wrestlers roll off the president, he scrambles on his hands and knees, gathers his coat and satchel, and crawls back to the door next to the AD. He slides up to his feet, staying as close to the wall as he can. Adam and Kruger move and counter in front of the president. They hand fight and maneuver for position. Their bodies slam into the president and pin him to the wall. Fatigue and frustration lead to a slap, which triggers a retaliation slap, and tempers ignite. Kruger throws a punch, and Adam answers with one of his own. Standing toe to toe, they pummel each other. Black-and-white clenched knuckles whiz by the president's face. Blood flies. The red fluid and chunks of flesh spray the president's face, white shirt, and tie. The wrestlers stand and pound.

Dan approaches and pats the brawlers on the back. "Okay, back to the center." They break. Blood runs from Kruger's nose and mouth and a cut above his eye. Adam's right eye is already closed shut. They move to the center of the mat and resume wrestling. Dan opens the door. "Let's step into the hall." The foursome files into the corridor. "Okay, what can I do for you?"

The president is soaking wet. Blood speckles and beads of perspiration cover his face. He strokes his sagging hair, straightens his soused shirt and tie, and removes a report from his leather satchel. His trembling hands hold the report up, and he reads. "I want to address a couple of issues. First, running out on bills."

"What are you talking about?"

"We have a documented trail that leads from the national duals to Dover."

"A trail of what?"

"A trail of unpaid hotel, food, and gas bills."

"Why do you think it was me?"

"You left a trail from Chicago to Dover."

"That doesn't mean it was me."

"The offenders were driving a university vehicle."

"University vehicles are off-limits to me."

"Exactly. We know you are breaking into the vehicle compound and stealing cars."

"Why? Are any missing?"

"No, but are you going to deny you're illegally using university vehicles and skipping out on bills while representing Dover University?"

The double doors burst open, and the Mangos spill into the hall. Mini D shoots in on Dickie's legs, picks him up, carries him back through the door, spins him upside down, and deposits his head in the spit bucket. Dickie rolls over, sits up, and removes the bucket. Spit, blood, and snot tissue cover his head. He throws the trash can at Mini D and charges him. Dan collars each one and holds them apart as they start swinging at each other.

"Heh, heh... brothers," laughs Dan.

Joe carries Bronk on his shoulder across the open double doors and impales the cowboy on the ranking board.

The president backs down the hall. "You're not going to get away with this. I know it's you. I know you steal the university vehicles, and you're responsible for these bills. And I'm going to prove it."

The AD wipes blood splatter from his face with his handkerchief and smiles at Dan.

"What?" asks Dan.

"They're looking ready," replies the AD.

"They're getting there."

Everyone stares in wonder at Bronk kicking and fighting to free himself from the ranking board.

"Never seen that before," says the AD.

Uncle Burt imitates Dan. "Heh, heh. I thought of that years ago."

Dan notices his eyeglasses on Uncle Burt. He grabs them and smacks him in the back of the head.

"You're supposed to be on my side."

Kruger slugs over and angles his bleeding brow at Dan. "What do you think?"

Dan spreads the cut with his fingers. "Looks like you're going to need some stitches. Go see the doc."

"What about this?" asks Kruger, pulling his lower lip down and opening his mouth.

Dan examines the gash. "Yeah, it's probably going to need some, too."

Kruger shakes his head and trudges down the hall.

Uncle Burt comments, "Adam fucked him up."

"What goes around comes around."

"What do you mean?"

"When Kruger was a freshman, he got in a fight with my stud senior and beat the shit out of him."

○○○○○○○○○○○○○○○○○○○○○○○○○●●●●

23. Popsicle

"OKAY, WE'RE DOWN one man tonight." The Dogs shift their eyes to Dickie, who leans on crutches. Dan continues, "That's an automatic six points for the other team, so I expect the rest of you to pick it up. It's alumni night, so there'll be a lot of former Dover wrestlers in the stands. Let's put on a good show for them. For you seniors, this is the last match you'll wrestle at Dover. Make the most of it and go out a winner. I have a special announcement: we have a new captain. Mini D will co-captain with Bronk."

The team shouts a verbal confirmation and signals a thumbs-up in Mini D's direction, while those nearby pat him on the back and head. He smiles and looks at Kruger, who nods and smiles back.

"This is a top ten team. We can't afford any letups," says Dan. He singles out Pump. "This is a big match for you. Your guy was a finalist last year. Beat him and it will set you up for a nice seed at nationals. Okay, let's get out there and get a good warm-up."

Dan leads the way. He marches to the door, swings it open, and exits. The team doesn't budge. A few moments pass, and Dan returns in a quick step.

"Let's go," says Dan, noticing the look on their faces. "What's going on?"

"We took a vote and we want Gorni to wrestle," says Bronk.

"This isn't a democracy."

"You weighed him in."

"That was in case there was a forfeit. Let's go." says Dan, leading the advance toward the door. The team stays put. Dan stops at the door, looks back, and no one moves.

"We're not going without Gorni," announces Bronk.

"Umm," stalls Dan, scanning the resolve on each face. "You don't understand." He looks to Uncle Burt for help. "This could...screw up his eligibility."

Uncle Burt mugs. "I could use a wrong name. It happens all the time."

Dan searches inside himself, examines the boys' expressions once more, and settles his eyes on Gorni. "Okay, get dressed and meet us in the wrestling room for warm-up."

***

Dan and Uncle Burt watch Balls lead the team through their prematch ritual.

"Let's go watch the other team warm up. Sometimes you can pick up something," says Dan, turning and hiking down the corridor.

"Did you get the honor guard to play the national anthem?" asks Dan.

"Not exactly."

"Well, the color guard or whatever it's called."

"Kind of."

"What's that mean?"

"Let's just say it's taken care of."

They enter the gym from the mouth of the tunnel. Two dozen ROTC cadets rappel from the network of catwalks suspended from the ceiling. Military students in full camouflage uniforms, helmets, gloves, boots, knee pads, and elbow pads zip down ropes and assault the visiting wrestling team warming up on a mat in the center of the gymnasium floor.

Wrestlers from the opposing team break from their drills and scatter, deserting the mat. Complaining and bitching to one another, they stand in disbelief as they watch the spectacle. The controlled descent resembles a military or SWAT team operation. The coach breaks from his bewildered team and yells at Dan, "What the hell is going on?"

"What the hell is going on?" asks Dan.

"I couldn't get the color guard, so I got the next best thing," answers Uncle Burt.

The fans scream as the Dogs trot in from the tunnel. Seated in a bleacher a few feet behind the visiting team, the school band breaks out in a deafening Dover fight song.

***

The small gym is packed for the contest. The buzzer sounds, ending a match. The contestants shake, and the referee raises Mini D's hand. He does a series of cartwheels accompanied by the Dover fight song.

Hobbling on his crutches, Dickie is the first to the edge of the mat to give his brother a high five. Gorni sprints out to the center circle, still wearing his warm-up. The official instructs him to remove his jacket and pants and points him back to the bench.

Balls addresses the student section of the stands. He rests his armpits on his crutches and frantically waves his arms for everyone to rise. The brown and black throng responds. Section by section, everyone stands, encircling the mat with a frenzied mass of stomping, clapping, and screaming supporters. The Dover band blasts the visitor's bench.

Up next, Bronk paces back and forth behind the team, cowboying up for his match. The Dogs sit next to the mat, yelling encouragement to Gorni. Joe stands behind his chair and watches the spectacle, soaking in the moment. His eyes wander the stands, lock, and take hold. He nudges Pump and nods his head toward the bleachers. Pump follows Joe's gaze and sends a signal along the bench until the entire team focuses on the striking blonde at the top of the first student section.

"That's what I call motivation," chimes Joe.

Kruger counters, "You want motivation, think Janet Jackson."

"How about that chick dancing in Flashdance?" offers Mini D.

Dickie shakes his head. "You're all missing the boat. It's got to be between Madonna and Paula Abdul."

"What about Cher?"

"That's lame."

"What's lame about Cher?"

"Look who she married."

"That's my point. She gives you hope, like anybody has a chance."

"They're all a distant second to my choice," brags Ben.

"And who's that?"

"Tara."

The whole team goes silent and casts a condescending look at Ben.

"Gotcha." Ben laughs at his joke.

Joe stands gazing into the stands. Uncle Burt tosses a towel and hits Joe in the head.

"You're up. Last home match, baby," says Uncle Burt, smacking Joe's rump as he walks out onto the mat. "Let's make it one to remember."

Pug glances at the mat and turns back to the discussion. "I'm not even thinking about girls. I have a list of every restaurant I'm going to eat at after the season."

Mini D. grabs a towel and wipes his face. "I've made myself a promise. When wrestling is over, I will never walk past a water fountain without taking a drink."

Doc closes his eyes. "I'm a chocoholic. Anything with chocolate."

"Hershey's."

"Nestle."

"Godiva."

"Dove."

"Cadbury."

"Ghirardelli."

"Chocolate-covered strawberries."

"Chocolate fondue."

"Chocolate truffles."

"French silk pie."

"Hot fudge sundae."

"Molten lava cake."

"A chocolate malt with French vanilla ice cream."

"Ice cream cake with vanilla ice cream, chocolate cake, and fudge."

"Ice cream by the gallon."

"Caramel mousse with cognac, sautéed pears, and cognac-soaked sponge cake," says Kruger. The whole team stares at him. He shrugs and explains, "I signed up for the recipe of the month club."

The referee raises Joe's hand in victory. Joe removes his headgear with his other hand, swings it above his head, and looks for his girlfriend in the stands. Dozens of girls stand, scream, and wave as Joe points to his girlfriend and releases. The headgear sails through the air but misses its mark by several rolls. A gang of girls led by the blonde beauty leaps for the bouquet.

Dan paces at the edge of the mat, hollering toward the action. Joe returns from the stands with a shoebox under his arm and sits next to Bronk. He opens the shoebox, and their eyes voraciously feed on stacks of chocolate morsels overflowing from the tinfoil-lined box. They reach into the box and make a selection.

Dan's eyes catch Joe and Bronk. He stops watching the match, marches over and snatches the gooey chocolate morsels from Joe and Bronk. "What's that?" he asks.

"My favorite. Mom made her gourmet brownies," answers Joe.

Dan confiscates the shoebox.

"Hey, you can't do that," complains Joe.

Dan holds the box above his head and away from their grasping hands. With a tone of finality, he barks, "You don't build a hot rod and then piss in the tank."

The boys think, look at each other, and back off. Dan tucks the shoebox under his arm and returns to the action. His purposeful strides cruise along the combat zone as he tosses a brownie in his mouth. *Mmmm.* His eyes bulge with delight at the flavor. Before he swallows what is in his mouth, he chomps down on another chewy chocolate piece, and then another.

***

Ben hand fights, circles, and shoots. He gets caught midshot with an underhook and sails through the air, landing on his back. He goes berserk, flies into a frenzied rage, bucks his opponent off, fights off his back, and goes on the attack.

Pump sprints, does his customary forward roll, and jumps to his feet like a lady gymnast. The routine elicits a roar from the crowd. The members of the girls' basketball team stand, pull up the front of their T-shirts, and slap their bare bellies in unison. Pump slaps his belly in response. Fans across the entire gym stand, lift their shirts, and slap their exposed midsections.

As the match winds down to its final seconds, the two drained behemoths lean and push each other around the mat. Sweat drips and sprays with every movement. The scoreboard reads 1–1. Out of nowhere, Pump explodes with a burst of energy and drives into his adversary like a Sumo, pushing him backward. When the big guy leans back to the counter the pressure, Pump swipes with his paw and slaps his opponent's head down. The heavyweight's whole body falls to the mat, and Pump spins behind for the go-ahead takedown. Pandemonium explodes in the small gym. Three...two...one—the buzzer sounds but can't be heard over the screams, and the wrestling action continues. The scorers' table throws in a towel for a visual signal. The referee sees the towel and taps the combatants, indicating the match is over. Pump jumps up, bounces on his feet, and extends his hand to his opponent, who is too exhausted to stand. Before the referee can lift Pump's hand in victory, fans rush the mat. The referee turns and runs as the fanatics flood the mat, trampling the fallen wrestler and hoisting Pump in the air.

Susan walks straight up to Joe. "Why didn't you throw your headgear to me?"

"I did," pleads Joe, "but it slipped out of my hand. Hey, I looked at you and pointed to you, didn't I?" She nods, and they hug. Joe cradles her in his arms, looks back over her shoulder, and winks at the tall, long-legged blonde with his headgear.

Dressed in their game uniforms, Carter and the basketball team confront Joe.

"Okay, we're square, right?" asks Carter. "I just don't get why you had us wear our uniforms."

"It's the most embarrassing thing I could think of," says Joe.

The opposing coach marches up to Dan. "You opened this can of worms. Remember, you come to our school next year."

Perplexed, Dan raises his arms. "But...uh...umm..." At a loss, he looks to Uncle Burt for help but gets only a shrug in response.

Pointing his finger in Dan's face, the other team's coach spouts, "Next year," and stomps off.

Tara sashays up to Ben. "Hi."

"Hi," says Ben, watching the team marching off to the locker room.

"You really looked good tonight. You want to hook up later?"

"I have to go," says Ben, running to catch up with the Dogs.

Tara watches Ben jog off.

***

Everyone huddles around Dan in the locker room. "Good job tonight. We had a solid effort from each guy. Pump, great match. Way to break that guy. You got anything to say?" asks Dan.

"This sport is a lot easier when you're in shape," responds Pump with a wide grin.

"You got anything to say?" asks Dan, munching down on a brownie and looking to Balls and Uncle Burt.

Uncle Burt grabs Gorni's wrist, raises his hand in the air, and shouts, "Let's hear it for Gorni, who won his first varsity match."

The locker room breaks into a cheer. Dan looks at his watch and nods, signaling Balls and Uncle Burt it is time for them to leave.

"That it? Okay, I have a meeting I have to go to," says Dan, tossing another brownie in his mouth. "You guys roll up the mat and put it away. Then, you can visit with your family and friends." Dan walks through the locker room toward the exit. "Make it an early night—and watch your weight. We got the qualifier next week," he says, sliding out the door.

Bronk and Joe look at each other, then at the team; everyone breaks into a celebration, cheering and high-fiving.

***

Dan cruises down the corridor, rounds the corner, and rumbles toward Uncle Burt standing in an open doorway next to an alumni gathering sign.

Dan tosses another goody into his full mouth as Uncle Burt approaches him.

"Perfect timing. The AD is just finishing. What's that?" asks Uncle Burt.

Dan extends the shoebox, and muddles "Here, have one," through a mouthful of goo.

Uncle Burt grabs the shoebox and looks into the empty tinfoil lining. "Thanks," he says, depositing it in the trash can.

Dan settles in the doorway and looks at the alumni present. *Okay, the team wrestled great, and these guys are feeling great. This is the perfect time to hit them up for a donation to the wrestling program.*

"Don't forget to invite them all up to my place," instructs Uncle Burt.

Dan swallows and listens to the athletic director speak while checking out the meeting room. Each table is covered with a crisp, white tablecloth and accented with a subtle light from a candle centerpiece. Strings of small white lights blink like fireflies along the walls at the ceiling line.

Bill Bohr glances at the entrance and sees Dan leaning against the doorframe. He announces, "And now here's the man of the hour, coach of the number four-ranked team in the nation and one of this year's candidates for the coach of the year, Dan Sangha." The applause swells, as a spotlight follows Dan to the podium.

"Thank you, Bill, and a special thanks to the athletic department and my assistant coach, William Burt, for all the work that they did in putting together this event." Dan takes a moment to look around the room. "I want to thank all our distinguished alumni for coming tonight. Your presence made the boys' job a little easier and a lot more exciting. I see a lot of familiar faces. They're a lot rounder and have less hair than when you went to school here." The alumni chuckle. Dan continues, "And I'm guessing no one is prouder of this team's achievements than you. And you should be—it was you who laid the foundation for what we accomplished this season, and I want to thank you."

"I don't want to go on too long, so I'll get to the point so we can eat dinner and tell war stories. I'm sure you know the important impact wrestling has on a young man's life. But I don't know if others outside the wrestling community understand or realize the vast impact that people with a wrestling background have had on our society. Dover University fields twenty-two athletic teams, and due to Title IX and budgetary concerns…" Dan freezes. Everything begins spinning. He continues, "…Dover University has decided to…" The entire room dances, sways, and rotates. Light trails streak.

Dan feels himself losing it. "Dover University has decided to…" He looks directly into the crowd. Each person's head is the size of a beach ball. He closes his eyes, shakes his head, and tries to focus. "Eh…eh…" A creepy buzzing fills his ears. When he looks back at the alumni, the beach ball heads float up and away like helium balloons. Diverting his eyes, he looks at the paintings hanging on the walls. All the still scenes in the frames come to life as if they are televisions.

He redirects his eyes to the room. The round tables turn into Pacmen and begin munching the screaming people. Their giant heads deflate, hissing colored musical notes into the air. The notes surround Dan's head, burst and shower his face with a jelly-like substance. He feels the spray melting his face and begins pushing his face back into place. He looks up at the spotlight for help, and it turns into the moon. The small white blinking lights surrounding the room turn into bumblebees and swarm down on the podium. Dan clutches his chest and dives under the side table to escape.

Bill Bohr is the first on the podium, followed by Cindy and Uncle Burt. He pulls back the tablecloth, takes one look at Dan gripping his chest, and yells, "Call 911. Someone call 911! Burt, we need a trainer immediately." Uncle Burt takes off running. Bill turns to the assembly. "Is there a doctor here?" No one responds. "I'm sorry, but I'm going to have to ask everyone to clear the room. Please move to the corridor and leave a path for the paramedics." Bill turns to Cindy and asks, "Have you seen him behave this way before?"

She shakes her head, staring at Dan as he rolls into a fetal position under the table.

Bill leans over and whispers, "He's behaving as if he's on drugs or something."

***

Cindy blasts into the locker room and bellows, "I want everybody in here. Now!"

Kruger flaunts his nakedness. "This is the men's locker room."

"Shut up. You don't have anything I haven't seen. Where is everyone?"

"Some of the guys have left," Balls explains.

"Anyone in the showers?" Cindy confronts the stragglers. "Okay, I want everyone seated here on the bench." Looking from face to face, Cindy explains, "Dan just collapsed, and we need to know if you know anything about it."

A silence falls over the locker room as the boys look suspiciously at each other.

"You guys think you're tough. You think you know about pain?" They smile at her empty threats.

"Ever see a woman give birth? Ever see a vagina stretched this big?" says Cindy, holding her hands up the size of a basketball. "Want to know what that's like?" She waddles down the bench, looking each wrestler directly in the eyes. "Think about shitting a watermelon."

As the image races through their minds, their faces distort out of shape.

"I want you to know who you're dealing with," says Cindy, pointing her index finger at her globular belly. "I'm about to shit my third."

"We made a batch of brownies, knowing if he saw them, he'd eat some."

"Brownies?"

"But he took the whole box and ate them all."

"Okay, he ate the brownies," comments Cindy, looking at the culpable faces. "Is that it? Am I missing something? You're going to have to connect the dots for me."

The boys look back and forth at each other, wondering who is going to speak.

"They're party brownies."

"What's a party brownie?"

"You know, we load them up with goodies."

"What kind of goodies?" asks Cindy.

A long silence hangs over the boys as they look around at each other, wondering if they should say anything else.

Cindy breaks the logjam. "Look, we have to know what was in the brownies. You know Dan has a heart condition. The doctors need to know what they're dealing with."

"We kind of all put something in."

"Like what?"

"Some pot."

"Marijuana?" asks Cindy.

"And acid."

"LSD?" asks Cindy, making a mental note.

"Speed."

"Speed?"

"Yeah, you know, Black Beauties."

"Anything else?" asks Cindy.

All the boys look at Doc. "You better tell her."

"And an experimental drug my Dad has been developing for one of the drug companies. It's for guys who have ED."

"ED?"

"Erectile dysfunction. You know, they can't get it up, so this gives them an erection."

***

Cindy fast waddles down the corridor and battles her way through bodies crowded in the doorway fighting to get a glimpse. She pops through the doorway just as the final strap is pulled tight around Dan, securing him to the stretcher. EMS attendants roll him toward the door. Dan lies on his back. A giant, bulging erection creates a tent over his crotch. As the observers split to form a path, Dan sees Cindy and screams, "I want a blow job! I want a blow job!" The attendants pick up their pace scrambling through the human passageway and down the hall with Dan bellowing, "I'm a Popsicle! Don't let me melt! I'm a Popsicle! Don't let me melt!"

○○○○○○○○○○○○○○○○○○○○○○○○○○○•••

24. God Loves Wrestlers

THREE OUTBUILDINGS, A carport, and a repair shop sit on a lake of asphalt. A dozen vehicles are anchored around the parking lot. A tall chain-link fence borders the black surface. Workers scramble around the lot complaining.

"This is bullshit."

"Orders from the top."

"You mean from the supreme moron."

"The way you mean it, it would actually be from the number one idiot."

"Whatever. They're stupid orders. We just have to pull them all back out on Monday."

Dan, Uncle Burt, and Gorni sit in Uncle Burt's van parked across the street from the university motor vehicle compound and watch the attendants pulling all the cars, vans, and station wagons inside.

"What the hell are they doing?" asks Dan. "They've never done this before."

"Which one's yours?" asks Uncle Burt.

"See the one parked on the side of the garage, under the carport?"

"And how are we supposed to start it?"

Dan holds up his specially tagged key and shakes it.

The crew members pull one vehicle after another into the garage, doubling up in the service and repair stalls until they fill every available space. As the storage buildings fill, the workers scramble from vehicle to vehicle, removing the keys and locking the car doors. Two station wagons remain.

One attendant whistles and yells, "There's room for one more over here." His partner runs to the one parked under the carport and starts it.

"That's my wagon," mutters Dan.

The crew member backs up, cuts the wheels, and steers the wagon through the open garage door, filling the final space. Workers scramble, locking everything, turning on the security lights and closing all the garage doors.

"What are we going to do now?"

"We'll check that last vehicle. Sometimes they leave the keys in them."

One by one, the attendants start their cars and exit through the open front gate. The last vehicle stops, the driver gets out and locks the gate behind him. He raises his right hand, aims a garage door opener, and pushes the button. One of the garage doors rolls open.

"All right," chime Dan and Uncle Burt.

Two graceful, muscular Dobermans prance out.

"Oh, shit," grumble Dan and Uncle Burt.

The Pinchers execute an intelligent, territorial gaze.

Dan figures, "We're going to need a distraction." He and Uncle Burt turn and look at Gorni.

A defiant Gorni shakes his head. "No. No dogs." His eyes are glued to the black and tan duo.

"I wouldn't put you in any danger. Look at them," explains Dan, pointing toward the compound. "They're guard dogs. They're trained to patrol the grounds and detain anyone who comes in their domain."

"Detain?" asks Gorni. He can't look away. Every sound perk the sinister pair's cropped, pointed ears and focuses their lively, dark eyes.

"Yeah, they're not going to hurt you unless you do something stupid. They're just going to hold you there." Dan lets his last comment sink in, then continues, "Look at their bodies. Watch the way they move. They just look vicious and bloodthirsty, but they're really big babies."

"Babies?" asks Gorni. He studies the dogs. Their eyes detect movement, their elegant, straight legs break into a pompous, energetic gait.

"They're just like guys in hairy bodies. All they want to do is eat, fuck, and fight."

"Yeah, if we had a hunk of meat, a bitch in heat, or a pit bull, we wouldn't be having this conversation," adds Uncle Burt.

"Like guys?" asks Gorni.

"Pretend they're guys on the team. Or better yet, pretend they're someone you're going to wrestle. You size them up and look at them as a whole—analyze their body language."

Gorni looks at the dogs. "No."

"Remember, these dogs are trained. They're just doing a job. They're not going to hurt you."

"No." The security lights reflect off the dogs' short-haired, black-and-tan coats as they patrol the lot, giving them a ghostly, devilish aura. Gorni shakes his head. "No dogs."

"We need you to go around back, climb the fence, make some noise, and get their attention. When the dogs come, don't run. Stand your ground and don't look them in the eyes. Act like you belong there and don't acknowledge them. You look away and turn sideways but don't turn your back to them. Keep your hands at your side and in a deep, low, loud voice give them a command to 'Stop' or 'Sit.' Use authority, but don't yell and don't show fear. When the dogs back off, you back off. Keep taking steps backward until you are out of danger. By that time, we should be around to pick you up. Got it?"

Gorni sees his life pass before his eyes. "No."

Uncle Burt opens his door and steps out as Dan shoves Gorni out of the van. Uncle Burt climbs back in and locks his door. Gorni jerks the door handle. Terror seizes his face, but Dan and Uncle Burt pay no attention. He ceases tugging on the door and looks across the street at the dogs standing at the fence staring at him. He looks back at Dan and Uncle Burt. They take no notice. Gorni takes one more gander at the devilish pair, contemplates his fate, lowers his head, and trudges off.

Uncle Burt smirks and asks, "So, how was your trip?"

"Fuck you, asshole."

"No really, how you doing?"

"Okay, I guess."

"What was it like?"

"Un-fucking-believable."

"You having any flashbacks or anything?"

"What?"

"You know, have you reexperienced any episodes from tripping?"

"Is that what that is?"

"Probably."

"What do you mean probably? You know about this stuff or what?"

"I know a little. I'm not a specialist. It's like I have a high school diploma, not a doctorate."

"I've been trying to figure out what it all means."

"What all what means?"

"When the clinic released me, Cindy brought me home and deposited me on the couch. As I sat there, all of these white balls popped up out of the carpet. There were dozens of them, all different sizes, as small as a golf ball and as big as a full garbage bag. They started cracking open like something was hatching, and the broken pieces turned into flower petals. Each one was a different color, and when it fell on the floor, it melted into the carpet.

"Then I had to take a piss, so I stood, and the next thing I knew, I was flat on my face on the floor. I didn't know how I got there—I was just there, and strands from the rug wrapped around my arms and legs like tiny, long octopus arms and tried to pull me down into the carpet. But I couldn't stay down because I had to go really bad. So I fought to my feet, walked to the bathroom, and stood over the toilet for what seemed like an hour before I could go. And then, when I pissed, I pissed a rainbow. It wasn't just a rainbow. It had dozens of colors and sparkling jewels. It was the most beautiful thing I've ever seen. I was the king of the leprechauns pissing into my pot o' gold.

"When I finished, I looked in the mirror on the way out, and I couldn't take my eyes away. I looked into my face, and it was like I could see it for the first time. It was fascinating, like a three-ring circus. I could see everything ... each hair in my hairline and eyebrows, each eyelash. I looked into my eyes and saw the cornea, the lens, the iris, the colors and veins, and everything in the center of my eyes was moving and shifting like a kaleidoscope. I looked at my nose and lips, and then I saw all the flaws and imperfections in great detail—every pore, hair, pimple, scar, everything.

"When I looked deeper, I saw through my skin, and I saw my muscles, skull, brain, the blood and cells, and then the parts of the cell. And then I saw down to the molecules and atoms—and then shit I couldn't even identify—and when I couldn't see anything any smaller, when I reached the end of the line, I saw myself. Not my physical self but my real self. It was like I removed all the layers and masks and looked at the guy hiding under all that shit. I saw who I really was, the real me. It wasn't pretty. I may have been a great wrestler, but I'm failing as a father, husband, and friend. I'm only okay when I'm by myself.

"After I saw my true self, I walked into the shower with my clothes on. Cindy said I was in there for hours. All I remember is I was trying to figure something out. I was walking down this path, and I came to a crossroad with three choices. I had to decide. Only one path led to my life. Then I got hungry, and Cindy made me a burger. I sat down to eat, and the burger looked like a Muppet, and it started singing David Bowie's *Changes* to me. I was up all night and the next day, thinking about which path to take, and I decided to have some hot tea before practice. I put the teapot on the stove and forgot about it and went to practice. When Cindy came home from picking the kids up, the teapot had melted into a clump. Any longer and it could've started a fire and burned the house down."

Uncle Burt continues staring at the fence surrounding the university vehicles. "Sounds like a typical Saturday night. So what else is happening?"

"I don't know. What's happening with you?"

"Nothing. So what's new?"

"Nothing. What's new with you?"

"Nothing. So what else is new?"

"Nothing. So what else is new with you?" asks Dan, watching the dogs snap their heads to attention and break into a sprint to the back of the buildings. "That's our cue. Let's go," says Dan, grabbing an eighteen-inch long black-and-red bolt cutter.

Dan and Uncle Burt run across the street and scale the chain link fence. "I've been watching Gorni in practice," says Uncle Burt.

"Yeah, so?" Dan tosses the bolt cutter over the fence.

"I think he can beat Dickie."

"He can kill Dickie," replies Dan.

"So, when are you going to give Gorni a shot?"

"I'm not."

"He could help the team. With him in the lineup, we beat everyone."

"Probably," answers Dan, dropping inside the compound. He picks up the bolt cutters and runs to the station wagon.

"You have to let him challenge for a spot."

"Can't."

Uncle Burt nods his head. "Right, you got it too good with him. He's like your little slave."

"Best manager I've ever had, but it's not like that," says Dan, opening the only station wagon not locked up in the garage.

Uncle Burt sits in the front passenger seat. "This year is a once-in-a-lifetime opportunity. You have to do whatever it takes."

"I know," says Dan. He looks and sees no keys in the ignition.

"So let's get Gorni on the team."

"Can't do it," says Dan, flipping down the visor. A set of keys falls into his lap. "Bingo."

"I'll never understand you."

Dan turns to Uncle Burt. "Gorni would put us over the top, but I can't use him, and I'll tell you why. But first you have to promise me something, okay?"

"Okay."

Dan inserts and turns the key. The engine turns over but doesn't start. "This is just between us. What I'm going to tell you could jeopardize people's lives. You have to promise not to say anything to anybody. Promise?"

"I promise."

Dan pumps the accelerator with his foot and turns the key again. "I met Gorni's dad at the world championships about the time Gorni was born. His dad was a silver medalist for Iran, and we hit it off. After the tournament, I went to Iran and hung out with him and his family for a while." Dan continues pumping and turning the key, but the engine won't start. It turns over slower and slower. The battery wears down until it grinds to a halt.

"Anyway, over the years, his dad got involved in politics, protesting for reform and shit. One day, he comes home and discovers government troops have dragged off his best buddy and fellow activist. He and his entire family just disappear off the face of the earth. So, Gorni's dad sees the writing on the wall and goes underground. To protect his family, he hides them with people he knows. So Gorni's hiding here, but he doesn't know it. He thinks his dad sent him here for me to coach him. He has to keep a low profile until things straighten out back at home. And who knows when that's going to happen in that part of the world? It's a powder keg."

"You're kidding, right?"

"I'm as serious as a heart attack."

"Wait 'til the guys hear this one."

Dan gives it one more pump and turns—nothing—the engine roars to life. Dan guns the accelerator, the engine backfires and blows a cloud of smoke out of the tailpipe, and then it purrs like a kitten.

Uncle Burt looks down at the floor. "You can't take this—there are holes in the floor."

"It must be the lot car. I can stop by the lumber yard and get some plywood."

"If it's the lot car, does it have plates?"

"We can take the front plate off your van. Let's get Gorni."

"Geez, the gas fumes are coming right into the car."

"We'll crack the windows open."

The station wagon pulls alongside Gorni, who lies on his stomach with his arms wrapped over his head and face. The Dobermans stand over him showing their teeth, growling, and dripping saliva on his head. The slightest movement ignites a series of barks. Dan gets out of the driver's seat with the bolt cutter, walks around the front of the car and without breaking stride, makes for Gorni. The Dobermans turn on him and attack.

"Heel," commands Dan.

The guard dogs fall in line and follow slightly behind Dan. He stops. "Good job," he tells Gorni.

Gorni uncovers his head and looks at the Dobermans. They growl.

"Don't look at them. Sit," orders Dan. The pair obediently sits. Dan lifts Gorni to his feet and hands him the bolt cutter. "Take this and cut the lock," says Dan, pointing to the back gate. Gorni takes off running toward the gate. The Dobies start to give chase. "Stay," instructs Dan. They stop.

***

A bear head turns sideways, opens its mouth and snaps. Fangs just miss Dan's ducking head. Dan dodges the swipe of the bear's claw, dives, tucks, rolls, and jumps to his feet a safe distance away. Faking to his left and then the right, the beast closes in. Dan doesn't know which way to break. The bear corners Dan, juts out his jaw, and growls. Dan yowls back, and the bear retaliates with a monstrous roar that blows Dan's glasses off.

Dan stands, raises both hands in the air, and roars in its face. The bear stands on his hind legs, spreads his claws, tilts his head, and lets out a deafening—

POP!

A short, sharp, explosive bang wakes Dan sleeping in the back of the wagon. Before opening his eyes, he shouts, "Don't hit the brakes."

Ben, the driver, instinctively jams the brake pedal with all his might. The steering wheel shakes violently, vibrating Ben's arms and upper body. Screams drown out the tires' screeching. Pitching toward the blowout, the vehicle's weight shifts, plants over the flattened tire, and the metal frame nose-dives into the pavement. The bumper and grill break down and cave in, the hood crumples, and the windshield shatters and explodes from its frame. The wagon's rearend pole-vaults up and over through the air.

"We're going down and I'm an Olympic and national champion. What are you?" shouts Dan.

CRASH! The wagon slams on its roof and becomes a metal pinwheel, whipping around out of control down the highway on its roof. The gyrating mass twirls off the pavement, coasts down the shoulder, and then winds down, slower and slower, until the whirling wagon skids to a stop. A shroud of dust and smoke engulfs the still vehicle. The van and other cars following it pull to the shoulder behind the wreck.

Inside, the smashed roof of the wagon has collapsed down to the dashboard and headrests. As Bronk opens his eyes, he sees a white sock dangling next to his head and watches as it begins to move. He slithers between the ceiling and the front seat through the gap between the headrests and follows the sock, which hangs half off a foot. The sock belongs to Dan, who crawls to the back and kicks out the rear window. One by one, each occupant scrambles from the wreck on their hands and knees.

Dressed only in his shorts and socks, Dan helps them to their feet as they emerge and asks, "You okay? You okay? Anybody hurt?" Dropping on his hands and knees, he looks into the wagon. "Is that everybody?" Once he's sure everyone is accounted for, he leaps to his feet. "All right. Give me five—no, give me ten." He moves from wrestler to wrestler getting two high fives at a time and bumping chests. After the last man, he jumps, leaps, and dances down the highway, shouting, "God loves wrestlers! God loves wrestlers!" He runs back to the crash. "All right, everybody listen up. I was driving. Everybody got that? I was driving." Looking around, he yells, "Ben. Ben." He spots Ben kneeling on the side of the road and runs to him. "Ben, you weren't driving. I was driving. You got that?"

Ben remains on his knees. He stares off with a blank look on his face and then bursts out crying, "We could've been killed. We all could've been killed." He drops his bawling face into his hands, and his whole body shakes.

Dan watches Ben crumble into a slobbering lump beside the road and turns to the rest of the survivors with a laugh. "Heh, heh, heh ... we destroyed a twenty-thousand-dollar car, heh, heh ... and it didn't cost us a thing. You can't pay for experiences like that and come out okay. They just happen. We're so lucky." He takes off dancing down the side of the highway, looking at the twinkling heavens and shouting, "God loves wrestlers!" Distant sirens penetrate the night air.

Dickie asks, "Where's my brother?"

Everyone runs to the back of the wreck and looks in. Several cars have stopped and have their lights pointed at the wreck. Down on their knees, the team looks and calls out, "Mini D. Mini D. You in there?" Movement gets everyone's attention. A hand reaches down from behind the seats. "Mini D, you okay?" He pulls himself from between the seats and crawls along the ceiling and out the back window with a cassette player in his hands.

Dickie grabs his brother and helps lift him to his feet. "You scared the hell out of me."

Mini D stands and fidgets with the buttons on his cassette player. "Geez, I just got this for Christmas."

"Hey, we're lucky to be alive."

Mini D shakes and slaps his cassette player, trying to get a sound out of it. "Yeah, that was one hell of a wreck, huh?"

Red flashers violate the night. Two police cars arrive and pull into the lane next to the wreck with their headlights and spotlights focused on the scene. Two officers approach.

The first asks, "Everybody okay?" He examines the wreck and says, "You're lucky you ain't in the morgue." The second patrolman helps Ben to his squad car. The first officer looks over everyone and asks, "Who was driving?" Everyone points to Dan. The officer stares at Dan, looks him over from his head to his shorts and down to his socks. "We're going to have to fill out a report. Where's your clothes?"

"Let me show you our trophy," says Dan, climbing into the back of the wagon as he mutters to himself, "snowball effect ... snowball effect."

"Are you aware it's illegal to drive without shoes in this state?"

"We're returning from the qualifying tournament," says Dan, emerging with a piece of the broken trophy in each hand. "We won. We won. We steamrolled them. We snowballed them." Dan fits the two pieces of the three-foot trophy together and holds it up.

"Why weren't you wearing shoes?"

Dan dances around waving the trophy above his head. "We qualified nine to nationals. We set a new record. We're from Dover. Where are you from?"

"Can you tell me about the shoes?"

"My name's Dan. How are you doing?" asks Dan, trying to shake the officer's hand and simultaneously hold the trophy together. "What's your name?"

"Sir ... the shoes?"

"They came off in the accident," sings Dan, running and leaping down the highway.

The second patrolman joins his fellow officer, and together they watch Dan skipping and hopping down the highway. They look at each other, nod, and confirm their suspicion. "Sobriety test."

"Get those boys away from that vehicle. Dan ... Dan, I need you to step over here." Dan walks over, grins, and stands at attention in front of the officer. "Dan, have you had anything to drink tonight?"

"No, I've been wrestling bears."

"Okay." The officers' eye contact acknowledges the suspicious behavior. "Dan, please put the trophy down."

Dan sets the trophy on the side of the road as the second officer corrals the boys to the far side of Dan, away from the wreck. He gives them a command to remain there as he returns to the wreck.

"Dan, I'm going to ask you to perform some skill tests." The officer demonstrates as he explains, "First, I want you to close your eyes and tilt your head back, like this. Keep your arms at your sides."

The boys become Dan's cheering section. "C'mon on, Dan. You can do it."

Dan closes his eyes and tilts his head back.

"Now, hold that position," says the officer, noting the time on his wristwatch. He checks for Dan to take a step, raise an arm, raise his head, or open his eyes. After the required time, the officer makes a note and orders Dan to relax. The boys cheer elicits a disapproving look from the patrolman.

"Now, raise one foot and balance on the other foot." Dan lifts his left foot off the ground to the cheers of the Dogs. "Begin counting from one hundred backwards."

"One hundred, ninety-nine, ninety-eight..."

The officer observes and listens, looking for any swaying, hopping or inability to count. "Okay," says the patrolman, scratching another note on his pad. The Dogs cheer louder. The officer turns his head toward the boys and silences them with his piercing eyes. Returning his attention to Dan, he commands, "Okay now, stretch your arms out to the side away from your body, tilt your head back, and touch the tip of your nose with your index finger. Take turns alternating hands."

The rest of the team from Uncle Burt's van joins the group, and the cheers build. "Go Dan, go. Go Dan, go. Go Dan, go." The officer looks at them, and they go quiet.

Dan leans his head back, extends his arms, and alternates fingers as he touches the tip of his nose. Cheers, claps, and whistles egg him on.

The second patrolman climbs from the wreck with Dan's pants and confers with the tester. When they turn their backs to Dan, he shows off. Standing on one leg and closing his eyes, he tilts his head back and alternates touching his nose with the index finger from each hand, and then for the crowd pleaser, he does a one leg deep knee bend. With his butt inches from the ground, he continues performing all three tests simultaneously. His cheering section explodes, but by the time the policemen look back at Dan, he's standing there in his shorts and socks, scratching his head. The uniformed pair looks at the Dogs, muting them. People from the stopped vehicles join the team, doubling the group's size.

The first officer turns and walks back to Dan while the other one removes Dan's wallet from his pants and begins searching through it. The testing deputy extends his right index finger to the white line on the highway. "You will walk this line in a heel-to-toe fashion from where I'm standing to that reflector," says the deputy, pointing. "Then, you will turn and walk heel-to-toe back to me. If you stumble or step off the line, it can indicate you may have been drinking or using drugs, and we'll have to take you in."

Dan looks at his cheering section, then focuses on the white line and begins. He holds his arms out for balance and places one foot in front of the other, heel to toe, heel to toe, heel to toe. The crowd cheers each step, to the chagrin of the highway patrolmen. Dan does the heel-to-toe walk to the end, turns and repeats the performance halfway back, then reverses and does a toe-to-heel walk and moves backward on the line. The crowd hoots and hollers, claps, and whistles at the performance.

Dan stops, does a heel-to-toe walk forward to the halfway point, stops again, bends at the knees, and launches his frame into the air. He tucks into a ball and spins backward, executing a backflip. He sticks his landing with both feet on the white line but loses his balance. To stop from stepping off the white line, he waves his arms in a frantic, excessive manner, turns sideways in an effort to gain his balance, waves and leans forward, overcompensates, and then waves and leans backward. He turns again, regains his balance for a moment, and runs the rest of the way down the white line on his tiptoes and throws his arms around the officer. Everyone stands, cheers, claps, and whistles.

The cop pushes Dan away, points his finger in Dan's face. "You're borderline."

The other officer reads Dan's license and calls his partner over. He points to something on the license and accidentally drops it while handing it to his partner. Both patrolmen bend over to pick it up. Dan uses the opportunity to pantomime a ride-the-pony gyration on the nearest officer's buttocks. The fans break out screaming, whistling, jumping up and down, and punching the air. The officers jump to attention and look at Dan standing in his socks and underwear, picking his nose.

"According to this, you wear glasses. Where's your glasses?"

Dan takes his slacks, searches the pockets, and pulls out a pair of glasses.

"How'd they get in your pocket?"

Dan puts his glasses on, and a huge billboard behind the policemen and cheering section comes into focus. It features a picture of an angry bear standing on his hind legs, his threatening paws spanning the width of the outdoor sign, his snarling mouth baring fangs, and his menacing eyes warning of danger. Above the picture, it reads "The Coliseum presents Yukon the Wrestling Bear, undefeated in over 10,000 matches." Below the bear, the sign advertises the prize in flashing lights: "WIN $20,000."

"How'd your glasses get in your pants pocket?"

Dan reads the sign again, then again. He shakes his head, blinks eyes, reads the sign one more time, and then takes off running and jumping down the highway, screaming, "God loves wrestlers! God loves wrestlers! God loves wrestlers!"

***

Dressed in a shirt and tie, Dan sits in an ornately carved high-backed wood chair with a brown leather seat. He looks at giant paintings hanging in the century-old hall of all the great men recognized for the founding, heritage, and traditions of Dover University. Opposite Dan, two ten-foot-tall doors swing open.

Bill Bohr walks out, looks Dan in the eye and shakes his hand. "Good luck," he says and then looks down. "I wish I could have done more."

"Hey, it's okay. I'm sure you did all you could. It'll be fine."

President Hardon steps out into the hall and smiles at the twosome. "You're next," announces Hardon.

Dan and Bill give each other a final nod. Bill shuffles down the hall. Dan strides into the room. Hardon closes the doors behind him. "Have a seat."

The only empty chair sits at the end of a long executive meeting table. Four elderly board members are seated down the left side. At the far end of the meeting table, a black high-backed leather chair is spun around, hiding its occupant. Another four mature men line the right side. A dark suit and a red power tie prop up each curmudgeon's face. The men sit at the table with interlocked fingers resting on a thick file in front of them. Their judgmental, wrinkled eyes observe an unkempt Dan walking to the chair. His hair sticks up in the back, and his glasses rest cockeyed across his face. The corner of his shirt collar is turned up, and although he wears a tie, the knot is off center. A full view of his outfit reveals that his belt has missed a pant loop, a shirttail hangs out of his tan pants, and he's wearing white socks and running shoes. As Dan sits, the oversized, overstuffed piece of furniture absorbs his body, making him appear half his size and a head shorter than everyone seated.

President Hardon addresses the board of trustees. "I'm sure everyone here knows of Dan Sangha. He was a national champion when he wrestled for Dover. After graduation, he went on to glory, winning the Olympics and then returning to coach wrestling at his alma mater."

The room is silent. All eyes focus on Dan. The president continues, "This meeting has been convened to evaluate Dan Sangha and his program to determine the future of wrestling at Dover University. I'm sure you are all aware that the university dropped the wrestling program at the beginning of the school year for budgetary reasons and to comply with the federal law, Title IX. As you heard from our athletic director, Bill Bohr, Mr. Sangha was given permission to continue the program if he assumed financial responsibility and there were no rule violations. The information in your folders will prove that Dan has failed on both counts. Each of you has before you documentation of all the complaints, rule violations, and a list of state and federal laws broken by Mr. Sangha and his wrestlers."

"Alleged," pipes in Dan.

"You'll get your turn," responds Hardon. He continues, "Plus, they are prime suspects in the theft of our beloved Dover Dog, stolen in the dark of night on Halloween from our main gate entrance." The president walks around the table and delivers a sheet of paper to each board member. "This meeting has been prompted by their latest escapade. Last weekend, Mr. Sangha and his wrestlers put the final nail in their coffin by breaking into our motor vehicle compound, stealing a university vehicle, transporting it across state lines, and demolishing it. This is the insurance report," says the president, slapping down a piece of paper and turning to Dan. "I'm sorry, but we've had enough of you and your ruffians and your total disregard for the law and Dover University. This is the proverbial last straw." All eyes finish scanning the insurance form and then focus on Dan.

"There's just one week left in the season," says Dan, shifting in his seat. "Let us finish the season, and then you can do whatever you want."

The board member seated closest to Dan speaks up. "From the looks of these reports, I'm afraid it's too late for any leniency." All the heads nod in agreement.

Seizing the moment, President Hardon steps in front of Dan. "You and your wrestlers are done at Dover."

Dan fights to sit up in his chair. "Look, I don't care what you do with me, but you can't do this to the kids," he says, sinking back into the cushions.

"Someone always gets caught in the pinch," answers Hardon.

"The kids haven't done anything wrong. You cancel their season now, and you're screwing with their lives, their dreams."

"We repeatedly warned you to shape up," says Hardon, pulling a handful of papers from his bag. "You've had more complaints than all the other teams combined, and this is just from this year."

"So are we keeping count of complaints?" asks Dan, pulling himself up to the front edge of the chair. "How many complaints does President Hardon have to date?"

"I'm not the one being evaluated."

"Maybe you should be."

President Hardon turns and appeals to the men seated around the table. "I'm just stating the obvious."

"He's right. We have more complaints than all the other teams put together because I have more All-Americans on my team than all the other teams put together."

"You mean criminals," adds Hardon.

Ignoring Hardon, Dan addresses the board. "Face it—athletically, Dover doesn't rate. None of your programs or facilities belong in Division I. You can't recruit a couch potato to come here. I did what I had to do to get tough kids and put together a team that can win on the highest level."

Hardon walks around the table. "The fact is, you recruit criminals, drug addicts, and social deviants who don't belong at Dover University or any university, for that matter." He leans in Dan's face. "Wrestlers are bad people."

"These kids are stallions. They got spirit and they're wild, but that's what makes them tough. But they're not bad," Dan says to the board, then directs his words to Hardon. "Bad is going out of your way to hurt other people and destroy what they've built."

"That sounds like the wrestling team," chides Hardon.

"You want me to kiss your ass, Hardon? You can fucking forget that," says Dan, turning to the men at the table. "Hardon says these kids don't deserve this. That's because he doesn't care. He doesn't know these kids the way I do. To him, they are just a file, a report."

Hardon cuts in, pointing his finger in Dan's face. "This man will say anything. He is a lying, deceitful, and troublesome employee. He lied to me about using university vehicles and running out on bills while representing Dover. He denied it to my face when I confronted him."

"Now, that's a lie," retorts Dan, slapping Hardon's hand away from his face. "And I'm not an employee."

Hardon walks around the table. "Dan Sangha and Bill Bohr conspired to cover up the fact that Dan was stealing university vehicles."

"What are you talking about?" asks Dan, sitting up straight. "Bill's a good man. He had no idea what I was up to, and I never denied your accusations."

"That's a lie."

"You calling me a liar?" challenges Dan, lifting himself from the chair.

"Isn't that what you call someone who makes a false statement with deliberate intent to deceive?" asks Hardon, puffing out his chest.

"I never lied to you," replies Dan, marching around the table toward the president. "And if you call me a liar again ... we're going to have to settle this another way."

"See," says Hardon, backing away and pointing at Dan, "this is a perfect example of what I'm talking about."

Dan closes, "This isn't about my wrestlers, is it? You're using them to get me, aren't you?"

President Hardon turns and makes a quick withdrawal, retreating to the head of the table. Dan stalks him. "Tell them ... tell them." The chair at the head of the table blocks Hardon's escape. "Tell them you're still pissed about the broken nose. Aren't you?" demands Dan, cornering the president.

The black leather chair spins. "What are you talking about?" asks a distinguished-looking silver-haired man.

"Checkmate," says Dan, reaching for the president's throat.   Hardon raises his arms and covers his head like a defensive boxer about to get pummeled against the ropes.

"What happened?" asks the tailored old man in the chair.

Dan freezes over a cowering Hardon. "When I was a freshman, Hardon was the football coach. He had done a little wrestling in high school, so he asked my coach who the toughest guy on the team was, and my coach pointed at me. So I'm on the mat stretching and Hardon sneaks up behind me, like Pearl Harbor, and jumps on me. I don't know who's jumping me, so I give him an elbow to his face and break his nose. He's hated me and the wrestling program ever since."

"Is this true, President Hardon?"

"That has no bearing on this case."

"Is it true?"

"Yes, Chancellor, but I have long since let go of that incident."

"President Hardon, I believe we know where you stand regarding Coach Sangha and the wrestling team. We need to speak to Dan alone, if you don't mind." says the chancellor, extending his manicured hand toward the door.

President Hardon gathers his briefcase and papers and walks to the door. "Thank you for your time. I'll wait in the hall for your decision." He walks out and closes the door.

The chancellor spins his chair to Dan. "Dan, I was president when you went to school here. I watched you win your national and Olympic titles. I was very proud of you and the way you represented this university. You have to understand, Dover University is my family, my life, as I am sure wrestling is yours. So I need to know what's going on."

"I'm trying to win."

The chancellor pauses, opens the file, and looks through it. "Dan, these are pretty serious charges. How about if we sort through them one at a time? Let's start with all these incidents in the file."

"Everything you have in front of you about the boys is just an allegation. The only crime committed was by me."

"Surely, with the sheer number. They can't all be allegations."

"It's just kid stuff. They're doing the same things I did when I was in school, the same things you did when you went to school, and probably the same things the next generation will be doing in twenty years."

"I'm sorry, that's not good enough."

"It's like when I went to school here, and you were president. There was that story going around about you, about how you pulled this prank with a horse when you were in the fraternity—"

"Dan, stop. Let's not go there." The chancellor flips a couple of pages. "Almost every wrestler has been cited for underage drinking."

"Is there anyone at this table who didn't try alcohol before they were legal?" Everyone sheepishly looks at each other. "If you're going to shut them down for that, you'd have to shut down every sports team, fraternity, sorority, any club, and two thirds of the students."

"What about the assertion that you recruit criminals and drug addicts?"

"I don't have choices. I get leftovers, the ones no one else wants. There are reasons why nobody wants them. A couple of them have problems, but they're not criminals or drug addicts. Not yet, anyway."

"What about Adam Robbins? He's been to prison."

"He did his time, paid his debt, and now he's trying to go straight."

"He has a record. He's a thief."

"Isn't that like the kettle calling the pot black?"

"What?"

"You charge twenty grand a year to come to school here, and you make it impossible to graduate in four years. So you get over a hundred grand from these kids for a degree, and then over half of them can't get a decent job."

"That's absurd. Utterly preposterous."

"Tell that to some kid who has your hundred-thousand-dollar degree and works at McDonald's."

"One more comment like that and this meeting is adjourned."

"What are you getting so sensitive about? It's the truth."

After a long pause, the chancellor tries to break the stalemate. "So, we're supposed to sit back, look the other way, and let your boys run wild?"

"No, that's not what I'm saying."

"Enlighten us."

"When I started recruiting these kids, I did it to win. But after you get to know them, they're just like me and you, except they got some bad breaks. Most of them just need time. They have no idea where they're going or what they're doing. Their energy has to be harnessed and focused. Their parents haven't done it. Neither have their schools, their communities, or the justice system. They need to find something. Some find wrestling, have some success, and they start feeling good about themselves. And when they feel good about themselves, they grow and change, and anything's possible. I've seen it."

"Dan, this is a school of higher learning. We're in the education business, not rehabilitation."

"Every one of these kids has leadership potential and could make a significant contribution to society. Isn't that what it's about, making the world a little better with each generation?"

"Have you proof of this?"

"There's stuff that's not in their files. Pump mentors the girls' basketball team. They're tied for first in the conference. Kruger and Mini D work with stranded, injured animals and nurse them back to health and find good homes for them. Pug and Doc mentor students with drug and alcohol problems. Bronk, Dickie, and Ben play cards with seniors. Balls has been helping me as a volunteer assistant. Joe teamed with Carter, and together they provide support for Dover athletic teams. Adam hasn't found anything yet. And they pass their classes and stay eligible."

"That's another concern, their grades. Their level of academic achievement as a group is very low."

"Some of these kids could barely read or write when they came here. I think they're doing great, considering where they came from. How come no one's mentioned the basketball team's grades?"

"Originally, the decision to end the wrestling program was made to satisfy two criteria. One was fiscal, and the other was compliance with federal law. Title IX requires gender equity. We simply followed the strategy employed by colleges across the country and dropped wrestling because there was no comparative women's program."

"It's my understanding that Title IX is not an athletic law. It is an institutional law that applies to the university as a whole and requires gender equity when hiring new faculty members, researchers, and administration—everyone." Dan takes a drawn out look around the table at each face of the all-white male board. "If you're serious about trying to maintain equity between men's and women's sports, why not institute more women's programs? Football doesn't have a comparative women's program, and you're not going to cut that, right?"

"There are fiscal limitations. Plus, there are not enough female athletes to field the teams we have."

"Exactly. That's why Title IX's a bad law. Its intention is to give more opportunities to women, not take away from men."

"Why do you think we should keep wrestling?"

"Look, I could sit here and tell you about how wrestling builds character and leaders and all that crap. About how it's more than books, degrees and titles and how it teaches about life, but you gave the best argument when you said Dover was your family. And if it's your family, then every program is like one of your kids. If you have a budget problem at home, do you solve it by killing one of your children? And if you start cutting programs when you have a problem, where does it end?"

"Is that it?"

"There's a reason for wrestling that's beyond our understanding. It's the oldest sport known to man. It's been around as long as man has. It has been used throughout history to train kings and presidents. Over twenty five percent of our presidents have wrestled, and two of our most famous, Washington and Lincoln, were both renowned for their wrestling prowess. It's one of the reasons man exists today. Without it, we'll be worse off, not better."

The chancellor turns to the next page. "Why did you steal a university vehicle?"

"I didn't steal it. I borrowed it to get the boys to the qualifier."

"But why?"

"I've had to sell both of my vehicles to get money to keep the program going, and I was too broke to rent a vehicle."

"It's obvious you have to make amends for the bills you owe."

"I've kept a list and plan on repaying every one of them, with interest," says Dan, removing a folded piece of paper from his back pocket.

"How do you plan to raise the money?"

"I'm leaving the moment this meeting is completed to do a fundraiser."

"What kind?"

"It's a competition, and I figure I can win enough to set things straight."

"When are you supposed to leave for nationals?"

"Tomorrow."

The chancellor looks around the table and then back to Dan. "Could you step out in the hall? We need to discuss this."

***

Dan sits next to Hardon in the hall. Hardon glances at Dan. Dan ignores him.

"I want you to know this wasn't personal." injects Hardon.

"Shut up."

"I had to do what was best for the university."

Dan turns to Hardon with a hard, cold stare. "Don't talk to me. I hate hippies and pussies, and you're not a hippie."

Bill Bohr enters and does a slow run down the hall to Dan. "When I got back to the athletic office, there was a message for you. Cindy has gone into labor and went to the hospital."

Dan jumps to his feet, takes a quick glimpse at the tall doors, and turns to Bill. "Let's go," he says.

"This also came for you," says Bill, handing him a large clasp envelope. "I think it's the results from your heart assessment at the Cleveland Clinic."

The tall doors swing open, and one of the board members pokes his head out. "Dan? We'll see you now."

Dan stops and looks back and forth between Bill and the board member. "Can you let her know I'll be there as soon as I can?" asks Dan. "And I'll take this." He snatches the envelope from Bill.

***

The chancellor leans forward, sets his elbows on the table, rests his chin on his interlocked fingers, and studies Dan. "Okay, we're going to give you a chance to set things straight. You make amends to Dover and Chicago, the hotels, restaurants, and gas stations on this list," says the chancellor, holding up a page of paper, "and present proof that you have the necessary funds for nationals, and you can take your team to the contest. Plus, we'll reconsider our decision to drop the wrestling program. The future of Dover wrestling rests upon your shoulders. Anything else you want to say?"

"Yeah, Bill is one of the good guys. He tried to find out what I was up to, but I lied to him. He didn't know anything. He's one of the best things this school has going for it."

"Dan, can I give you some advice?"

"Sure."

"All of these things are happening to you for a reason. You can take this for what it's worth, but it's been my life experience that what happens in the world around you is usually a reflection of what's going on inside you. The outside just reflects it back like a mirror."

○○○○○○○○○○○○○○○○○○○○○○○○○○○○○••

25. Wish I Could Fly

SHAFTS OF BRIGHT light wave back and forth across the dark sky like wipers on a celestial windshield. The random searchlight beams pierce the night, attracting attention and showing the way.

"Hoooly movie premiere," says Joe to his teammates as he steers his car to the end of a long line of vehicles waiting to pull into the parking lot. A parking attendant with a flashlight guides each set of wheels into the entrance just below a lit Vegas-style roadside sign in pronounced white lettering:

THE COLISEUM PRESENTS
YUKON THE WRESTLING BEAR.

Flashing letters advertise the prize: "WIN $20,000."

Joe turns into the lot and navigates from attendant to attendant to attendant to a parking space. Another car with the rest of the team parks in the next space. The Dogs climb from the cars, stretch, and straighten.

"Look at the size of that place," says Dickie.

The converted aircraft hangar spans several football fields. Giant black sport figures are painted and spaced along the outside walls. Each action image spans the height of the wall from the ground to the roof.

A multicolored lit marquee projects from the building over an all-glass front entrance. Red, yellow, and blue lights flicker, blink on and off in a pattern creating the impression they are circling around the large, white letters spelling "YUKON." A sudden burst of color illuminates the marquee as all the lights flash simultaneously, go dark and then start all over repeating the sequence. Above the marquee, a fifty-foot-tall picture of the ferocious, growling Yukon is swarmed by a half-dozen moving spotlights.

Promoters wait just inside the glass doors, accosting everyone coming through the entrance and hawking an encounter with the bear. "Twenty dollars gives you a chance to win twenty thousand."

"We're here to see a friend wrestle Yukon," says Balls, hobbling on his crutches.

"Just twenty dollars and five minutes, and you could go home twenty thousand richer."

"Are you looking at me?" asks Balls, balancing on one foot and holding up his crutches.

"How about one of your friends?"

"No, that's okay. We're just here to watch."

"Can't win if you don't play."

"We just want to watch."

Giving up, the pitchman directs the boys to a circus tent pitched in the center of the giant hangar for the main event and moves on, stopping the next set of ears willing to listen.

"Do you believe this place?" asks Bronk.

The team looks at the colorful sports murals decorating the inside perimeter of the enormous hangar. At ground level, a half-dozen bars are interspersed among game rooms, restaurants with live entertainment, and food buffets. An array of games, sports activities, and performing acts run simultaneously under the huge enclosure: video games, pool tables, golf simulators, batting and pitching cages, golf pitching and putting challenges, football punt, pass, and kick skills, basketball hoops, soccer kicking and dribbling tests, a go-cart track, a putt-putt course, a high-diving exhibition, and a variety of caged wild animals. Clowns, musicians, jugglers, and magicians roam the floor as they perform. Signs promote a special appearance by the Dallas Cowboys cheerleaders.

A photographer flashes his camera to capture the Dogs' entrance and then presents them with a card telling them where they can view and purchase the photographs.

The house lights go down. The arena falls silent as two spotlights come up. One light circles an older cowboy dressed in white. He twists the end of his handlebar mustache and covers the grip of his holstered six-shooter with the palm of his other hand. "Throw up your hands, kid, I want your guns," he says over the public address system.

The other light illuminates a young gunslinger in all black. He brushes back his shoulder-length hair and pulls the glove tight on the fingers of his shooting hand. "Back off, Sheriff, or you'll be pushing up daisies."

"You need to learn some respect for the law."

"I believe in respect ... for the dead."

"I like you. You remind me of me when I was young and stupid."

"No law against stupidity."

"But there's a law against packing a firearm in my town."

The young gunfighter pats the white handle of his six-shooter. "Pearl never leaves my side."

"Appears there's nothing under your hat but hair. I'm glad you set aside some time for some schooling."

"Ain't nothing I can learn from you, old man."

"I can always tell when you're lying, kid."

"How's that?"

"Your lips move."

"Read my lips. I'm visualizing your tombstone."

Piped-in music increases in volume and intensity as they begin pacing toward each other.

"Varmint." The sheriff steps closer.

The youngster continues to advance. "Yellowbelly."

"Skunk." They draw. Bang. Bang. The sheriff grabs his stomach, drops his handgun, looks at the kid in disbelief, and falls dead. The lights go out.

"Whoa, do you believe they killed the sheriff?" asks Ben.

House lights unleash the hucksters, who hustle in and corral everyone they can before the audience members can make their escape. Then, they begin herding up contestants who have signed up to wrestle Yukon and escort them to a waiting area.

Approaching the tent, the boys pass a series of moving message signs that update the latest Yukon results.

YUKON: 10,341 WINS and 0 LOSSES

Two attendants carry a huge farm boy from the tent. His clothes are shredded, and blood drips from his red-soaked head of hair. A third attendant walks next to them and talks into his walkie-talkie. "Have the ambulance meet us at the front door. We have someone who needs medical attention."

The sign flashes again:

YUKON: 10,342 WINS and 0 LOSSES. NEXT SESSION BEGINS AT 9:15.

"That's in fifteen minutes. Let's go check out the Dallas cheerleaders," suggests Pump.

"No, I want to get a good seat," counters Balls.

"Hey, you got me. I can clear out any seats you want." reminds Pug.

The Dogs respond together, "Cheerleaders."

***

Inside, the tent looks like a regular arena with bleachers surrounding an elevated ring in the center. All the seats are full. House lights dim, and a spotlight shines on the ringmaster dressed in a red sequined tux and black top hat.

"Ladies and gentlemen, welcome to the greatest phenomenon of our time. Every age has its extraordinary marvel, a supernatural anomaly, a spectacle so great it's called a wonder. We would like to introduce this generation's offering," he says, removing his tall cylindrical hat and pointing it across the arena. "Yukon, the next wonder of the world."

Spotlights bounce and ricochet around the ring and come to rest on one of the corner entrances. Horns announce his approach. Yukon and his trainer step from the shadows of the tunnel into the spotlight. The trainer leads the way to the ring, accompanied by pounding drums timed to Yukon's lumbering steps. Boom. Boom. Boom. The trainer spreads the ropes, and Yukon squeezes into the ring. With a wave of the trainer's hand, Yukon stands on his hind legs, and four beams of light flood him from all directions.

The ringmaster announces, "He stands over seven feet, weighs more than thirteen hundred pounds. He has three-and-a-half-inch canine teeth. Undefeated in 10,342 matches. Bigger, stronger, and faster than any human on earth. I present ...Yukon!" Music blares and lights flash.

Spotlights follow Yukon as the showman struts to center ring, stands tall, spreads his paws, and shows off his stuff.

Dan and Uncle Burt stand in a waiting area with a dozen other challengers. Uncle Burt stands behind Dan, rifling through some papers. "Did you read this medical report?"

Dan spins and snatches the report. "Where did you get this?"

"It was with your stuff. Did you read it?"

"Doctors don't know everything."

"But—"

"I know what I can do."

Uncle Burt massages Dan's shoulders. "Okay, I paid the entry fee and filled out the release forms—now the rest is up to you. Just five minutes with this furball, and you're going home with twenty grand."

"Did you find out when they pay?" asks Dan.

"They pay immediately upon conclusion of the match after all the officials confirm the outcome."

The spotlight shifts back to the ringmaster as he announces, "The rules are simple: you last five minutes, and you win $20,000. If Yukon holds you down on your back for a three count, he wins all the Coke he can drink—and he loves Coke. Yukon's next opponent this evening is Mark Olney. Mark is a practicing martial artist. Let's have a big hand for Mark from Cincinnati, Ohio."

The crowd enthusiastically cheers and whistles as a short, wiry man makes his way to the ring. Yukon's trainer takes his place in his corner, and the ringmaster starts the match. Above the ring, a giant four-sided clock begins ticking down the seconds. Mark moves in, angles to the side, and grabs the bear's arm. He locks down on the hairy limb with all his might and attempts various holds and throws, but the bear does not budge. Yukon breaks the hold and just stands there as the man circles away and plans his next move. The bear looks the man over and extends his other arm, giving it to the human as if he has done this a thousand times before and gestures as if to say, *Go ahead and try this one, but we know you do not have a prayer.* The man tries to leverage the bear's arm but fails to challenge Yukon's incredible strength and weight advantage. The trainer's eyes shift back and forth between the match and the clock. When he thinks the show has gone on long enough, the trainer slaps the mat to get Yukon's attention and gives a thumbs down signal. The bear grabs the man, flips him on his back, and places his paw on the man's chest. The ringmaster counts, "One. Two. Three. You're out."

After the match, Yukon bounces to his corner and sits on his haunches. His trainer hands him Coke after Coke. The bear takes each bottle, turns it straight up, drains the liquid contents down his throat, and reaches for another.

The ringmaster announces the next contestant. "Next, hailing from Detroit, Michigan, Matt Bundy. Matt is pursuing a career as a professional wrestler. Let's give it up for Matt."

Cheers raise the tent when the spectators see the next challenger is three times the size of the first man. The large, rotund fellow splits the ropes as he enters the ring and stands in his corner, facing the post. He grabs the converging ropes with both hands, leans back and stretches. Yukon finishes his Coke, expels gas from his stomach with a loud, blatant burp, and walks to center ring. The giant of a man walks straight into the bear and grabs its head, attempting to tie up as professional wrestlers do. Using his weight, he drives into the bear and then tries jerking, but all attempts to move the bear in any direction fail. The human behemoth tries to headlock the bear and ends up swinging from his furry neck.

The professional wrestler backs across the ring and runs at Yukon, striking him across the chest with a forearm smash and then grabs his own arm in pain. Moves that look so effective on other human beings are almost comical. The mountain of fur tolerates the silly human's feeble attempts until his trainer slaps the mat and gives the thumbs down signal. With a swipe of his paw, the bear flips the man to his back, holds him down for the count, and then rambles to his corner for Coke.

The ringmaster offers a rote response before giving the next introduction. "Good try, Matt. Let's hear it for Matt. Our next opponent comes to us from Chicago—the Chicago Bears that is—professional football player and fan favorite for his ferocious play on the field, the legendary linebacker Ted 'Rhino' Granite."

The muscle-bound football player goes straight for the bear. He runs across the ring, extends his arms and attempts to lock them around the hairy chest. Rhino's confidence angers the bear. He picks him up and slams him on the mat so hard everyone can hear the thud and feel the vibration. Rhino bounds back to his feet as if he just made a big play on the gridiron. He lowers his level and rushes with all he's got. He buries his shoulder and whacks the bear with his best tackle. Yukon sweeps him in the air and throws him down, bouncing him off the ring floor. Climbing back to his feet ever so slowly, he attempts another strategy and runs. Running away arouses Yukon's wrath. He chases the agile man around the ring until he closes in and corners him. This time, the bear shows no mercy. Without a signal from his trainer, he slams the football player and holds him down with his paw. After the count, Yukon flings the former football player around like a rag doll. He picks him up, repeats the beating in each corner before throwing him out of the ring and running for his Coke.

Next, the ringmaster introduces two young women for a tag team match with the bear. They leap on the fuzzy playground jungle gym and climb all over him. When the trainer senses the comic relief has run its course, he slaps the mat and gives a thumbs up. Yukon nuzzles his nose up their T-shirts, exposing their breasts. When the crowd hoots and hollers, Yukon rolls out his footlong tongue and licks the girls as they scramble out of the ring.

Dan and Uncle Burt stand out of view in the entrance tunnel, watching Yukon chugging Coke and waiting for Dan's introduction.

"Are you sure you want to go through with this?" asks Uncle Burt glancing at the envelope with the medical report.

"Don't you get it? This is all meant to be. I've been dreaming of wrestling the bear to prepare me for this moment. I wrestled this match a hundred times. I know exactly what I'm going to do. I've never been more ready for anything in my life."

The announcer breaks in. "And now from the world of amateur wrestling, it's our honor to present Olympic and national champion, Dan Sangha."

The Dogs scream and the fans follow with a tent-flapping roar. Dan marches down the aisle, climbs between the ropes into the ring, and looks across at Yukon guzzling another Coke. Yukon looks back with a hint of recognition; he senses this man is different. He lowers the half-finished Coke bottle from his drooling mouth, casts it aside, and plods from his corner. Dan gets his first close-up look at Yukon's face. *It's the bear from my dream.*

The ringmaster starts the match with a slash of his hand, and the clock begins ticking. Dan carefully gauges his distance to stay out of Yukon's reach. The sly old dog moves in, out, and around Yukon until he maneuvers the bear to the center of the ring, and then begins skipping sideways, encircling the giant furball. Dan circles Yukon to avoid any contact, slow at first, then faster and faster. In the beginning, the crowd laughs and points, but when they tire of the antics, their snickers turn to boos. The Dogs look at each other, questioning Dan's strategy and wondering if he is afraid.

The spinning bear playfully consents to this dizzy game. Dan senses Yukon beginning to become a bit woozy and continues circling until the bear's back is to his trainer.

No hand signals this time. Dan stops and strikes the classic bear pose. He raises both hands in the air in a threatening manner and growls a deep guttural growl. Yukon's eyes twinkle at Dan's comical and nonthreatening rendition. The lack of any type of reaction from the bear provokes Dan to smack the bear in his snout, sending the slobber hanging from his jowls splattering across the mat. Now, Yukon accepts the challenge. He raises his massive, furry frame. On his rear soles, he strikes a frightening, formidable posture to show off the real thing and win this silly contest. The awed spectators lean backward and gasp as Yukon lifts his huge, menacing claws skyward, flashes his threatening fangs, and tilts his fury head to bellow a dreadful, deafening, rolling thunder roar. A vibration like the precursor to an earthquake sends a chill through the observers' bones and renders them mute.

The trainer slaps the mat and the instant Yukon looks, Dan lowers his level and shoots headfirst on the bear's short, stubby legs. His hands cup the heels below the ankles, and he drives his shoulders through the bear's knees with all his might, tripping the showoff backward. In midair, the athletic bear flips from his back and lands on his stomach. Dan leaps onto Yukon's back, wraps both legs around the torso and buries his heels into the bear's groin. At the same time, he clamps his arms around the husky neck, locks his hands, and squeezes. The action breaks the silence dam, and screams spread throughout the assembly. The Dogs rush forward, and the overflowing throng tsunamis to the edge of the ring.

The bear is miffed by the nuisance strapped on his back. Baffled by the novel position, the animal struggles for an appropriate counteraction and begins pawing at Dan. The heavy, powerful swipes barely miss Dan's tucked head but snag his shirt and shred it from his torso like wet tissue paper. Dan adjusts his wrestler's grip, squeezes harder, and puts a clamp on the windpipe. Yukon paws at Dan until he realizes he can't inhale. He forgets the human backpack and struggles for a breath. He violently slings his head back and forth, his silent mouth gaping open and his perplexed eyes cast to an unavailing heaven. Terror overwhelms the panicking beast. He thrashes about the ring uncontrollably, throwing his furry frame into the ropes as he tries to scrape Dan from his back. The choke is on. The mob shoves and crams forward, packing ringside to witness a first. Led by the Dogs, the squashed mass begins pounding the outer edge of the ring and chanting, "Dogface! Dogface! Dogface!"

Absence of air takes its toll and slows the majestic beast. The sluggish mammal summons all his power from every fiber. Straining his entire network of muscle, he flexes and mimics a prolonged scream, pumping blood to every cell. An all-out exertion of the silent cry enlarges his bulging neck muscles. The severe pressure of his expanding neckline stretches the two steel hooks forged from Dan's interlocking fingers. His clutching hands vibrate and shake as his hold begins to melt. Fingers slowly extend and straighten until he is holding on by his fingertips. Exertion distorts his face. Yukon's incessant flexing continues pumping blood into his swollen, constricted neck. Dan's face grimaces as the sinew that knits his knuckles and finger joints begins popping and snapping. A finger joint dislocates. In a full-blown panic, Yukon slings his head around, emitting a soundless Godzilla bray. Another knuckle pops out of joint ... and then another. *No pain, no gain.* Dan wills his four-finger stranglehold to endure. Banished air dissipates the beast's power; he deflates as his movements retard to a suffocating slow motion. After a couple of staggered steps, he collapses to all fours. The stunned arena falls silent. Yukon holds himself up for a final moment, then crumbles to the ring floor and lies motionless.

Dan's face is an ashen void. He slowly releases his white knuckled grip, fights to stand erect, ready to regrab at the slightest movement. Straddling the furry mound, the remains of his shredded shirt slip from his drenched torso. The ring's lights reflect off his glistening upper body, producing a golden, ethereal glow. The fans snap out of their funk and unleash series upon series of uncontrollable screams and cheers that are soon drowned by the "Dogface" chant. The trainer runs to his bear. Dan slides his leg over the bear and aims his wasted remains toward his corner, which is mobbed by the Dogs pounding their hands on the mat and screaming, "Dogface!" Dan labors with every wobbly step. Uncle Burt climbs into the ring to greet the victor. Dan strains to take one more step, covers his chest with his hand, and then drops, collapsing to his knees. Uncle Burt rushes toward Dan as his eyes roll up into his head, his body goes limp, and he falls forward, slapping the canvas floor with his comatose face.

***

Dan's unconscious body lies on an examination table in the center of a makeshift locker room. He is surrounded by Uncle Burt and the Dogs. They watch as a doctor administers smelling salts; the pungent aroma of ammonia jars his senses. His head jerks, his face flinches, and his eyes blink open.

"Where am I?" asks Dan, sitting up.

"Easy does it," cautions the doctor.

"You passed out. We thought you were a goner," injects Uncle Burt.

"I was just resting my eyes," says Dan, feeling the pain and lifting his hands to his face. "I'm fine now," he says, examining his knuckles and fingers. "I won, right?" He pulls a finger and resets the knuckle and joint.

"I'll say," replies Uncle Burt, followed by the rest of the team. "You were awesome, Coach. Un-friggin-believable. The whole place went nuts."

The door flies open. Two security guards step in and post themselves on each side of the door as an entourage files in and clusters.

One man steps forward, "How's the man of the hour doing?"

"He's coming around," says the doctor.

The very plain, unassuming man in a conservative suit and tie approaches Dan, grabs his hand, and shakes vigorously.

"Let me be the first to congratulate you."

Dan grimaces, pulls his broken hand free from the man's grip and cradles it in his other hand.

Reading from a card, the man asks, "It's Dan—Dan Sangha—am I right?"

"That's right," says Dan, opening and closing his hand. "Who are you?"

"Benny Shapiro. This is my place, and in all my days, I've never seen anything like this. You gave everyone the thrill of a lifetime. There's a buzz in the Coliseum I've never witnessed," he says, patting Dan on the shoulder with one hand and pointing at his face with the other. "They'll be talking about this for years. You are going to be a legend, my man."

"Thanks. When do I get the money?" asks Dan, pulling and elongating another finger.

"That's why I'm here." Pointing to one of his assistants.

The assistant reads from a binder. "To win the monetary prize, a contestant must wrestle the bear for a full five minutes. During that time, the contestant must stay in the ring without running away and without being pinned or injured."

The promoter continues, "And according to our official timekeeper ..." He points to another assistant with a stopwatch.

"Mr. Sangha expired and could not continue at 4 minutes and 57 seconds."

The promoter finishes, "You did not complete the five-minute requirement, and since you're okay and Yukon is okay, we are officially calling this match a draw. There will be no prize money."

Uncle Burt and the Dogs rage, "That's bullshit. You can't do that. Coach beat Yukon fair and square."

The promoter raises his hand and snaps his fingers. Four very large, armed security personnel step to the front as the promoter and his entourage dance out the door.

"You're a crook. Cheat. Swindler," yell the Dogs as the security guards back out and close the door.

All eyes refocus on Dan sitting up with his legs dangling over the side of the table. His head hangs. He stares at his hands resting in his lap. His blank, expressionless face is frozen. A stream of thoughts flows behind his empty eyes. Everyone can hear his deep breathing. He lifts his head. His vacant, sagging eyes look around the room into each of the boy's faces. In a subdued tone, they have never heard, he admits, "I haven't been ... honest with you." He has trouble concentrating and searches for the right words. "The university ... dropped ... the program, the wrestling program ... ." One hand rubs his stomach. "There's no ... money." The other hand covers his chest. "I had to ... win tonight to get you to nationals ... ." Both hands cover his face.

Dan slides off the table. The boys part and make a path. Uncle Burt grabs Dan's arm before he can take a step. "C'mon, we can—"

Dan jerks his arm free from Uncle Burt's grip and turns on him. Grabbing two fistfuls of his shirt, he runs his assistant backward into the wall. Lifting him off the ground, he shouts in his face. "I can't do any more—"

Sensations like jagged daggers stabbing a raw nerve radiate from his finger joints and knuckles. He releases his grip. In agony, he lifts his wrists, palms, fingers, and thumbs and supports them in the air like a surgeon preparing for surgery. Uncle Burt drops back to his feet. Dan feels an uncomfortable heaviness in his chest. He turns toward the door. An acute heartache squeezes his rib cage. He stabs the center of his sternum with his right wrist and reaches out blindly, finding the wall with his left forearm and leaning against it, preventing his unstable frame from collapsing.

"You okay?" asks Uncle Burt, reaching out.

Removing the hand from his breastbone, he waves off Uncle Burt, takes a few slow, deep breaths, and stands erect. Everyone watches Dan limp across the room and lean his head against the door. He opens his mouth and protracts his jaw from side to side while simultaneously turning his head and extending one side of his neck and then the other. He shakes the fuzziness from his head and blinks repeatedly. An ugly, contorted expression masks his face when he takes the doorknob in his hand.

"I need your keys," says Dan, extending an open hand.

"Where are you going?" asks Uncle Burt, setting the keys in his outstretched mitt.

Dan turns the doorknob. "Where I should have been all along." He opens the door and gimps out.

○○○○○○○○○○○○○○○○○○○○○○○○○○○○○•

26. Dare to Come Out

DAN'S PROFILE IS backlit in the doorway. His iconic burr head and cauliflower ears are unmistakable.

"Dan? Dan is that you?" asks Cindy from her bed in the dark room. "What are you doing here?"

"I came to be with you." His black slouched, deflated frame remains motionless. "What are you up to?"

"I'm having a baby."

"Am I in time?"

"In time?"

"You know, for the baby."

"What?"

"Am I in time for the baby?"

"My contractions stopped, so we're in wait and see mode."

"Good, I made it." Dan drags his feet across the room to her bedside.

Cindy turns on the lamp next to her bed and sees Dan's gaunt, drawn face. "What happened?" asks Cindy, wrapping her arms around him.

"I screwed up."

"What else is new?"

"No. I really screwed up."

"Well, you're here now."

"I lost everything."

"What?"

"I don't want to lose you and the girls."

"What are you talking about?"

"I screwed up really bad. I don't know how to tell you."

"Tell me what?"

"I lost my job."

"Oh, Dan." Cindy squeezes Dan tight.

"I lost the program."

"No. I'm sorry."

"I let the boys down."

"I'm sure you did your best."

"I'm probably going to lose our home."

"What?" Cindy pulls away and opens her eyes and ears.

"I've been so stupid. I can't believe I did what I did."

"You're not making any sense."

"At the beginning of the year, the school fired me and dropped the wrestling program, so I've been keeping it going in secret."

"What do you mean you're going to lose our home?"

"I can't believe I put things before my family. I promise from this day forward, you and the kids will come first."

"The house—"

"I need you and the girls."

"Tell me about the house."

"I couldn't make the mortgage payments. They're going to foreclose."

Cindy looks at the family photo on the night stand.

"I've been so stupid. I'm sorry. Please forgive me."

She twists and twirls her wedding band.

"Please."

"Shhh." says Cindy, reaching out. She pulls Dan's head to her bosom and rocks. "Of course, I forgive you."

Dan's arms swathe her. "I'm just glad I'm in time."

"For what?"

"I missed the first two, but nothing in this world is going to stop me from being here for the birth of this child." Dan clings to her, wrapping his arms snugly around her.

"You're home." She hugs tight and tears roll from her closed eyes, cascade over her cheek, and splash on the back of Dan's head. "Everything's going to be okay. Rest now." She cradles his face with one hand and strokes his hair with the other.

Unwilling to let her out of his grasp, Dan climbs into the hospital bed and clings to her. Cindy's womblike embrace dissolves life's hold on Dan. Each narcotic breath relaxes his muscles, unknots his stomach, and empties his mind. Their hearts synchronize. Immersed, his eyes close. He drifts off.

***

Three nurses cackle, scurry past the open door, and scamper down the hall. Cindy listens, trying to overhear what the commotion is about, but Dan's snoozing murmur is just loud enough that she can't make out what they are saying. A figure carrying a large brown paper shopping bag with loop handles appears in the doorway.

"Excuse me, ma'am, could I have a moment of your time?"

"Carter? Is that you?"

"Yes ma'am," says Carter. "Mrs. Sangha? Is that you? What are you doing here?"

"I'm bringing another little creature of joy and mirth into this crappy world."

"I'm sorry to bother you. I'll just be moving on."

"No, what is it?"

Carter looks down at the snoring Dan. "You probably already know the university dropped the wrestling program, and the team doesn't have the money to go to nationals. Balls rallied all the Dover athletes at Uncle Burt's place, and we agreed to knock on every door in town and on campus and ask for a dollar from everyone."

"Carter, I thought you hated the wrestlers."

"No ma'am, I just like competing with them. Coach Sangha's got it going on. I wish I had a coach like him. The team deserves to go to nationals, and we're going to get them there."

"Hand me my purse," says Cindy, pointing to the nightstand. Carter retrieves her purse. Dan's head erupts with a harsh snort when Cindy lets go to reach for her purse. She removes a dollar and drops it in the open bag. Cindy looks down at the top of Dan's head for a moment, kisses and hugs it, and asks, "Before you leave, would you hand me the phone?"

***

Dan's arms wrap around Cindy, his head nestled between her plump belly and breasts. His sprawled body hogs up most of the bed. She hangs over the edge of the mattress and clings to him, so she doesn't slide off. Two doctors enter the room, accompanied by a nurse. They are dressed in masks, caps, and gowns, ready for the delivery room.

The nurse nudges Dan's shoulder. "Mr. Sangha, it's time." He lies motionless. Her gentle push intensifies into an aggressive jab. "Mr. Sangha ... Mr. Sangha, it's time."

Dan mumbles in his sleep and slobbers on Cindy's belly. Grabbing his shoulder with both hands, the nurse shakes vigorously. Dan responds to the prodding and sits up with his eyes closed. His mouth hangs open, and drool leaks from the corner.

The nurse holds up a garment. "You need to put this on."

Half asleep, Dan stands and holds his arms out like Frankenstein. The nurse slides the long-sleeved garment over each of his extended arms, circles behind, pulls the gown snug to his body and ties the straps down the back.

Dan opens his eyes and looks at each sleeve dangling from the end of his arms down to the floor. "Aren't these sleeves a little long?"

One of the doctors steps forward. "No problem. We can take care of that." The two doctors each take an arm and wrap the extra material around Dan's body.

Dan feels his arms being pulled across his chest. "What's this?"

The doctors jerk the material and tie it behind Dan's back, binding his arms tight against his body.

Dan tugs against the restraint. "What's going on?" he asks.

One doctor raises his hands in front of Dan's face. "Calm down. This is standard procedure."

The other doctor hurries into the hallway, puts his arm in the air, and waves. Dan fights the constraint, but the device has totally retarded the use of his arms.

"It's just a formality, Mr. Sangha. You have to relax," cautions the doctor.

"Hey, I recognize your voice. I know who you are," says Dan, regaining his faculties.

The Dogs rush through the door and surround Dan. He begins kicking and headbutting whoever comes in range until the team swarms him and lifts the human burrito on their shoulders.

He struggles. "What are you doing? No, stop. You can't do this." They carry him out of the door twisting, wiggling, and straining. "My wife is having a baby. No, no, I promised. You don't understand." He kicks and lashes out with his head and feet as they turn the corner and disappear. "You can't do this. I promised. Cindy ... Cindy, help me," pleads Dan as he is carried down the hall. "Cindy! Help me! ... Cindy!"

"Thanks for the call, Cindy. We owe you big time," says Uncle Burt, removing the doctor's mask.

"I know who I married."

"Jas thought up the straitjacket. I don't think I've ever seen Dan that mad before."

"He'll get over it. And if he doesn't settle down, tell him," she looks at Jas, then back at Uncle Burt and waves him to come close.

Uncle Burt walks over and leans his ear to Cindy's lips, and she whispers. Uncle Burt grins and blushes. "I could listen to that kind of talk all day. Anything else?"

"Yeah, kick some butt."

***

Bound in a straitjacket and gagged, Dan squirms under the seat belt strapped across his lap and latched in the flight seat. His body expands and strains until his head burns, glows red and breaks a sweat. Then he goes limp, takes some heavy, deep breaths and explodes again, exerting every muscle to its utmost until he shakes uncontrollably. After a while, he goes lax, breathes, and investigates. He slowly stretches, twists, and wiggles inside his restraints. Feeling for a change, a weakness of any kind, he puts pressure against the seams. *Nope, nothing there.* Exploring the shape of the jacket with his elbows, he searches for looseness. *Oh, c'mon ... Anything.* Dan sits still as his arms shift and hunt around inside the jacket. *C'mon. Whoa. What was that?* Dan rechecks with his right elbow. *That's about an inch more movement than last time. Go ballistic.* Dan takes a gulp of air and detonates.

In the seat next to Dan, Uncle Burt stretches his legs as much as possible and slouches his head over an airline magazine. Dan strains. His deep, guttural grunts break Uncle Burt's focus. He shifts his eyes from the publication and watches Dan shiver, turn purple and go flaccid again. Uncle Burt looks around the plane. Everyone watches Dan's struggle. Some passengers whisper to each other.

Finding the disturbance impossible to ignore, the stewardess approaches and asks, "Is everything all right?" Realizing he has her attention, Dan struggles against his seat belt and tries to communicate with his head movements, bulging eyes, and muffled gagged sounds.

Uncle Burt studies Dan and downplays it. "He's afraid of flying. We have to go through this every time we fly."

"Some of the passengers are concerned. Maybe next time you should try a sedative."

"You don't happen to have a sedative, do you?" he asks the stewardess.

She takes a long look at Dan's pleading face. His eyes widen, and he frantically shakes his head back and forth and groans.

Uncle Burt interrupts her stare. "He usually calms down about this time. Can we give it a few more minutes?" She nods to Uncle Burt, takes another once-over of Dan, turns and walks up the aisle to the front of the plane.

"Okay, we're going to give this a try," says Uncle Burt, loosening the gag. "If I remove the gag, are you going to be civil?"

Dan listens and sits still.

Uncle Burt pauses and waits for a response. "Well?"

Dan nods.

"If I remove the gag, you promise to stop all the thrashing about?"

Dan doesn't answer, so Uncle Burt begins retightening the gag. Dan grumbles, nodding hard and fast that he agrees.

Uncle Burt loosens the cloth muzzle. "And you promise to be mellow?"

Dan nods yes.

"And keep your voice down?"

Dan nods yes.

"And not say anything that will disturb anybody?"

Dan nods yes.

Uncle Burt removes the gag.

"HELP!" screams Dan.

Uncle Burt puts a hand over his mouth. "You promised."

Dan jerks his mouth free. "I confided in you. I trusted you."

"What?"

"I told you I was claustrophobic and look what you did to me."

"That's right, you did," says Uncle Burt with a smirk. "I forgot. It was the only way we could figure to get you out of the hospital. I wasn't thinking."

"Let me out of here."

"I want to, but you have to cooperate."

"I have to get back to the hospital."

"Look, you can't do anything about that now. They're not going to turn the plane around. You have to wait until we land."

"HELP!"

"What are you yelling about?

"You kidnapped me. You're holding me against my will. I have to get back to Cindy."

"You know, that's the one thing about you that puzzles me. You always focus on what you don't have."

"What are you talking about?"

"You got everything you wanted. We raised enough money to take care of all the bills."

"Yeah."

"We're taking the team to nationals."

"Okay."

"And you have a wife who loves you."

"I have to get back to the hospital," says Dan. "I promised."

"There you go again. Cindy said if you don't settle down, I should tell you something."

"Yeah? What's that?"

Uncle Burt leans across the seat and whispers in Dan's ear.

"Bullshit," exclaims Dan.

Uncle Burt shakes his head.

"You're just saying that."

Uncle Burt shakes his head.

"She said that?"

Uncle Burt arches his eyebrows and nods.

"You're sure that's what she said?"

Uncle Burt nods with an envious, evil grin.

"You're just saying that to get me to go along."

Uncle Burt shakes his head and adds, "She actually said ... you know ... that."

"She said that if we win ... she'll ... you know ..."

Uncle Burt's nods with a sly smile. "You got everything you wanted. You lucky dog."

Dan stops. He looks over his shoulder and then bows his head in contemplation. His face explodes with a sudden insight. "Okay, you can untie me." Uncle Burt hesitates. Dan sees the skepticism in his eyes. "It wasn't the bear. It wasn't me. It was this. No, really, I get it. It's about all of us, and I'm getting everything I wanted. Heh, heh, I get it. I really get it."

The plane rolls into its gate and slows to a stop. An airport employee wheels out a portable set of stairs and locks them into place. The exit door swings open. A free Dan is the first to step out. "Okay, enough of this jet set bullshit."

***

Dan turns a brand-new red station wagon from the airport drive. Uncle Burt turns after him and follows in the latest model white passenger van. Streaking down the highway, Dan's vehicle breaks, yanks left into the turning lane and pauses. At the first opportunity, he makes a sharp turn across traffic and darts through an open gate in the black wrought iron fence.

"Where's he going?"

Uncle Burt follows. "Beats the hell out of me."

Dan follows the roadway meandering through the cemetery.

"What are we doing in a bone orchard?" ask Bronk.

He winds between the gravestones and pulls off the road onto the edge of the grass near the heart of the burial ground. Dan orders everyone to get out, take a walk around, and read the headstones. After a few minutes, he calls everyone together around a freshly dug grave.

"What did you see?" Dan asks.

Ben shrugs. "Dead people." He corrects himself. "Well, not dead people but their markers—you know what I mean."

"That's right. Dead people's tombstones. Anything else?"

"They all have a name," Pug offers.

"That's right, and ..."

"And dates," Mini D finishes.

Dan holds up two fingers. "Two dates that everyone who looks at the gravestone is going to read—one marks the beginning and the other the end, but all that matters is that little dash in the middle. It represents their lives." Dan points down at the rectangular resting place. "That's where I was yesterday. I was ready for someone to throw the dirt on, and you guys pulled me out." Dan stares into the permanent, black refuge. "I thought I'd seen it all and done it all. But, this is new. I felt it was me against the world. Everyone was the enemy. Anyone I was nice to was keeping me from winning. I had it all wrong. That's not what it's about." He looks around at the team. "It's about us. It's about struggling together, fighting together, standing together, and supporting each other. It's about brotherhood. We're a team. A damn good one."

Dan waves his arm over the graveyard. "In the end, everyone loses. We're put in a hole, they throw dirt on, and it's our permanent address. Alone for eternity." Dan looks into their eyes. "But for the next three days, we have each other, and if you're not going to try to pack the next three days of your dash with great memories, well ... you may as well crawl into one of these holes right now, because you ain't living. It's your choice."

Everyone stands staring down in the dark hole. Joe slips behind Dan and pushes. Dan hops over the pit. Laughs out loud, grabs a handful of dirt and wings it, covering Joe's face with muck.

Handfuls of earth spray and splat.

Dan jumps in the middle of the fray. Everyone pelts him. He wallows in the dirt shower and bellows, "This has been the best year of my life—a dog year." He extends his hand forward. "Dogs."

One by one, they add their soiled hands.

"No breaks."

"Be an ax."

"Be a hammer."

"Dominate."

"Finish number one."

"Beat people up."

"Make your man succumb."

"Think pin."

"Be the ultimate competitor."

Dickie hesitates. "Only head shots count." He slumps and complains, "You guys took all the good ones. It was the only thing I could think of."

"It works." Balls adds the final hand. "Run to the roar."

They bark.

"All right, Uncle Burt's going to take you to the gym so you can get a workout and check your weight." Waving a handful of note cards, he explains, "I prepared a card for each of you. I've written what you need to focus on in your workout. Here—pass these around."

Uncle Burt spouts, "Okay, you Dirty Dogs, get your card and let's get going."

Dan pulls Uncle Burt aside. "I have to make an appearance at the arena for media day. I'll meet you back at the hotel."

"Hey, Coach, there's no card for me," complains Bronk.

Dan hesitates. "Why should I make you one?" he asks. "You let Ryder kick your butt, and then you whine that you can't beat him, so why should I waste my time?"

Bronk stands in shock.

"Well?"

Bronk doesn't answer.

"I thought so," says Dan walking to the car.

"I can beat him," murmurs Bronk.

Dan opens the car door.

"I can beat him."

Dan climbs in. "Huh?"

Bronk takes ownership. "I can beat him."

Dan leans his head out the car window. "What was that?"

"I said, I can beat Ryder."

"Based on what?"

"I'm hankering for a good fight."

"Okay, I believe you."

"Hey, Coach," interjects Ben, holding up two note cards. "I got Bronk's card by mistake."

"Give it to Bronk," says Dan, pulling away. *That's the best mistake I ever made.*

***

A crew of journalists surrounds Dave Kane's table. He sits behind a microphone, answering questions. All the other coaches' tables are deserted.

A lone reporter queries Dan. "What do you think your chances are?" asks the writer. He tries to disrupt Dan's focus on Kane by waving a hand in front of his face.

"Cut it out." Dan pushes the reporter's hand away.

"I think you can make a run at them. What do you think?" The reporter waits for an answer, then begs, "C'mon, answer my question."

"You're from the Dover paper. I see you every week. Sometimes more."

"So, what are your chances?"

"I don't make predictions. It's up to the guys now."

"So, what are their chances?"

"Nationals are the ultimate pressure cooker. Emotions run high and tempers flare."

"So, what are the team's chances?"

"I don't know. We could poop in our pants, or we could come out fighting? If we fight we'll do good. Now shut up. I want to hear what he has to say."

"Should I write that?"

"Start writing something, so I can hear what he's saying." warns Dan, watching the clamor around Kane.

The reporters anxiously wave their arms. Kane looks around at the field of hands and selects one.

"How do you feel about your number one ranking?"

Kane answers, "We've won nine championships in a row, and we're unbeaten this season. It's exactly where we expect to be." He points to a waving hand.

"After being number one for so long, do you ever feel like you're wearing a target?"

"Of course, but being number one is what we're all about. That's what we're here for. We're willing to do whatever it takes to do it better than anyone has ever done it before. This weekend, we are going to win a record tenth straight national championship, which has never been done by any sports team in college history. Plus, we are going to break the record we set three years ago for most team points scored."

"Is Bobby Ryder the second coming?"

"Everything he's gotten in the sport, he's earned. It's who he is. He brings a mindset to the mat that is hard to deny. He stands for domination, and he embodies that. He goes all out every practice and every match. He epitomizes what this sport is all about. If I could clone nine more like him,

I wouldn't have to coach—I'd just open the room when it's time to practice, lock up after them, and show up for the matches."

"Why is Chicago the best?"

"We are committed to whatever it takes. Discipline, commitment, and passion. We love being number one and not just challenging another team," Kane waves his arm, "but the whole damn country. Okay, one more question."

"How do you do it year after year? What's your secret?"

"When I say whatever it takes, that's exactly what I mean. To be the best, you must be driven to go beyond your abilities. You must see what no one has seen before and then do what has never been done. Why so many people cannot be number one is because they don't have a strong enough desire. Most live in their comfort zone, and it becomes their prison. They never give themselves a reason to climb out of their rut and rise above the field. If you want to be the best, you must have a dream. You have to be able to visualize the end of that dream and live in it now. There is no tomorrow. You must be able to experience it with all your senses in the *now*. When you sleep, you dream about it. When you wake, you rush out the door and live it." Kane stands. "Speaking of rushing out, I need to end here. I'll see you boys tomorrow."

Followed by his entourage, Kane walks around the table and heads for the exit. He pulls up at Dan's table and extends his hand. "Dan, you ole dog, welcome to Chicago country. Heard you did real well at that qualifier of yours. You got eight boys here, right?"

"Nine."

"We didn't do too bad, either. We qualified all ten," says Kane, slapping Dan on the shoulder. "What do you think of that?"

"You're going to need them."

The comment wrinkles Kane's brow. He grins. "I noticed you have some Oklahoma and Iowa boys in the early rounds."

"Got some Chicago, too."

Kane laughs, "Oklahoma and Iowa's been pressuring us all year, and I know you did real well against them. You could help us and knock a few of them off."

"If we knock off too many ... you're going to have to worry about us."

"You never change." Kane forces a laugh and walks away. "See you on the mats."

***

Dan and Uncle Burt lounge on their beds. Gorni and Balls fiddle with the TV antenna, trying to get a picture on the snowy screen. Peeling wallpaper and faded, stained paint surround the foursome. Uncle Burt's bed is lopsided, one corner lower than the rest. Worn and tattered bedspreads provide flimsy cover. Above, chunks of the textured ceiling hang in haphazard flakes. Someone knocks. Gorni opens the door, and the whole team streams in behind Bronk.

"We talked it over, and we want to stay at a nice place," says Bronk.

"It's bedtime. We'll talk about it tomorrow."

Bronk strides to the closet. "Come here." He opens the door and points down at the floor. "Look at that." Dan slides off the bed and sluffs over next to Bronk. The team clusters around them.

Dan stares at the floor where Bronk is pointing. "Yeah, what about it?"

"That's rat shit," announces Adam.

"There's rat shit in your closet," explains Bronk. "There's rat shit in our closet. There's rat shit in everyone's closet."

Dan thinks it over. "Uh, it's just added pressure."

Joe steps forward. "What the hell, Dan. It's the nationals. It's the last go-round for some of us, and we got the money."

The whole team chimes in. "Yeah, Dan, what do you say? Come on, let's go for it."

***

The rented station wagon cruises down the highway followed by the van. They turn into a high-tower luxury hotel and drive up a wide, pure black driveway lined on each side with white brick and decorative lighting. Beyond the lights, exotic plants and clusters of small trees adorn the immaculately manicured grounds. They follow the drive in a large circle winding to the front entrance. They pull up and stop next to a couple of limos. The doorman runs from the front door to the car, opens the door, and welcomes everyone to the Crystal Towers.

Everyone piles out. "All right. Oh, yeah. This is what we're talking about. Cha-ching, baby."

The doorman makes a quick assessment and delivers a string of hand signals back to the front door. Several bellhops rush out, pushing luggage carts.

***

"Shut up," shouts Dan. "Stop your bitching. It was your idea to stay in a nice place."

"Yeah, but all of us in one room?" complains Joe.

They are all crammed into one large bedroom with a heart shaped bed, and mirrors on the walls and ceiling.

"It was the only one left. These rooms have been booked for years. You asked to stay in a nice place, and this is a suite, a penthouse bridal suite. You got to be careful what you ask for—you just might get it."

The Dogs scatter about the suite. Dressed in their warm ups, they pack their backpacks and gear bags, and engage in a variety of last-minute preparations. One ties, unties and then reties his shoes searching for the supreme fit. Some bounce around in their stances moving in and out, making level changes, fakes and circling. Others find-tune for combat by fiddling with their socks, adjusting headgears, cracking their necks and taping fingers.

"Don't tape your fingers. That's the first thing they'll go after."

"Have to. They're really bad."

"Then tape both hands."

Dan shouts, "We're running late. Is everybody ready? Dan looks around to make sure he has their attention. "I got a few words, and then we'll load the elevator. Today is the first day of a new season. Everyone starts this tournament with a 0–0 record. Everyone trained all year for this. The next three days is going to be a pressure cooker. It doesn't matter whether you're seeded or not seeded—every guy in the weight class has a chance to win a national title. You have to get that in your head right now. Every match is the finals. It's not how good you are in one match, but it's who is the best for five matches. Do what you do best. When you wrestle, wrestle hard. Above all, be excited, focused and execute.

At media day yesterday, I watched Kane. Chicago is overconfident. We can win this thing. But, they aren't going to give you anything. You're going to have to take it, like taking a bone from a hungry, snarling dog. Scrap every second to the very end. When you are up, show no mercy. If you are down, fight your way back into the match. We need a big first day. Seniors, this will be your last time wrestling for Dover. I think you should say something."

The seniors look at each other, turn to the team, and break out barking. Everyone joins the chorus of deep, harsh, guttural dog noises. "Woof. Woof. Woof."

"Okay, whose turn is it to say the prayer?" asks Dan.

"Your turn, Coach."

Dan reaches out and takes the hand of the man to his left and then the right, and they in turn take a hand until everyone has joined hands in a circle.

Dan thinks for a moment and offers, "I can't help but think everything happens for a reason. If that's so, then there's a reason You've brought us all together at this time and in this place. I come to You now because I've failed trying to do it on my own. These guys deserve better. Together, I know we can do this. Please fill us with the strength for the task ahead. Help us cope with the unexpected and protect us from injury. Fill each man with the mind-set to see this through. Thank You for surrounding me with a great wife and kids, a team of warriors, and everyone in my life. Thank You for this opportunity. Amen." After a moment of silence, Dan lets go of the hands in his grasp and floats toward the door. "Okay, let's put some more names on the wall." He opens the door and strides out into the hall.

Adam follows Dan and points down at his legs. "Coach."

Dan looks down at his bare legs. "You guys load in the elevator and hold it for Gorni."

Dan rushes back in and comes out zipping up his slacks. A ball of gear bags duck-walks down the hall. Dan buckles his belt and closes the door. He squeezes past the human beast of burden and then sprints down the corridor to the elevator.

Dan counts heads. "Everybody here?" He casts a look back down the hall at the toddling Gorni. "If we're late, it's your fault." Gorni accelerates to a fast toddle.

Dan addresses the team. "You guys take the elevator down to the main lobby, and I'll take the stairs and meet you there."

Uncle Burt rationalizes, "We don't have time. You have to take the elevator."

Dan looks at his watch. Gorni shifts, turns, and adjusts to fit in the elevator. The doors close, hit the sphere of bags and reopen. Dan lowers his shoulder and drives into Gorni, trying to squeeze everyone tight to make room, but half of him hangs out into the hallway.

In futility, Dan pulls Gorni from the elevator. "You'll have to catch the next one." He gulps and steps into the space left by Gorni. He pushes the down button, instructs Gorni, "Meet us downstairs."

The doors close less than an inch in front of Dan's nose. The elevator is packed like an Irish bar on St. Pat's day. The tight space silences Dan as the elevator begins to drop. He turns clammy, and beads of sweat break out on his forehead. Everyone shuffles, adjusting to the space and fighting for more shoulder room.

Dickie notices Dan's uncomfortable look. "Coach, you all right?"

Dan shuts his eyes, nods, and fills his lungs.

A disguised voice shouts, "Roughhouse." A fist slugs Dan in the middle of the back, driving him forward and smashing his face into the elevator door. A bevy of knuckles pelts Dan's back and shoulders. A rapid, continuous fire of fists, pin him against the closed door panels. He can't move. The trapped punching bag endures the pounding floor after floor as the elevator descends to the ground level. A ding announces their arrival, and the lift comes to a halt. The doors crack open and glide apart. Enraged, Dan leaps from the ambush and swings around into a cocked stance, ready to discharge. He's aglow as if on fire. The sweaty contents of the elevator politely empty and stroll past the wild rogue elephant. Dan has murder in his eyes and kill etched on his face. He looks down the single file of innocent, cherubic faces, glances at the empty elevator, and then back to the childlike mug shots.

Uncle Burt brings up the rear. "Forget about the claustrophobia?"

The elevator next to Dan dings and opens. Sweating profusely under the strain of his load, Gorni marches past Dan, who remains frozen in his tracks as he glares at the team. He snaps out of it, runs up behind Gorni, winds, and smacks him in the back of the head with his open hand. "Hurry up." The slap pitches Gorni forward momentarily losing his balance. He wobbles down the hall as if he's about to fall from a ledge before recovering his equilibrium at the door.

BOOK 3

Post Season - The Nationals

○○○○○○○○○○○○○○○○○○○○○○○○○○○○○○○

27. Moving Pictures

DAY ONE - THURSDAY
THE PRELIMINARIES

SWARMS OF FANS infest the arena and overrun the corridor surrounding the enormous beehive, indulging in refreshments, wandering among display stands exhibiting the latest in wrestling news and paraphernalia, and waiting in lines to meet former wrestling greats who promote their cutting-edge gear, videos, and camps.

Supporters march up the ramps to the inner sanctum and join their team's color-coded section in the preliminary warm-up cheers. Chicago's red section is the largest, but their volume is rivaled by several enthusiastic roars from blue, black, orange and green factions. Each group is armed. Shouting through megaphones, bizarre, kooky costumed mascots lead their factions by blowing on horns, beating drums, ringing bells, sounding sirens, waving signs, fluttering banners, or shaking colored pom-poms.

Below, the floor is a patchwork of a dozen distinctive, brightly colored wrestling mats. The aroma of new mats satiates the arena. Small contingents of wrestlers run the perimeter, circling hundreds of bodies sparring for space to warm up. Just as ancient army camps claimed their territory before battle, each team stakes out an area and goes through a prematch warm-up ritual.

Joe gathers the Dogs in a huddle. "Chicago's over there," he says with a nod. "Let's get in their heads. We'll jog around them and everyone mad-dogs the guy in their weight. Bronk, you lead the way."

"But—"

"You're the captain. Lead us."

Bronk takes off running, and the Dogs follow in a single line. They circle around the Chicago team spread out on the mat doing their stretches. Each Dover wrestler finds his opponent and stares him down. Joe brings up the rear. One by one, he taps each teammate on the shoulder and has him pull out and gather to the side. Unknowingly, Bronk pounds around the Chicago team alone and rivets his eyes on Bobby Ryder.

Ryder feels the fixed gaze and looks back at Bronk's wrinkled brow and inflamed eyes. The bold, conspicuous glare becomes uncomfortable and bristles Ryder. He directs his teammates' attention to Bronk's steady gaze. In unison, they rise, troop across the mat, and block his path.

Bronk pulls up, thinking, *Well, we got their attention,* and smiles as he looks over his shoulder for the Dogs, who are missing in action. The Chicago ten surround Bronk and begin poking at him.

Joe and the boys watch the confrontation. The hunting party swallows Bronk. The Dogs rush forward and push the Chicago team off Bronk.

The loud speaker blares, "Attention, wrestlers. Please clear the mats. Please clear the mats. We will begin wrestling when the mats are cleared."

A collective roar from the spectators swells as the wrestlers evacuate the mats, revealing the Chicago and Dover teams squared off in the center of the arena floor. Finger pointing, bumping, pushing, and shoving escalate into name-calling and rough, aggressive jostling.

Bobby Ryder pokes Bronk in the chest. "I don't even know who you are. What's your name?"

"You will," says Joe, stepping in front of Bronk.

Three officials plunge into the middle of the commotion, driving a wedge between the two teams. Their bullying thrusts separate the squads. The two teams shuffle off in opposite directions with their heads angled toward each other and their eyes doing the talking.

Joe puts his arm around Bronk's shoulder. "Don't let him in your head."

"It's hard not to."

"Well, you just got in his."

"You reckon so?"

"I know so. You're ready for him now. You can take him. Just don't lose to him up here," says Joe, tapping his index finger on Bronk's head, "before you step on the mat. Remember, you're not wrestling his rep. Hell, I can beat him, and if I can beat him, you sure as hell can."

In the stands above, fans in each cheering section take turns yelling their school's traditional chants. Several boisterous fanatics jump up and join the mascots, inciting the noisemakers to shout louder. Back and forth, the deafening cheers build and climax in a finale with each school's fans screaming their fight song in an earsplitting pitch.

*** *** ***

The reporting crew scrambles into place on the center mat. Three announcers put on their game faces. A production assistant counts down with her fingers. Three ... two ... and then she points at them. Their images appear on the giant four-sided screen hanging from the center of the domed ceiling.

"Hello, and welcome. This is Chet Avery with wrestling champions Barry Smart and James Smith reporting from the College National Wrestling Championships in Chicago."

"The atmosphere is electric," observes Barry Smart.

"You could cut the intensity with a knife. I know that's a cliché, but it's the most accurate description of the atmosphere here," adds James Smith.

Chet Avery pipes in, "I've been covering national and world championships for more than twenty years, and year in and year out, this is my favorite event."

"That's right," says Barry. "The College National Wrestling Championships always deliver. Every championship develops its own personality that manages to inspire, amaze, and surprise like no other."

"And this year's promises to be the most entertaining ever," says James Smith.

"Chicago is the clear favorite, but look for schools from Iowa, Oklahoma, Michigan, Pennsylvania, and Ohio to challenge," says Chet.

"And you can't forget that spunky Dover team," reminds James. "What a storybook year they've had."

"Is that another cliché?" asks Barry.

"Yes, yes it is," answers James. "Guilty as charged."

"Of course, the big story is Chicago. Undefeated and ranked number one from start to finish," responds Chet, getting back on track.

"They have clearly made a quantum leap this year with freshman sensation Bobby Ryder leading the way," responds Barry.

"You heard that right, folks," adds James, "he's a freshman, undefeated, and the number one seed."

"Amazing. His stiffest competition is expected to come from the number two seed, Michigan's Ralph Terry. He had a couple of losses at a higher weight early in the season but is undefeated since he dropped," chimes Barry.

"Is it premature to say Bobby Ryder may be the biggest thing to ever hit college wrestling?" asks Chet.

James and Barry raise their eyebrows, look at each and nod a confirmation as they digest that comment.

Chet continues, "And of course, the biggest story of all, Coach Dave Kane and the Chicago Cats are going for their record tenth straight national title. If they pull this off, they will be the first college team to ever win ten national championships in a row."

"Mind-boggling," say Barry and James together.

"After a miracle come-from-behind finish at last year's tournament to capture their ninth consecutive title," says James. "I'm sure the rest of the country thought they saw a chink in the Chicago armor."

Barry points at James. "Cliché."

James responds, "Touché," and high-fives Barry.

Chet takes control. "But Coach Dave Kane has brought back the program to the familiar dominating style it's known for. Many think they have the talent to intimidate their way to another title."

"And having home-court advantage doesn't hurt either," adds James.

"No matter what team you root for, this tournament promises to be the most entertaining wrestling experience you'll have," responds Barry.

"Let's hear a word from Coach Kane. Run the clip," directs Chet.

Kane's face fills the four-sided screen. Instantaneous cheers and boos vibrate through the arena.

Kane boasts, "Our guys are wrestling the best they have all year. We come here to wrestle with intensity and emotion and to dominate and win, and that's what we are going to do."

An announcement comes over the loud speaker. "Let's get ready to wrestle. On mat number one—"

A roar from the attendance drowns the broadcast.

***

Kane stands before his team.

"Well, studs, it's time. The whole season comes down to the next three days. No team in the history of college sports has done what we are about to do. This is our tournament. The championship comes through us. Everybody has two matches today. Now, we can't think ahead. We've got to take it one match at a time and wrestle each match like it's the finals. Don't save anything. Leave it on the mat."

Assistant coach Duray bursts through the locker-room door. "They're starting."

"Okay, hands in," says Kane, extending his hand.

The Chicago team packs in a tight circle. They add their palms to a mound of hands and bow their heads.

After a few moments of silent prayer, Kane lifts his head. "Okay, on three. One ... two ... three."

"Chicago!" shouts the team in unison.

"Okay, this is what we train for. This is what we look forward to. This is showtime. Let's go take some hardware."

They break. Kane opens the locker-room door, and the team struts out in single file. Kane brings up the rear, catches up to Bobby Ryder, and wraps an arm around his broad shoulders. "How do you feel?"

"Great."

"Let's take it to them. Today, we rewrite history."

"I've waited my whole life for this."

***

Every action, score, or result on the floor ignites a simultaneous shout of approval and a groan of disappointment from the stands above. Each mat plays its own drama, an encounter with the same rules and structure, but with an improvised performance. Every match is a one-of-a-kind battle, a controlled violence that ultimately leads to the same ending. There's always a winner and always a loser.

The battles are fast and furious. A whistle blows, hands grab, heads butt, and bodies clash. They fight, they sweat, they bleed until there is a pin or the time expires, and a point system determines the winner. A plethora of moves, positions, and situations covers the floor. Each mat has two wrestlers, a referee, and two coaches from each team are seated on both sides of the scorer's table.

A wrestler shoots. He is in on his opponent's legs. He lifts, spins, and slams the body to the mat, applying a Turk leg lock in one continuous move. Driving and arching his back, he wraps his arm around the bottom man's neck and twists him to his back. The referee's arm slashes the air for a five count, indicating back points, and then as sudden as thunder, his hand slaps the mat, signaling a fall and the end of the match.

On another mat, time is running down. The bottom wrestler looks gassed. His coaches and teammates scream for him to move, but his exhausted limbs can't respond. Time is out. He drops his forehead onto the mat. All his supporters stand and watch, feeling helpless, disappointed, and angry.

A noisy uproar disrupts the focus as Bobby Ryder takes the mat. When the whistle blows, he buries an underhook, and his other hand slaps the adversary's head down. He uses his leg to hook his opponent's leg and inside trips the man to the mat, trapping him on his back until a pin is called. The Chicago fans and everyone in his corner celebrate his quick victory, but his attention is on the next mat.

Ryder watches as a wrestler struggles on his back, straining to fight to his stomach. The official slaps the mat and blows his whistle, signaling the pin. The winner, Ralph Terry, leaps up and punches the air, celebrating his victory. His eyes meet Ryder's. Ryder points at Terry to let him know it is on.

As the final seconds tick off the clock, a losing wrestler on the mat across from Terry's takes a desperation shot. He's in and scores as the buzzer sounds. In one second, the loser becomes the winner and explodes in celebration. The winner becomes the loser and sits in disbelief, covering his face with his hands. They shake. The victor runs into the waiting arms of his coaches, and dances off surrounded by his team. Defeated, the other opponent walks to his corner, collects his warm-ups, and walks off alone.

In a far corner of the arena, feet arc through the air and slam to the mat. Scrambling, the referee positions himself to look for the fall. In one corner, the coaches explode, leaping off the ground and swinging their fists in the air. In the opposite corner of the mat, dead silence consumes the slouching, motionless coaches as they look on.

On the next mat, two combatants pound on each other. They push each other around. Their shoves escalate to slaps, the slaps escalate and ignite a fight. The referee steps in, and the coaches run onto the mat and grab their combatants. They separate the pair and bring the situation under control.

Wrestlers who are not wrestling are scattered throughout the stadium. Some sit with their teammates and families and talk, snack, and drink. Others watch and cheer their teammates on. And others prefer the solitude of reading, listening to music, working a Rubik's cube, playing solitaire, knitting, or napping wherever they can find a spot to stretch out.

A referee's call catapults a coach from his seat. He runs to the scorer's table and waves for the official to meet him. He waits with crossed arms and a stern look on his face. After a brief conference, the coach explodes and gets in the referee's face, mouthing his disapproval of the call. A shouting match breaks out. Another coach steps between the two and restrains his fellow coach. He drives the barking coach back to his corner.

A dominant cheer erupts as Bobby Ryder takes the mat again. Within seconds, he is in his underhook, moving his opponent. He drives across and knee picks the far leg, tripping the man to his back. A smack on the mat and a whistle indicate a fall and the end of the match. Ryder records his second pin. After the customary handshake, the referee raises Ryder's arm, signaling the victor. The Chicago fans blow up in a wild frenzy. Ryder's eyes search for Terry's mat. When he finds it, the wrestlers are shaking hands, and the official lifts the winner's hand. With his arm stretched into the air, Bronk stares intently at Ryder. Their eyes meet and lock as they walk to their corners. Ryder points to his wrist and taps, indicating his pin time was faster, and then he curls his arm and flexes his bulging bicep.

With seconds left in a match on the other side of the arena, the winning wrestler backs up. The referee warns him for stalling, and then with one second left on the clock, he is warned again and penalized a point, tying the match and sending it into overtime. In overtime, the other wrestler shoots in on the penalized wrestler, and when he sprawls, the referee penalizes him a third time and awards the winning point. Boos follow the call.

The losing wrestler's mother cries. His father runs down the steps from the stands, leaps the barrier, and confronts the official leaving the mat. Security guards surround the father, restrain him, and escort him from the floor.

One wrestler screams midway through a match in a far corner near the arena's exit. The referee stops the match and circles his finger in the air above his head, signaling the scorer's table to start injury time. Trainers hustle to the fallen athlete. An announcement blares over the speakers. "Doctor to mat nine … Doctor to mat nine ..."

A wrestler wins a hard-fought match in a mat underneath the four-sided screen, and his team piles on him. In the other corner, tears roll down the cheeks of the loser, and his coach and teammates don't know what to say or do.

***

The final session of the day draws to an end. Fans begin leaving.

In the coverage booth, Chet wraps up the day's broadcast. "With more than three hundred matches in the books, we're down to the last minute of the final match of the first day."

"Dover's Ben Wussle has a one-point lead over Chicago's Ken Howard," observes Barry.

"This round pits the losers from this morning's round. So, if you lose here, it's hasta la vista, baby," says James.

"That's right. Losers here are 0–2 and out," adds Chet.

"It's a lousy way to end a season," says Barry.

"That doesn't mean you're not a good wrestler," says James. "I've seen returning all-Americans go 0–2 and out."

"It just shows how tough this tournament can be," summarizes Chet.

On the mat, Ben and his Chicago opponent move in and out, circle, hand fight, and pound on each other's head, trying to create an opening. They take a step back, lower their levels, and shoot at the same time, colliding heads. Stunned, Ben drops to one knee. Chicago's Howard seizes the opportunity. Before Ben can recover, Howard charges forward. The whistle sounds. Howard lowers his forehead and rams it into Ben's skull. Ben falls to the mat, grasping his head. The referee steps in and blows his whistle a second time in a series of short blasts. Howard staggers and weaves back to his corner. Kane and Duray greet him with high fives. He smiles, and collapses to his knees. Kane studies the condition of his woozy wrestler, then looks over and compares Ben's state.

Dan is the first to Ben. "Good, now you got him right where you want him."

Ben holds his head and writhes about. "Something's wrong."

Seeing Ben's condition is worst, Kane leaves his corner and approaches the official. "We're ready to continue."

The referee walks over to Dan and Uncle Burt. "Are you ready to go?"

Uncle Burt watches Ben squirm in pain and tells the referee, "We need injury time." He turns to Dan and says, "This is bullshit ..." but before he finishes, Dan is up and marching to the scorer's table.

He confronts the referee. "You going to let him get away with that?"

"What?" asks the official.

"That was an intentional head butt, and it was after your whistle."

Kane nudges his assistant with an elbow. Duray flies out of his chair, and when he gets in range of Dan and the referee, he yells, "Sit down."

"I'm not talking to you," responds Dan.

"Sit down," orders Duray. Turning to the official, he counters, "Hey, ref, don't let him talk you into anything."

Another assistant from Chicago signals their cheering section, and they start a chant. "Sit down, clown!" "Sit down, clown!" "Sit down, clown!"

"I can't stand their fans," explodes Uncle Burt, rocketing to his feet. "They drive me crazy."

In the broadcast booth, Barry pipes in with commentary on the wrestlers' collision. "Wow, that looked like it was after the whistle. You could hear their heads clunk like a couple of coconuts."

"Now that was an NFL collision," says James.

"That's one for the highlight film," concludes Chet.

"Check this out—the coaches seem to be having some sort of verbal exchange," says Chet.

"I don't believe this," says Barry. "They're leaving their wrestlers unattended and squaring off in the center of the mat. They're nose to nose, jawing at each other."

"This is nuts. It looks like they skipped the discussion went straight to an all-out argument," says James.

"They are really going at it," says Chet. "This could turn violent."

"Boy, what I wouldn't give to be down there and hear what's going on," says Barry. "Look—the officials are trying to separate the coaches."

"They better get this under control," warns Chet.

"Here come the reinforcements," announces James. "They actually have two referees for each coach, pushing them back to their corners."

Barry stares in disbelief. "What is going on down there?"

"Did you see that?" asks James. "Dan Sangha just threw his arm in the air. Did he flip Kane and Duray the bird, or was he signaling them to come and get some more?"

Barry shakes his head. "Your call is as good as mine."

"This is crazy," summarizes Chet.

On the mat, the referee approaches Dan. "Coach, injury time is up. He has to continue or forfeit."

"You heard him, Ben. What's it going to be?" asks Dan.

"Huh?" asks Ben, removing his hands from his head and lifting his face.

Dan takes his head in his hands. "Your injury time is up. It's your call."

"I didn't come here to forfeit," says Ben, struggling to its feet.

"You got thirty seconds left. Circle and stay away from him. Got it?" asks Dan.

Ben stands and walks unsteadily back to the center. He shakes his head and blinks his eyes. Each wrestler gets in his stance and places a foot on the starting line. On the whistle, Howard smacks Ben in the head and shoots. He snatches him off his feet, spins him, and drills him headfirst into the mat, driving him to his back. Ben fights. The official counts. Ben can't see the time through his blurry eyes. The referee looks for a fall. Ben bridges on top of his head. Howard flattens him. Ben goes ballistic. He bridges and every time the ref positions himself to make the call Ben turns and the ref has to scramble to the other side. Back and forth, back and forth until the buzzer sounds. The referee awards takedown and nearfall points.

Howard leaps into the air and jogs around the mat with both fists raised above his head in exultation. As he passes Dan and Uncle Burt, he lowers his fists, transforms them into six-shooters, points them, and fires. "A Dog a day keeps the doctor away."

In the booth, "Here we go again," pipes in Barry.

"Both coaching staffs and now the teams are pouring onto the mat," reports Chet. "They've surrounded the officials at the scorer's table. There are a lot of exchanges going on. Everybody is getting into it. And listen to the Chicago fans' chant."

"Sit down, clown!" "Sit down, clown!" "Sit down, clown!"

"After Howard's win, he appeared to make some sort of gesture and say something to the Dover coaches," says James.

Chet nods. "There's a lot of jabbering and pointing going on."

"Uh-oh, there's some pushing and shoving," says Barry through nervous laughter.

"This could get ugly," responds James. "One spark could ignite this into a real donnybrook."

"Here comes the cavalry," announces Chet.

Barry fills in the details. "Security has been called. A dozen or more security guards and policemen are on the mat and jumping into the fray. They're separating the teams and clearing the mat."

Chet leans forward. "Okay, here's the ref's call. There's one team point deducted from Chicago for unsportsmanlike conduct, and Dover loses a team point for unsportsmanlike conduct."

"What an ending to the first day of action," summarizes Barry.

"That call makes it awkward for coaches Kane and Sangha," adds James. "It's only the first day, and if either of them or any of their coaches get another unsportsmanlike conduct call, the head coaches are removed from the arena for the remainder of the tournament."

"The team scores are coming in now," relays Chet. "Oh my, get a load of this. Dover is in first with twenty-seven points and guess who is in second?"

James and Barry shrug. "Chicago?"

"It is Chicago with twenty-six and a half points. And the next place team is nine points away. This looks like it's turning into a two-team race."

"Well, from what I've seen, Dover isn't going to let Chicago intimidate them," cautions Barry.

"Let's see ... Chicago has nine going into the quarters and one in consolation, and Dover has eight in the quarters and no one in consolation," tallies Chet.

"Dover is leading because of the number of pins they had today," calculates Barry.

"I don't think Dover has the firepower to hang with Chicago," predicts Chet.

"Time will tell. That's why we wrestle the matches," concludes James.

***

Dan stands next to the door in his T-shirt and underwear with his hand on the light switch. "Okay, shut up and go to sleep." Lights out are followed by a series of thuds. The lights immediately go back on in the middle of a torrent of pillows barraging Dan.

"Okay, who doesn't have a pillow?"

Everyone pretends to be asleep.

"Quit screwing around and get to sleep."

The moment the lights go off, the onslaught resumes. Dan turns the lights back on and stands with his hand on the switch. Removing a water-soaked towel draped over his head, he groans, "Wrestling starts in six hours. Let's get some sleep."

Dan flicks the switch off and waits. It's quiet. He's ready to make his way to his bed when he hears someone moving. The lights go on. Joe is caught red-handed removing Dan's wallet from his pants. Dan gives chase. Pillow fights, towel fights, and wrestling matches break out. Oranges sail across the room. A loud knock at the door goes unnoticed. The door opens.

A coach from another team walks in and roars, "Hey! Let's keep it down."

Everyone freezes. When Dan looks to see who it is, Joe seizes the opportunity, smacking Dan in the head and escaping from his grasp.

"Okay, everybody quiet," shouts Dan, walking to the uninvited guest.

The visitor directs his scowl at Dan. "I don't know about you, but my boys have a tournament to wrestle tomorrow. And they can't sleep with all this noise."

"What do you want me to do smack their wrists?"

The whole team barks and unleashes a volley of pillows, towels, and oranges, driving their uninvited guest back out the door.

Dan's stern face turns back to his team. They go mute. They see his grave expression and hold their poses like statues. Dan maintains his angry expression until he finds Joe. "Okay. Where were we?" He bolts across the room in hot pursuit.

The bedlam resumes. Bronk slips out in his shorts, tiptoes down the hall, and knocks on a door. After a few moments, the door opens.

Squinting and adjusting her eyes to the light from the hall, Jas asks, "What do you want? Do you know what time it is?"

"You gonna invite me in?"

"No. Go to bed."

"That's what I had in mind," says Bronk.

"You need your rest."

"C'mon, just for a spell."

"Can't."

Bronk drops his head. "So, you're giving me the mitten."

Jas lifts his face with a stroke of her hand on his cheek. "You looked great today."

"We're ahead of Chicago."

"I was talking about you—two matches and two pins."

"I got lucky with the last one. He could buck off a man's whiskers."

Jas looks into his eyes, unsure if she should speak. "Head trainer told me I'm not a trainer for the wrestling team next year."

"Does that mean what I think it means?"

"Maybe, if you grow a few inches."

***

Bronk opens the door, steps in, and slowly closes it behind him. He tiptoes across the dark room, placing each stealthy footstep with caution. Slipping into his spot, he gets comfortable, and readies for sleep. Light floods the room. Balls limps in with a half-empty bottle of Jack Daniels dangling from his hand. When the door closes, it pitches the room back into darkness. He hobbles to Dan, engulfed in sleep's vulnerability. He's curled up, clutching his wallet to his chest with both hands and his chin,

Balls squats, and blows lightly on Dan's face until he releases his wallet and rubs away the tickle. Balls slips the wallet from Dan, opens it and thumbs the wad of bills. "You can give these guys everything but the one thing they need. They have to choose to be a champion."

Bronk watches Balls lift Dan's limp hand, and replace the wallet. "Once you choose there's only one course, you put yourself through hell every day until you're the baddest man alive. You chose. I chose. To the choosers." He straightens, lifts his bottle skyward and drains the contents down his throat. "The worst thing about this is ... this might never happen again. This place, this time, and these people. That's the worst thing. I just hope that next year we are still doing the same crazy things." Balls breathes heavy and stares down at Dan. Shedding tears, "I did everything you said." He spouts, "Dogface," and then staggers to bed.

A tear swells in the corner of Dan's closed eye. It releases, and streams down his cheek.

DAY TWO - FRIDAY MORNING
THE QUARTERFINALS

Dan and Uncle Burt yell from their seats, "Jerk your hands to your chest. To your chest and up."

Mini D has his hands locked around the man's head and leg in a cradle. A violent jerk pulls the man from his stomach to his side. From there Mini D works him to his back.

"Put your belly on his face."

"Settle. Now stick him." shouts the corner.

The opponent kicks and rocks, fighting the hold, but Mini D grips and squeezes for the fall. The Dogs scream their approval. Mini D's performance is infectious. His teammates start bouncing and swinging their arms around, channeling pent-up energy in preparation for their upcoming matches.

***

Bronk waits on deck as the Chicago 126-pounder, Andy Mason, puts the final touches on a major decision. Kane and Duray greet him as he comes off the mat. "Way to go, stud. Now go get some rest. You got a big one tonight."

On the whistle, Bronk attacks, bulling in and pushing his opponent back. When he feels resistance, Bronk lowers his level and shoots. Gathering in the legs and hips, he lifts him off his feet and spins, drilling him into the mat. Bronk pounces. Sinking in a bar and a half, he traps his man. No matter which way he turns, it is the wrong way. Twisting limbs to their breaking point, Bronk enforces his will until his foe gives up and turns to his back.

In the stands, a dozen brown T-shirts jump to their feet and whoop and holler. As soon as his hand is raised, Bronk pulls free from the referee's grasp and breaks into a run. He sprints across several mats with matches in progress and pulls up at the edge of Bobby Ryder's mat just in time to see him get his hand hoisted. When he has Ryder's attention, Bronk points and taps his wrist.

***

Joe Kerr moves in, circles, and moves away, sucking his man in. When he steps forward, Joe fakes a shot, then slaps his adversary's head down and locks around the man's head and arm in a front headlock. Circling hard, he yanks, drives his head under the man and loads the body on his shoulders. He has the head trapped in one arm and a leg in the other. Throwing the leg and holding the head, he flings his opponent to his back and covers him for the count.

Dover coaches, wrestlers, and fans jump to their feet and begin high-fiving.

***

Pug locks up. He and his opponent take turns twisting, snapping and tugging each other's heads. He peeks to see how much time is left, in the same instant his opponent attacks and slips past Pug's defenses. He's in deep. Pug dives and grabs an ankle. They scramble and trade the advantage position. One moment Pug is on top, and the next, his opponent fights back on top. Back and forth, back and forth, they jumble and squirm around until the opposition pops on top with control for two points and rides Pug out for the win.

***

Doc walks straight in, pummeling for hooks.

"You got plenty of time. Work it. Work it," coax Dan and Uncle Burt.

Doc forces his hook in and rushes forward to try and suck up his man and take control. His opponent backs away and blocks off, prompting the official's whistle and a stall call.

Coaches spring from their seats clapping and shouting, "Good job. Good job. Keep the pressure on. Another stall call ties the match."

On the whistle, Doc rushes forward and buries a deep hook, pressures in, and fights for an over and under. When he feels the resistance, he sucks the man up, back arches and launches. His opponent doesn't fight the move but goes with it, using Doc's momentum to roll through and put Doc on his back. The period ends with Doc fighting off his back.

Uncle Burt's deflated body droops over the chair. "I don't get it. He didn't have to do that. He should have gone for another stall call and taken it to overtime." He looks up at Dan. "The guy was tiring. He had him."

"I know he had him," says Dan, "but he went for the big move." Dan shakes Doc's hand as he comes off the mat. "You can't force a move. When it's not there, you have to eke out a win."

"Win with a big move," mutters Uncle Burt. "That sounds like more Duray bullshit."

***

Kruger is putting on a clinic. Everything he does works. Every move puts points on the scoreboard. Double leg, two points; ankle pick, two points; duck under, two points. With less than a minute left in the match, Kruger is running up the score.

"One more time. Try to take him down to his back," yells Dan.

Kruger shoots and walks up a single leg. His weary challenger tucks his foot in Kruger's groin, grabs his chin and sinks a deep underhook.

"Let go of the leg! Let go of the leg!" screams Uncle Burt.

Before the words sink in, Kruger's opponent sits, kicks his foot and elevates Kruger's body, extends the chin and rips the underhook across Kruger's spine, lifting and twisting him to his back. Kruger's eyes bulge and every vein swells, covering his skin with snakelike protrusions. He strains and resists the pin.

"Fight it. You have less than a minute. Fight it," plead Dan and Uncle Burt.

Kruger's assailant sinks the half. He cups Kruger's chin in his hand and turns it out to Kruger's shoulder, then lifts the head with his elbow, driving a knuckle into Kruger's Adam's apple and cutting off his air.

"Thirty seconds. And you win. C'mon, you can do it."

Kruger turns one way, then the other. Lack of oxygen plus the strain begins to take its toll. He channels the strength of every muscle to keep his shoulder up. His eyes flash black ... white ... black ... white. When he feels his shoulder going down, he posts his hand against his opponent's hips. Dozens of sparkling, twinkling stars span the height and width of his eyeballs. The high-pitched, warbling tweet of the referee's whistle fills his ears. Stunned, he remains seated to shake hands and watch his challenger break into a bouncing, jumping victory dance back to his corner. He looks at Dan and Uncle Burt, who stand bewildered.

"I don't believe what I just saw," stammers Uncle Burt. "That's three in a row. This can't be happening."

**

Adam circles in a crouched stance. He and his rival study each other's movements and cautiously feel each other out.

"Look at the size of this guy."

"They could be twins."

Abruptly, they stop and just stare. Using an invisible communication, they stand straight, and with a mutual understanding, they walk up and lock their hands in a bear hug around each other's chest and start wrestling from a clinch.

"What the hell are they doing?" asks Dan.

"This is the guy who has been telling everybody he could crush Adam."

"Oh, geez."

"Here we go."

The two behemoths squeeze. Back and forth they teeter like two arm wrestlers of equal strength. Their veins pop, their muscles puff. Globules of sweat break out and balloon into droplets rolling down their foreheads and dripping from their faces. The challenger makes his move. He clutches and compresses with an all-out crush. The Herculean bodies tremble and begin to change colors from the total exertion without a breath. Adam bends backward. His eyes jut from their sockets. He bears down, digs in, and stops the breach. Now it's his turn. Straining his muscles to the utmost, he constricts his boa arms and squashes the pretender's defense, bending him over backward, squeezing him to the mat, and trapping him on his back for a quick pin.

"Holy orange juice," says Uncle Burt. "Did you see that?"

***

"Do you believe this?" asks Uncle Burt in a whisper to Dan. "Pump is up 3-0 and is two minutes away from the semis. That would give us five guys in the semis. We could win this thing, Dan. We could really do it."

"Shut up. You talk too much," replies Dan.

The Chicago heavyweight has Pump in double underhooks. Pump fights back with double overhooks, buries his head into the neck, and drives up into the chin.

"Stalling! Stalling! Stalling!" chants the Chicago fans.

The referee clenches his hand into a fist and straightens it above his head and points at Pump with his other hand. The Chicago giant sees the stalling warning and drives into Pump, forcing him to back up. As they leave the wrestling area, the official dings Pump with another stalling warning and awards Chicago a point.

The Chicago cheering section explodes.

Uncle Burt springs to his feet and yells at the referee in disbelief, "What's that all about?"

"Your man is blocking and backing."

"The other man isn't doing anything with the hooks except pushing," responds Uncle Burt. He turns to Dan and complains, "Why do referees always penalize the guy who's winning in the last period?"

When the match resumes, the Chicago mammoth rushes forward, buries two hooks, and plows, forcing Pump back off the mat for a second time. The referee awards a second point to Chicago.

Uncle Burt leans forward and shouts, "Pump, stay out of those hooks. No hooks. No hooks."

"If he gets them, don't back up. You have to circle," instructs Dan.

The two Goliaths pound away at each other. The Chicago opponent does everything he can to get a hook in, and Pump counters every attempt.

"Stalling! Stalling! Stalling!"

With seconds left, Chicago gets the hooks, lifts, and charges. Pump drives both hands under the attacker's chin, circles hard, and slips out of the hold at the buzzer. Dan and Uncle Burt leap from their seats in celebration. The referee's fist punctures the air for a fourth time, awarding Chicago two points and a 4-3 victory.

Uncle Burt screams at the referee, "I don't believe it. We weren't backing. And the other man wasn't doing anything with the hooks but blocking and pushing."

The official addresses Dan. "Coach, you've been warned and penalized. If we penalize you or any of your coaches again, you have to leave the arena for the rest of the tournament."

Dan looks at Uncle Burt as if to ask, "What do you want to do?"

Uncle Burt concedes, but as he walks off, he can be heard saying, "There's something wrong with our sport when a wrestler rides his man out and scores the only takedown and escape and loses to the other man who didn't score a point."

Kane hands his heavyweight wrestler his warm-up, wraps his arms around his sweaty neck, and hugs. Duray gives a congratulatory slap on the rear.

DAY TWO - FRIDAY EVENING
THE SEMIFINALS

Kane and Duray stand before their team gathered in their meeting area off the Chicago dressing room. It's laid out in a red and silver color scheme with plush chairs and couches. Kane presides at the head of a long executive meeting table in front of a large-screen television flanked by a bulletin board on one side and a presentation board on the other. His wrestlers are bundled in their warm-ups and ready to go.

"We can win this tournament right now. How bad do you want to be a national champion?" he asks, looking around the room. "Do you want to be an all-American? We have six in the semis, and we wrestle Dover in three matches. You all have to win. We sweep Dover and get more men in the finals, and this tournament is ours. The only reason they have stayed so close is because of all the pins they have. If anyone has a chance for a pin, go for it. Dwayne, you have a rematch with Joe Kerr. You stop his fireman's carry, and you can beat him. No inside ties. You got that?"

Dwayne nods.

"Anything else?"

Duray steps up to the table. "I was at Dover for three years. I'm telling you, these guys are soft. You push them hard for the entire match, they'll put their tail between their legs and cower like a scared dog."

Kane extends his hand. "Okay, everyone gather around."

***

"Are you ready?" blares Barry from the broadcast booth.

Chet jumps in. "The semifinals are about to begin. Many consider this the most exciting round."

"That's right," adds James. "A lot of the top seeds meet, plus the low seeds and no seeds that made it through the quarters have upset on their minds and a chance to break out and capture some of the spotlight."

"We have some fascinating match-ups," announces Barry, "but what everyone is talking about is the team race."

Chet takes control. "Chicago came in as the heavy favorite. Surprisingly, little Dover University had the lead after the first day, and then Chicago took control this morning in the quarters, putting six in the semis while Dover has four in the semis."

"The exciting thing is Dover meets Chicago in three of its semis at 118, 142 and 177," adds James, "and if Dover can sweep, they can put a huge dent in the Chicago machine and take back control."

"At 118, Chicago's Joe Daniels meets Dover's Johnny Mango, known by his teammates as Mini D," declares Chet. "Joe Daniels is the favorite here. He had an impressive victory over Mango during the season."

"That's right," says Barry, "but I wouldn't put it past Mine D to pull it out. He's really stepped it up this tournament."

Chet continues, "At 126, Chicago's Andy Mason is the defending champion and clear favorite. This brings us to 134 and Bobby Ryder. His challenge was expected to come from Michigan's Terry, but he got knocked off by Dover's Bronk Pokard, who is in the other semifinal."

"Have you been watching these guys?" asks James. "There seems to be some sort of personal animosity brewing between Ryder and this Bronk kid."

"And that's interesting, because at the start of the season, Dover had the number one-ranked Rick Ballsinger, a returning finalist from last year," informs Barry. "But he goes down with a season-ending injury, and the backup steps in, and now he's one win away from the finals."

"But he has the number three seed, a very tough Bill Johnson from Iowa," relays Chet. "He has to get past him first. At 142, Dover's Joe Kerr takes on Chicago's Dwayne Kelly."

"Kerr is a scoring machine," says James. "He's one of the most dominant and entertaining wrestlers we've seen at this tournament."

"Kelly hasn't had much luck against him, dropping a couple of lopsided decisions," says Chet.

Barry adds, "Well, for that matter, no one has had much luck against Kerr this year. Every match, he runs the score up with a fireman's carry, which is almost obsolete in college wrestling. The guy's a freak."

"And then we have another doozy at 177," says Chet. "Dover's freshman sensation, Adam Robbins, is going against defending champion Russ Harvey."

"What makes this so intriguing," adds Barry, "is in their only meeting, Harvey lost his only match of the year to Robbins in overtime at the national duals but has since beaten a couple of ranked wrestlers who have victories over Robbins."

"So that begs the question, did Robbins catch Harvey napping, or does he have his number?" asks James

"They are both beasts," declares Barry, "so it should be a great match."

"And the final wrestler for Chicago is heavyweight Ben Ryan. He squeaked by Dover's Willie Kinsman in a controversial quarterfinal," says Chet.

"Controversial is putting it mildly," says James. "They need to check that referee's address and family tree."

"Well, he has his hands full now," pipes in Barry. "He goes against the number one seed."

"On paper, it looks like Chicago should have four in the finals and Dover one, maybe two," projects Chet. "This could be the end of Dover's run."

"But we don't wrestle the tournament on paper. We wrestle it on the mats," injects James.

"That's why you just never know until the last second has ticked off the clock," sums up Barry. "And that's why we come every year and watch."

***

Mini D and Joe Daniels are going at it.

Dan leans forward in his chair, holding a program rolled up like a megaphone to his lips and screaming, "Pressure. Pressure ... keep the pressure on."

Mini D clubs Daniels with a head tie.

Kane counters from his corner, "Get two, Joe, get two. It's there—take it. Take it!"

Daniels pulls Mini D's elbow and drops in on his legs. No sooner does his knee touch the mat than he explodes to his feet and runs, lifting Mini D in the air and driving him to the mat for a two-point takedown and a 6-5 lead.

Uncle Burt catapults out of his chair and leans and twists as if he can help Mini D fight. He looks at the clock. "Twenty seconds!"

Kane is on his feet, screaming through his cupped hands, "Now ride him!"

"Got to score. Score!" yells Dan. He stands as his eyes shift back and forth between the clock and the match.

Duray counters, "Fifteen seconds. Hold him down."

"Back pressure. Back pressure," bellows Dan.

Mini D pushes back and builds to a tripod on his hands and feet.

"Hit it. Hit it!" scream Dan and Uncle Burt.

Mini D tucks and dives into a shoulder roll under Daniels. Not wanting to risk a two-point reversal, Daniels lets Mini D go. But instead of breaking free, Mini D makes a surprise lunge in on Daniels' legs. Mini D powers forward on his knees and drives. He walks up and lifts Daniels off his feet and carries him on his shoulder.

Kane hollers, "Five seconds. Fight it! Five seconds!"

Uncle Burt hollers, "Score. You got to score!"

Duray screams, "Hold on. Squeeze!"

Dan roars, "Break him!"

Daniels locks his hand in Mini D's crotch. Mini D slides him off his shoulder, drops him to the mat, and covers him. He grabs the far ankle, leg laces the near ankle, applies a crossface and drives Daniels to his far hip. The referee's hand cuts the air, signaling two points as the buzzer sounds. Mini D explodes to his feet and jumps and skips around the mat. Dan and Uncle Burt dance and hop along the side of the mat. Kane stands and throws Daniels' warm-up to the floor and walks off. Duray watches Kane strut off toward Andy Mason's mat with his focus already on the next man up. Duray kicks the warm-up from the floor onto the mat and follows Kane.

***

Bronk strains to hold his opponent still long enough for the pin call. His eyes shift from his foe's raised shoulder across the floor to the mat Ryder is wrestling on. He adjusts his chest, circles his hips, tightening his hold and increasing his pressure, all while keeping his eyes on Ryder, until a whistle blast and mat slap signal the fall.

Bronk yanks his raised hand free from the referee's grasp and breaks into a sprint. He darts across the connecting mats, dodging the other grappling wrestlers in the shifty, evasive style of a football running back, making a zig-zag beeline for Ryder's mat. He pulls up matside and paces back and forth along the edge of the out-of-bounds line. He directs his eyes and fastens them. Ryder holds his opponent down for the count. They shake, and the referee lifts Ryder's hand. Bronk's and Ryder's eyes lock on each other. They stand like sculptures frozen in time until Ryder's coaches lift him on their shoulders and carry him off the mat to the cheers of the Chicago fandom.

***

Joe circles, moves in and out, and steps forward into an inside tie.

"Dwayne, no inside ties." Kane bolts out of his seat and runs around the edge of the mat screaming, "Watch the carry. Watch the carry!"

Joe pulls his opponent's arm with a violent jerk and drops. He pulls his opponent's body on his shoulders, wraps it around his neck, and launches. Vaulting feet arc through the air, creating a blurry rainbow. His head and shoulder crash into the mat, followed by the loud thud of his feet. Joe drives and covers, securing his hold, and then looks up at Kane standing matside and says, "That's five points." Dwayne arches his back and bridges on top of his head.

Dan and Uncle Burt yell, "Stick him. Stick him!"

Kane watches with both hands on his hips. "Dwayne, get off your back." Joe breaks Dwayne's bridge. "Dwayne, you get pinned and I'm putting you on a plane home. Dwayne ... Dwayne ..."

The referee's hand spanks the mat. Joe jumps to his feet and stands over his challenger with a hand extended. Dan and Uncle Burt run to Joe.

Kane grabs Dwayne by the arm as he comes off the mat. "I told you to watch the carry. If you don't want to wrestle, take off that uniform. Now, get out of my sight."

Duray tosses Dwayne's warm-up in his face and tags behind Kane.

***

Dan and Uncle Burt stand off to the side as Adam paces back and forth like the king of beasts behind bars.

Uncle Burt nudges Dan with an elbow. When Dan shifts his gaze, Uncle Burt murmurs, "You know, I was just thinking, if Adam wins this, we'll have two freshmen in the finals. Has any team ever had two freshmen in the finals before?"

"You think too much."

The buzzer sounds, ending the match in progress. Both sets of coaches hover around their seats, waiting for the current coaches to vacate. Adam and defending champion Harvey walk in a deliberate manner to the scorer's table and check in. They jog to the center of the mat and bounce around while the referee, timers, and scorers make their final preparations.

A police officer followed by a small entourage of policemen marches past Dan and Uncle Burt to the scorer's table.

The referee brings the two combatants together for the customary handshake. They get in their stances and step on the start lines. A buzzer blast calls the official to the scorer's table. They call both the wrestlers over.

Each wrestler is identified, and the police inform Adam Robbins he is under arrest. The officer removes his handcuffs from his belt and instructs Adam to put his hands behind his back. He refuses, and the other four policemen grab him.

Dan barrels in. "What the hell is going on?" Everyone freezes.

"Who are you?" asks the officer in charge.

"I'm his coach. My name is Dan Sangha."

"There's a warrant for Adam Robbins' arrest."

"Are you sure you have the right Adam Robbins?"

"He's been positively identified."

Dan pulls the officer aside. "What's he being arrested for?"

"Apparently, he was caught on surveillance cameras last month, burglarizing a locker room right here in the Chicago arena."

"You can't wait until tomorrow?" asks Dan.

"Sorry."

"I promise I'll bring him in Saturday night after the finals."

"Sorry."

"C'mon, he's busted his ass all year for this. Can't you give him a break?" pleads Dan.

Shaking his head, the officer replies, "I'm sorry, but I can't. He has a previous conviction. Being his coach, you had to know."

Dan turns to Adam. "I'm sorry. I know what this means to you, but you have to cooperate. I'll get to the bottom of this." He turns back to the officer. "Can I have your card, so I know where to go?" The officer digs a card out of his wallet. Dan watches Adam being handcuffed. "Adam, don't say anything to anyone. I'll get down there when I'm done here."

The other officers read Adam his rights and escort him away. Duray stands across the mat, waiting. When Uncle Burt's eyes locate him, he shrugs as if to say, "Too bad" and then cracks a grin. Uncle Burt drops and slouches in his seat, dumbfounded.

Dan prods, "We can't lose our focus. We still have four more in the wrestle backs. They're depending on us."

"That's it. We can't win now. It's over."

"Hey, it ain't over 'til it's over. Get the team together for a meeting. And after this round, we'll run down to the station and find out what's going on."

***

Dan leads the team through a series of dim hallways running under the stadium. They follow him through the maze, and when he finds an isolated hall, he begins trying to open doors. Locked. Locked. Locked. Open.

"Okay, we have twenty minutes," announces Dan. "Team meeting. Everyone in here."

The Dogs squash into in a combination broom closet and storage room.

"I found out something this year. It's easy being a winner, when you're winning," says Dan. "But when you lose, it's tough. Pain and failure do funny things to your head. Your first thought is to give in and give up. Like when you're a kid learning to ride a bike, and you fall, and it hurts and you look around to see if anyone saw you fail. For an instant, you consider going without a bike, but after that moment of weakness, you jump back on and try harder—and that's the key. You guys who lost, you have a choice. Are you going to suck your thumb and pout, or are you going to come back with more determination?" Dan scratches his sweaty head and looks around at a bunch of cramped bodies and uncomfortable faces. "You never want to forget what you are doing here. This tournament represents almost sixty years of tradition and is the pinnacle of our sport.

You're wrestling in front of 15,000 of the best and most knowledgeable fans from around the country.

"I remember a guy losing his first match here and then winning seven matches in a row to take third place. After his final match, the entire arena gave him a standing ovation—longer than any champion got that year. They understood his feat, they appreciated it, and they let him know. He'll never forget that moment, and neither will anyone in the arena that day. You do something here, and it's yours for the rest of your life. No one can ever take that away from you."

Dan lets that simmer, and then he turns up the heat. "This last round knocked us down and bloodied our noses. If you don't mind it, it's going to happen again, but if you don't like it, you're going to do something about it. The team championship is going to be determined right now by the decision you make. The true champion is the guy who loses and comes back, and comes back stronger. It's what this sport is about. It's what life is all about. From here, every match is about you. You get to show everyone watching who you are and what you are about." Dan extends his hand. "How do you want them to remember you?" The Dogs slap their hands on top and grip tight.

***

Alone, Dan meanders down a secluded concrete tunnel in deep thought. At the corner, he makes a sharp turn and collides with another body.

"Excuse me," says Kane, looking up and realizing he crashed into Dan. "You're beginning to make a habit of running into me."

Kane looks around and realizes they are alone. He studies Dan's face and tries to read it. Dan just stares. A polite, not-so-sure smile cuts across Kane's face. He slowly backs away. Dan bears forward. Kane quickens his pace.

"That was a real shame, what happened to your boy Robbins," says Kane, shuffling his feet in reverse. He comes to a sudden stop when his back smashes into a closed door. He lifts his hands in front of him, signaling Dan to stop. "I had nothing to do with it." He prepares himself for an attack.

Dan pulls up and takes a deep breath. "I want to thank you."

"Thank me?"

"Without you, this year would have never happened."

"Huh?"

"When I beat you off the national team and won the Olympics, I thought I was going to get the Chicago job. When you got it, I ... I hated you. All these years, I felt you were living my life. But what I've come to realize is I hated myself for coming up short. It had nothing to do with you. It's funny—I thought when I beat you, and my team won the nationals, I would celebrate, but it feels more like a funeral."

"What are you talking about? This tournament isn't over."

"It was over when we got off the plane. You can't beat us," says Dan, reaching into his jacket pocket and handing a folded piece of paper to Kane. "Here—I don't need this anymore." Dan turns and laughs to himself as he walks away. *That'll fuck his head up.*

Kane watches the door close behind Dan, checks the other end of the empty corridor, and unfolds and opens the shabby, dog-eared page. Well-worn white creases mark the fold lines like a tic-tac-toe game grid. His fingers smooth out the magazine cover photo of the Chicago team carrying Kane on their shoulders above a large Roman numeral X. The headline reads "KANE'S CHICAGO TEAM FAVORED FOR UNPRECEDENTED 10th STRAIGHT NATIONAL TITLE." A smile creeps across his face as the image fills his eyes. The weakened wrinkles disintegrate, and the cover crumples into giant snowflakes that swirl and glide their way to the floor.

DAY THREE - SATURDAY
THE FINALS

"Welcome to the College National Wrestling Championships coming to you from Chicago," says Chet. In the background, numerous spotlights swirl around the jam-packed arena. Hundreds of cameras flash. The floor has been cleared except for one mat on an elevated platform in the center of the floor.

"This is the college wrestling national finals in all its grandeur," says Barry.

"This is what college wrestling is all about. You really owe to yourself to experience this in person at least once in your life," says James. "I know you can see it on television, and we're going to try our best to keep you in the action, but nothing is like being here. There's an indescribable feeling when you're right in the middle of it. You can't explain it."

"There's Steve Sheets of Olympic fame who went on to a professional wrestling career," interjects Chet. The camera zooms in on Steve Sheets waving to the crowd.

A camera focuses on a man signing autographs. "And there's Ben Fraser," adds Barry. "After his college wrestling career, he went on to be an action star in the movies, and to this day, he gives wrestling credit for his ability to do all of his own stunts."

Realizing a camera is on him, Ben Fraser looks up from signing, cracks a bright white smile, and coaxes a fan to pose with him. They wave at the camera.

Another camera scans a long line of men walking around the arena floor. Young and old, they walk and talk, and wave to the crowd. Some move with vigor, and a few hobble and struggle to the complete the walk.

"This is always my favorite part, the Parade of Champions. All the former champs present are invited to come down on the floor and walk the perimeter before the first match," says Barry, with a tear in his eye.

"You should be down there," points out James.

"So should you," replies Barry.

"The game has definitely changed in the college wrestling scene," redirects Chet. "A new rivalry has shaken the college wrestling seismograph."

"And this isn't a tremor," adds Barry, "it's a quake."

"The question is—is it the big one?" asks James.

"Dover stormed back in the consolations, taking two thirds, a fourth and a fifth," explains Chet.

"Dover is a great story. They came in as huge underdogs and wrestled their butts off. Every round except the quarterfinals, their wrestlers have exceeded expectations, and every round, we hear another story from their camp," announces Barry. "And here's another one—their one-hundred-fifty pounder, Billy 'Pug' Pugliano, actually broke his back in a motorcycle accident in high school and was told he would never walk again. Four years later, he's taking fourth in the college nationals."

"I guess Dan has added the hospitals' intensive care units to his recruiting circuit," pokes James.

Barry continues, "Next, Blair 'Doc' Borne finished fifth on the strength of a headlock everyone is still buzzing about. And then Phil Kruger, what can you say?"

"You can say he crushed the competition," exclaims James, "and he very well may be the best third placer in the whole tournament."

"And finally, the fan favorite, the charismatic Willie Kinsman, aka Pump—and his belly thump—got a rematch with Chicago's Ben Ryan and avenged an earlier loss to finish a strong third."

"Do you believe this guy? He's awesome," calls out James. "Before each match in the consolation, he pulled up his T-shirt and beat his belly with both hands like he was playing a bongo drum."

Barry laughs and shakes his head. "By the time he got to the third-place match, he had half the fans in the seats pulling up their shirts and playing along with him."

"And if you look around the arena tonight, you'll see an awful lot of brown T-shirts. It appears the Dogs have won over this crowd and taken away the home court advantage."

"As of now, Dover is ahead in team points, so every match is crucial," reports Chet. "And no matter how you figure it, the team championship will be determined by the outcome of the 134 finals, the only finals match where Dover and Chicago meet."

The house lights begin to dim. "Here we go," alerts James.

The light is muted. The noise level diminishes until the arena is pitched into dark silence. An occasional shout is the only sign of life. A warm glow appears above the center of the floor as a spotlight burns to life, illuminating the elevated mat.

Mini D and his Oklahoma counterpart sprint out from opposite ends of the dark auditorium, leap the steps to the lit platform, circle to their corners for a final word from their coaches, and meet in the center. They shake, the whistle blows, and it's on.

In the shadow of the corridor leading from the sports center floor, Gorni warms up Bronk, and Joe and Balls watch Mini D's match.

Joe cautions, "Remember, stay out of his hooks."

Balls adds, "But if he does get the hooks in, just execute what we worked on."

"C'mon, you guys are makin' me nervous," complains Bronk.

"You're going to be fine," says Balls, rubbing Bronk's shoulders. "Give it all you got and let the chips fall where they may."

"Remember, you're in better shape," reminds Joe.

"That's right," adds Balls. "Push him hard the first two periods, and the third period is yours."

Joe steps to the edge of the floor and just stands, staring across the arena floor to the other side. "Look at him," he says, watching Bobby Ryder warming up. "In this light, he looks like a wuss."

Everyone joins Joe gawking at Bobby Ryder. They look intently.

Balls with a revelation, claims, "He looks like Horshack from *Welcome Back, Kotter.*"

Joe continues to stare at Ryder. "I never noticed it before. He does look like Horshack."

"From the neck up, he is Horshack."

They are all struck by the uncanny resemblance and burst out laughing.

"You can't lose to Horshack," asserts Joe.

"Look at the size of his nose."

"Hello. How are ya? I'm Arnold Horsha-a-ck," imitates Joe.

Everyone laughs out loud.

Joe continues, "That was ver-ry impressive, Mister Kotter-r-r." They're laughing uncontrollably. Joe's on a roll. Balls can't take anymore. He tries to grab Joe to quiet him.

"G'head, G'head," says Joe, dodging Balls. Joe raises his hand and imitates Horshack in class. "Ooh-ooh-ooh." He breaks into a Horshack wheezing laugh.

Balls gives up and watches Joe continue his act. "You sound like a hyena."

***

Mini D shakes with one hand and gets his other hand raised in triumph. With both hands lifted above his head, he runs a victory lap around the mat. He stops in the opposite corner from his coaches and then breaks into a sprint toward them. He does a handspring followed by a backflip, sticks his landing, and leaps into Dan's arms, wrapping his arms around Dan's neck and his legs around Dan's body and hugs. Uncle Burt slaps and pats Mini D's back with both hands.

Unsure of what do with his hands, Dan reminds Mini D, "Uh ... we're on national television."

Dickie is the first one to his brother as he jumps from the platform. He grabs him in a bear hug and carries him down one of the tunnel exits.

Bronk observes Mini D's sweat-soaked, drained opponent enter the hallway. His weary legs stop. Cramped forearms have disabled his hands. He drops his warmups and headgear, and slumps to the floor across from Bronk. His body pulses with the thumps of his heart. His "What the hell?" is rendered inaudible by the crowd's cheers for the great match.

***

"Well, one down, two to go," says Uncle Burt, looking in the mirror and grooming himself. "Do you believe Mini D? He wrestled the tournament of his life."

Dan stands at the wall urinal. "He always had it in him. He just had to believe in himself." Dan zips up, walks over, and stands next to Uncle Burt at the mirror and sinks.

"That was a good move making him captain." Uncle Burt meticulously combs every hair in place.

"It was Kruger's idea."

"He should've been in the finals. He should've won the damn thing," says Uncle Burt straightening his chocolate brown suit coat and black tie, and then looking at himself in the mirror from different angles. Every pose looks like a mannequin in the front window of a fine clothier shop.

"What, you got a hot date after the tournament tonight?" asks Dan.

"Are you kidding?" asks Uncle Burt. "This next match is the highlight of the evening. And when that camera broadcasts my close-up across the country, I'm going to look good. Do you know how much pussy this is going to get me over the next few years?"

"Here we go."

"I have a friend taping this for me, and if Bronk wins, I could probably play this for years at the bar. Do you know how many girls will want to relive this experience vicariously through me?" Uncle Burt holds his hands under the faucet and wets them, then shakes them and runs them over the back of his head. He takes a step back, takes a final gander in the mirror, and proclaims, "Perfect." He strides toward the door. "Better get a move on. Bronk is going to be up in a few minutes."

"Hold on."

"What?"

"There's something I want to tell you."

"Yeah?"

"You were the best I ever coached," says Dan.

"I know," says Uncle Burt.

"It just wasn't in the cards for you. I wanted you to know how I—"

"It means a lot coming from you," interrupts Uncle Burt. "Thanks. You're a hell of coach."

There is an awkward silence.

"I told you we would have fun, didn't I?" asks Dan.

"It's been a hell of a year."

"A hell of a year."

"I'll see you outside," says Uncle Burt, heading to the exit with a bounce in his step.

Dan turns and stares at his reflection. His disheveled, undersized black suit jacket hangs open at his protruding belly. A crooked, off-center, stained brown tie yokes the collar of his wrinkled white shirt. A brown belt pulls together the two sides of the outgrown waistband of his crumpled, tight, dark blue slacks. He slants his burr-cut head to one side and looks, then tilts it to the other side and looks. His finger pushes his eyeglasses up and straightens them on his smashed nose and cauliflowered ears. When he removes his hand, his glasses slide back down to the bottom of his nose. He raises his hand to his mouth, exhales into it and then sniffs, checking his breath. Satisfied, he turns, looks at the profile of his body, and parades out.

***

"Chicago's Andy Mason wins his second national title and keeps Chicago in contention," announces Chet. "Well, folks, after three days of wrestling and more than six hundred matches, it all comes down to one match: Bobby Ryder of the Chicago Cats versus Bronk Pokard of the Dover Dogs."

"It's the Cats versus the Dogs," puns James, "natural enemies."

"It's winner take all," warns Barry.

"The winner of this match will determine not only the national champion of the weight class but also the national team champion," informs Chet.

"Two freshmen for the title," exclaims James. "This has to be a historic moment."

"Clean your glasses—and you folks watching TV, don't you dare leave," cautions Barry. "You're seeing history in the making."

"Bobby Ryder, of course, is the heavy favorite," clarifies Chet. "They've had one meeting during the season, and Ryder majored Bronk."

"But the way this tournament has gone, anything is possible, even the impossible," says Barry, winking at James.

"The improbable happened last night," agrees Chet. "Dover was about to wrap up the team title when their 177-pounder, Adam Robbins, was arrested before his semifinal match and forced to forfeit to sixth and lost a lot of team points."

"The Dover coach, Dan Sangha, was recognized as the best wrestler in the world in his day," says Barry. "It's taken him almost fifteen years to put together a team to challenge for the national title."

"But the question everyone is asking is where does he get these guys?" asks James. "And how does he get them to go to Dover?"

"We've heard all sorts of stories," adds Chet.

"He goes into the ghettos and recruits the winners of gang fights," explains Barry. "He waits at the prison gates when prisoners are released."

"And don't forget the hospitals," chuckles James.

"The rumors have been flying," admits Chet.

"However he's done it, you got to hand it to him," acknowledges Barry. "No small university has ever made a run at the national title."

"Let's hear some words from the finalists," says Chet. "Roll the tape."

Ryder appears on the large screen, barely able to contain himself. "I'm excited for it. Since he beat Terry, everybody's been waiting for it. It's on. Let's do it."

The screen goes black, and then a close-up of Bronk's chin fills the monitor. The camera adjusts from his ear to his nose and then pulls back until his face is centered. He looks around, not sure when he's supposed to talk.

"Now?" he asks. He looks off-camera to the left, then the right, and then into the camera. "Now? Okay...Let's kick up a row and let fly. I'm game as a banty rooster."

"Did you guys get that?" asks Chet.

"What language is that?" asks Barry.

"Is this kid for real?" asks James. "Where does Dan find these guys?"

***

Uncle Burt strides across the mat to the referees huddled at the scorer's table. When they look up, he extends his hand, and they shake. "Have a good match tonight. It's been a great tournament. I'm glad we got you guys for our match. You're the best."

"Thank you."

"Now, you know I can't say anything to the Chicago coaches—they're a bunch of hotheads," says Uncle Burt, nodding at the Chicago corner. "But it would be different if you have a word with them and warn them about the cheap shots."

The referee extends his hand and points to the Dover corner. "How about if you return to your seat and let us referee the match?"

Uncle Burt walks off and delivers the last words loud enough for the Chicago corner to hear. "Okay, I'm just warning you. You let them get away with the cheap shots, and we'll retaliate."

The Chicago coaches jump to their feet.

In the announcer's booth, "Whoa, here we go again. The match hasn't even started, and the coaches are going at it," observes Chet. "Look at them chatter. The refs were ready for this one. They jumped in and separated the coaches before it got going."

"It looks like they are ready to start," pipes in Barry.

"Here we go. Better fasten your seat belts, this match is taking us off-road," warns James.

***

Bronk and Ryder shake. On the whistle, they come out of the gate and clash. Moving in and out, up and down, and side to side, they paw and slap each other. Abandoning caution and forsaking good position, they rip and tear to send a message. Standing forehead to forehead, they pound on each other. An all-out assault continues with forearm smashes, quick, sharp blows to the head, and open-hand smacks to the face. Each clashing skirmish ignites waves of cheers from the crowd. Ryder backs Bronk to the edge of the mat, rams into him, and shoves him off. The referee blows his whistle, warns Bronk for stalling, and orders the wrestlers back to the center.

"That was quick," says Uncle Burt.

Dan races to the scorers' table and signals for the referee. The official orders the wrestlers to stay in the center of the mat. He walks to the scorer's table.

As the referee approaches the table, Dan asks, "I'm not disputing the call, but what was the stalling warning for?"

"Your man was backing up."

"Could you tell him, so he knows why you called that?"

"Okay, I'll do that," answers the referee as he walks back to the center.

"One more thing," says Dan, halting the referee in his tracks. "You're going to call it that way the rest of the match, right?"

"That's right."

After a brief explanation, Bronk nods. On the whistle, Ryder rushes in, buries his underhook and goes straight to an inside trip, setting Bronk on his rump and taking him to his back. Bronk turns one way and then the other. Each time he moves, Ryder's arms coil tighter. Trapped, Bronk detonates. He explodes in to a high bridge, arching his back up from the mat and balancing on his head and toes. Ryder stays chest to chest and rides Bronk off the mat at Dan's feet.

Uncle Burt claps and cheers Bronk on. "Good job. Way to fight. Now, let's get those points back."

Ryder bounces to his feet and stalks back to the center. Bronk looks up at Dan as he climbs to his feet.

"I'm waiting," says Dan.

"Waiting?"

"What are you going to do?"

"I'm at sea on that."

"Look, forget the national championship, forget the cameras, forget the fans. It's just you and another guy in a fight."

When the referee starts them, Ryder pushes Bronk away and lets him back to his feet. Within seconds, Ryder has another hook in, driving Bronk across the mat. The referee's fist punches the air, signaling another stalling call and a point. Ryder drives across, reaches and knee picks Bronk, tripping him to his back. Bronk bridges off the mat again at Dan's feet.

Uncle Burt jumps in Bronk's face. "What the hell are you doing? The whole country is watching. Is that the way you want them to see you?"

Dan holds up his hand in front of Uncle Burt, and he retreats. Dan turns to his wrestler. "I'm still waiting."

"For what?"

"Hanging out isn't going to get it done. Let him know you're here."

Bronk is down. On the whistle, Ryder kicks Bronk free and immediately shoots in on a single-leg. He drives forward and walks up from his knees to his feet and jerks Bronk's leg up while trying to trip the other leg and take Bronk to the mat. Bronk bounces around on one leg. He posts the heel of his hand against Ryder's head and pushes it away and drives into him, backing him up. Then, hooking Ryder's arms, he kicks down and frees his leg. Ryder repenetrates and makes a level change, dropping on the lower part of Bronk's leg. Bronk dives and hooks one of Ryder's legs with an arm. They scramble, counter, and recounter. Fast and furious. It's a dogfight. Just when one is about to gain control, the other slips from underneath. The momentum shifts back and forth. The fans are on their feet, leaning and screaming when time expires. Ryder runs back to the center. Bronk doesn't move.

Dan studies Bronk for a second. "I need some time."

Uncle Burt gets the official's attention and circles his finger, asking for injury time.

The Chicago coaches appeal to the referee. "He can't take a time-out."

"It's injury time."

"I can't believe you're letting him have injury time." Looking over at Bronk, they continue to work the official. "He's not hurt. Nothing happened to him. Look at him—he's fine. We're ready to continue."

Dan looks deep into Bronk's glassy eyes. He turns to Uncle Burt. "Distract them. I need a minute."

Uncle Burt heads for the scorer's table and confronts the Chicago coaches and barks, "Worry about your guy."

"Pussy," bellows Duray.

"Crybaby," responds Uncle Burt.

Uncle Burt and Duray go nose to nose. The referees approach.

Dan asks Bronk, "You okay?"

"I'm lettin' the team down."

"Forget the team. This is about you."

"He's cleanin' my plow."

"Can you live with that?"

"Yeah, but I don't want to."

"Then do something about it."

"I'm trying to stay out of the hook."

"Forget that. Get into a scrap. If he gets the hook in, make him force it and do what Joe showed you. You'll feel it."

"You have lots of time. Keep the pressure on. You're down 10-2. Remember, you come back one point at a time. Escape, takedown and you're back in the match."

Uncle Burt returns to the corner and yells, "Suck it up," at Bronk as he trots back to center mat.

It's Bronk's choice of position, and he takes down. Ryder kicks him and lets him get to his feet and then comes at him with an all-out physical attack, clubbing his head and shoulders with open-hand slaps. Bronk adjusts, Ryder shoots. Bronk fights him off. Ryder repeatedly smacks and shoots, smacks and shoots. Bronk counters each attempt. Ryder smacks, sinks in a deep hook, and charges. Bronk knows if he backs up again, it means another point. Ryder lifts with his underhook arm and drives across for another knee pick. Bronk's body spins in the air and heads to its back. In midair, he goes with the pressure and spins under the arm, turning Ryder's knee pick into an arm spin and sends Ryder flying through the air. Caught off guard, Ryder knows the only way to stop from going to his back is to take it on the chin. He lifts his head and gets face planted. Ryder is stunned for a moment. Without hesitation, Bronk slips out to the front and tries to spin behind. Ryder's instincts respond. He catches Bronk with an arm, squares up, and walks back to his feet. Bronk fights back and resists the pressure until he feels Ryder force another hook. Bronk fights against the hook. Ryder forces it. Bronk pulls on the arm, drops in, and throws the dizzy Ryder with a fireman's carry. Ryder flies through the air. Bronk drives with the intention of spiking Ryder's head into the mat. Again, Ryder raises his head to stop from going to his back and takes it on the face. When he doesn't go over, Bronk re-cocks and pile drives Ryder's face into the mat again and again. On the fourth attempt, Ryder ducks his head and screams. The referee breaks the action, calls an injury time for Ryder, and awards Bronk two points for a takedown.

Uncle Burt goes ballistic and stomps across the mat, waving frantically at the referee. "What's that all about? He's going to his back, and you stop the match."

"He screamed," answers the referee.

"This isn't high school. Let them wrestle."

"Return to your corner, Coach."

"At least give him the back points. They were imminent."

"Sit down," orders the official.

Uncle Burt turns and walks back to his corner. He sits and watches the Chicago coaches make a fuss over Ryder. Duray glares at Uncle Burt. Uncle Burt smiles, drops his hands between his legs out of view of everyone but Duray, and puts the two thumbs and two index fingers of each hand together, forming the shape of a vagina.

"Up yours," shouts Duray.

"You talking to me?" asks Uncle Burt, acting innocent but motioning Duray forward with his fingers.

"How's it going?" asks Dan.

"I think I'm figurin' him out," answers Bronk.

"You think you can do that again?" asks Dan.

"I reckon."

"He's fading. Time to turn it up," coaches Dan. "You're down by five, but you have time." Dan looks at Uncle Burt and Duray go at it and laughs. "Look at those idiots." He turns back to Bronk and leans toward him. "He's fighting for you—we all are. Okay, ride him out the rest of this period and then kick him at the start of the third period and go on your feet. Remember, if you need a stall call, you have to back him up."

The referees restrain Uncle Burt and Duray.

"You should talk," spits Uncle Burt, pushing in nose to nose. "You had these guys for three years, and I'm still working the bad habits out of them."

Duray takes a swing. Uncle Burt ducks, steps in, and locks his hands around the body in a bear hug. He lifts, spins, and slams Duray to the mat. Fists fly. Security personnel sprint to the mat from all directions. Uncle Burt springs to his feet and dances around the mat, playing to the cheering fans.

"I've been covering the nationals for decades, and I've never seen anything like this," says Chet.

"Some bad blood there," summarizes Barry.

"I did a little research," interjects James. "Apparently, Burt beat Duray for third place at this tournament when they were freshmen. And then Duray went on to win three national titles, and Burt was never heard from again."

"I seem to remember that," adds Barry. "I think Burt was plagued with injuries and eligibility issues."

"I still can't believe this," mumbles Chet. "Do you believe this feud is playing out on national television?"

"It isn't over yet," says James.

A close-up of Uncle Burt's face fills the overhead big screen. He looks at the screen and sees himself being grabbed by two security guards. He jerks an arm free from each guard.

"I know you guys are doing your job, but I can walk out on my own."

The guards try to grab an arm again.

Uncle Burt yanks free. "I can walk out on my own. You touch me again, and the paramedics will be carrying someone from the arena—and it isn't going to be me. It's your call."

The guards look at Uncle Burt and then look at each other. Uncle Burt straightens his suit and walks. "Okay, let's go."

The referees inform Dan and Kane that they have to leave, and they fall in line behind Uncle Burt, the security officers and Duray. Each coach yells to an assistant to take his chair.

Kane looks at Dan. "This is un-fucking-believable."

"Welcome to my world," snorts Dan. "Just rat shit in the closet."

"Huh?"

"Nothing."

"I've been thinking it over," says Kane. "I feel bad about this Robbins mess. I know it was some sort of prank. I'll get the school to drop the charges."

"You're a good man."

"You had a great year. And this tournament is one for ages. Hey, wasn't that a great match between Daniels and Mini D?"

"It was un-fucking-believable."

Uncle Burt marches across the floor toward the exit. When he walks in front of the Chicago section, they begin wagging their fingers and chanting.

"BAD dog. BAD dog. BAD dog."

Uncle Burt unbuckles his belt and saunters faster, increasing his lead on the guards. He stops, turns his backside to the heckling fans, drops his trousers and shorts to his ankles, bends over, and flips the tail of his jacket up, exposing his chunky buttocks, touching off an eruption of cheers and jeers from the rest of the arena.

The guards rush forward, grab Uncle Burt by the arms, and drag him off the floor with his slacks and underwear bundled at the bottom of his naked legs. He looks up at the monitor and watches the scene play out on the big screen. Right before his exit, he smiles and gives a thumbs-up to the audience.

"I think we've seen <u>all</u> of Coach Burt," jokes James.

"That's the first time the Chicago section has been quiet all weekend," comments Barry.

"And now the assistants are filling the seats in the corner," informs Chet.

"There's Rick Ballsinger," observes Barry. "He was the favorite to win this weight, but an injury cut his season short, and now he's coaching his backup to win the title that was supposed to be his."

"Now, that's irony for you," reflects James.

As he takes his seat, Balls yells, "This is your period. Nobody can hang with you in the third period. NOBODY!"

Bronk burns the few seconds left in the second period by grabbing an ankle and holding on. Last period, it is Ryder's choice. He takes down.

Balls howls from the corner, "Keep the pressure on. Stay solid."

Bronk lets Ryder back to his feet and then ratchets up the intensity by increasing his pace and going on the attack. They flail at each other, trading pushes, pulls, and swats to the head. They trade shots and counter shots in a standoff. Fatigue takes its toll. Both are out of their stances and leaning on each other.

Ryder takes a lackluster shot. Bronk catches him midair with a chin and underhook and rips. He nails his cow catcher, pancaking Ryder to his back. Ryder rips Bronk's hand off his chin and bridges on the top of his head. Bronk fights to reclaim his hold, Ryder blasts into another high bridge. The only way Bronk can stop from going over is to bail. Ryder escapes. He circles to catch his breath and get his bearings.

Bronk goes after him, fighting for a grip. Ryder backs up and gets banged with a stalling warning. Bronk fakes a shot and head snaps Ryder down to the mat and spins hard. He gets the angle on Ryder but cannot get behind for the points.

Balls jumps out of his seat, yelling and pointing, "He's holding the singlet! He's holding the singlet!"

When the referee circles to get a look, Ryder lets go of the uniform, and Bronk slips behind for the takedown.

"You're tied. Hold him down," screams Balls. "Hold him down! Ten seconds!"

Before the referee's fingers signal two points for the takedown, Ryder blasts to his feet and begins ripping at Bronk's hands. Bronk feels he is losing his grip and drops to grab a leg. Ryder senses the drop and limps his leg free from Bronk's grasp for an escape. Bronk rushes him. Ryder circles. Bronk runs at him and pounces, diving in at his legs. Ryder backs up and catches the lunging Bronk with an underhook and holds him off. Bronk keeps driving and driving. The sound of the buzzer fills his ears. *Shit. Ran out of time.*

The referee's fist makes a sharp thrust and jabs the air above his head. "Stalling on Chicago. One point Dover. Reset the clock for overtime."

The Chicago assistant curdles, "Stalling? How can that be stalling?"

"Your man was backing," responds the referee.

"It's called a sprawl. That's what you do when a man shoots on you," complains Chicago's corner.

The whole stadium is up on its feet, booing and cheering the call.

"Bronk. Bronk!" shouts Balls, through his cupped hands. Bronk looks. Balls checks the Chicago corner to make sure no one is spying, then tells Bronk, "Shoot a low single and rotate hard, fake a limp arm and when you feel him square up, bury that cow catcher and rip with all you've got."

The two gladiators stagger back to the center.

"Bronk!" shouts Balls. Bronk looks to his corner. "Fake shot. Fake snap and then a hard low single."

The referee blows his whistle. Ryder barrels forward. Bronk circles, fakes a shot, and reaches for the head snap. Ryder remembers the previous head snap and sets, so he cannot be pulled down to the mat. Bronk fires a low single leg. He is in deep. Ryder sprawls and applies a whizzer, hooking his arm over the arm wrapped around his leg. Bronk drives his shoulder into the thigh and circles his hips hard. Ryder applies pressure with his hips and the overhook. Bronk fakes the limp arm, and Ryder bites. He whizzers hard and squares up, bringing his head around and down. In a blur, Bronk slips the arm he has around the leg across the back to the far hip, hooks his chin on top of Ryder's near shoulder, and buries his free arm elbow deep over Ryder's head, around his neck. Ryder fights and turns his chin into Bronk's waiting hand. Bronk hooks his hand around the chin and jawbone and cranks. Ryder posts his far foot to stop from going over. Bronk torques Ryder's body across his chest and buries Ryder's far shoulder into the mat. Ryder's face fills with the shock of the realization that he cannot stop the move. Bronk drives him to his back.

***

The Dogs surround the championship trophy and put on their game faces as the cameras unleash a bevy of flashes. The boys' families are scattered around the perimeter of the photo shoot. Some take their own snapshots. They beam and can't wait for the pictures to end and the smiling and hugging to begin.

"Hey, Coach can we get a shot of you with your three champs?" asks the photographer.

"They're all champs." Dan pulls Gorni into the shot and puts his arm around Ben. "We won this because of you."

"Me?"

"When that Chicago guy put you on your back, you fought—you didn't get pinned. If he had pinned you, they would have gotten bonus points, and they'd be raising this trophy right now."

"Telegram for Coach Sangha!" yells a special delivery person in a fast march across the gym floor. "Telegram for Coach Sangha!"

"Here," responds Dan.

The carrier performs an exaggerated turn, scampers over, and extends the telegram to Dan. He tears open the message and reads, then proclaims with unabashed pride, "Unbelievable! It's a boy! It's a boy!"

The Dogs gather around Dan, surrounding him with congratulatory words and pats on the back.

Dan asks, "What would you guys say if I said, 'Let's do it again'?"

Everyone barks, "Woof, woof, woof ..." and lifts Dan.

He raises the trophy high and signals number one with his other hand. "Enjoy tonight. Practice on Monday. We have to start getting ready for next year."

DIRTY DOGS

If you like this story

Go to:

DirtyDogsWrestling.com

Write A Review

Join The Team

Like And Share

or

Share A Story/Anecdote

www.ingramcontent.com/pod-product-compliance
Lightning Source LLC
Chambersburg PA
CBHW071647260626
47170CB00001B/268